W9-CCD-479

FATAL FLAW

FATAL SERIES, BOOK 4

MARIE FORCE

Fatal Flaw
Fatal Series, Book 4
By: Marie Force
Published by HTJB, Inc.
Copyright 2012. HTJB, Inc.
ISBN: 978-1952793608
Cover Design: Kristina Brinton
Cover photography by Regina Wamba
Models: Robert John and Ellie Dulac
Layout by The E-book Formatting Fairies

Thank you for respecting the hard work of this author. To obtain permission to excerpt portions of the text, please contact the author at *marie@marieforce.com*. All characters in this book are fiction and figments of the author's imagination.

MARIE FORCE and FATAL SERIES are registered trademarks with the United States Patent & Trademark Office.

marieforce.com

The best way to stay in touch is to subscribe to my newsletter. Go to *marieforce.com* and subscribe in the box on the top of the screen that asks for your name and email. If you don't hear from me regularly, please check your spam filter and set up your email to allow my messages through to you so you never miss a new book, a chance to win great prizes or a possible appearance in your area.

The Fatal Series

Sam and Nick's Story Continues....

More coming soon!

AUTHOR'S NOTE

Thank you once again to Capt. Russell Hayes (retired) of the Newport, Rhode Island, Police Department for reading, reviewing and providing valuable insight. To Julie Cupp, Lisa Cafferty, Jean Mello, Tia Kelly, Nikki Haley and Ashley Lopez, thank you for taking this wild ride with me, Sam and Nick.

To my beta readers, Anne Woodall and Kara Conrad, you ladies are the best, and I appreciate the astute comments and insight. And to all the readers who've embraced Sam and Nick, I so appreciate your support and enthusiasm. I can't remember a time when they didn't live as real people in my imagination, and I look forward to many more adventures with them.

xoxo
Marie

CHAPTER ONE

On the night before she was due to return to work, Lieutenant Sam Holland lay awake watching the bedside clock count down to midnight, the hour she'd officially be back on call. Five minutes to go. Sam had expected to be itching to get back to work after two weeks of constant togetherness with her new husband, U.S. Senator Nick Cappuano. But as the final minutes of their blissful interlude slipped away, she was filled with despair, wondering when they'd ever get that much time alone together again.

"What's the matter, babe?" he asked from behind her.

Sam used to hate sharing a bed, and now she couldn't imagine sleeping without his strong arms around her. Conceding defeat to the clock, she turned over and snuggled into his chest. "I'm not ready to go back to work."

"You've got a few hours yet."

"Is it after midnight?"

He raised himself up to peer over her shoulder. "One minute past."

"They can call me in anytime now."

"Maybe you'll get lucky and the criminals will take a night off."

"Let's hope so." She pressed a kiss to one of his well-defined pectorals, and slipped an arm around him. "You've totally ruined me, you know."

"How's that?"

"Before this, before us, I used to hate vacations. They'd make me take one twice a year whether I wanted to or not, and the whole time I'd be bored and jonesing to get back to work. But now..."

"I feel the same way." He tipped her chin up and kissed her. "We've got much better things to do than work."

"Exactly." She gave herself over to the kiss, powerless to resist him even though they'd both be tired in the morning if they didn't get some sleep. The trip home from their honeymoon in Bora Bora had left them jet-lagged.

Without breaking the kiss, he shifted on top of her.

"Nick..."

"Hmm?"

"We already did this tonight—twice if I recall correctly," she reminded him, as he trailed kisses from her jaw to her collarbone.

"Is there a daily sex limit law on the books?"

"Not that I'm aware of."

"Then shut up and kiss me."

She was still laughing when her cell phone rang, making them moan with dismay.

"Ignore it," he said, capturing her lips for another kiss.

That she was half-tempted to pretend she hadn't heard the phone was so wildly out of character it scared her. Clearly, she'd gone soft in the head since she got married. "Let me go, Senator. Back to reality."

"Don't wanna," he said as he released her.

Sam grabbed the phone from the bedside table and flipped it open. For the first time in two weeks, she said, "Lieutenant Holland."

"Lieutenant," the dispatcher said, "I was told you're back on duty as of midnight."

Since Nick was awake anyway, Sam turned on the light and reached for the pad and pen she kept handy. "That's correct."

"We have a report of a double homicide at Carl's Burger World on Massachusetts Avenue."

She wrote down the address. "I'll be right there. Can you call Detective Cruz?"

"Will do."

Sam ended the call and turned to give Nick a quick kiss. "Sorry."

"Duty calls," he said with a long-suffering sigh. "What've you got?"

"A double at Carl's on Mass Ave."

"I don't know that place."

"A friend of mine worked there when I was in high school, but I haven't been there in years." She pulled on jeans and a long-sleeved T-shirt since it was still chilly at night. Sitting on Nick's side of the bed, she glanced at him as she put on socks. "Best vacation ever."

"For me, too."

"We should do it again sometime."

His face lifted into the sexy half smile she adored. "Absolutely."

Sam tied her sneakers and got up to grab a sweatshirt. In the bedside table drawer, she unlocked the box where she kept the gun, badge and cuffs she hadn't touched in two weeks—the longest stretch of time off she'd had since joining the District of Columbia's Metropolitan Police Department twelve years earlier.

Before leaving the bedroom, she gave her husband one last kiss. "Have a good first day back."

"You, too." He tugged on a strand of her long, toffee-colored hair. "Be careful out there, babe."

"Always am. See you later." She wasn't even halfway down the stairs before she was hit by the urge to turn around and run back to him. If someone had told her a year ago she'd be so stupidly in love that she'd be mooning over a guy when there were dead bodies to tend to, she probably would've beat the shit out of the person.

"I may be stupidly in love," she said as she went out the front door and down the ramp her husband had installed for her paralyzed father, "but it's time to get back to work."

SAM ARRIVED on the scene at the same time as her partner, Detective Freddie Cruz. He'd donned one of the signature trench coats he claimed were necessary to staying in character and Sam claimed were proof he'd watched too much TV as a kid. He offered her a powdered donut from a six-pack as he jammed another in his mouth.

Shaking her head, she looked up at him. "Do you buy those things in bulk or something?"

"Never hurts to be prepared for middle-of-the night calls."

"I hope I'm around when your metabolism slows down."

He held up the yellow crime-scene tape for her, and she scooted under it. "Nice to have you back, Lieutenant. I've missed your sparkling wit."

"I'm back one minute, and you're already sucking up?"

"I see you still can't take a compliment. Good trip?"

"*Great* trip. Went by too fast."

The Patrol officers who'd responded to the initial call showed them to the restaurant's back room, where the sub-zero freezer door was propped open. Inside were two people who looked as if they'd frozen to death.

"Ugh," said the District's Chief Medical Examiner, Dr. Lindsey McNamara, as she joined them. "What a way to go."

"No kidding," Freddie said, putting the rest of the donuts in his coat pocket. Apparently, he'd lost his appetite.

"How do we know this is a homicide and not an accident?" Sam asked the Patrol officers.

"The door locks from the outside," one of them said, pointing to the mangled padlock that had been broken open.

"Who did that?"

"The boy's father." The Patrol officer pointed to the young man in the freezer. "Daniel Alvarez, age seventeen. When he didn't come home after work and wasn't answering his phone, his father came looking for him. The door was unlocked, so he came in and found the boy's stuff sitting here on the counter." He pointed to a wallet, keys and cell phone next to an unzipped bank bag that bulged with cash, which ruled out robbery as a motive. "The father went crazy when he saw the lock on the freezer, found a hammer and went to town on it. By the time he got in there it was too late."

"So not only did he pound the fingerprints off the lock, but he also compromised our crime scene by touching the vics, too. Am I right?"

The patrolmen shuffled from one foot to the other. "Yes, ma'am."

"Fabulous," Sam muttered as she stepped into the freezer for a closer look at the two victims. She recognized the second one as Carl Olivo, the owner and proprietor. He'd aged since the last time she saw him during her senior year of high school when her friend Melissa had worked for him. Both victims had a bluish tint to their skin, and their eyes were open.

Freddie grimaced as he squatted for a closer look. "No obvious sign of other trauma."

"The lack of oxygen in here could've gotten them before the cold did," Lindsey added. "I'll know more after I get them back to the lab."

Sam studied both victims and took a good look around the freezer. "Go to it," she said to Lindsey. "I'd like to talk to the kid's father."

"Joseph Alvarez," the patrolman said. "He's outside with Officer Gentile."

Sam followed the officer through the kitchen and out the back door to an alley behind the restaurant.

Joseph Alvarez was tall and broad-shouldered, and those broad shoulders were heaving with sobs as Officer Gentile did her best to comfort the grief-stricken man. Looking relieved to see help arriving, she stepped aside to make room for Sam.

"My only son," Joseph said to no one in particular. "My boy."

Dealing with the families of murder victims was the most difficult part of Sam's job, and it never got any easier. "I'm very sorry for your loss, Mr. Alvarez."

"I don't understand. Who would do such a thing to my Daniel? Or Mr. Olivo? Everyone loved them both."

"Is it possible another worker locked the freezer without knowing they were in there?" Sam asked, still not entirely convinced this was a homicide.

He shook his head. "It was only the two of them closing for the night. As soon as I saw Danny's phone sitting on the counter I knew something was wrong. My son is *never* without that damned phone. I was always after him about it. If he wasn't looking at it between customers at work, it was in his pocket. Someone had to have threatened them to get him into that freezer without his phone."

"How long after closing did you wait to come check on him?"

"A couple of hours. They close at nine, and he usually goes out with his friends after. He has to be home by eleven, so when he wasn't home at eleven-thirty and wasn't answering his phone, I came looking for him." Mr. Alvarez rooted around in his shirt pocket and withdrew a pack of cigarettes. His hands shook as he lit one. "I don't know what drew me to the freezer. Just a feeling I had." Shuddering, he broke down again. "I'll never forget seeing the two of them in there."

"Did you notice if anything in the kitchen area or restaurant was disturbed?"

He shook his head. "Everything looked normal to me. At first I thought I was losing it for storming down here like an over-protective father, but when I saw that phone...I knew something was wrong when I saw Danny's phone." Wiping his face, he leaned back against the wall and looked up at the sky. "I lost my wife a year ago. Breast cancer. Danny and I... We were getting back on track. I can't believe this has happened."

Moved by his despair and more certain now this had, in fact, been a homicide, Sam laid a hand on his arm. "We'll do everything we can to find the person who did this." Not that an arrest would bring much comfort, she thought. His son would still be gone forever.

Nodding, he took another deep drag on his cigarette.

"Did Danny have trouble with anyone at school or outside of school?"

"No one. My boy was popular. Everyone loved him. He had a nice girlfriend, lots of good friends. Played sports. A good kid." Joseph gestured to the back door, which was propped open. "This was his first real job."

"Did he say anything about Mr. Olivo having trouble with anyone?"

"Not that I ever heard. His wife died last year, too. We had that in common. Had a few talks about it here and there while I was in to see Danny at work."

"Did Mr. Olivo have any other family in the area?"

"I don't think so. He said something once about his kids being scattered and not getting home much since their mother died. I got the feeling there was some strain between him and the kids. Nothing that would've led to this though."

"You've been very helpful. Is there someone I could call for you? A family member maybe?"

He shook his head. "It was just me and Danny. My family's gone, and since my wife died, we haven't seen much of her people."

"I can't leave you here all alone."

"I'll call my buddy from work. He'll come get me. Go ahead. I'll be okay."

Sam needed to get to work figuring out what'd happened here, but a quick glance at Joseph Alvarez's shattered expression told her he was anything but okay. Standing next to him, she put her hands in her pockets and leaned against the same wall that propped him up. "I'll wait with you until your friend gets here."

CHAPTER TWO

*S*am and Freddie spent the rest of the night interviewing Carl Olivo's other employees, his regular customers and tracking down his scattered children. By the time the sun began to rise over the capital city, they had put together a portrait of a man who was well liked by his employees and customers but not particularly close to anyone.

Of all the people they talked to only Joseph Alvarez had related anything even remotely personal about the intensely private man. From what they could gather, Carl was a workaholic who poured all his time and energy into his restaurant and hadn't had much left over at the end of the workday for his children, which explained the estrangement.

"I hate cases like this," Sam said to Freddie as they rode in her car to HQ. They'd dropped his rattletrap Mustang at a garage for service. Apparently his on-again-off-again girlfriend Elin Svendsen was on again and had complained about the car's propensity to backfire without warning. Sam had held back a laugh when he told her Elin always thought they were being shot at when it happened. "Two seemingly nice, unassuming people killed for no apparent reason."

"Where do we even go from here?"

"I guess we wait to hear from Lindsey and the Crime Scene detectives." When Sam and Freddie left the restaurant, the

Crime Scene officers were still sifting through the freezer where the bodies had been found. "Until then, we've got diddly squat."

"Lindsey said something about having to wait for the bodies to thaw before she could do the autopsy. So gross."

Since Sam couldn't argue with that, she didn't try. "I've got something I need to do when we get back to HQ."

"You'll want to see Gardner."

Surprised he knew exactly what she was up to, Sam glanced at him. "You think you know me so well, don't you?"

Amused, he shrugged. "Am I wrong?"

"You're not wrong."

"Want me to go with you?"

"Thanks, but I'd better go alone. He's already stonewalled you and Gonzo. I might have a better chance on my own."

"Whatever you want, Lieutenant. The whole squad is pulling for a break on your dad's case. I hope you know that."

"I do, and I appreciate the support." She'd devoted a ridiculous amount of time on the beach in Bora Bora imagining her showdown with Darius Gardner, who'd shot at her and Freddie the week before the wedding when they'd gone to ask him some questions about her father's unsolved shooting.

At HQ, they headed to the pit. Sam went into her office to get the Gardner file and noticed a huge stack of mail on her desk. "What the hell?" she muttered. Whatever that was about she'd deal with it after she had her moment with Gardner.

Standing outside one of the city jail's interrogation rooms a few minutes later, she studied Darius Gardner through the observation window. At just over six feet tall, Gardner had dark hair and eyes and a muscular build. It would be rather easy, she deduced, for him to overpower a young woman and brutally rape her, which was another of the charges he faced.

While he waited for Sam in the sterile room, his posture was full of insolence and attitude. He looked a lot less threatening than he had the last time Sam crossed paths with him—the day he'd shot at her and Freddie. Thanks to her partner's quick thinking, neither of them had been hit.

Sam reached up to run her fingers over the healing wound

on her scalp. After Freddie tackled her to get them out of the bullet's way, she'd conked her head on a rock in the yard next door. The injury had been worth the outcome—SWAT had stormed Gardner's house and arrested him for shooting at cops.

Later that day, the rape victim Gardner had intimidated years earlier came forward to finally press charges. They had him nailed on both counts, but that wasn't why Sam had spent a big chunk of her honeymoon thinking about him. No, she'd thought about him because there was a good chance he might've shot her father more than two years ago.

With her wedding days after the confrontation with Gardner, she'd had to put off this meeting for two long weeks and had made it a top priority on this first day back to work. Rolling her shoulders, she prepared to do battle. This was her battlefield, her war room. This was where she shined, and if ever there was a time when she needed to shine, this was it. Some nameless, faceless bastard had shot her father and left him a quadriplegic. If it was the last thing Sam ever did, she'd make that person pay.

"You don't have to do this," a voice behind her said.

Startled, Sam turned to find her mentor, Detective Captain Malone, standing with hands on hips. His warm gray eyes studied her intently.

"Yes, I do." She returned her attention to Gardner, who tapped his fingers on the table as if he had much better things to do than wait for her. "Why're you here so early?"

"I had a feeling this might be your first stop today. Thought you might need some moral support."

"It wasn't quite my first stop." She briefed him on the murders at Carl's.

"Oh, jeez. I love that place. I know Carl."

"How well did you know him?"

Malone thought about that for a minute. "Not that well, come to think of it. We passed pleasantries whenever I was in there, but that's as far as it went."

"I got the same story from just about everyone who knows him. Looks to be another head-scratcher."

"Aren't they all?" Malone stepped farther into the small

observation room. "Cruz and Gonzales didn't get anywhere with Gardner."

Sam rolled her shoulders again, fighting the tension that wanted to settle there. "I know."

"So what's the plan?" Malone asked.

"I'll offer him leniency on the incident at his house in exchange for information about my father's shooting."

"You talk to the USA about that?" he asked, referring to the U.S. attorney.

"Nope. I have no plans to do shit for that scumbag, no matter what he might have to tell me."

Malone chuckled. "Are you the same gal who made for such a lovely bride a few short weeks ago?"

"One and the same." She took another hard look at Gardner. "Well, here goes nothing."

"Sam." Malone put a hand on her arm, forcing her to look at him. "If you don't think you're going to get him, walk away. Let him spend a little more time rotting in jail. Your offer will start to look a whole lot better to him the longer he's in."

Knowing the captain was right, she nodded, took a deep breath and stepped into the room.

Gardner sat up straighter but eyed her with disdain. "You again."

"That's right."

"What'd you want?"

"Same thing I wanted that day at your house. If you hadn't shot at me and my partner, we could've cleared up this whole thing then."

"What whole thing?"

"I want to know where you were on December 28, 2008."

Snorting, he rolled his eyes. "I'll tell you the same thing I told you the last time—I got no fucking clue."

"Think about it. What did you do for Christmas that year?"

He shrugged. "Same thing I do every year. Nothing."

Sam opened the file she'd brought with her to the interrogation room. "A run of your credit cards and ATM records shows you were in the city that day."

"What's that prove? I *live* here." He slouched into the chair, an arm hiked up on the back as if he was hanging out in someone's living room. "What's so important about that day anyway?"

That day, Sam thought, *changed my life more profoundly than almost any other.* She withdrew her father's department photograph from the folder and placed it on the table in front of Gardner. "That was the day Deputy Chief Skip Holland was shot on G Street." Pulling out a second photo of her father in his wheelchair, she placed it next to the first one. "That's him today."

Gardner gave the photos about three seconds of his attention. "I still don't see what that's got to do with me."

"You lived for a time in Washington Highlands." She recited an address on First Avenue.

"So?"

"We found clippings, photos and other items referring to the shooting at that address after you lived there."

Gardner propped his elbows on the table and leaned in. "I'll tell you the same thing I told those other detectives the day you arrested me—I didn't shoot no cop on G Street."

"If you expect me to believe that, you'll need to tell me where you were that day."

He slapped his hand on the table. "I don't fucking know!"

"Let me refresh your memory." She listed his credit-card transactions for the day in question. "Ringing any bells?"

"Nope."

"Too bad." Sam relaxed into her chair. "I was willing to offer up a deal on the charges of assaulting police officers with a deadly weapon in exchange for information about the 2008 shooting. But now…" She shrugged.

"You can take your deal and shove it up your ass."

Sam put the photos of her father back in the folder and closed it. "Then I guess we're done here." She stood up. "The deal expires in forty-eight hours." Leaving the room, she tried to ignore the subtle tremble in her hands. She'd love to plow her fist into his sanctimonious face, but that wouldn't get her any closer to the answers she needed.

"You did everything you could," Captain Malone said.

Sam nodded.

"Take a deep breath."

She took two of them.

"We'll keep digging. We'll keep looking. We'll never stop until we close this case."

The captain was one of her father's closest friends. Unable to trust herself to make eye contact with him, she nodded again. She couldn't escape the overwhelming feeling that she was letting everyone down by not being able to solve this most important of cases. To the deputy standing guard, she said, "You can take him back."

"Yes, ma'am, Lieutenant."

"Do you know what that pile of crap on my desk is all about?" Sam asked the captain as they made their way to the detectives' pit.

"Wedding cards, I believe."

Startled, Sam stared up at him. "Get the hell out of here."

"We were inundated. They came in all last week. I heard there's another bag in the mailroom."

"God," Sam said, "how embarrassing."

"Think of it this way," Malone said, laughing, "your under-cover days are over."

"There is that." Sam hated working undercover—never more so than during her tumultuous investigation into the Johnson family's drug ring, which had resulted in a child being shot and killed. Many months later, thoughts of that night still had the power to make her sick.

"So how was the trip?"

"Good."

He raised an eyebrow. "Just 'good'?"

"Nice try, but that's all you're getting."

Entering the pit, Sam received a warm welcome back from her detectives. Even though she was still smarting from the unsuccessful confrontation with Gardner, Sam accepted the good-natured ribbing about her tan, the honeymoon, the wedding and everything else they could think of.

"All right, everyone," Sam said. "Playtime's over. Get to

work." She went into her office, flipped on the light and took a closer look at the enormous pile of cards she'd barely glanced at earlier.

The last thing she felt like dealing with on her first day back to work was a stack of mail, but since she had no choice but to wait for autopsy and crime scene reports from Carl's, she sat at her desk and flipped through the cards. They were addressed to Sam Holland, Mrs. Nicholas Cappuano, Mrs. Senator Cappuano, Mrs. Sam Cappuano and Lt. Sam Holland. The many identities amused her. For the record, she might be married now, but she wasn't changing her name at work.

Her *husband*—she still got a kick out of saying that—was fine with that, which was all that mattered to her. She'd told him on their wedding night that she planned to be Samantha Cappuano at home, which had taken him completely by surprise.

As she sifted through the hundreds of congratulatory cards, letters and messages, Sam continued to be amazed by how popular she and Nick had become throughout the Capital region during their whirlwind romance.

"May your life be filled with all the love and joy that brought you together," one message read.

"Amen," Sam said. She was onboard with a lifetime of the love and joy she'd experienced with Nick over the last few months. She could, however, do without the spate of drama that began with the murder of his boss, Senator John O'Connor, continued with Nick's appointment to complete the last year of John's term, the murder of O'Connor family friend and Supreme Court nominee Julian Sinclair, Nick's decision to run for the Senate in the fall election, and the investigation that led to the abduction and assault of Sam's colleague, Detective Jeannie McBride.

Life, she had assured Nick during the blissful days of their honeymoon, surely couldn't continue to be as crazy as it had been lately. He'd been skeptical, but he had good reason to be.

She followed her nose to a pink envelope that reeked of cheap perfume. When she opened it, she scowled at the confetti that spilled onto her desk. Why did people think anyone wanted a card full of shredded paper to clean up? "As you begin your married life, may you know good luck, good health and good fortune," the card proclaimed.

Under the printed message, the sender had handwritten in block letters, "Dear Sam, So happy to hear you now have everything you've ever dreamed of—a job you love, a family you love and a man who loves you as much as you love him. No one deserves such happiness more than you do. I hope you both live long enough to enjoy all that good luck, good health and good fortune." It was signed, "An Old Friend."

She dropped the card onto her desk and scooted her chair back from the desk. Rising, she went to the door and signaled to Cruz in the pit. "Bring me an evidence bag," she said.

Freddie came into the office holding the bag in one hand and a half-eaten candy bar in the other.

"Find some gloves"

"What're you up to?"

"Just get them, will you?"

Shooting her a puzzled look, he left the office.

Sam stared at the card on her desk, her mind whirling with possibilities. In twelve years on the police force, she'd made her share of enemies. In a matter of seconds she compiled a long list of possible suspects.

Freddie returned with the gloves. "What've you got?"

"A thinly veiled threat." She relayed what the card had said. "Or so it seemed to me."

"Let me see."

She nodded to the card lying open on her desk.

He took a bite of his candy bar. "I don't get it," he said, his voice muffled by caramel and nougat.

"Read it again."

"Okay. So what?"

"They hope we *'live long enough'* to enjoy our happiness? Is that something people normally write in a wedding card?"

"Hmm. You may have a point."

"Gee, really? And here I thought you were one of my best and brightest."

He scowled at her and took another bite of candy.

Donning the gloves, she lifted the card and envelope into the evidence bag. "Get that to the lab and tell them I want a full workup ASAP. Don't get chocolate on the bag."

He rolled his eyes at her. "What about the rest of it?"

Sam glanced at the huge pile of unopened cards on her desk. "Until we have more to go on with the Carl's killings, I guess we glove up and go through each one."

"You think Nick got one, too?"

Sam sucked in a sharp deep breath. "Christ, I never thought of that. Maybe there's hope for you yet." As he scowled at her for using the Lord's name in vain, she reached for the phone to call her husband. Thinking of him that way made her buzz with happiness even if the reason for the call was unsettling.

"Hey, babe," he said. "How's it going?"

"Okay, I guess. The thing at Carl's was rough. Carl and a seventeen-year-old kid who was his father's only living family."

"Jeez."

"No kidding."

"How'd it go with Gardner?"

Of course he would assume she'd already taken care of that piece of business. He knew how badly she'd wanted her moment with that scumbag. "Nowhere fast."

"Sorry to hear that. Are you okay?"

"Yeah. Another dead end. For now."

"So what's up? Miss me already?"

What would he say if she told him she'd missed him from the minute she left him? "You know it. So while we were gone, did you get any mail?"

"*Tons* of it. You?"

"Same. Did your office open it?"

"Not all the cards and stuff they could tell were personal."

"Listen, do me a favor and don't touch any of it until I can get there."

"What's going on, Samantha?"

He was the only one allowed to call her that and usually only trotted out the dreaded name at the most important of moments. "I'm not sure, but I'll tell you about it when I see you."

"And here I thought I had to wait *all* day to see my lovely wife. What a nice surprise this is."

She smiled. "I'll be right over."

CHAPTER THREE

"*A*re you *kidding me?*" Sam asked as she took in the mountain of cards that occupied the meeting table in Nick's Capitol Hill office. There had to be thousands of envelopes. "You're *way* more popular than I am."

"It's because I'm far more charming than you are," her handsome husband said. At six foot four with soft brown hair that curled at the ends, gorgeous hazel eyes and a mouth made for sin, Nick turned female heads everywhere they went. No doubt more than a few of the cards were from his admiring public.

"I can't deny you're more charming than I am," she said. She'd never been known for her charm and was fine with leaving that trait to him. "Perhaps the eight million citizens you represent might have something to do with why more people are happy for you than they are for me."

"All these people," he said, gesturing to the pile, "are happy for *both* of us."

"Not all of them." While it still went against her nature to share everything with him, especially stuff she knew would upset him, she told him about the threatening card she'd received.

Hands on his hips, face set in an unreadable expression, he stared at the pile of cards.

Sam went to him and rested a hand on his back. "What're you thinking?"

He glanced at her. "It never ends, does it? Just when we've neutralized one threat against you, another pops up."

Sam knew he was referring to the recent murder investigation that had uncovered a prostitution ring reaching the government's highest levels. As she'd closed in on the man who'd raped and murdered two women and kidnapped and raped Detective McBride, Sam had been warned to back off or face a similar fate.

"We don't know for sure this is a new threat. Maybe it's someone thinking they're being funny."

"You don't believe that or you wouldn't be here."

"I don't know what to believe yet. Could be nothing, could be something. I have to take all these cards and go through them, okay?"

"Whatever you need to do."

Sam reached behind her and closed the office door. Sealed off from the prying eyes of his busy staff, Sam took his left hand and kissed the platinum band she'd recently placed on his finger. The sight of that ring never failed to stir her. That the one who'd gotten away now belonged to her forever was still hard to believe. "I don't want you to worry until we know we have something to worry about."

He put his arms around her and rested his chin on the top of her head. They fit together like two halves of a whole. Sam closed her eyes and took a moment to breathe in the scent of starch in his dress shirt as well as the citrusy cologne that suited him so perfectly. She concentrated on remembering the blissful days and nights they'd spent together in Bora Bora.

"I always worry about you," he said. "You know that."

"The card mentioned both of us living long enough." She looked up at him. "If this turns out to be something to worry about, would you consider requesting protection, especially on campaign stops?" When she thought about the hordes of people he'd been attracting on the campaign trail, she shuddered at how easy it would be for someone to take a shot at him.

"Let's cross that bridge if and when we come to it."

"It may come to it, and I won't need you being mulish about asking for protection."

"And who will protect you, my love?"

She flashed a big grin and rested her hand on the service weapon on her hip. "I've got my protection right here."

"Samantha…"

"I'll be careful," she assured him, going up on tiptoes to kiss him. "I've got so much to live for these days. No point in being reckless."

"I'm glad to hear you say that." He glanced again at the pile of cards. "Is it possible this could be Peter's handiwork?" Her ex-husband had tried to kill them both with crude bombs strapped to their cars. He'd recently been released from jail on a technicality that rankled Sam because it was partly her fault. She'd let her detectives enter his apartment before they obtained a search warrant. Stupid mistake she was now paying for by having that lunatic on the loose again.

"I suppose it's possible, and it's certainly his style. Good old Peter *loves* the passive-aggressive game."

"And it would piss him off that we're married now, especially after all he did to keep us apart."

Six years ago, after Sam and Nick met at a party and spent a memorable night together, Peter, her platonic roommate at the time, had gone to great lengths to make sure she never saw Nick again. She still couldn't believe she'd fallen for his games and ended up spending four miserable years married to the controlling bastard when she could've been with Nick all that time. The night before her wedding to Nick, Peter had confronted her on the street outside their home. Violating a restraining order, he'd pulled a gun on her and let her know their relationship would "never be over." He'd gotten a two-week slap on the wrist for the stunt and was now walking free again.

Nick kissed her forehead and then lingered at her lips. "Don't think about it or him," he said, tuning into her thoughts as he often did. "The past is the past, and all that matters now is the future."

"I swear to God, if he's got the balls to threaten us, I'll kill him with my own hands."

"You'll do me no good in prison, babe," he said with a devilish grin that calmed her. "Even though you'd look awfully sexy in an orange jumpsuit."

"Very funny. Can you grab me a couple of garbage bags for all these cards?"

"I'll see what I can find," he said. "I'll need them back when you're done with them."

"What for?"

"I have to acknowledge them all."

Sam stared at him. "Seriously?"

"Such is the glamorous life of a politician."

"What about the hundreds that were sent to me?"

"I'll need any that came from Virginia."

"Better you than me."

While he went to get the bags, she plopped down at his desk and studied the tidy piles of reports, file folders and other desk paraphernalia, which, as always, was arranged with the neat precision that drove her bonkers. Taking a quick look to make sure he wasn't on his way back yet, she turned the pile of reports so they were all upside down and knocked them out of whack so they wouldn't be anally aligned the way he liked them. Then she turned the picture of the two of them from the White House state dinner—the night they'd gotten engaged—upside down. Finally, she scrawled "Sam loves Nick" on a sticky note and put it inside his desk drawer. She loved the idea of him finding that later. By the time he returned, she was sitting with her feet up on the desk and hands folded in her lap, the picture of innocence.

As he crossed the threshold with the bags, he stopped short. "What're you doing over there?"

"Just waiting for you, my love."

He eyed her warily. "And that's *all* you're doing?"

"What else would I be doing?" It took all her self-control not to descend into laughter. Messing with his need for rigid order was one of her favorite pastimes.

Sam got up to take the bags from him and gloved up to fill them with the cards. Because the bags were too heavy to carry on her own, he walked her to the car she'd left illegally parked outside the Hart Building.

Holding the car door for her, he leaned in for a kiss. "Gonna be a long day, huh?"

"Looks that way."

"Here we go again."

DETECTIVE JEANNIE MCBRIDE sat in the window seat in her boyfriend Michael's bedroom, which overlooked a leafy street in the city's Foggy Bottom neighborhood.

"Coffee?" he said, handing her a steaming mug.

She worked up a smile for him. "Thanks."

"Got any plans today?" he asked as he knotted his tie.

"Nothing special." How could she tell him it took all she had to get out of bed, to breathe, to eat, to function? Forget about sleeping. Every time she closed her eyes she was back in the yellow room, tied to a bed while a monster attacked her.

How could she tell Michael that the thought of him or any man touching her made her sick? Or that the overwhelming love she'd once felt for him was gone? It had been replaced by numbness so deep and so pervasive she'd begun to wonder if she'd ever feel anything but nothing ever again.

"Want to meet me for lunch?"

Since that would require showering, getting dressed and leaving the cocoon of his comfortable home, she shook her head. "No, thanks."

He sat next to her and reached for her hand. "I'm worried about you, Jeannie. Every morning I wake up hoping this might be the day you start to feel a little better, but it seems to be getting worse."

"I need some more time."

"I hate to see you in so much pain. There has to be something we can do. Maybe that counselor Sam suggested—"

"No," Jeannie said sharply—more sharply than she'd

intended. He'd been a pillar of strength and comfort in the dark days following the attack. He certainly deserved better than her snapping at him. "I'm sorry, but the last thing I need is to relive it all again." Reliving it once with her lieutenant had been more than enough. Eventually, she'd have to relive it in court, too. So no, a counselor was the last thing she needed.

"Whatever you want."

He looked so tired and sad, which only added to her guilt over what she was putting him through. The days when they'd been blissfully happy and newly in love seemed like a long time ago rather than a few short weeks. She reached out to caress his face. "Maybe I should move back to my place. I'm not all that much fun to have around these days."

He took her hand and kissed the palm. "That's not necessary. You feel safer here because of the security system. I want you to feel safe."

She didn't feel safe anywhere. She was a cop, a Homicide detective, and she'd been nabbed off the street in broad daylight. Would she ever feel safe again?

"I had hoped you'd feel better once they caught him."

"I do." How could she tell him that knowing her attacker was behind bars didn't do a damned thing to erase the memory of what he'd done to her?

"I thought you'd want to get back to work, back to something that feels normal."

What was normal anymore? In her eight years as a police officer she'd learned you could lock up one monster but there were thousands more like him roaming the streets looking for someone else to attack, someone else to change forever.

"I'm not ready yet," she said. How could she tell him she didn't think she'd ever be ready to return to work or any other part of the life she'd had before?

The doorbell rang, startling them.

"I'll get it," he said, kissing her forehead before he left her.

She wondered how long it would be before he left her for good.

He was back a minute later. "Someone here to see you." The determined look on his face set her nerves on edge.

"I don't want to see—"

Michael stepped aside to admit Lieutenant Holland into the room. She dropped a huge trash bag on the floor next to her.

Jeannie ran trembling fingers through her hair, wondering if she looked as awful as she felt.

"Sorry to bother you, Detective," Sam said, all business. "But I could use your help."

"Oh. Really?"

Sam told her about the threatening card she'd received and about the thousands of cards they now had to go through to see if there were others. "I thought you might be willing to lend a hand with the investigation."

Since that would require effort and focus, Jeannie wanted to say no, but the pleading expression on Michael's face stopped her from uttering the single world that hovered on the tip of her tongue.

"Can I count on you?" Sam asked.

Jeannie thought of the hours her lieutenant—and friend— had spent by her bedside as she endured the rape kit examination, the setting of her fractured wrist and the trauma of reliving the attack for the sake of the investigation. Now someone was threatening her sister officer, her friend. How could she say no to helping her? Clearing her throat, Jeannie said, "Of course."

Smiling, Sam withdrew several pairs of gloves from one pocket and a fistful of evidence bags from the other and held them out to her.

Hoping her trembling legs would support her weight, Jeannie got up from the window seat and made her way across the room. Halfway there, she realized she couldn't remember the last time she'd showered. She took the gloves and bags from Sam.

Sam waited for Jeannie to look up at her, to make eye contact. In her lieutenant's eyes she saw a touch of sadness along with determination. "Let me know if you find anything."

Jeannie nodded.

"Thank you."

"No problem."

After Sam left the room, Jeannie stared at the huge bag on the bedroom floor. All at once, a wave of panic hit her. Why had she agreed to help? She was on leave. They couldn't make her work. What had Sam been thinking coming to her home and dragging her into an investigation when all Jeannie wanted was to be left alone?

Possibly sensing her growing panic, Michael put his arms around her, drawing her into his embrace.

Jeannie took deep, calming breaths of his familiar scent and fought back the panic that threatened to consume her.

"You can do this, Jeannie. I know you can. Sam must need your help or she never would've bothered you."

Jeannie nodded.

"Why don't you take a nice, hot shower, and I'll fix you some breakfast before you get started?"

"Okay." She did as he suggested, but only because she was tired of seeing that worried, desperate look on his face. For the first time in weeks, he seemed a little hopeful.

Standing under the hot water, she thought about Sam and her senator husband and how happy they had been on their recent wedding day—the only time Jeannie had left the house since the attack. The idea of someone threatening them made Jeannie good and mad, which she decided was better than the numbness. Anything was better than that.

CHAPTER FOUR

*S*o much for a nice easy return to work, Sam thought as she set up the murder board in the conference room. A double murder and some hate mail would complicate any day, but the post-vacation gods had been particularly harsh on her.

Crime Scene had scoured the kitchen in Carl's restaurant and hadn't found a shred of useful evidence. After autopsies, Lindsey reported both victims had asphyxiated from the lack of oxygen in the freezer. She placed time of death at right around ten-thirty. From what Sam could deduce, someone had come into the restaurant, maybe pulled a gun on Carl and Daniel, ordered them into the freezer and locked them in. By the time Daniel's father arrived at eleven-thirty, they were long gone.

What bothered her most was the bag of cash left sitting on the counter. Why hadn't the perp taken it?

"What're you thinking, boss?" Freddie asked as he came into the conference room with sandwiches for both of them. His was an extra-large meat-lovers while hers was a small veggie. And she'd be the one to gain weight from the meal. Life wasn't fair.

"I'm thinking about the money."

"What money?"

"The deposit bag full of cash on the counter at Carl's. If someone came in there and forced them into the freezer, why didn't they take the money?"

"Because they weren't there to rob the place?" he said over a mouth full of sub.

"Who couldn't use a couple thousand extra dollars?"

"So you're saying regardless of why they were there, they should've taken the money."

"Not so much *should've.* It's weird to me they didn't. Hell, I would've."

Her phone chimed with a text message from Nick. *Very fitting you should turn the picture upside down since you've already turned my life upside down. Revenge is sweet, my love.* Sam's insides went all fluttery. How many more hours until she could go home to him?

"What's with the goofy grin?" Freddie asked, bringing her back to reality. "Must be the *husband.*"

Sam snapped her phone closed and jammed it in her pocket. "We need to find out if Carl had any disgruntled former employees."

"How do we do that?"

"We go through his office and see what we can find. Eat up." She downed the last of her sandwich and chased it with a bottle of water, all the while wishing it were a diet cola. Nick's doctor friend Harry had made her give up diet soda when she'd gone to him complaining of vicious stomach pains. She still hadn't forgiven Harry for that diagnosis, even if it had cured her stomach ills. Stepping into the pit, she gestured for her colleague Detective Tommy "Gonzo" Gonzales and his partner Detective Arnold to join them.

"What's up, Lieutenant?" Gonzo asked.

Sam noticed he looked tired, no doubt from the late nights he was keeping with the infant son he'd recently learned he had fathered with an ex-girlfriend. The baby was now living with him and his fiancée, Christina Billings, who also happened to be Nick's chief of staff. Sam *loved* the way her personal and professional lives kept butting into each other. Not.

"I need a favor." She told the detectives about the threatening card that had cropped up in the mail she'd received while she was away on her honeymoon. "I need some help going through the rest of it."

Gonzo and Arnold took a long look at the huge piles of cards on the conference room table and then glanced at each other.

"I know, believe me. It sucks. But if someone is threatening a police officer and a U.S. senator, we can't ignore it."

"Well, we could ignore it," Freddie added, flashing her his best ingratiating smile, "but because the police officer is our lieutenant, and because the senator happens to be her husband, we're not going to ignore it."

"That's not why," Sam snapped. "We'd investigate no matter who was being threatened."

"Of course we would," Freddie said, contrite. "Joke gone bad. My apologies."

"No, no," Sam said. "I know you were kidding, and believe me, it burns my ass to have to devote department resources to something so stupid. Maybe we should ignore it."

"We're not ignoring it," Gonzo said. "Go work your homicide. We'll dive in here and see what we've got."

"Thank you," Sam said, relieved he got it. He always did, which made him one of her most valued colleagues and closest friends. "I, um, I need you to make sure you're careful with any of the cards that came from Virginia." She could feel her face heating with embarrassment. "Nick has to…you know…acknowledge them."

"Got it," Gonzo said without blinking an eye even though he probably had something he was dying to say about her high-profile love life.

"Let's hit it, Cruz."

When they were in the car on their way back to Carl's, Freddie turned to her. "Sorry about the crack back there. I didn't mean anything by it."

"I know that. I *hate* all the attention Nick and I get in this city. I wish they'd get tired of us and move on to bothering someone else for a change."

"I doubt they'll get tired of you guys anytime soon, especially with him running in the November election."

"It's maddening. I want to live my life in peace. Is that too much to ask?"

"Because you're you and he's him and people are interested in the two of you, I'd say that is indeed too much to ask."

Sam scowled then moaned when her phone rang with the tone she'd set for the one reporter she'd learned to tolerate, Darren Tabor from the *Washington Star*.

"What?" she barked into the phone, wondering if the guy was psychic or something.

"I can see two weeks in the tropics didn't do a thing for your surly disposition," Darren said.

"What do you want, Darren?"

"While I was hurt to not be invited to the wedding, I wanted to say congratulations."

"Thanks. Anything else?"

"What've you got on the murders at Carl's?"

"Not a goddamned thing."

"You're not usually so forthcoming, Lieutenant."

"I'd ask you not to quote me on that, but I suppose it's too late to go off the record now."

"I won't quote you if you tell me it'll compromise the case."

And that, Sam thought, is why she took his calls. That and a favor he'd once done for her that she wouldn't soon forget. "Go ahead and quote me this time. Maybe it'll generate some leads. We can use all the help we can get."

"May I soften the *goddamned* to just *damned?*"

Sam snorted. "By all means."

"Keep me in mind if you have an exclusive or two you can share with your favorite reporter."

"Bye, Darren."

"I think he's growing on you," Freddie said after she ended the call.

"The way fungus grows on a tree."

That cracked up her partner. "You have a way with words, Lieutenant. Speaking of which, I'd prefer if you wouldn't use the one that starts with *G* and ends with *D*."

"You mean *good?* Or are you referring to *gonad?* Then there's always *Galahad.*"

Freddie's scowl made her laugh.

They spent the afternoon pouring over Carl's tidily kept books, bank accounts and personnel records and discovered that the last person he'd fired had been let go more than eight years earlier.

"Rules out a disgruntled ex-employee," Sam said, frustrated. Rarely did she find herself in the midst of a homicide investigation without a single idea of what to do next. "We need a thread to pull, and we've got nada."

"Maybe we should dig deeper into the kid," Freddie said. "Perhaps he wasn't as squeaky clean as his father thought."

"Entirely possible. Still, I can't shake the feeling he was in the wrong place at the wrong time. But let's go find out what we can about him."

They spent three hours talking to teachers, coaches, the parents of Daniel's friends as well as his devastated girlfriend and came away with an impression that was exactly in keeping with what his father had told them—a good kid on the right path with a bright future ahead of him.

"Depressing," Freddie said on the way back to HQ. "The kid had everything in the world to live for."

"This wasn't random," Sam said. "Someone went in there looking to take out one of them and the other was collateral damage. Since Daniel was as squeaky clean as it gets, my money is on Carl."

"The guy was totally innocuous. Who'd want him dead?"

"I have no freaking clue," she said.

Joseph Alvarez was waiting for them when they returned to HQ.

Sam's stomach clenched the way it used to when she was strung out on diet cola.

"Lieutenant," Joseph said, his face lined with grief and exhaustion. "Tell me you've figured out who killed my Danny."

"Come into my office, Mr. Alvarez."

She gestured for him to have a seat and leaned back against

her desk. "I wish I could tell you we have something, but we don't."

His face fell with disappointment, which tugged at her. He'd already had more than his share.

"We suspect this wasn't a random crime, but rather something planned and calculated. We believe one of them was targeted and the other was in the wrong place at the wrong time. What we don't know is what either of them could've done to bring this about. From all reports, both were well liked and respected. Mr. Olivo was low-key and tended to keep to himself." She took a deep breath. "I'm afraid we've hit a dead end. We don't have a shred of evidence pointing to a third person in that kitchen last night."

Dejected, he looked down at his feet. "So the person who did this to my Danny could get away with it?"

"Not if I have anything to say about it. I'd like to go through Danny's room. While it might seem invasive, we need to do it anyway. If he has a computer, we'll remove it for analysis. It would be quicker to have your permission so we don't have to get a warrant."

"Whatever it takes."

"We'll work every angle we can, but we'll never give up. I promise you that."

"I've read about you in the paper. I know how tenacious you can be."

"I'll put that tenacity to good use on Danny's case, and I'll keep you informed of every development. I'll do my best for you, Mr. Alvarez, and for Danny."

"I suppose I can't ask for anything more than that."

After he left, Sam stood there for a long time rethinking every second since she arrived at Carl's just after midnight. Finally, she turned and called for Freddie.

THEY TORE apart Daniel Alvarez's bedroom as well as the basement computer room where he liked to hang out. The computer was sent to the lab for further scrutiny, but they found nothing else useful to the investigation. Unlike many of his peers, Daniel had no deep dark secrets he kept hidden from his father. Sam was relieved they didn't find anything that would add to Joseph's grief, but the search hadn't done a thing to further the investigation.

They had similar luck—or lack thereof—at Carl Olivo's small house. All his paperwork was in perfect order. The house was neat and tidy and held absolutely no hints to explain why someone might want him dead.

Defeated and running on fumes after the night without sleep, Sam and Freddie returned to HQ to relieve Gonzo and Arnold who'd spent the day opening Sam's mail. The grand total, at the end of the long day, was 4,132. More than thirty-five hundred cards had been sent to Nick's office, the rest to Sam's. Not one of the other 4,131 cards had contained a threat—thinly veiled or otherwise.

"Is it weird I read maybe ten of the cards sent to me and managed to find the single threatening one?" Sam asked Freddie as they polished off a pizza around nine.

"You think someone put it right on top where you were sure to see it?"

"It's possible."

"Which would mean it came from someone here. Who else besides Lieutenant Stahl would do something like that to you?"

"No one probably, but who knows? Someone could've walked in the front door, handed the card to an admin who dropped it on my desk. Or handed it to any cop and asked them to give it to me. Because of the wedding, no one would think twice about tossing it on my desk."

"But it had been through the postage machine, so that rules out hand delivery."

"Baffling," Sam said. She rolled up the paper towel she'd used as a napkin and sent it arching into the garbage can. "Let's clean this up and get out of here. I need to go home and tend to these paper cuts."

"The hazards of this job never end."

"I hear ya. Thanks for staying late."

"No problem."

"So how's it going with Elin?"

"We've been seeing each other here and there since the wedding."

"Define 'seeing each other.'"

"Why do I have to define it?"

"Are we talking going out to dinner or all sex all the time?"

Flustered, he scowled at her. "None of your business."

"Ahhh, sex fest revisited. I get it."

"Whatever you say."

"Did you ever go out with that girl your mother fixed you up with? The one from church?"

"Yeah. No spark. She didn't do it for me. She was a perfectly nice girl, though."

"I'm sure she was if your mother liked her." As they talked, they boxed up all the cards and letters. "So let me get this straight—while you continue to burn up the sheets with Elin, you're dating these girls your mother fixes you up with."

"Don't make it sound like I'm cheating on Elin. She knows I've been out with other women, and she's fine with it."

"And are you fine with her going out with other guys?"

"As long as she doesn't sleep with them, I don't mind."

Except he looked like he minded. He looked like he minded quite a lot. "Freddie, come on. Of course you do. You're playing with fire."

Throwing up his hands, he said, "What do you want me to say? My mother still hates her, and I'm sick of being in the middle of it."

"I thought you were ready to tell your mother Elin is the woman you want."

"I thought I was, too," he said, dejected. "Every time I try to broach the subject she comes up with another girl she wants me to meet. It's like she knows what I want to tell her but doesn't want to hear it."

"In the meantime, the woman you might or might not love is dating other guys. But as long as you're fine with that—"

"I'm *not* fine with it!" He ran his hands through his dark hair, leaving it disheveled. "I hate it! But how can I ask her to be exclusive when I'm not?"

"You didn't ask my opinion, but it's high time you took control of this situation. It's making you crazy."

"I know," he said, slumping into his chair.

"You're almost thirty years old, Freddie. At some point you have to live your own life and not necessarily the life your mother has in mind for you."

"I'm not entirely a mama's boy. If she'd had her way, I never would've stepped foot in the police academy."

"And what a waste that would've been. You proved my point."

"Huh," he said. "I hadn't thought of it that way before."

"Go home and get some sleep. I'll see you in the morning."

"See you then."

CHAPTER FIVE

*F*reddie walked the boxes of cards to Sam's office and piled them in the corner as she'd requested. As he was locking the office door, Lieutenant Stahl came around the corner.

"You're working late tonight, Detective," Stahl said, his jowls quivering with every word.

"As are you, Lieutenant."

"What's kept you here so late?"

"Nothing special. Just taking care of some paperwork." Sifting through four thousand cards certainly counted as paperwork. Rather clever if he did say so himself. "You?"

Stahl glanced at the closed door to Sam's office—the office that used to be his—and then back at Freddie. "Nothing."

"Did you need Lieutenant Holland for something?"

Stahl's fat face twisted into a scowl. "Absolutely not."

The animosity between the two lieutenants was no secret to anyone in the department. Stahl had made more than a few threats toward Sam, especially since he'd tried and failed to punish her for hooking up with Nick during the investigation into Senator O'Connor's murder. Sam believed Stahl had fed information to her ex-husband's defense attorney that led to Peter's release from jail, but they'd been unable to prove that. Yet.

"I'll see you later then," Freddie said, getting out while the getting was good. The last person on the entire police force he wished to spend any extra time with was the lieutenant who used to oversee the detectives' squad. No one had anything good to say about the guy.

As always after an encounter with Stahl, Freddie gave Sam a quick call to let her know the unsavory lieutenant had been skulking around the detectives' pit after hours.

"What the hell is he doing?" she asked.

"Who knows?"

"I wouldn't put this card thing past him. How awesome would it be if the lab came back with his prints all over it?"

"Extremely awesome, but we'll never get that lucky."

"Sad but true. He knows I've got my eye on him. We'll trip him up eventually."

Freddie got into his Mustang, which was no less dilapidated after an expensive day in the shop, and turned on the engine to start the heat. The night was chilly for mid-April in Washington. "Can't happen soon enough for me."

"I hear ya. Thanks for the heads-up. See you in the morning."

"Later." Waiting for the car to warm up, Freddie contemplated the phone in his hand and the conversation he'd had earlier with Sam. Yes, he loved Elin. He loved everything about her. He loved her quick wit, her astute observations, those light blue eyes that looked at him with such desire and yes, he loved the sex, which was flat-out amazing. Not that he had anything to compare it to since she'd been his first, but he had a feeling he could sleep with an army of women and never find the kind of connection he had with her.

Then he thought of his mother and how completely she disapproved of his relationship with Elin, who she'd deemed too racy and worldly for her sainted son. She'd raised him alone, and their church had been central to their lives. When he was fifteen he'd taken a vow of celibacy that he'd stuck to for fourteen long years—until he met Elin and all vows went rushing out the window in a haze of lust. He'd been stunned to discover he was like every other guy who let his little brain do the thinking for his big brain.

Before the interlude with Elin, he'd liked to think he was superior to other men who lived in constant pursuit of their next bed partner. Finding out that, despite his deep Christian faith, he was no better than the next guy had been a revelation, to say the least.

Which was why he was sitting here in the dark wanting to call her and knowing if he did, he'd end up at her place and they'd be going at it in under five minutes. And that was bad how, exactly? His cock hardened as he thought of her soft skin, the firm, toned muscles from hours at the gym where she worked, those amazing breasts with the pierced nipples that hardened to sharp points and brushed against his chest as he thrust into her.

Freddie groaned and pressed the speed-dial number he'd assigned to her. He hoped she wasn't out with someone else. They'd been taking it day-by-day since she agreed to go to Sam's wedding with him, and of course Sam had been absolutely right when she concluded he and Elin were still mostly about sex.

"I wondered if you would call tonight," she said when she answered. Her voice sounded hoarse from sleep. Imagining her in bed did nothing to help the situation in his lap.

"What're you up to?"

"Nothing much. How about you?"

"Just getting out of work."

"Long day. You want to come over?"

His erection surged in answer to the question, but he forced himself to ignore the lust. "We could go out," he said, even though he had no interest in going anywhere other than her bed. "Hit a club or something."

"I'm tired. I don't feel like going out."

"We can get together another night."

Her soft laughter had him starting the car and driving toward her place. "I'm not *that* tired."

"I'm coming."

"Not yet, but you will be soon."

Freddie swallowed hard. It was official—he was addicted to her, and it was time to take this relationship to the next level, with or without his mother's approval.

SAM WAS in the car on the way home when her cell phone rang. She pressed the speaker button to take the call. "Holland."

"Other Holland," her father Skip said with a husky laugh. "I thought you were Cappuano now."

Sam smiled. "Only at home."

"Can you swing by on your way home? There's a ton of mail for you here, and Celia has some questions about some of the stuff you have upstairs."

Sam's belly took a nosedive at the mention of mail. "Sure. I'm almost there. Why do you sound all stuffed up?"

"Just a slight cold. See you in a few."

She used the remaining minutes in the car to place a call to her friend Roberto, a young man she'd met while undercover with the Johnson family.

"Is this my favorite lady cop?" he asked when he answered the call.

"One and the same. How are you, Roberto?"

"Gettin' by. Saw some wedding pictures. I had no idea you were so *fine.*"

Sam hooted with laughter. "Save the bullshit. How's the job?" She'd arranged for him to work as a clerk at city hall after he'd been caught in the spray of gunfire that killed young Quentin Johnson.

"Boring but safer than dealing drugs."

"That's what I want to hear."

"So what can I do you for?"

"The killings at Carl's."

"Heard about that. True they was found in the freezer?"

"Yep."

"Tough way to go. What'd ya wanna know?"

"Anything you hear. We've got dick, so I'll take whatever you've got."

"I don't spend much time these days talkin' to guys who'd lock people in a freezer. You saw to that."

"I'm glad to hear you're staying on the straight and narrow. Just keep your ears open for me, will you?"

"Anything for you, Lieutenant."

"How's your girlfriend? Still standing guard over you like a pit bull?"

That made the young man laugh—hard. "My Angel takes good care of me. Don't forget you want me to meet your dad. Us paralyzed guys gotta stick together."

"I'll make that happen. Soon. Call me if you hear anything?"

"You know I will."

After parking on Ninth Street, she retrieved latex gloves from the trunk of her car and stuffed them into her coat pockets. On the way up the ramp to her father's house, Sam told herself there was no reason to worry about one random card among thousands of others. It was someone's idea of a sick joke, she decided as she entered the house to find her father and stepmother in the living room.

"There's my wayward daughter who used to visit her paralyzed old man once in a while." Her father sounded hoarse and congested.

"What's the matter with you?" Sam asked as she bent to kiss his warm forehead. She glanced at Celia. "Does he have a fever?"

"Low grade. I think he's got the same crud I had at the wedding."

Except, Sam thought, for a quadriplegic, a cold could quickly turn into pneumonia. A ripple of fear worked its way through her.

"Don't worry," her stepmother the nurse said, tuning into Sam's worries. "I'm all over it."

"I'm sure you are," Sam said. "Have you called the doctor yet?"

Knowing how close father and daughter were, Celia sent her an indulgent smile. "Tomorrow, if he's not better."

"Quit hovering," Skip said. "I'm fine. What've you got on the murders at Carl's?"

"Not a damned thing. Less than nothing if that's possible." Like she often did, she went through the details of the case, hoping he might have an idea she hadn't considered.

He listened and thought it over for a long quiet moment. "What about civic organizations? Business owners are often involved in the Chamber of Commerce or the Rotary. Maybe someone knew him through one of those groups and can shed some light."

"It's something," Sam said. "I'll check it out tomorrow. I've been working since midnight. I'm about to drop."

"Then we won't keep you," Skip said. "Celia, what'd you want to ask her about the boxes in the attic?"

"Oh right. Do you want all of that to go to Nick's, too?"

"Nah, if it's okay with you guys, that can stay here. It's stuff from school and the academy. If I bring all that on top of everything else, he'll divorce me."

"Probably better to leave it here then," Celia said.

"I still can't believe I agreed to this plan of yours."

Celia laughed. "With your crazy schedule, if I hadn't packed for you, you'd be married five years and still living between two houses."

Sam kissed her stepmother's cheek. "I can't deny that, and I can't thank you enough."

Celia's pretty face radiated with happiness. "It was my pleasure, honey."

"It's been a long time since I've been mothered. I didn't realize how much I've missed it."

"Oh, well." Celia's green eyes went all misty. "That's a lovely thing to say."

"Yes, it is," Skip said. "All that paper over there is yours and your husband's." Using his eyes, he directed her to the pile of mail on the table inside the door.

Sam's eyes bugged at yet another huge stack.

"The cards have been *flooding in*," Celia said. "We can't get over it!"

Sam surveyed the pile and wondered if she'd find another threat in there. She also wondered how she'd manage to get them bagged without her father noticing. "Can you believe we got more than *four thousand* cards at work? Or I should say thirty-six hundred at Nick's office and six hundred at HQ. He's far more popular than I am."

"And why do you know those exact numbers?" Skip asked, his shrewd eyes studying her intently.

Oh crap, Sam thought. She should've known the former chief of detectives would hone right in on what she'd planned to keep from him until she knew more. "No reason."

"You expect me to believe, after being away on a rather long vacation, you had time today to count the number of wedding cards you received while you were gone? Excuse me if I don't buy that."

Cornered by the best detective she'd ever known, Sam squirmed.

"Spill it, Lieutenant. This minute."

"For a guy in a wheelchair, you can be rather intimidating."

He seemed pleased to hear that. The eyebrow on the side of his face that wasn't paralyzed lifted to let her know she'd better start talking.

"One of the cards I got contained a threat."

"What kind of threat?"

Reluctantly, Sam told him what the card had said.

"You're running it through the lab?"

She nodded. "Could be nothing."

"If you thought it was nothing, you wouldn't have gloves hanging out of your pockets so you can put that pile of mail into evidence bags."

Sam stared at him, incredulous.

He smirked. "Nothing wrong with my eyesight, baby girl."

No, she thought, wincing at the wheeze she heard coming from his chest. *But there's definitely something wrong with your lungs.*

CHAPTER SIX

*S*am took the garbage bag full of cards to the home she shared with Nick, three doors down Ninth Street from her dad's place. She had, finally, moved the majority of her clothes and a good chunk of her prized shoe collection into the spare bedroom Nick's builder friend had made into a closet for her.

The items currently crammed into a storage unit—including the other two-thirds of her shoe collection—would be delivered at a later date. She figured she needed to do this in stages so she wouldn't overwhelm Nick's anal-retentive sensibilities with her utter disregard for order.

Celia had saved Sam a ton of time and aggravation by packing up the room she'd occupied at her dad's since he was shot. No doubt her stepmother was right—without her help, Sam probably would've still been living between the two houses years from now.

Approaching the ramp that led to her front door, she glanced back at her dad's place, wondering if she should've stayed to help Celia in case he worsened during the night.

The front door swung open. "Hey, babe," Nick said. "You coming in?"

Celia had promised to call if she needed help, so Sam tore

her eyes off the house down the street and let her husband usher her into their home, a renovated double-sized townhouse he'd bought so she could be near her dad and work. Of course its Capitol Hill location put him in close proximity to his office, too.

"What's the matter?" he asked, taking her coat and hanging it in the closet when Sam would've tossed it over the sofa. Why hang it when she'd need it again in the morning?

"I think my dad is sick. He's all congested and wheezy sounding, and he has a fever."

"What did Celia say?"

"She's on it, but I'm worried about pneumonia."

"And what's this?" Nick asked, gesturing to the garbage bag full of wedding cards sitting on the floor next to her.

"More well wishes that went to Dad's house—at least I hope they're well wishes."

Nick kissed her forehead and then her lips. "My poor wife's first day back to work was far more stressful than it should've been, wasn't it?"

She nodded. "And now this with my dad. Maybe I should go back over there. Just in case."

"If that's what you want to do, I'll go with you. We can sleep over there tonight."

"Really? You wouldn't mind?"

"I'd rather have you there where you can be near him than watch you wear out a path in the carpet over here worrying about him."

Sam hadn't realized she'd been pacing as they talked. She stopped and looped her fingers together, filled with nervous energy. "Sorry. Anything with him totally freaks me out. We've been so lucky to get two pretty good years since the shooting. All that time we've known how precarious his health is now. A simple cold is anything but for him."

Nick came to her and put his arms around her. He unclipped her long hair and combed his fingers through her curls. Breathing in the scent of Nick, the scent of home, Sam closed her eyes and rested her head against his chest. At times like this, she could no longer remember what it had been like to live without him.

"Sometimes I feel guilty because I'm so grateful he survived the shooting even if I hate the way he has to live now," she said.

"I think he's come to terms with it. In his own way."

"Yeah, but it still sucks." What really sucked was the case remained unsolved more than two years later, despite ongoing effort by Sam and all of Skip's former colleagues at the Metropolitan Police Department. "I'm beginning to give up on ever solving his case."

"You will."

Sam drew back to look up at him. "You sound awfully sure of that."

"I'm awfully sure of you." Keeping his eyes firmly on hers, he lowered his head and captured her mouth.

Sam linked her hands around his neck and teased him with her tongue, making him groan.

"This was the *longest* day," he said. "I spent most of it missing you and daydreaming about Bora Bora."

She kept her lips close to his. "Me, too."

His hands found their way to her bottom and squeezed. "How soon until we can go back?"

Sam laughed. "Not soon enough."

He surprised her when he suddenly lifted her and arranged her legs around his waist. "No reason we can't relive some of the magic right here at home."

"Is that so?"

"Mmm-hmm." His kisses became more urgent as he lowered them to the sofa. "I feel like I'm going through withdrawal or something."

"Just think," she said, running her fingers through his hair, "we get to stay on this drug for the rest of our lives."

"Do you promise the same number of daily doses I received in Bora Bora?"

Sam laughed and brought him down for more of those heated kisses he was doling out.

"So that's a 'yes'?"

"You're rather persistent this evening, Senator."

His hands were busy divesting them of clothes. "I'm rather horny, too."

Normally, he was the epitome of finesse, but tonight he was all about urgency. The moment they were both naked, he surged into her and dropped his head to her chest. "God, I needed this."

She loved watching his legendary control waver and then break as he took fierce possession of her. Sweat dampened his back and brow. Sam gave herself over to him, loving him more than she'd ever imagined possible.

"Babe," he whispered. "Can't…" He moaned and tightened his hold on her.

"It's okay." She ran her hands down his back and clutched his backside, which seemed to send him careening completely out of control.

His face was tight with tension as he came hard. His fingers gripped her arm and shoulder so tightly she suspected there would be bruises, not that she cared.

"Sorry," he said, breathing hard.

"For what?" She brushed the damp hair off his brow.

"You didn't come."

"You can make it up to me next time."

"And I will. I promise." He ran his hand down her arm and linked their fingers. "I wish we'd never had to leave Bora Bora."

"Is that so?"

"They were the best days of my life. I could've stayed there with you forever."

"You would've missed work and your friends and your life here after a while."

"I had everything I needed right there with me."

"You would've gotten fat and lazy and slovenly."

He chuckled and brushed his lips over the side of her breast, sending a shiver of sensation rippling through her. "We found a good way to burn off calories."

"We certainly did."

"More than anything, I liked having you all to myself."

"You'll have me all to yourself every night."

"Not the same. Not nearly enough."

Sam placed her free hand on his face, urging him to look at her. "What's this all about?"

Hesitating, he looked away for a moment before he brought his gaze back to meet hers. "Having you all to myself showed me how little time together we get at home."

"It'll be better now that we're officially living together."

"It won't be better. We'll always be competing against a million other demands for time to ourselves."

"True, but as long as we make our relationship the top priority we'll work it out."

"I told Christina today that from now on I'm only giving two nights a week and one weekend day to the campaign."

"Can you do that?"

"I have a sixty-five-point lead over my Republican opponent, so I'm willing to risk it."

"Is that an unusually high lead?"

"I guess so," he said modestly. "We got a nice bump out of the wedding."

"Glad to be of assistance."

That sexy grin of his made her go weak in the knees even when she wasn't lying naked in his arms. "Anyway, since we've got a pretty solid lead, I don't see the need to spend so much time campaigning. Especially," he added, kissing her, "when I have so many other things I'd rather be doing."

"You won't get any argument from me."

"I had a feeling you might approve." He propped his chin on her chest. "So do you want to go over to your dad's?"

Sam thought about that for a minute. "Celia said she'd call if anything changes, so I guess we can stay here."

"Want some help going through the cards?"

"Sure. The faster I get that done, the faster I can go to bed."

"Why do you think I offered to help?"

"And here I thought your offer was entirely unselfish."

"Oh no, babe. Not entirely."

. . .

TERRY O'CONNOR PACED on the sidewalk outside Lindsey McNamara's stylish townhouse in the Adams Morgan neighborhood, working up the nerve to take the next step. They'd met at Sam and Nick's shower and engaged in some harmless flirtation. At the wedding, they'd danced the night away. After a couple of weeks of exchanging texts and emails and more than a few multiple-hour phone calls, tonight was supposed to be their first official date. Except she'd been detained at work, so here it was close to eleven and he'd been invited over for a glass of wine.

Which was why he was pacing. He had to tell her. His sponsor had helped him see that waiting any longer would be unfair to both of them. The sponsor had also warned him, repeatedly, he was endangering his recovery by becoming involved with someone so soon after leaving rehab. Terry had agreed to proceed carefully, and being honest with her was an important first step.

He rubbed damp palms over his jeans, summoning the courage he'd need to get through this. At the end of it, she'd either want to take a chance on him or she wouldn't. All he could do was share the truth. The rest was up to her. Putting it off wouldn't change the outcome. This was the story of his life now—and forever.

As the district's chief medical examiner, he figured she probably knew he'd briefly been a suspect in his brother's death, but she probably didn't know the details about his years-long battle with alcohol.

"Let's get this over with," he said to himself. Stepping through the gate, he walked up the sidewalk and knocked on the door. While he waited for her, he took a series of deep breaths to calm his nerves.

And then there she was—all long legs and that lithe dancer's body she'd wowed him with at the wedding. She had coiled her long red hair into a bun, and her green eyes danced with the mischief he was coming to expect from her. In typical Lindsey style, she took his hand and all but dragged him inside.

"This has been the longest day!" She led him into a contemporary living space that was warm, welcoming and entirely *her*. The open floor plan allowed him to see her in the kitchen uncorking a bottle of wine. "What's your pleasure? Red or white?"

"None for me, thanks."

As she spun around to maybe gauge whether he was serious, he thought, *here it comes*. They'd been so busy dancing at the wedding she hadn't noticed he wasn't drinking.

"Are you sure?"

He nodded and took a seat on the sofa.

She joined him, curling those endless legs under her.

Terry made an effort to keep his eyes on her face and not on the creamy expanse of skin above her pale pink tank top.

"Everything okay?" she asked.

"Yes. Of course."

"Then why are you so tense?"

"Am I?"

She nodded.

Terry sat back and released a deep breath. "I have something I need to tell you."

"Okay."

Here goes nothing. "I recently spent two months in rehab."

The statement hung in the air between them for what felt like an hour.

"Say something. Please."

She put her wineglass on the coffee table. "What were you treated for?"

"Alcoholism."

Her face had lost all expression. "How long have you been sober?"

"Eighty-six days."

She blew out a long deep breath.

"That part of my life is over, Lindsey. I swear to you. I nearly lost everything, and now… The senator has given me a chance at a whole new life, and I'd never risk that." He still couldn't get over Nick asking him to be his deputy chief of staff. Terry was loving every minute of being back in the game of politics.

"I, um... It's a lot to take in."

His heart beat wildly as he slid closer to her on the sofa, took her hand and linked their fingers. "On the night my brother was murdered, I was so drunk I couldn't remember who I'd been with. Because of that, the investigation focused on me for a time. Sam thought it was possible I'd *killed* my brother. And the worst part was I couldn't say for sure I hadn't because I didn't remember."

"I don't know all the details, but I knew she looked hard at you. Murders often involve family members."

"The only reason John was a senator was because I blew my chance before I could even declare my candidacy."

She eyed him tentatively. "What happened?"

"I got a DUI days before I was due to declare. All those years of preparing and planning down the tubes. My little brother, who didn't even *want* the job, was suddenly the golden one, and I was the disappointment." He dared to look directly at her and noticed her eyes had lost the animation he so enjoyed. "Do you know what it's like to be a disappointment to Graham O'Connor?" His father had served forty years in the Senate. All his life, Terry had prepared for the day he would run for his father's seat. But one big night out had changed everything—for him and his brother.

Lindsey remained quiet, so Terry kept talking. "Sometimes I wonder if what happened to John was sort of my fault."

That got her attention. "How in the world could that be your fault?"

"If he hadn't been forced to run for the Senate, maybe he would've moved to Chicago to live with the woman he loved and their son."

"How old was he when he was elected to take your father's place?"

"Just thirty. He barely qualified to run." That was another galling fact of Terry's life.

"So he was thirty years old and hadn't yet moved to live with his son and the woman he supposedly loved, right?"

"My father put a lot of pressure on him to keep a lid on that situation. In those days, the fifteen-year-old son of a United States senator fathering a child would've been a huge scandal."

"If he hadn't taken a stand against your father's directive by the time he was thirty, he probably wasn't going to. You can't blame yourself for the fact that his son killed him when he found out John was seeing other women. That's not your fault, Terry."

While he appreciated what she was doing, the weight of guilt was something Terry carried with him every day. "Where does this leave us?"

She looked down at their joined hands and then back at him, sadness radiating from her. "I need to think about it."

"I suppose that's better than 'I never want to see you again.'"

Her smile didn't quite reach her eyes. "I didn't say that."

He held her hand between both of his. "Take all the time you need. You know where I am when you're done thinking."

When he would've withdrawn his hands, she tightened her grip. "Thank you for telling me."

"I should've done it sooner."

"When exactly is the right time for a conversation like this?"

"Damned if I know," he said with a laugh. "This is all new to me." Taking a big gamble, he leaned in to kiss her cheek as she turned her face. Their lips collided and since his eyes were wide open, he watched hers flutter closed. Encouraged, he raised his hand to her face, keeping the kiss light and undemanding.

By the time he finally pulled back from her, his heart was racing again. She seemed to have that effect on him. "Sorry about that."

"No, you're not," she teased.

"No," he said, laughing, "I'm really not." Reluctantly, he released her hand and stood. "I hope you'll call me."

"I will. When I'm ready."

"Fair enough," he said as she walked him to the door.

Terry stepped into the cool air and took deep breaths. In eighty-six days of sobriety, he'd never wanted a drink more than he did just then. But rather than head to one of his favorite watering holes, he reached for his cell phone and called his sponsor.

CHAPTER SEVEN

*S*am and Nick worked their way through the pile of cards and a bottle of wine.

"This one's nice," Nick said. "'You're a gorgeous couple. Can't wait to see the gorgeous children.'"

Sam glanced at him. "Must be one of the six people in the region who hasn't heard about my fertility issues." The miscarriage she'd suffered just after Valentine's Day had proven two things—one, that she was able to conceive despite what she'd been told after an earlier miscarriage, and two, she was not ready to try again. Before their wedding she'd had a contraceptive shot, which bought her three months of not thinking about "the issue" that loomed large over her entire life.

"They would be beautiful, you know—especially if they look like their mother."

Taking a long sip of her wine, she studied him over the glass. "Something you want to say?"

He shrugged. "Just wondering."

"About?"

"What happens at the end of the three months?"

Sam's stomach sank. She *almost* preferred the days when she still thought the plumbing didn't work anymore. "What about it?"

"Have you given it any thought?"

Sam stared at him. "Are you seriously asking me that? Like I don't think about it *all the time?* I can't remember what I used to think about before I knew it might be possible..." Her voice caught. Damn if this subject didn't always get to her!

He wrapped his gloved hand around hers. "I'm sorry. I shouldn't have asked it that way. I know you've thought about it."

"Obsessed about it, you mean."

His face set in an unreadable expression, Nick released her hand, reached for another card, used a letter opener on the envelope and scanned the message. He tossed it aside and reached for the next one.

"That's it? End of conversation?"

"I wish I hadn't said anything." Sighing, he sat back against the sofa, took off the latex gloves and ran his fingers through his hair. "I can't deal with how sad you get when we talk about this. It kills me."

"When I think about getting pregnant again, I picture a baby growing inside me." She rested her hand on her belly. "They say the quickening, when the baby starts to move, is like butterfly wings fluttering. Can you imagine what that must feel like?"

"Sam..."

"I've never gotten that far, so I don't know what it's like to feel the baby move. But because of what I've been through in the past," she said, swiping at a tear that rolled down her face, "when I think of being pregnant, I also have to think about losing it. And it was bad enough losing your baby once. If it happened again..."

He drew her into his arms. "I want you to know what it feels like to have a baby move inside of you. I want that more than anything."

"Somehow I've managed to get through four miscarriages. I don't know if I could survive it again."

"Then let's not risk it. It's not worth the gamble."

"It's just that knowing I *can* get pregnant again... That changes everything." Desperate to finish the job and get to bed, she sat up and reached for another card. "Oh man."

"What is it?"

She stared at the card.

"Sam?"

"It's from my mother."

"What does it say?"

"Um...That she saw the pictures, I looked beautiful, you're so handsome, we look wonderful together." She tossed the card aside. "Yada yada."

Nick reached for it. "You left out the part about how she'd love to hear from you sometime and would like to meet me."

"Like that's going to happen."

"When was the last time you saw her?"

"At my first wedding. She started a big fight with my dad—right in the middle of the wedding. After that, none of us wanted to see her again." Sam stared at the card on the table for a long moment before she glanced at Nick. "*She* left *him*—for another guy. What right does she have to show up again years later and act like it was all his fault?"

"No right."

"What? I can tell you're dying to say something."

"Just that only the two people in it know what goes on in a marriage."

Sam tossed the card into the pile they planned to trash. "He was totally devoted to her, which was way more than she deserved."

"That's what he wanted you to see, but who knows what really happened?"

Sam stared at him. "You can't seriously be defending her."

"I don't even know her. I'm only saying there could be more to the story than what he's told you."

Before Sam could respond to that outrageous statement, her cell phone rang. Seeing Jeannie's number on the caller ID, Sam took the call. "Hi, Jeannie."

"I'm sorry to call so late, Lieutenant, but I thought you'd want to know I found another one."

Sam let her head fall forward as she absorbed the implications. No longer was this about a single threat. Rather, they were dealing with a calculated, intentional campaign. "What's it say?"

"'Rose are red, violets are blue, bang, bang you're dead, who will miss you?'"

Images of the massive crowds Nick's campaign had been attracting flashed through Sam's mind, leaving a sick, nauseous feeling in the pit of her stomach.

"Lieutenant?"

"I'm here."

"Like the other, this one smelled like flowers—carnations, I think, and there was confetti."

"Bag it all."

"Already done."

"Who was it addressed to?"

"Nick."

Sam ran her fingers through her hair, hoping to buy a minute to absorb this latest development before she had to face him.

"Are you okay?" Jeannie asked.

"Yes, just thinking. Have you been working all this time?"

"Except for a dinner break."

"Thank you, Jeannie. I appreciate the help."

"I appreciate the nudge."

"Any time you're ready to come back…"

"I might be getting closer. It felt good to be back in the game today, even if it was from the sidelines."

And that, Sam thought, had been the goal of involving the traumatized detective. "I'm glad. I'll be by in the morning to pick up the card."

"I'll be here."

Sam put her phone down on the table.

"What'd it say?" Nick asked.

She relayed the message, glancing at the handsome man who'd become the center of her world. And now someone was threatening his life. But *why?* "You need security."

"So do you."

"This one was directed at you. They're talking about *shooting* you."

"Why would someone want to shoot me? I haven't been in office long enough to piss off anyone that badly."

"If it's someone I've put in jail and they're out for revenge, what better way to get at me than to have someone take a shot at you?"

"Or if it's someone who's bitter that I got handed a Senate seat without doing a damned thing to earn it, what better way to get at me than to take a shot at you?"

She scowled at him. "I carry a gun. I work with a partner who carries a gun. I'm trained to be observant and vigilant. It's not the same thing."

"I'll request security only after you tell me what special measures the department is taking to protect you—and not one minute before."

"Fine."

"Fine."

"God, I'm tired." She contemplated the two or three hundred unopened cards that remained in the pile. "My eyes are crossed." While they finished going through the remaining cards, Nick polished off the wine.

"Can we go to bed now?" he asked when the last card had been opened.

Even though she was itching to go get that card from Jeannie, she said, "I guess so." Back in the day she would have rushed off to take care of something that would keep until morning. But now she had a good reason to stay home—the best reason.

She followed him upstairs, going through the routine of brushing her teeth and getting undressed as she ran through the disturbingly long list of people who might want to do her—and her husband—harm. Tomorrow she'd start looking into the whereabouts of each and every one of them as well as others she'd no doubt forgotten all about.

In bed, Nick reached for her and brought her into his embrace. The heat of his skin against hers, his endlessly appealing scent, the brush of his chest hair against her face—that was all it took to make her want him—again.

"I know you're tired," he said as he bit back a yawn. "We don't have to do anything."

Sam wrapped her hand around his erection and stroked him. "We don't have to do *anything?*"

He gasped and tightened his hold on her. "Keep that up, and we'll be doing something."

"I have a headache."

"Want me to get you some pills?"

"I'm joking. Now that I'm your wife, I can't be as easy as I was when I was just your girlfriend. And I've been pretty damned easy since our wedding."

Laughing, he said, "Easy is good." He shifted so he was on top of her. "In fact, easy is preferred."

Sam looped her arms around his neck and held on tight, steeped in the magic that never failed to amaze and astound her.

"I didn't realize," he said, brushing his lips softly over hers, "what I was missing until you came along and showed me."

"Nick," she whispered, moved by his words. He'd been so alone for most of his life, but now they had each other, and she wanted to give him everything he'd missed out on—especially a family to call his own. "I love you."

"Love you, too, babe." Entering her in one smooth thrust, he stayed perfectly still. "This is what I live for now. *You* are what I live for."

Arching into him, she urged him to move. "Me, too. What does it say about us that we can't get enough of this?"

"That we're pretty damned lucky," he said, keeping his movements slow and deliberate.

"Yes, we are." Sam's orgasm built like a wave rolling toward the beach, and when it broke, she cried out, taking him with her. After, when he would have rolled to his side, she held on tight, determined to do everything in her power to protect this man and this love from whomever would do them harm.

JEANNIE STOOD under the shower and let the pulsing water work out the kinks in her neck and back from the long day spent opening mail at Michael's dining room table. She'd meant what she'd said to Sam, that being useful again had made her feel slightly better than she had since the attack.

Maybe it was time to get back to it, to rejoin her life already in progress, to stop hiding out in Michael's comfortable home, sealed away from the world.

With her hand propped against the shower wall, she took another blissful moment to let the shower massage her shoulders. Emerging from the bathroom a few minutes later she found Michael already in bed, his eyes closed. She took a moment to study his broad shoulders, muscular chest and smooth dark brown skin. The first time she met him she thought he was the most handsome man she'd ever beheld. Struck by his six-foot, six-inch height, she'd been dazzled from the start. Add in the successful career in finance, his unfailing sense of style and the tenderness he'd shown her since day one, and it hadn't taken her long to fall for him.

He'd been about to propose. Before. The signs had been hard to miss. Since then, he'd been a rock of support, unfailing patience and more of that legendary tenderness, even as she'd flinched under every touch, every caress. Not once, though, had they spoken of the future that had seemed so assured before the attack.

Without opening his eyes, he extended his hand. "Come to bed."

"How did you know I was here?"

"I always know where you are." He patted the bed again. "Come on. You worked hard today. You have to be tired."

She was tired. Tired of hiding, tired of being a victim, tired of reliving the nightmare over and over again. Dropping the silk robe he'd bought her into a puddle at her feet, she slid between the cool sheets. Before she met Michael, sheets had been sheets. Now she was spoiled by Egyptian cotton. She snuggled up to him, and felt him tense as he realized she was naked.

"Baby, what're you doing?"

"Holding you," she said, even as her entire body was seized by panic reminiscent of that day. "Is it okay?"

He released an unsteady laugh. "Sure is. Could I hold you, too?"

She appreciated he'd asked, that he sensed what the effort was costing her. Nodding, she raised her head so he could slip an arm under her.

He drew her in close to him, but not so close she would feel confined.

She rested her head on his chest, remembering all the nights she had slept like this, snuggled up to him, embraced in his strong arms, breathing him in. Telling herself he was nothing like the man who'd attacked her helped to calm her overactive imagination and her rampaging nerves.

"You're okay, baby," he whispered as his lips brushed her forehead. "You're safe. You're loved. Everything is fine."

Tears spilled from her tightly closed eyes, wetting his chest and her face. He'd been so good. So patient. So understanding. She wanted to give something back to him, to regain some of what they'd lost at the hands of a monster. If only she could be sure it wouldn't somehow make things worse.

Tentatively, she moved her hand over his chest to find his abdominal muscles rigid with tension.

"Jeannie?"

If she spoke, if she said a single word, she might lose her nerve. So she stayed quiet as her hand relearned the body she had come to know so well—as well as her own.

Michael stayed so still she wondered if he was breathing.

Even as she caressed him, the tears continued to leak from her eyes. Summoning the courage to continue, she sent her hand under the covers. She found him fully erect and throbbing.

"Sorry," he said through what sound like gritted teeth. "Can't help—"

"It's okay." She raised herself up to trail kisses over his stomach as she stroked him.

He sucked in a sharp deep breath when he realized her intention. "Jeannie, honey, you don't have to...Oh...*Jesus.*"

Taking him into her mouth, she used her tongue the way he liked, all the while telling herself this was not the man who had hurt her. This was the man who loved her, who had stood by her through the darkest days of her life. This was the man she loved. She let her hair cover her face so he wouldn't see the tears that kept coming despite her desire to get through this without them.

"*Oh*, that's good, baby. So good." His fingers combed through her hair, encouraging her, but the rest of him remained still—even his hips, which would normally be contributing to this act. Without moving a muscle, he gave her exactly what she needed. Total control.

Jeannie had forgotten the power that came with taking a man in her mouth, of bringing him pleasure with her lips and tongue and hand.

"*Jeannie...*"

She recognized the note of warning in his tone.

"It's been so long...I can't..."

Rather than retreat, she used her free hand to cup his balls and lightly squeeze, sending him—as she knew it would—into intense release.

His chest expanded with each deep breath he took as she kissed her way to his lips. Strong arms encircled her, again not too tight, not confining. "Wow," he said after a long period of silence. "Didn't see that coming."

"Are you complaining?" she asked, attempting a playful tone.

"No. No complaints." He ran his hands over her back, soothing rather than seducing. "I've missed you."

"I've been right here."

"No, you haven't."

"I'm sorry."

He shook his head. "Don't apologize." Brushing the dampness from her cheeks, he studied her face. "Could I...maybe...return the favor?"

"I don't know if I can."

"We could take it super slow. So slow."

She could see the yearning in his face and hear it in his voice. "What if I can't?"

"Then we stop and try again another time. And we keep trying until you don't feel the need to stop."

Her damned eyes filled again, and Jeannie brushed impatiently at the tears. They were putting a damper on her attempt to reclaim this important part of her life.

"Hey," he said, using his thumbs to sweep away the tears. "We don't have to."

"I want to. Just ignore the tears. I can't seem to stop them."

With his big hands framing her face, he kissed her gently. When she thought of the devouring way he used to kiss her, his show of restraint made her sad once again for all they'd lost. But they would get it back. If it took the rest of their lives, they would find their way. That determination was new and, perhaps, an indication she might be recovering a small bit of who she'd once been.

"I want to turn over," he said. "Can we do that?"

The new position would put him above her, over her.

"It's okay if you don't want to," he said, tuning into her immediate anxiety.

"No, we can." She rolled off him and settled on her back, looking up at him.

He stayed on his side, his head propped on a pillow as he placed his hand on her quivering belly. "Just say stop," he said softly. "At any point."

Jeannie bit her bottom lip and nodded as his hand began to move. Even though *this* man's touch couldn't be confused with that of any other, she kept her eyes open so there would be no mistaking whose hand took a slow journey over her belly, arm and neck. He made the same patient trip three times before he included her breast.

She reminded herself that she knew exactly whose hand caressed her, whose fingers coaxed her nipple to life, and *this* man loved her. Despite her best efforts to control the panic and keep it from taking over, it closed in on her anyway. As if an elephant were suddenly sitting on her chest, Jeannie fought for every breath.

Michael quickly removed his hand. "Breathe, honey."

Try as she might, she couldn't seem to get any air to her lungs.

He grabbed her shoulders, forced her to sit up and gave her a gentle but insistent shake. "Breathe!"

Spots danced before her eyes, and then as suddenly as the panic had seized her, it let her go. She sucked in deep, gulping breaths, grateful for every one.

"Christ almighty," Michael whispered as he reached for her.

Despite her fear of the panic, she clung to him. "Sorry," she said when she could speak again.

"No, no. It was me. Too much too soon. I shouldn't have—"

Jeannie tightened her arms around him. "You didn't do anything wrong. I thought I was ready."

Now she had reason to wonder if she'd ever be ready. And if she eventually got there, would he still be waiting?

CHAPTER EIGHT

*O*n the way to pick up the card from Jeannie in the morning, Sam's thoughts were full of her father and his rapidly deteriorating health. She'd been alarmed earlier to see how much sicker he'd gotten overnight. Celia had assured Sam she would be taking him to the doctor first thing, and there was no need for Sam to stay home from work—except she probably should have because she'd be good for nothing today. Listening to him struggle for every breath had filled her with overwhelming anxiety.

She knocked on Jeannie's door, wondering if she should've called first. Probably. Hearing the series of deadbolts disengaging, she stood up a little straighter, trying to shake off the dread that hung over her after seeing her dad.

The door swung open, and Sam was sorry to see that Jeannie looked like she hadn't slept a wink.

"Come in." She led Sam to the dining room table where the nonthreatening cards had been boxed up. "Here's the one." Jeannie had opened the card before she put it into the evidence bag so Sam was able to read both sides.

A chill traveled through her as she read the message. The "bang bang you're dead" line certainly got her attention. Nick would be so vulnerable on the campaign trail.

"Why would someone do this to you guys?" Jeannie said. "I don't get it."

"Neither do we."

Jeannie went into the living room and sat on the sofa, curling her legs under her. "So what's the next step?"

"I suppose I have to inform the brass."

"And arrange for some sort of security for Nick, I hope."

"It's on the agenda." Sam sat in the chair across from Jeannie. "Everything okay?"

Jeannie shrugged. "Define *okay*."

"I, um…"

"Don't worry about it," Jeannie said, waving her hand.

"If there's something you want to talk about, you know you can talk to me."

Jeannie shook her head. "You don't want to talk about this. You want to get that card and get the hell out of here so you can start figuring out who's threatening you and your husband."

"I'll admit I'm quite anxious to start looking into that, but if you want to talk, I'll stay for as long as you need me."

Jeannie eyed the lieutenant suspiciously for a long moment. "Why do you suppose we were never really friends? Before?"

Sam relaxed into the chair, resigned to sticking around for a while. "I, ah, I don't know, but I suspect it probably was more a failing on my part than yours."

Laughing, Jeannie said, "I'd have to agree with you there."

Even as she raised her middle finger in protest, Sam was relieved to hear her detective's laughter again. "Since we're BFFs now, why don't you tell me what's got you so down when you seemed to be doing a little better."

Jeannie brushed a hand over her black yoga pants. "I was doing better, or I thought I was, until I tried to…you know… with Michael."

Sam winced. "What happened?"

"I freaked out. Hyperventilated. It was quite a show."

Sam wanted to say the right thing, but damned if she had any idea what the right thing was. "I know it's not the same—at all—

but Nick and I had a heck of a time getting back on track in that regard after I miscarried."

Jeannie gasped. "When did you miscarry?"

Sam wanted to shoot herself for bringing it up, because confronting the man who'd attacked Jeannie had led to the miscarriage. She knew she needed to tell her detective the truth before she heard it from someone else. "When I arrested Sanborn, I caught an elbow to the gut. One thing led to another." Sam shrugged. "I was barely pregnant, but it knocked us for a loop."

"Oh, God. No one told me." Jeannie shuddered. "That bastard. What he took from both of us…"

Sam leaned forward, arms propped on knees. "He took a lot from us. No question about that. But we have to try to keep living our lives so we don't let him win."

"I know that, and I'm trying," Jeannie said. She paused before she added, "I thought you couldn't get pregnant."

"That's what I thought, too. Surprise."

"Oh, Sam! That's great news! You can try again. When you're ready."

Trying again was the last thing she wanted to talk about. "The point is, it takes a while to get back in the saddle after something traumatic happens—especially what happened to you."

"How long will it be before Michael decides he's had enough of waiting for me to get better?"

"I doubt he's put a time limit on it."

"He has to be getting sick of having me moping around his house."

"Then why don't you get dressed and come to work with me for a while?"

"Oh. I don't think I could."

"Why not?"

"I just…I'm not ready."

Even though she was dying to get to work, Sam crossed her legs, folded her arms and got comfortable.

"Don't you want to get going?" Jeannie asked.

"Yep."

"Well, then go already!"

"My dad is sick."

Clearly startled by the sudden change in direction, Jeannie sat up a little straighter. "What's wrong with him?"

"I suspect we're going to hear he has pneumonia when Celia gets him to the doctor this morning."

"Oh my God. I'm so sorry to hear that."

"Pneumonia is doubly complicated for a quadriplegic."

"I can only imagine. You must be freaking out."

"I'm trying not to," Sam conceded. "Do you remember the Tyler Fitzgerald case?"

Seeming puzzled by the shifting conversation, Jeannie thought for a moment. "The boy who was nabbed from a park and murdered. Years ago. Unsolved, right?"

Sam nodded. "It was my father's case—the only one he wasn't able to close. I'd like to take another look at it. Maybe a fresh set of eyes will see something we missed the first time around." After seeing her father so sick earlier, Sam felt a sense of urgency to tie up this loose end for him. She pushed aside the nagging doubt about whether he'd *want* her to look into it. All she could think about was being able to tell him they'd finally caught Tyler's killer.

Jeannie sat perfectly still for a long time—so long Sam suspected she wasn't going to take the bait. Then she stood. "Give me ten minutes."

Watching her head upstairs, Sam smiled. *"Yes,"* she whispered to the empty room. Then she sent a text to Freddie, asking him to give everyone a head's up that McBride was coming back— and to play it cool.

THE SERGEANT WORKING the front desk stopped Sam on her way into HQ. "Lieutenant, the chief is looking for you," he said, nodding respectfully to Jeannie.

Sam debated for a moment, and then turned to Jeannie.

"Come with me. He'll be so happy to see you he'll forget what he wants to get all over me about."

Jeannie rolled her eyes. "You know what he wants."

The man she'd called Uncle Joe as a child would no doubt be up in arms about the threatening mail she'd received.

"That's why I want you with me." Sam led the way to the chief's office where the administrative assistant waved her right in.

"He's been waiting for you, Lieutenant," the perky assistant said.

"Fabulous," Sam muttered. She swore she heard Jeannie snicker, but when she glanced over her shoulder the other detective was straight-faced.

In the chief's office, she discovered he'd called in the cavalry. Deputy Chief Conklin and Captain Malone were seated in front of the chief's desk. All three men rose when Sam came in with Jeannie.

"Detective McBride," Chief Farnsworth said, walking around the desk to shake hands with Jeannie. "It's so good to have you back."

"Thank you, sir. I'm not sure I'm *back*, but I'm here today."

"We'll take what we can get."

"I appreciate the support of the department during this difficult time, sir."

"We appreciate your sacrifice in the line of duty."

Sensing Jeannie's composure was in danger of cracking, Sam said, "You wanted to see me?"

"Yes, Lieutenant, have a seat please."

"That's okay, I have to—"

"Sit," Farnsworth said sternly, pointing to the available chair. Conklin jumped up to offer his seat to Jeannie.

"What've you got there?" Farnsworth asked Sam, nodding to the evidence bag she was holding.

Reluctantly, Sam handed it over to him and watched his rugged face take on an infuriated expression. He handed the bag to Conklin who took a good look before passing it to Malone.

"I'll pass this on to Tremont," Malone said, referring to the chief of detectives, who rarely got involved in Homicide cases.

"To do what?" Sam asked.

"To oversee the investigation," Malone said.

"So let me get this straight—I'm the one being threatened, and someone *else* is going to investigate? Yeah, that makes a lot of sense, especially since they'd know firsthand who'd have a beef with me."

"Save the sarcasm, Lieutenant," Farnsworth said. "It's a conflict of interest for you to investigate this case, and you know it."

"What I know is no one could do it faster or better than I could. I already have a list of twenty possible suspects. How many days will be lost while another detective digs into my life and gets us to where I already am?"

Farnsworth and Conklin exchanged glances.

"She's right, you know," Malone said, and Sam sent him a grateful look. "This could be anyone—someone she arrested, someone she knew years ago, someone one of them dated."

"Or was married to," Sam said with a scowl, thinking of her vindictive ex-husband who'd love nothing more than to give her something to worry about during the early weeks of her new marriage.

"Or was married to," Malone agreed.

"You think it could be Gibson?" Farnsworth asked.

Just thinking of her ex-husband was enough to make Sam sick. "I suppose anything is possible," she said. When Peter pulled a gun on her the night before her wedding and said their relationship would never be over, was this what he'd meant?

"He'd be foolish to do something like this when he knows we're watching him like hawks," Malone said.

"That didn't stop him from showing up outside my house the night before the wedding," Sam reminded him.

"Let's give him a good hard look," Farnsworth said.

"Are you going to let me run this investigation?" Sam asked.

The chief's face was unreadable.

Sam had begun to sweat by the time Malone spoke up.

"She does have an advantage over anyone else in this case," he said.

"What about the investigation into the murders at Carl's?" Conklin asked.

"At a total standstill at the moment. We've done everything we always do and have nothing. We're hoping one of our informants will come through."

They all looked to the chief expectantly.

"All right," he finally said. "I don't like it, but I'll give you a week on this. After that we'll reevaluate."

"Thank you, sir," Sam said, relieved.

"I want regular updates," Farnsworth added.

"Of course. No problem."

"Get to work."

"Um, Chief, before we go, I wanted to let you know I've asked Detective McBride to reopen the Tyler Fitzgerald case."

"Why now?"

"My father is sick."

Chief Farnsworth sat up a little straighter. "What do you mean?"

Sam hated to put words to her fears, but she needed to make him understand. "I'm worried he may have pneumonia."

"That can be treated."

She was afraid she'd end up bawling in front of them if they talked about it any longer. "I want to give it a fresh look."

He held her gaze for a long moment before he nodded. "Keep me in the loop—on both cases and your father's condition."

"Me, too," Malone said as Conklin nodded in agreement.

"I will," Sam said, gesturing to Jeannie to follow her.

"Wow," Jeannie said on the way to the detectives' pit. "Are they always so intense?"

"Pretty much."

"Better you than me."

"You get used to it after a while," Sam said, surprised to realize at some point she'd become accustomed to being grilled —frequently—by the chief and his deputies.

As they navigated the corridors, the officers they passed seemed surprised but pleased to see Jeannie.

"I feel like a monkey at the circus," she whispered to Sam.

"It'll be weird for an hour or two, and then it'll be business as usual."

"Promise?"

Sam stopped and faced her detective. "Do whatever you feel like doing. Don't answer any questions you don't want to answer. You're calling the shots. We'll do this your way."

Jeannie's eyes filled but she blinked back the tears. "Thank you for all the support."

Sam squeezed Jeannie's arm, led her into the office and opened a file cabinet. Sam pulled out two thick folders and handed them to Jeannie. "These are my dad's files on Fitzgerald. The case went cold about ten years ago, but my dad was on it right up until the day he was shot. I've had good intentions of getting back to it, but life keeps getting in the way."

"You've been a tad busy, Lieutenant."

"This is important to me."

"I'll give it everything I have."

"I appreciate that. If you'd like to work in here, that's fine."

"I'll see how it goes in the pit, but I might take you up on that."

"Whatever works for you."

Jeannie glanced at the pit, which was unusually quiet. "Did you warn them I was coming?"

"Maybe."

Jeannie nodded and squared her shoulders.

"Remember—do only what you feel comfortable doing. If you'd rather work from home, let me know and I'll take you."

"I think I'm okay."

"All right then."

Freddie came to the door and stopped short when he saw Jeannie. "Detective McBride. Nice to see you here."

"Thank you." She stepped around him and headed for her cubicle. The other detectives offered subdued greetings and went right back to work.

CHAPTER NINE

*W*hen Sam was certain Jeannie was okay for the time being, she turned to Freddie. "Thanks for laying the groundwork."

"No problem. We're all happy to have her back." He gestured to the conference room. "Come with me, will you?"

"What're you up to?"

"You'll see."

Sam was dismayed to find another huge pile of cards on the conference room table along with three towering stacks of file folders.

"More mail?" she said. "You gotta be kidding me."

"Sucks to be so popular, huh?"

"Seriously. What's with all the files?"

"All your cases."

"*All* of them?"

"Every one. I figure we go through them and maybe we can figure out who might have a beef with you."

"They *all* have a beef with me."

"Until we get the report on the cards from the lab, we can narrow the list of suspects to who might've gotten paroled recently."

Eyeing the huge pile of files, Sam yearned for the beach in Bora Bora. She so didn't feel like dealing with this.

"Lieutenant?"

"I appreciate what you've done, gathering the files and the thought you've put into this."

"But?"

"I'm afraid we're spinning our wheels. In about four seconds last night I thought of a hundred people who'd never want me to know a minute of happiness."

"We'll look at every one of them," he said fiercely. It bothered him, she knew, that someone was threatening her.

"It's a waste of time, Freddie."

"How can you say that? Someone is threatening you—*and your husband.* You can't ignore that."

"I don't plan to ignore it." She thought of the week the chief had given her to investigate the threats, but the sheer magnitude of the task hadn't settled on her until she saw the huge stacks of file folders on the table. "I'd much rather investigate Gardner's role in my father's shooting."

"No reason we can't do both."

Sam felt like her head was going to explode. Her phone pinged with a text message. She reached for it and flipped it open, her heart sinking as she read the text from Celia: *Pneumonia. They are admitting him to GW's ICU. Call when you can.*

When her legs seemed to liquefy beneath her Sam sank into a chair.

"What?" Freddie asked.

"My dad. He's got pneumonia."

"Oh God."

"Yeah."

"What do you need?"

"I have no idea." The mountain of file folders seemed to get larger as she absorbed the news about her dad. Her phone rang, and Sam flipped it open. "Holland."

"Sam," Celia said, her voice wavering. "Your dad is asking for you. They're talking about putting him on a vent and he wants to see you before then. Can you come?"

Sam's stomach began to ache fiercely. "I'm on my way."

"Hurry," her stepmother added before ending the call.

"I'll drive," Freddie said after Sam filled him in.

With his hand on her shoulder, he urged her out of the chair and steered her from the conference room. In the hallway, they ran into Lt. Stahl.

"A moment of your time, Lieutenant," Stahl said with a glare for Freddie.

"Not now," he snapped.

Stahl's beady eyes narrowed with rage. "Watch your tone, Detective."

Freddie ignored him and propelled Sam into her office. "Get your stuff."

Sam wanted to shake off her overly concerned partner the way she normally would when he tried to hover, but somehow she couldn't seem to form the words. She grabbed her keys from her desk drawer.

Freddie was locking the office when Gonzo approached them. "Everything all right?"

"The lieutenant's father is in the hospital. We're on our way over there now."

Gonzo turned his gaze on Sam. "What can I do?"

"Go through the unopened cards in the conference room. See if there are any others that need to go to the lab," Freddie said. "Put some pressure on the lab for results on the first two."

"Will do. Keep me posted?"

Sam nodded and glanced at the pit. "Keep an eye on McBride. Don't let her do too much today. See her home after a while."

"No problem. Just so you know, I've been doing some more digging on Gardner. I don't have anything new yet, but I feel like I'm getting closer."

"I appreciate that. Thank you." Sam felt the eyes of everyone at HQ on her as she and Freddie headed for the main door. It wouldn't take long for news of her father's illness to whip through the ranks. A popular, decorated officer, Skip Holland had been three months shy of retirement when a gunman's bullet changed their lives forever. Finding that gunman had turned out to be one of the more frustrating challenges Sam had faced in her life.

As Freddie drove them to George Washington University Hospital on 23rd Street, Sam called Nick and got his voice mail. Hearing his voice made her long for him. "Hey, it's me. They're admitting my dad to GW ICU with pneumonia. That's where I'll be for now. Freddie's with me. I, um, I guess I'll see you when I see you." She closed the phone and returned it to her pocket.

"You know he'll be there the second he gets that message," Freddie said.

Sam looked out the window as the city raced by. "Yeah." Just over two years ago, they'd come so close to losing Skip. Since then, he'd done an admirable job of adapting to the hand life had dealt him. At some point, Sam realized, his family had accepted his limitations and learned to live with them. To lose him now, especially before she caught the person who shot him, would be unimaginable.

They arrived at the Intensive Care Unit where Celia waited with Sam's sisters Angela and Tracy as well as Tracy's husband Mike. Celia's green eyes were rimmed with red. She hugged Sam and then Freddie.

"What're they saying?" Sam asked. Seeing her stepmother and sisters in tears didn't do much to help her already out-of-control anxiety.

"They're putting him on a ventilator, but he wants to talk to you first." Celia put her arm around Sam. "He sounds awful, so prepare yourself."

Sam nodded and let Celia lead her into the room where monitors were beeping and a nurse was typing into a computer. Her father's labored breathing was all Sam could hear.

Celia leaned over the bed and kissed her husband's forehead. "Honey, Sam's here."

Skip's eyes fluttered open. "Sam."

Sam rested a hand on his arm and was startled by the heat radiating from his skin. "I'm here, Dad."

Skip shifted his eyes to Celia. "Give us a minute, hon."

"I'll be right outside," she said.

Sam turned to the nurse. "Could we have a minute?"

"The doctor wants him on the vent ASAP."

"We'll be quick."

The nurse left the room, and Sam focused on her father. She brushed the hair off his forehead because she wanted him to be able to feel the caress. It occurred to her this could be the last time she ever spoke to him, a thought so overwhelming she had to force herself to take the next breath.

"You remember," he said between wheezing breaths.

Sam knew exactly what he meant. She thought of the prescription bottle she'd stashed in a safety deposit box.

"Sam. Please." He gulped in a deep breath. "Don't let this go on. Promise me."

Her heart felt as if someone was squeezing it. "I promise. Don't worry about anything." Years ago she'd agreed to help him if the time came, but now... The thought of doing it was beyond devastating.

"Love you, Sam Cappuano," he whispered, saying words they rarely uttered out loud.

Sam bent to press her lips to his forehead, tears spilling from her eyes. No doubt he could feel them, too. "Love you, too, Skippy. You're going to beat this. I know it."

"If I don't..."

"I'll take care of it. I'll never stop looking for the person who did this to you."

"Stop looking." His eyes fluttered closed. "Live your life, baby girl."

"Get some rest." She wiped the dampness from her face and stayed with him until the nurse returned. Outside the room, she leaned against a wall, eyes closed, heart beating fast. The last two years had been a nightmare for him in so many ways. He had to be tired of such a limited existence. But Sam wasn't ready. If she had another twenty years to prepare herself, she'd never be ready to lose him.

"Sam."

She opened her eyes to find Freddie watching her with concern etched into his adorable face. He too was very fond of her father.

"How is he?"

"Not so good."

"What can I do for you?"

She shrugged, helplessly. "Since you have a direct line to God, maybe, you know…"

"Already done."

"Thanks. You don't have to stick around. You can go back to work if you want."

"If it's all right with you, I'd rather be here. I'll take vacation time."

Grateful for his presence, she nodded. They rejoined the others in the waiting room where the doctor found them half an hour later. He reported that Skip was being given massive doses of antibiotics and had been put on a ventilator to help him breathe. They'd sedated him to keep him comfortable.

"It's more or less a waiting game at this point," the doctor concluded. "We'll have to see how he responds to the medication."

"So he could be all right," Angela said hopefully.

"I don't want to make any promises I can't keep," the doctor said. "The next twenty-four hours will be telling."

"Thank you, Doctor," Celia said.

"I'll check on him again later. In the meantime, one visitor at a time, please."

As the doctor left the room, Nick came in, his eyes seeking out Sam.

She got up and went to him, leading him into the hallway.

He put his arms around her. "I got here as fast as I could. I was in a meeting."

"Glad to see you." With her face pressed to his muscular chest she brought him up to date on her father's condition.

"God, it happened so fast," he said.

"I know."

"I was thinking I should call Scotty and let him know we might have to postpone the trip." Nick had befriended the adorable twelve-year-old in a state home for children in Richmond, and the boy had since become a close friend of theirs. In fact, before their wedding, Sam and Nick had discussed the idea of adopting Scotty, who they'd both come to love. Sam's wedding gift to Nick had been tickets to opening day at Fenway Park in Boston for him and Scotty who, like Nick, was a huge Boston Red Sox fan.

"You can't disappoint him," Sam said. "My dad helped me get the tickets. He'd want you to go."

"I can't leave you with this going on."

"I'll be all right. I've got Celia and my sisters. Freddie will stay close. It's okay. Really."

Nick released a deep sigh. "Let's see what tomorrow brings."

Sam's eyes burned with tears she fought to contain. Blubbering all over her husband wasn't going to make her father any better. "Are you still going to talk to Scotty this weekend?" While on their honeymoon, they'd agreed Nick would broach the subject of Scotty coming to live with them during the Boston trip.

"I was planning to, but we'll see what's going on."

She knew he meant with her father. Everything was on hold until Skip recovered.

Nick tightened his arms around her. "Whatever happens, Sam, I'm here. I'm right here."

She'd managed to contain the tears until he said that.

He kissed her forehead. "It'll be okay, babe."

While she'd never be ready to lose her dad, knowing Nick would be by her side somehow made this awful situation a little more bearable.

JEANNIE WENT through the Tyler Fitzgerald file page by page. Skip Holland's notes were thorough and detailed. He'd interviewed people who'd known the seven-year-old and his family, who'd frequented the school playground where he'd vanished on a Saturday night in June of 1986 and children who'd attended second grade with the boy. Jeannie read every word on every report. The family's heartbreak was palpable, and her own heart ached imagining what they'd been through in the ten days from when he went missing until his body was found in a Maryland landfill. There were photos of the adorable child from before and after his death and a medical examiner's report that detailed death by asphyxiation.

Skip had included articles from Washington newspapers and from papers around the country that had picked up the story that summer. Immersing herself in the file helped to keep her mind off her own troubles. For that she had to give her lieutenant credit. Coming back to work had been a good move.

"I heard you were here," a familiar voice said.

Jeannie looked up at the smiling face of her partner, Detective Will Tyrone. Tall with close-cropped blond hair, a muscular physique and a sweet baby face, Will had been a pillar of strength in the dark days after the attack.

"Hey there," Jeannie said. "What're you doing here?" They normally worked third shift, 11:00 p.m. to 7:00 a.m.

"The LT has had me on days lately."

"Who've you been partnering up with?"

"Cruz while she was on vacation, but now I'm not sure. Are you back to stay?"

"I don't know yet. I'm taking it an hour at a time."

Will grabbed a stray chair from another cubicle and straddled it. "What're you doing?"

Jeannie explained about the Fitzgerald case and how Sam had asked her to take a fresh look at it.

"Can I help?"

"I was thinking I'd like to talk to the parents, but I don't have my car."

"I can take you."

"That'd be great. Thanks." She reached for a notebook in her bottom drawer and ran a hand over her hair to make sure it was under control. "Just let me tell Gonzo. Sam left him in charge of me."

"Before we go…"

Jeannie took a closer look at his tormented expression. "What is it?"

"I want you to know I can't stop thinking about that day,

about whether there was something I could've done to change what happened."

Seeing him so distraught saddened her. "It wasn't your fault, Will. We'd gone our separate ways. There was nothing you could've done." She put a hand on his forearm. "I've come to the conclusion that this happened to me for a reason. I don't know why yet, but I hope down the road at some point it'll become clear to me."

"No one deserves what happened to you."

"No, but sadly it happens far too often. Perhaps I'll be a better cop because I understand the victim's point of view now."

"I'm glad you're able to see some positives coming out of it. I've been hard-pressed to think about anything other than how I'd like to kill the son of a bitch who did this to you."

"As tempting as that might be, it won't change what happened. It wouldn't do much for your career, either."

At that, he finally cracked a small grin.

"I appreciate your friendship and all the support. It's meant a lot to me." She smiled when the compliment made him blush. "How about I give the Fitzgeralds a call to let them know we'd like to talk to them?"

"Sounds like a plan."

CHAPTER TEN

*D*uring four hours in the ICU, Sam got a total of fifteen minutes with her dad. Listening to a ventilator breathe for him had shredded her nerves as she wondered if she'd ever again be able to bounce a case off him when she was stuck, to consult with him about every aspect of her life. He'd been her touchstone, and in many ways her very best friend for so long she couldn't begin to entertain the notion of having to spend the rest of her life without him. Being back in the ICU also brought back grim memories of the horrible days that followed his shooting when they'd been told to expect the worst.

Maybe now, like then, he'd defy the odds. In the meantime, the waiting was making her crazy. Nick had gone home to change out of his suit and to pick up a change of clothes for her. Listening to her sisters and stepmother run the scenarios of how her father's illness could play out had driven Sam from the waiting room, and now she was doing laps of the long corridor outside the ICU.

Nick returned with the clothes just as Freddie came bursting through the double doors from the ICU.

"What's up?" Sam asked him.

"We've got a murder."

"Where?"

"Chevy Chase, near the Alice Deal Middle School."

"A kid?"

Freddie shook his head. "Stay-at-home mom, discovered by her daughter when she got home from school."

Sam glanced at Nick who watched her intently.

"There's not much you can do here, Sam," he said.

"I probably shouldn't leave, though. Even for a little while."

"Is there anything you need to say to him that you haven't already said?"

He knew her so well it was frightening at times. "No."

"Then go. That's what your dad would want you to do. I'll stay with Celia and the others, and I'll call you if anything changes."

"Are you sure you don't mind? It's not like you don't have things to do, too."

"I cleared my schedule for the rest of the day, and I don't mind."

How, she wondered, had she ever managed without him? She went up on tiptoes to kiss him. "I'll be back as soon as I can."

"I'll be here." He ran a finger over her cheek. "Be careful out there."

"Always am."

"Be extra careful today. You've got a lot on your mind."

"You'll tell Celia where I've gone?"

"Absolutely."

"Thanks." She kissed him once more and then followed Freddie to the elevator, still not entirely certain she should leave. If the worst should happen while she was gone, Sam would deal with it because Nick was right—her father would want her to go. The job, he'd say, pauses for no one and nothing. She hoped her stepmother and sisters would understand. If they didn't, Nick would smooth things over with them.

Sam and Freddie arrived a short time later at a two-story colonial home on a leafy street in Chevy Chase. Emergency vehicles lined the street, and the usual crowd of concerned neighbors had gathered outside the yellow crime-scene tape. Flashing their badges, Sam and Freddie pushed their way through and ducked under the tape. A patrolman greeted them.

"What've we got?" Sam asked.

The officer consulted a notebook. "Crystal Trainer, age thirty-five, found on the back patio by her daughter Nicole, age twelve, when the daughter arrived home from school." He gestured to the yard where a female officer was comforting the distraught girl. "No sign of forced entry, and as far as we could tell, nothing had been disturbed inside the house. Mrs. Trainer's purse and cell phone were found on the kitchen table. The cash in her wallet seemed to be untouched. The deceased's son, Josh, age eight, is due home from school momentarily."

Where, Sam thought, he'd learn his life had been permanently changed. "Husband?"

"Was notified by his daughter and is on his way home from work."

"Neighbors?"

He gestured to the tapeline where two other officers were interviewing the people who'd gathered there. "So far no one has reported seeing or hearing anything out of the ordinary."

"Good job," she said to the patrolman. Sam snapped on latex gloves and headed for the open front door. To Freddie, she said, "Check on the canvass."

"On it," he said.

Inside the nicely furnished home, Sam nodded to the officer who greeted her.

"This way, Lieutenant."

She followed him from the living room to a spacious kitchen that boasted modern appliances in brushed stainless. A designer purse sat on the kitchen table next to keys and a smartphone.

"I was sorry to hear your father is ill," the officer said, jarring Sam from her thoughts about the case.

"Thank you."

"We're all pulling for him."

"I appreciate that, and I'm sure he will, too."

They stepped through a sliding glass door to a stone patio that boasted a glass table and wrought-iron chairs with green-and-white-striped pads. Pots of well-tended blooms added a cheerful dose of color.

The officer pointed to the dead woman, who was sprawled facedown on the far side of the table. "Hit from behind with a blunt object is my guess," he said, pointing to the back of her head. She'd bled so profusely it was almost impossible to tell her hair had been blond.

A gasp from behind them caught Sam's attention, and she turned in time to watch the color drain from the face of a man in a dark business suit as he caught sight of the dead woman. He staggered and gripped one of the chairs to steady himself. Something about him was familiar to Sam.

"Oh my God," he said. "*Crystal.* What happened?"

"We don't know yet. What's your name?"

"Jed. Jed Trainer."

"And she's your wife?"

"Yes." He nodded and then glanced at Sam. "We've been separated for a few months, but we'd been working on it." His voice caught, and his eyes filled. "God. Crystal. I can't believe this."

"One of the officers said your son is due home momentarily," Sam said.

He raised a shaking hand to consult his watch. "Yes, any minute. How will I tell him? They were so close. And poor Nicole to come home and find this…"

"Go meet your son, and we'll discuss this further when you've had a chance to tell him what's happened."

"Yes. Yes, okay." He took another long look at the woman on the patio before he turned and went inside.

Lindsey McNamara came through the slider next. "We meet again," she said to Sam, shaking her head with dismay as she took in the scene. She squeezed Sam's arm. "I was sorry to hear about your dad. He's a fighter."

"We're counting on that."

"If there's anything I can do—anything at all—you know where I am."

"Thank you."

Lindsey tugged on gloves, knelt on the patio and went to work examining the body.

"I need a time of death to get me started," Sam said.

"Judging from the clotting and rigor, I'm guessing about three hours ago." Lindsey lifted some strands of hair to better expose the wound on the back of her scalp. "Looks like one lethal blow from behind. Probably took her by surprise."

An anguished scream came from inside the house, and Sam shuddered. "That'd be the son hearing the news."

"How old?" Lindsey asked.

"Eight."

"God. Poor kid."

"Kids, plural. The twelve-year-old daughter found her."

"Ugh."

Sam had so many competing emotions storming around inside her—worry about her father's health, thoughts of the new case and the poor children who'd lost their mother—she had to force herself to focus on her job. She was concerned about McBride and whether she'd made a mistake bringing her recovering detective back to work so soon after the egregious attack. Then there was the matter of Gardner and the offer she'd made him hoping to gain some new information about her father's shooting. And not to be forgotten were the threats they'd found in the wedding cards. It was all too much for one brain to process.

"Sam?" Lindsey jarred her out of the pensive state she'd slipped into. "Are you okay?"

"Yeah, thinking it through."

"When you have a spare minute in the midst of the madness, I could use some advice."

"About?"

"You want to do this now?"

"We've got a minute. What's going on?"

"Terry O'Connor."

"Ahh. What about him?"

"He told me about the alcoholism."

"And?"

Lindsey glanced at the officer who was canvassing the yard. "We should probably talk about it another time."

"I've got time now while I wait for the husband."

"Well, he's put the ball in my court. It's up to me to call him."

"So what's stopping you?"

"I grew up surrounded by alcoholics. My father, grandfather, uncle. I'm not sure I have it in me, you know?"

"I can see how it would be daunting."

As they spoke, Lindsey sealed Mrs. Trainer's hands in plastic bags to preserve evidence and prepared the body for transport. "How well do you know him?"

"Not all that well. We didn't get off to the best of starts with me accusing him of his brother's murder and all that."

Lindsey continued to prepare the body for transport. "And since then?"

"I see him once in a while when Nick and I go to Sunday dinner at the O'Connors'. For what it's worth, he's a much different person now than he was when I first met him."

"How so?"

"For one thing, he's sober and seems committed to staying that way. Nick made rehab and daily AA meetings a condition of his job offer."

"He's thrilled to be Nick's deputy chief of staff," Lindsey said.

"Nick has been pleased with his contributions so far. That's all I can tell you."

"That's quite a lot." She glanced up at Sam. "If you were me, would you give him a chance?"

Sam thought about it for a minute. As much as it drove her crazy to have her people dating Nick's people, she liked Lindsey and wanted her to be happy. "In light of how hard he's worked to reclaim his life, I'd guess he's a pretty good bet right about now. Of course, I can't know anything for sure, but since you're only talking about dating not marriage, I can't see what a few dates would hurt."

At the word *marriage*, Lindsey made a grimacing face. "No talk of marriage."

"Then I guess it's up to you to decide whether he's worth the risk."

Escorted by Freddie, Jed Trainer stepped through the sliding door, his eyes red from crying. "That was the most brutal thing

I've ever had to do," he said, his voice catching on a sob. "I've sent the kids next door so they won't have to see their mother removed from the house."

"That's a good idea," Sam said. "However, I'll need to speak with both of them."

"I'll take you over there when you're done here."

"I sent a Patrol officer with the kids to keep them from talking to each other about their mother or speculating about what might've happened until you have a chance to talk to them," Freddie said.

"Good, thank you."

Crime Scene detectives arrived, and Sam turned to Jed. "Mr. Trainer, could we please step inside for a few minutes?"

"Of course," he said, taking a last look at the body on the patio before leading them into the living room to sit on the sofa. He tugged at his tie and released his top button.

Sam took a seat across from him on a love seat. Freddie sat next to her. "Can you tell me when you last saw Crystal?" she asked.

"The day before yesterday. I took the kids to dinner and saw her when I brought them home."

"What was your custody arrangement?"

"They lived with her and spent every other weekend with me. I travel a lot for work, so I see them when I can during the week."

"And Mrs. Trainer was okay with that?"

"We went out of our way to keep things cordial for the kids."

"Who initiated the separation?"

"She did."

"What was her reasoning?"

He ran a hand over his mouth as his posture tightened with tension. "I had an affair. She found out about it, and that was that."

"You said you'd been working on the marriage. Were you in therapy?"

Nodding, he said, "We were making some progress, but now… I can't believe she's gone."

"Where were you today?"

The implication of what she was asking settled on him all at once. His expression went from cooperative to angry in a flash. "At my office."

"All day?"

"Except for twenty minutes when I went to get a sandwich."

"We'll need to confirm your alibi so we can rule you out as a suspect."

"Fine." He got up, went into the kitchen and returned with a pad of paper. Withdrawing a pen from his shirt pocket, he wrote down a name and number. "My assistant can confirm my whereabouts for the entire day."

"Thank you."

"I didn't kill her. I loved her, and I wanted to fix our marriage. I screwed up. I was doing what I could to make amends. What am I supposed to do now?"

"You take care of your kids the best you can," Freddie said.

"Mr. Trainer, did your wife have problems with anyone in her life? Family members, friends, anyone in the community?"

He shook his head. "Everyone loved Crystal. She had tons of friends and was president of the PTO at Nicole's school. People liked her."

"Is it possible she had problems with someone and didn't tell you?" Freddie asked.

"Doubtful. Even though we were separated, we talked often. She would've told me if something was wrong."

"Did she work?" Sam asked.

"No, but she did a ton of volunteer work."

"Can you give us a list of the organizations where she worked as well as friends we might speak to?"

Jed added the names and addresses to the page he had given them.

"If you can think of any problem she might've had or anyone she was at odds with, please let us know." Sam handed him her card. "Even the smallest thing can make a difference."

"The officer outside said there was no damage to the doors,

so does that mean it was someone we know?" he asked. "Did she let in a friend not knowing they'd come to do her harm?"

"That's possible," Sam said. "Or the door was unlocked, and this was totally random."

"Do you really think that?"

"My gut tells me this wasn't random," she said, standing to take a closer look at some family photos. She knew this couple from somewhere. "Have we met before now?"

"I was thinking you seem familiar, but of course I saw the coverage of your wedding."

"What was Crystal's maiden name?"

"Martin."

The name, like the face, was familiar, but Sam couldn't place it. "Where did she go to high school?"

"Roosevelt."

"College?"

"Maryland. College Park."

That ruled out school. Sam had gone to Wilson High, American University and George Washington for graduate school. "Is there any chance she was romantically involved with someone else?"

Jed recoiled from the question. "No."

"None at all?"

"Absolutely not. We were working on our marriage."

"Tell me the circumstances of the affair."

"Am I a suspect, Lieutenant?"

"Everyone's a suspect until they aren't." Sam returned to the love seat and sat facing him. "Let me tell you how these things sometimes go. A husband makes a mistake—a mistake he regrets and goes home to put the pieces of his marriage back together. In the meantime, there's another woman out there who's in love with him. Maybe he made some promises, told her he planned to leave his wife. Maybe she took a huge gamble on this guy, fell in love, believed him when he told her she was 'the one.' You see where I'm going with this?"

Jed was shaking his head. "It wasn't Janet. It was a short-lived thing. I made no promises. She knew I was married and would never leave my wife."

"If you'd never leave your wife, why have an affair?"

"It sort of happened. It wasn't something I planned. And it didn't happen because I no longer loved my wife. It had nothing to do with her."

Um, okay, Sam thought. *Whatever you say.* "How did your wife find out about it?"

"She received a text message."

"From whom?"

"We were never able to determine where it came from. It was an unknown number."

"So either the woman you were involved with sent that message or someone else found out about it and sent the text."

"Janet wouldn't have done that. It's not how she's wired."

"We'll need her name, address and phone number."

"Do you really have to drag her into this?"

"Yes, we really do." She gestured for him to add the information to the page he'd started. "Who else might've had a beef with Crystal?"

Jed ran a trembling hand over his jaw. "I've told you— everyone liked her."

"Everyone. She never had words with anyone, a disagreement in the PTO, a meltdown in the mom's club."

"Not that I can think of. She got along with people and hated drama of any kind, so she avoided it." He looked over at Sam. "I'd like to be with my children right now."

"We'll walk you over so we can speak with them."

"You go easy on them, won't you?"

"Of course. I want to know what Nicole saw when she got home and if they know of anyone who might want to harm their mother."

Sam and Freddie followed Jed to the house next door where Nicole and Josh were under the care of an older couple. Josh got up and ran to his father.

"Martha, Larry, this is Lieutenant Holland and Detective

Cruz," Jed said to the neighbors. "They have a few questions for the kids."

"We'd like to speak with both of you, too," Sam said to the older couple. "If you could wait in the kitchen, we'd appreciate it."

Martha glanced anxiously at Nicole on the sofa. "But the children..."

"We'll be quick," Sam said. "I promise."

"It's okay," Jed added.

Larry put an arm around his wife and escorted her from the room.

Sam glanced at Freddie.

"Mr. Trainer, would you and Josh join me in the dining room?" Freddie asked.

"Nicole?" Jed said. "Honey, do you mind talking to Lieutenant Holland?"

The girl sat up and shook her head.

"I'll be right in the dining room with Josh, okay? Come get me if you need me."

When they were alone, Sam sat next to Nicole on the sofa. "I'm so sorry about your mom."

"Thank you." Nicole wiped tears from her face. "I can't stop crying."

"That's to be expected. You've had a terrible shock." Sam gave the girl a moment to get herself together before continuing. "Can you tell me what happened when you got home?"

Nicole nodded. "Since school is only two blocks away, my mom and dad said I could walk this year. A lot of days my mom meets me halfway, but she wasn't there today."

"Did you think anything of that?"

"No, because sometimes she's on the phone or something. She only gets worried if I'm not home by three."

"When you got home today, was the door open?"

Shaking her head, Nicole said, "I went in through the garage. We have this door opener with a code we can punch in to open it. I thought it was weird the front door wasn't open because she's usually waiting at the door, even if she's on the phone."

"So you came in the house, and then what?"

"I called for her, but she didn't answer. I saw the sliding door was open, so I went out there and she was… There was so much blood. I started screaming for her to wake up, but she wouldn't."

"Did you touch her?"

A sob hiccupped through her. "I shook her shoulder, but she didn't wake up." She rubbed at red, raw eyes. "I ran inside and called 911. I didn't know what else to do."

Sam reached for the girl's hand. "You did everything right. You saw your mom was hurt, and you called for help."

"But if I hadn't stopped to talk to Jessica, maybe I would've gotten here sooner…"

"It wouldn't have mattered. She'd been gone a while by the time you got home."

"Oh."

"Can you think of anyone who might've wanted to hurt your mom?"

Nicole's pretty brown eyes filled again as she shook her head. "She was so nice. All my friends thought so. They liked coming to my house because she was always there and made us cookies and snacks."

"If you can think of anyone she might've argued with or who was mad with her, will you call me?" She wrote her cell phone number on the back of her card and handed it to Nicole. "You can call me anytime."

"I'll think about it."

"Your mom would've been proud of the way you held up today," Sam said.

"You really think so?"

"I know so."

*a*s Freddie drove them downtown, Sam checked in with Nick and learned there'd been no change in her father's condition.

"How're you doing, babe?"

"I'm okay. Working takes my mind off it." Her conversation with the grief-stricken twelve-year-old had helped to bring some perspective to her own situation. It could always be worse. "You should go home and get some sleep."

"I'll wait until you get back."

"Could be a while."

"That's all right," Nick said. "I talked to my dad. He wants you to know he's praying for Skip."

"That's nice of him. Tell him I said thanks."

"I will. What's up with the case?"

"Thirty-five-year-old mother of two found murdered on the patio by her twelve-year-old daughter. The eight-year-old son came home right after we got here."

"Oh, man. Those poor kids."

"Yeah, it was rough."

"Any suspects?"

"Of course not. We talked to the estranged husband, the kids, the neighbors. They all said the same thing—she was the perfect mother, and everyone loved her."

"Another tough one."

"Aren't they all?" Sam glanced over at her partner, who seemed to be lost in thought. "I'll be there as soon as I can."

"Love you, babe."

"You, too."

Freddie brought the car to a stop at a light in the Woodley Park neighborhood where he lived.

"Want me to drop you at home?" she asked.

"Nah, my car's at HQ."

Sam glanced out the window at a couple walking arm-in-arm on the sidewalk and did a double take. "Hey, isn't that your mom?"

Freddie bent his head for a closer look and gasped. *"Are you freaking kidding me?* She's seeing someone at the same time she's busting my chops about Elin?" He continued to stare at the animated couple long after the light turned green and cars behind them started to blow their horns. The man with his mother turned toward the street to see what all the commotion was about, and Freddie let out a gasp. "Oh my God. That's…"

The driver of the car behind them laid on the horn.

"Freddie? What is it?"

"I can't even believe it." His face had gone pale and his lips were white with rage. Sam had never seen him so furious. "She's such a hypocrite!"

"Pull over," Sam said, pointing to a parking lot in the next block.

Freddie did as directed and killed the engine. He continued to grip the steering wheel so tightly his knuckles were white.

"Talk to me. Who's the guy?"

"The father I haven't seen or heard from in twenty years."

"Whoa," Sam said. "How could you tell it was him? Is it possible it's someone who looks like him?"

Freddie shook his head. "It was him. I'd know him anywhere. I've spent two-thirds of my life looking for him in every crowd, sidewalks…"

"What's he doing with your mother?"

"A very good question. While she's making me feel like shit

about dating Elin, she's seeing *him* behind my back? She's put me through *hell,* and this is what she's doing?"

"You need to talk to her before you jump to any conclusions."

"What do we need to talk about? You saw her. She was hanging all over him."

"There might be something else going on. You won't know until you ask her."

"I don't even want to talk to her right now. That son of a bitch left us without a word *twenty years* ago. What could she possibly have to say to him?"

"Why don't you go ask her?"

He shook his head and started the car. "I need to cool off before I talk to her."

Sam had no idea what she should say to him so she kept quiet.

Freddie drove faster than usual as he navigated rush-hour traffic.

At the downtown consulting firm where Jed Trainer was a managing director, Sam and Freddie took the elevator to the sixth floor.

Janet Nealson seemed shocked to have cops asking for her.

"What can I do for you?"

"Jed Trainer's wife was murdered in their home today."

Janet gasped, and her legs seemed to buckle beneath her. Gripping the table, she slipped into a chair.

"Where were you around noon?" Sam asked.

That seemed to snap Janet out of the stupor she'd slipped into. "I'm a suspect?"

"I asked where you were."

"Here. I've been here since seven-thirty."

"You never left for any reason?"

"No," she said, shaking her head. "We've been in meetings most of the day. We ordered in for lunch."

"And was Mr. Trainer here all day?"

"He left for a short time at lunch. He's a vegetarian, so he wanted something different than the rest of us."

"You were involved with Mr. Trainer?"

"Y-yes," she said.

"How did that end?"

"His wife found out, which upset him very much. He… He decided to go back to her, to commit to his marriage."

"How did you feel about that?"

"I was disappointed. We had a real connection." She folded her hands, maybe to stop them from trembling. "Those poor kids. Jed always said Crystal was a great mother."

"Were people here aware of your involvement?"

"No. We were extremely discreet."

"Do you have any idea who might've told his wife about the affair?"

"Neither of us had any idea. We didn't think anyone else knew."

"You didn't tell *anyone?*" Freddie asked with an unusual edge to his voice.

"No," she said. "As much as I cared for Jed, I was ashamed to be seeing a married man. It wouldn't have been good for me professionally if people here found out, and I certainly didn't want my friends or family knowing I'd become such a cliché."

"What was your professional relationship like after you ended the affair?" Sam asked.

"Cordial. We both went out of our way to maintain a collegial relationship."

"That couldn't have been easy."

She shrugged, the gesture full of defeat. "I knew what I was getting into. I was hardly surprised when he went back to his wife."

"Did he ever indicate he planned to leave her?"

"We didn't talk about the future."

"So that's a no?"

"He never indicated he might leave his wife for me."

"Where did your liaisons take place?"

Her attractive face flamed with embarrassment. "We went to a hotel."

"Which one?"

She named a hotel in Crystal City. Interesting, Sam thought, that he'd chosen a city for his trysts with the same name as his wife.

"Where did his wife think he was when he was with you?"

"He told her he was on travel for work. She never questioned him as far as I knew."

"Did he ever express anger toward his wife?" Freddie asked.

"Not to me."

"I can't help but wonder," Freddie said, "why he'd have an affair when he had such a great wife at home."

"I wasn't privy to his thought process. We didn't talk about the 'why' of it. At least he didn't share that with me. For what it's worth, I never heard him say a bad word about her."

Sam handed her a card. "If you think of anything that might help the investigation, give me a call."

Janet took the card. "I know you may not believe this, but I'm truly sorry this happened to her—and to their family."

"Thank you for your time."

They confirmed Trainer's alibi with his assistant and left the office.

"What now?" Freddie asked.

"We wait to hear from the lab and the autopsy," Sam said, checking her watch. "Tomorrow we'll look into her volunteer gigs."

"You want to go right to the hospital? I can grab a cab to HQ."

"That's okay. I'll drop you off and head over there."

"I can come to the hospital with you."

"That's nice of you, but go home and get some sleep so at least one of us can function tomorrow."

"If you're sure."

"About this thing with your mother…."

"I don't want to talk about it."

"I know her well enough to be sure she'd never do anything to hurt you. I bet there's a perfectly good explanation."

"There's nothing she can say that will make me understand what she was doing with him." He handed her the car keys. "One good thing about all this is now I don't have to give a shit what she thinks about Elin."

"Freddie… It's not like you to talk this way."

"Well, this is the new and improved Freddie."

"I liked the old Freddie," Sam muttered.

"The old Freddie was a pushover who let his mother have far too much influence over him. The new Freddie is his own man."

Before Sam could respond, her cell phone rang. A glance at the caller ID indicated Captain Malone was calling.

"Captain."

"Lieutenant, I understand you caught a murder this afternoon."

"Yes, sir." Sam brought him up to speed on the case thus far. "We're waiting on Crime Scene and the lab. First thing tomorrow we're looking at the places where she volunteered."

"The husband checked out?"

"We confirmed his alibi, but we're going to run the financials." She glanced at Freddie, and he nodded. Jed Trainer could've hired someone to kill his wife. A look at his bank accounts would tell that story.

"Excellent. Any word on your father?"

"He's the same—on a ventilator with massive doses of antibiotics being pumped in. It's a wait-and-see thing at this point."

"I'll be over to check on Celia in a while."

"Thank you, sir. I know she'll appreciate that. As do I."

"Hang in there, Sam. He's tough, and he's survived worse."

"Yes." She swallowed hard. "Sir."

"I'm also calling because Darius Gardner requested a meeting with you."

Sam sat up straighter in her seat. "Really?"

"That's the word from the jail."

"Would you ask Detective Gonzales to meet me there?"

"Will do."

"Thank you." Sam ended the call. "Well what'd you know?" she said to Freddie. "Gardner wants to see me."

"Wonder what that's all about."

"Maybe he's had a fit of conscience."

"Highly unlikely."

"Wouldn't it be nice to finally get a break in my dad's case? An honest-to-goodness *break?*"

"Yes, indeed. You're long overdue."

"Of course it would have to happen at a time when my dad is unable to appreciate it. Isn't that just my luck?"

"I know the situation with him is serious," Freddie said. "I get that. But I don't think this is it for him."

"How do you know?"

"Just a feeling I have."

"Normally I'd have no choice but to make fun of a statement like that, but right now it's damned comforting."

"I appreciate the show of restraint." Freddie parked outside the jail and walked in with her.

Gonzo was waiting for them.

"Go run those financials and then go home," Sam said to Freddie. "Meet you back here in the morning."

"I'll let you know if anything pops."

He walked away, and Sam watched him go, concerned new Freddie was going to make a mess of things for old Freddie.

"Everything okay?" Gonzo asked. As the senior member of her team, he was not only a good friend but often a sounding board, too.

"He's upset about something. Keep an eye on him, okay?"

They navigated the winding corridor to the city jail.

"Will do."

"Appreciate that."

"How's your father?"

"Same. Not good."

"I'm sorry. If there's anything I can do, just ask."

"Thanks. How's McBride making out?"

"She seemed to be doing okay. She went with Tyrone to talk to Fitzgerald's parents."

Sam nodded. "That's good."

"It's a wise move," he said.

"What is?"

"Easing her back in with a cold case."

"Oh, well." Sam never had figured out how to take a compliment. "Seemed to make sense."

"It's a good move."

"Anything else in the mail?"

"One thing I want you to look at, but it can keep."

"We'll do it after this."

At the jail they asked a deputy to bring Gardner to an interrogation room. When he was led into the room, Sam took perverse pleasure in seeing he'd been in a fight. One eye was swollen shut and his nose had been splinted. No wonder he'd been so willing to talk to her.

"Mr. Gardner," she said. "You remember Detective Gonzales." He nodded stiffly.

"You asked for this meeting. What can we do for you?"

"You want information about who shot your father, the cop."

An electrical current worked its way down her spine. "That's right."

"It wasn't me."

Sam eyed him skeptically. "And I'm supposed to believe that?"

"I swear on my son's life, it wasn't me. Anyone who knows me will tell you I'd never swear on his life if I was lying."

"It's good to know you're so ethical."

He glowered at her. "You want information or not?"

"I'm listening."

Gardner seemed to be thinking over what he wanted to say. "There was this other guy who lived in the First Avenue house about the same time I was there. He came home one night all hopped up and high, ranting about something to do with a cop."

Adrenaline zipped through Sam's veins, making her heart race. She had to work at hiding her reaction from Gardner.

"Did this guy have a name?"

"Leroy. That's all I know. I never caught his last name, and I don't know how he ended up there, but I heard him talking about a cop."

"And you think it was the week between Christmas and New Year's 2008?"

He nodded. "I know it was. Someone had made a Christmas tree outta beer bottles and covered it with lights. Those blinking lights drove me crazy. That's how I remember."

"How come you couldn't remember this the other day?"

His shrug was full of the insolence she'd come to expect from him. "It's a long time ago. I can't be expected to remember shit that happened years ago off the top of my head. I had some time to think about it."

The fist to the face no doubt helped to move things along, Sam thought. "Can you give me a physical description of this Leroy fellow?"

"He was a big black dude. About six-six, two-fifty. Muscular."

"You don't know anything else about him?"

Gardner shook his head. "He wasn't there for long."

Sam placed her hands on the table and leaned in close to him. "If I find out you're dicking me around, that mess on your face will be the least of your concerns, you hear me?"

"I ain't dicking with you. I'm telling the truth."

Strangely, Sam believed him. "You'd better be." She turned to leave the room.

"Hey! What're you gonna do for me?"

"Nothing," she said. "You're going away for a good long time on the rape charges. Not a damned thing I can do about that."

"You bitch! You said you'd get me a deal if I gave you something on your dad's shooting."

She glanced at Gonzo. "Does that sound like something I would say?"

"Not that I've ever heard, Lieutenant."

Sam smiled at Gardner. "You must've heard me wrong."

"Motherfucking cunt."

"I love when they roll out the C word, don't you, Detective Gonzales? It makes me all tingly inside."

Gonzo rolled his eyes at her. "Are we done here?"

Sam glared at Gardner. "We're done."

He screamed swears at her retreating back until the deputies subdued him. *That was for Faith Miller,* she said to herself, thinking of the assistant U.S. attorney Gardner had threatened.

"I'll dig into the new lead ASAP," Gonzo said. "I know you must be anxious to get back to the hospital."

"That'd be great." She checked her watch and couldn't believe it was already eight o'clock. "I do need to get over there."

"Go ahead. I'll let you know what I find out."

"Earlier, my dad suggested we look into Carl Olivo's involvement in civic organizations like the Rotary Club," Sam said. "It's a stretch, but he thought we should check."

"I'll look into that, too."

"Thanks."

On the way back to the detectives' pit, Sam was stopped by at least ten other officers wanting to know how her father was doing. Their concern bolstered her sagging spirits. In the pit, Freddie let her know he was still digging through Trainer's financials, but so far nothing unusual had appeared.

"Give it another hour and then get out of here," she said. "I'm going back to the hospital. Call me if you hear anything from Lindsey or Crime Scene." She started to walk out but stopped when she remembered the card Gonzo had mentioned. "Show me that card."

"Oh, right." He went to his cubicle and returned with the card, which was encased in an evidence bag.

"Dear Sam," the letter began. "After all you have done for others in your life, I hope you get absolutely everything you deserve. And then some. With much love from an Old Friend." The word *everything* had been underlined three times.

"Wow," Sam said. "That's creepy."

"I thought so, too."

"Get it to the lab," Sam said, rubbing her temples. "I was hoping this was someone's idea of a joke, but whoever it is, they're not giving up."

"I think it might be time for one of us to have a conversation with your ex-husband."

A headache that had been threatening all afternoon was quickly coming to fruition. "I'll do it. I don't want any of you dealing with him."

"Why not?" Gonzo asked with a glint in his eye. "Any one of us would love five minutes alone with him."

"No," she said. "I'll do it."

"Aw, you ruin all my fun."

"That's my job. I'm going. Call me if you hear anything."

"You got it. Give my best to your stepmother and sisters."

"I will." As Sam was heading out of the pit, Lt. Stahl came around the corner. She tried to dodge him, but he blocked her path. She came perilously close to bouncing off his fat belly. The near miss added nausea to her growing list of ailments. "What do you want?"

"A moment of your time."

"That's more than I've got." Ever since Sam had replaced him as the lieutenant in charge of the Homicide detectives Stahl had been making her life miserable. He'd even used his new bully pulpit as an internal affairs officer to call her up on disciplinary charges for getting involved with Nick during the investigation into John O'Connor's murder. Fortunately, he'd been unsuccessful, but he continued to badger her.

"Not so fast, Lieutenant," he said, his jowls jiggling with every word.

"I have somewhere I need to be. Could you please get out of my way?"

"Internal Affairs is looking into your wedding," he said with barely restrained glee.

What the hell? She kept the thought to herself to deny him any satisfaction. Pushing past him, she said, "Whatever."

He followed her. "Is that all you have to say about how you invited some members of your squad but not others?"

Sam spun around to face him and once again came far too close to that protruding belly. "What the hell are you talking about?"

"There's been a complaint." Stahl positively beamed as he broke the news to her. "As you well know, a commanding officer can't show favoritism to one of her subordinates over another."

"I didn't show favoritism. I invited my *friends*. Do you know what *friends* are, Lieutenant?"

His fat face went purple with rage as he pushed a sheet of paper at her.

Sam had no choice but to take the paper or be touched by him.

"Administrative hearing."

"*Again?* You're starting to become a bad cliché, Lieutenant. Don't you have anyone else to pick on?"

"Must suck for you to be in trouble—again—and dear old daddy can't do a thing for you this time."

Sam's blood went from simmer to boil in the flash of an instant. "Fuck you, you miserable excuse for a human being."

Somehow his purple face got even darker, but Sam didn't stick around to hear what he had to say. She'd had more than enough of this day.

CHAPTER TWELVE

S am called Gonzo from the car and told him about the encounter with Stahl.

"That son of a bitch," Gonzo muttered. "He seriously needs to get a life."

"Until he does, he's out to make mine miserable." Sam gripped the steering wheel, trying to contain the rage that threatened to consume her. "As much as I hate to dignify this with any kind of response, can you sniff around a bit and find out who complained about not being invited to the wedding?"

"Absolutely. For what it's worth, I haven't heard the slightest ripple about anyone being put out. But I'll find out who it was."

"Be subtle, and don't let on that I asked you to."

"Jeez, Sam, give me some credit, huh?" he said, his voice laced with humor. "I'm known for my smoothness."

Despite her anger, the comment drew a smile from her. "Did I screw this up, Gonzo? Should I have invited everyone?"

"Don't be crazy. How could you have done that?"

"I hate the idea that I might've walked right into another excuse for Stahl to dig into my business."

"I wouldn't sweat it. Whoever supposedly complained wouldn't dare testify against you in a formal hearing. There's not a detective in this squad who doesn't think the world of you. I know that for a fact."

"There's at least one."

"Go be with your dad. I'll take care of things here."

Sam appreciated his steady support and friendship. "Any word on the sergeant's list?"

"Nothing yet."

"I'm pulling for you, and I've already put dibs to keep you on my team."

"I love when you talk dirty to me, Lieutenant."

Sam snorted with laughter. "I talked kinda dirty to Stahl just now. I'm sure he'll add a smack for that."

"Eww, don't even put the image of dirty talk and Stahl in my head. I'll have nightmares."

Still smiling, Sam said, "Talk to you later." She grabbed the first parking space she could find at the hospital and half walked, half ran to the ICU. Nick was alone in the waiting room. He had his arms crossed and his head tipped back against the wall. Since he seemed to be asleep, Sam stepped out to find a nurse to get an update on her dad.

"No change," the nurse overseeing his case said.

"Should there have been a change by now?"

"Not always. Let's see what the next few hours bring. The antibiotics should begin to kick in soon."

Dejected by the less-than-encouraging report, Sam trudged back to the waiting room and crawled into her husband's lap.

His arms encircled her even as his eyes remained closed. "I sure hope you're my wife, or I'm going to be in big trouble."

"It's me," she said, burrowing into his chest and breathing in the comforting scent of home.

"Rough day?"

"Miserable day, and no change here."

"Yet. They said it could be a while."

"Where is everyone?"

"Angela took Celia to get something to eat. Tracy is in with your dad."

"Have you gotten to see him?"

"Briefly a couple of hours ago."

"Thanks so much for staying all this time."

"I didn't mind. It was a night off anyway."

Sam touched her lips to his, and he finally opened his eyes. His hand found its way to her face. "What's wrong?"

"What *isn't* wrong?" The frustration of the day threatened to boil over. "My dad is fighting for his life, we've got a murdered woman who everyone loved, and her poor kids are destroyed. I got a good new lead on my dad's shooting, but I had to turn it over to Gonzo because I needed to be here. Freddie saw his mom canoodling with his deadbeat dad, and now he's 'new' Freddie, and Stahl slapped me with yet another IAB summons because someone in my squad is pissed he or she wasn't invited to our wedding."

"Wow. All that today?"

Sam nodded. "I want to go back to Bora Bora. Right now."

"I wish I could wave a magic wand and make it happen."

"If you had a wand, I'd want you to use it to fix my dad. In fact, make him whole again, would you?"

He pressed a soft kiss to her forehead. "I'd do it in a second if I could."

"I love you for that—and many other things."

"I love you, too, babe. I'm so sorry you had such a shitty day."

"How long is Tracy going to be in there? I want to see him."

"You can go to the door and let her know you're here."

Sam snuggled deeper into his embrace, absorbing the comfort only he could provide. "I will. In a minute."

AFTER FINDING nothing compelling in the Trainers' financial records, Freddie texted Sam to let her know the results and headed for the parking lot. Since seeing his mother with his father earlier, Freddie had been grappling with the implications. He knew Sam was right—he should go talk to his mother and get to the bottom of what was going on. Except the last thing he wanted to hear was that his mother was giving that son of a bitch another chance.

How could she even talk to him after he'd left her alone with a young child? When Freddie thought about how they'd struggled to get by without the support of his father, he wanted to kill the guy. His mother had worked two jobs for years to keep a roof over their heads and food on the table. Without their church, they would've had no social life at all because they wouldn't have been able to afford it. And now she was seeing him again? Laughing with him? Walking down a public street without a care in the world as to who might see her with the man who'd caused them such suffering?

The whole thing made Freddie sick. And it made him furious. His mother's disapproval of Elin had been driving him slowly insane. Well, those days were over now. Never again would he allow his mother to influence his life or his decisions.

Normally, he would've called Elin to see if she was available, but tonight he was new Freddie, and new Freddie didn't ask. New Freddie just showed up, and if she didn't like it, too bad. By the time he arrived at Elin's apartment, he was in one hell of a mood. He knew he was hardly fit for company tonight, but that didn't stop him from taking the stairs to her place two at a time. It didn't stop him from knocking a little too loudly on her door. And when she answered wearing a short silk robe and not much of anything else, it didn't stop him from lifting her into his arms and carrying her straight to bed.

"Freddie, what—"

"Don't talk," he said. "Not now." Capturing her mouth in a deep kiss, he moved quickly to get rid of clothes, only breaking the kiss to pull the shirt over his head.

She looked up at him with big blue eyes. "What's wrong?"

"Nothing." He shifted his attention to her neck, leaving a trail of open-mouth kisses on his way to the breasts that dominated his fantasies. Her pierced nipples sprang to life under the attention of his tongue and then his teeth.

She cried out and her fingers burrowed into his hair so tightly it probably would've hurt if all his attention hadn't been focused on the burning need to possess her, to make her his.

He freed himself and plunged into her tight, wet heat. *Oh my God, did that feel good!*

"Freddie! Condom!" Her frantic tone snapped him out of the lust-filled haze he'd drifted into.

"Sorry," he muttered. Withdrawing from her he reached for the bedside table where she kept a ready supply and rolled on the ribbed kind she preferred. When he returned his attention to her she was looking up at him, her face set in a puzzled expression.

"Why won't you tell me what's wrong?" she asked.

"I told you. It's nothing."

She rolled out from under him and tugged her robe closed.

Groaning he landed face-first on the bed. "Come on, Elin."

"You come on. Tell me why you came in here acting like the big macho man when that's *so* not you."

"It's the new me."

Her face wrinkled up with dismay. "What the hell does that mean?"

"I'm tired of being so predictable and boring."

"You're neither of those things. Who told you that?"

"Doesn't matter. I realized it's time to make some changes."

"What kind of changes?"

"Can we have sex first and then I'll tell you?"

"Tell first, sex second."

Freddie let out a long sigh. Why did all the women in his life have to drive him crazy? Couldn't one of them be easy to understand and manage? He took a visual trip down Elin's long muscular leg, and his cock surged with renewed interest.

"Come here," he said.

She inched down the bed.

"Closer." He held out an arm to her. When she would've settled on his chest, he stopped her and turned to face her. He wanted to be able to see her for this.

She rested a hand on his belly. "You're acting weird."

"I'm sorry. I don't mean to be. I have something I want to tell you, but I'm afraid it'll freak you out. It's something I've wanted to tell you for a long time now."

"Okay."

As she watched him expectantly, Freddie ran his fingers over her gorgeous face, tangling them into her white-blond hair. "I love you."

Her eyes widened and her lips parted, as if there was something she wanted to say.

"I know you didn't sign on for serious and committed, but somewhere along the way I became very serious about you and extremely committed."

"But...I thought...You said you wanted to see other people."

"I never wanted to see anyone but you."

"Then why...? I don't understand."

"I was letting my mother twist me up in knots, but that's done now."

"What changed?"

"I've made up my mind you're the one I want, and I'm done playing games or doing what other people want me to do." He leaned in to kiss her. "I love you. I want to be with you. I want us to move in together."

She pulled back from him. "What did you say?"

"Which part do you need me to say again?" Freddie lifted up and moved so he was on top of her. "The part about I love you, or the part about I want to live together?"

"Both," she said softly, still looking slightly dazed.

He bent his head and kissed her. "I love you," he whispered. "I want to live with you."

She linked her arms around his neck. "I thought you were looking for a way out when you said you wanted to see other people."

"I never wanted out, and I've never wanted anyone else. Not since the first time I saw you."

She ran her fingers through his hair. "I love you, too."

For a second, Freddie wasn't sure he'd heard her right. Then the words registered and his heart skipped a happy beat. "You do?"

She nodded. "But I love old Freddie, not the guy who came in here tonight acting all alpha. That's not you."

Grateful to know she returned his feelings, Freddie reached between them to open her robe and reveled in the feel of her skin against his. Soft yet strong, sweet yet tough, she'd become everything to him. It was such a relief to be able to tell her how he felt and to know she returned the feelings.

He went out of his way to show her how much he loved her by worshiping every inch of her. Whereas before he'd been all about urgency, now he was about tenderness. She was the first woman he'd given his body to and now the first to receive his heart. He wanted to give her everything, to give her every reason to stay with him forever. Thoughts of his mother's disapproval would normally be taking something away from his enjoyment of being with Elin, but tonight he refused to think of anything but the warm, willing woman who made him burn with desire.

Cupping her breasts, he ran his tongue over one nipple and then the other. He added suction and the light biting that drove her wild.

She clutched his backside and raised her hips, urging him to take her.

Even though he'd planned to take his time, he couldn't resist her offer. Sliding into her, he sighed with completion. He was exactly where he wanted to be. As he moved slowly, prolonging the pleasure, he caught her gaze and held it.

He could tell by the trembling in her legs that she was close, so he picked up the pace. At times like this, when they were in total harmony, it was hard for Freddie to believe that only a few months ago he'd been a virgin. She suited him so perfectly, and as her legs tightened around his waist, it was all he could do to maintain control.

"Elin," he gasped, clutching her ass to hold her still for his fierce possession.

She let out a sharp cry in the second before she came hard, triggering an explosive finish for him.

As he lay panting on top of her, Freddie had never been more content. He had staked his claim on the woman he loved. Knowing she loved him, too, was the best gift he'd ever been given.

"Yes," she said so softly he almost didn't hear her.

He raised his head to meet her gaze. "What?"

"I want to move in together."

"Really?"

"Yes."

"You're sure?"

She nodded.

He hugged her tightly. "You've made me so happy."

CHAPTER THIRTEEN

eannie sat with Will in his car outside Michael's townhouse in Washington's Foggy Bottom neighborhood.

"What're you going to do?" Will asked.

"I honestly don't know."

"There has to be a reason why Deputy Chief Holland didn't fully investigate the brother."

"And we can't exactly ask him."

"Right," Will said.

Jeannie's mind had been racing since they left the home of Tyler Fitzgerald's parents. After walking the parents step-by-step through the day their son was abducted, it had become obvious to both detectives that their son Cameron might've had something to do with his brother's disappearance. But for some reason, Skip Holland had never dug into the brother who entered the army shortly after Tyler was kidnapped.

Cameron had had a contentious four-year tenure in the military, culminating in a dishonorable discharge. He'd been in and out of trouble ever since, all of it misdemeanor level, but he'd been escalating.

"What'll you tell Sam?"

"I honestly don't know."

"Maybe you shouldn't say anything until we know what's going to happen with her father."

"Good point."

Jeannie turned in her seat so she could better see her partner. "I can't imagine what he was thinking. It was such an obvious lead. How could he not follow up?"

"We need to talk to the other brother, Caleb. He was with Tyler and Cameron at the school that night."

"Did you read the statement he gave Skip?" Jeannie asked.

"Yeah and it left me with more questions than answers. What about a partner? Who was Skip working with?"

"The department was going through a major budget crunch, and they were seriously strapped. Most of the detectives were working alone during that period."

"What about the medical examiner who worked the case?"

"Tracking him down is on my to-do list for tomorrow."

"You know who might have some insight into Skip's thinking..."

Jeannie shuddered at the thought of it. "The chief."

"Yep."

"Let's keep that as an avenue of last resort."

"Agreed. What about Sam?"

"I'll tell her we're working the case and don't have anything yet. Let's keep all of this between us until we know more."

"You're the boss, Detective."

That drew a small smile from Jeannie.

"Feel good to be back in the game?"

"It's good to feel useful again."

"I'm awfully glad to have you back." His smile was full of shyness. "I missed you."

"I missed you, too." Her cell phone rang and Jeannie took the call from Michael. "Hey, I'm outside with Will."

"Okay. I was just checking on you."

"I'll be in soon." She ended the call and turned to Will. "See you in the morning?"

"Yes, you will."

Jeannie got out of the car and waved to him as he drove off.

The instant she realized she was alone on the same street where she'd been abducted her heart began to race. She wondered if the day would come when she could walk down a city street without worrying about who might be lurking behind her waiting to harm her.

By the time she took the eight steps to Michael's front door, she was convinced her heart might burst through her chest. Her hands were shaking so hard that getting the key in the door was an exercise in futility.

Michael opened the door and ushered her inside. "Are you okay?"

"I am now," she said, immediately comforted by his large, imposing presence. No one would get to her while he was around. That much she was sure of.

"Why are you trembling and sweaty?"

"Am I?"

"Jeannie, what's going on?"

"Just a little panic attack on the street."

He frowned. "I thought you said Will was with you?"

"He was. Happened after he left. I found myself alone on the street, just for a second, but that's all it took."

"Goddamn it. I should've gone right to the door to meet you, but I finished unloading the dishwasher."

"It's not your fault, and I'm going to have to be out there eventually. I may as well get used to it."

"I hate the idea of anything scaring you so badly you tremble."

Jeannie stepped into his outstretched arms and let him surround her with his unconditional love. He kept one arm around her and used his free hand to set the alarm. The beep, beep, beep of the alarm engaging took care of the last of her anxiety.

For the first time since the attack, she was able to remember the way he'd made her feel from the very beginning. As he held her she experienced a reawakening of sorts, as her body reacted to him in the old familiar way.

"Michael?"

"Hmm?"

"Will you kiss me? Really kiss me, the way you used to. Before."

"Are you sure? I don't want to scare you."

"You won't." Jeannie reached for him and brought his head down to meet her halfway. Their lips met and held for a long, breathless moment before he tipped his head to delve deeper. Jeannie let go of all the worries and fears and gave herself over to the desire. *This* was what she'd needed. *He* was what she'd needed. She held on tight to him, letting him take the lead as his tongue tangled with hers, and gave as much as she was getting.

By the time he finally broke the kiss, she was light-headed and the tingling sensation traveling through her body reminded her of better days.

"God, Jeannie," he whispered, leaning his forehead against hers. "I've missed you. I've missed *us*."

"I have, too." She took his hands and held on tight. "I'm sorry about what happened last night. You have to be getting so frustrated."

He straightened to his full height. "Come with me, will you?"

"Where are you taking me?"

His playful smile was infectious as he walked backward, leading her into the kitchen where the table was set for an intimate dinner for two. When her mouth watered, she released his hands so she could examine the stove and peek in the oven. "Did you make all this?" she asked, stunned by the effort he'd put into the meal.

"I can't take credit. As you're painfully aware, I'm a terrible cook, so I ordered the meal and somehow I've managed to keep it warm without screwing it up."

She laughed and followed his directions to be seated at the table.

He poured them both a glass of wine and sat next to her. "To you," he said, raising his glass to her. "The bravest, strongest, gutsiest gal I've ever known."

His words went straight to her heart. "I haven't felt so gutsy lately."

"We've had a tough go of it for a while now, but I want you to know there's nowhere else I'd rather be than with you." He placed a jeweler's box on the table.

Jeannie sucked in a sharp deep breath and stared at the distinctive blue box as if it were a grenade about to detonate.

"Now before you say anything hear me out. Okay?" When she didn't reply, he said, "Jeannie?"

"Yes, yes," she said, never taking her eyes off the box. "Okay."

"I bought this two weeks before."

That finally drew her attention off the box and back to him.

"I was going to ask you that weekend. I had it all planned."

She'd suspected as much, but hearing of yet another thing her attacker had taken from her had Jeannie fighting off a wave of fury. She wouldn't give him this moment, too, so she refocused her attention on Michael.

"I'm not going to ask you now."

An odd sense of letdown overtook her. "Oh. Okay."

"You're hearing me out, remember?"

Returning his smile, she nodded.

"I'm not going to ask you now, but I'm not going anywhere. No matter how long it takes, no matter how many bumps we hit along the way, I'm here, and I'm staying."

Jeannie bit her lip, hoping to hold back the tears that filled her eyes.

"Unless, of course, you're sick of me, and this is the worst possible thing I could be telling you."

Laughing, she reached for him and held on tight.

He tugged her closer, and she ended up on his lap.

"Thank you," she whispered.

"I know what you were thinking after last night. 'How long will it be before he's had enough?' Am I right?"

"Maybe."

"Now you have one less thing to worry about. I love you. I'll always love you, and nothing could ever change that."

"That's good to know."

"This is the part where the girl would usually say 'I love you, too, and when I'm ready I'll want that ring and everything that goes with it.'"

"Hmm," she said, playing with him a little, "could I maybe see the ring so I know what I'm agreeing to?"

With a playful scowl, he flipped open the box to reveal a breathtaking cushion-cut diamond in a platinum setting.

"Oh," she said, at a loss for words.

"Do you like it? Your mom helped me pick it out."

"She never said a word!"

"I swore her to secrecy." He kissed Jeannie's cheek and then her lips. "You didn't answer the question."

Jeannie was too busy staring at the *gorgeous* ring to remember what he'd asked.

"Do you *like* it?"

"I *love* it. It's spectacular."

"And it's all yours whenever you're ready. No rush, no pressure, no stress."

"Am I allowed to try it on?"

"Not until you're ready to leave it on."

"Oh, that's mean!"

He shrugged. "That's my final offer."

"You drive a hard bargain."

He kissed her again, closed the ring box and put it back in his pocket. "How about some dinner?"

LINDSEY FINISHED up the autopsy on Crystal Trainer, concluding she'd died of a single blow to the head, delivered most likely by a hammer or a similar flat-faced object. The senseless waste she encountered in her line of work often saddened her. Here was a young mother with everything to live for, and her life had been snatched away in the flash of an instant. No defensive wounds, no skin under her nails, nothing to indicate Crystal had any inkling her life was about to come to a quick and dramatic end.

After she cleaned up and returned the body to the morgue, she alerted the funeral home the family had chosen, typed up her report and sent it off to Sam and Freddie.

As she left work, she was oddly out of sorts, sad over the death of the young mother and thinking, nonstop, about Terry and what he'd told her.

Her better judgment told her to run as far and as fast as she could, but there was this other voice nagging at her, wondering if this might be "it," if he might be the elusive "one."

"Ugh," she said out loud as she unlocked her silver sports car and slid into the leather bucket seat. "So stupid. I'm an educated, professional woman sitting in the dark talking to myself about a guy. I suppose I could be more ridiculous but I'm not entirely sure how. Well, you could *not* call him. That would be kind of ridiculous. He's a nice guy. He told you the truth about what he's dealing with and didn't wait for you to find out from someone else. That ought to count for something, right?"

If she were being truthful, she'd admit to being lonely and ready for a meaningful relationship. The last one ended disastrously five years earlier, and she'd stayed away from anything that smacked of commitment ever since. How had five years managed to go by without her noticing? She'd been busy—working, building her career and reputation, nurturing friendships and spending more time with her family. So those years hadn't been a total waste. Figures the first guy to turn her head in half a decade was right out of rehab and putting his life back together. Was he even allowed to get serious with someone so soon? Didn't they have rules about that?

"I should drive home and not get involved. He's not even supposed to be dating." She was familiar enough with rehab to know that much. So why then was she still sitting here, cell phone in hand, wanting so badly to call him?

"You're probably going to regret this," she said with a sigh as she found his number in her list of contacts and pressed Send. Her heart beat a weird staccato as she waited for him to answer.

"Hi there," he said.

Lindsey couldn't think of a thing to say.

"Lindsey?"

"Yes, it's me," she said. "How are you?"

"I'm good." He sounded amused. "You?"

"Um, fine. Tired. You know, long day at work." She cringed. Really? Was that the best she could do?

"I'm burning the midnight oil myself. The senator came back from his honeymoon with new rules about the campaign, so I've been rearranging his schedule all day."

"What kind of rules?" she asked, grateful for the chance to talk about anything other than what the heck was going on between them.

"He's willing to give the campaign two nights during the week and one weekend day—that's all."

"So he can spend more time with Sam."

"Right."

"It's refreshing to hear of a guy who has his priorities straight," she said, then winced when she realized how that might sound to him.

"I agree."

"You do?"

"Why do you find that so hard to believe?" he asked, laughing. "He's happily married and wants to spend as much time as he can with his new wife. I get it."

"I'm happy for them." Sam had been through the ringer with her ex-husband and deserved every ounce of happiness she could find with her handsome senator.

"I am, too, although I have to admit I wasn't her biggest fan at first. She's grown on me since she accused me of killing my brother."

Lindsey chuckled at the ridiculousness of his statement.

"I'm glad you called," he said. "I wondered if you would."

"I needed some time. I hope you understand."

"Of course I do."

"My, um, my father was an alcoholic. It was, you know, a difficult situation."

"I can imagine, and I understand it's probably too much of a gamble for you to get involved with someone who's fighting the same battle."

"I didn't say that."

"Oh. Well, I assumed…"

"He never fought the battle. He never even tried. At least you're making an effort. That counts for something."

"It's a hell of an effort. A daily battle, but I seem to be winning. I've been going to the gym, I've lost thirty pounds at last check, and I feel better than I have in years. I love my job, and I'm enjoying my family in a way I never have before. I can't imagine ever going back to the way I was existing—day to day with no purpose and nothing much to live for."

Listening to him, Lindsey experienced a surge of hope. Maybe, just maybe, this could work.

"I don't mean to be trying to sell you," he added. "I'd understand if I was too big of a risk for you to take, especially growing up the way you did."

"I don't feel like I'm being sold anything. I appreciate you being truthful with me."

"I am, Lindsey. I swear I am."

"I believe you."

"So what now?"

"I'm not sure yet, but I've missed talking to you since you left the other night."

"I've missed talking to you, too."

"Have you eaten yet?"

"Nope."

Lindsey closed her eyes, sucked in a deep breath and took the leap. "There's a pizza place in my neighborhood that's to die for. Interested?"

"In having to-die-for pizza or seeing you?"

Her face heated the way it used to in middle school when Johnny Lubock tossed his hair in her direction. "Either. Both."

"I'm interested in both—one more than the other."

She felt her face flush with heat as she told him the name of the place and the address. "Twenty minutes?"

"I'll see you there."

CHAPTER FOURTEEN

*S*am stood over her father, watching his chest rise and
fall as the ventilator forced air into his lungs. All she
could think about was the promise she'd made to him more than
two years ago, shortly after the shooting when he'd pleaded with
her to not let him live in a vegetative or unconscious state. If it
ever came to that, he'd said, *do* something. At the time, Sam had
given her agreement more to pacify him than anything. But
she'd also taken steps to ensure she had what she needed should
that day ever arrive.

Was it here now? She thought of the prescription she had
stashed in a safety deposit box at the bank. She'd put it there
during the dark days that followed the shooting, never thinking
for a minute she'd ever use it. When it came right down to it,
how would she ever end the life of the man who'd meant everything to her all her life? Even knowing it was what he'd want
didn't make the idea of it any easier to handle. Imagining life
without Skip Holland was like trying to picture an existence
without air or water or food. Or Nick.

As if she'd conjured him up, he appeared behind her and
began massaging her shoulders. "We should go home and get
some sleep while we can."

Before Sam could reply, a nurse bustled into the room and
began checking the monitors. "How is he?" Sam asked.

"About the same."

Hearing that, Sam wanted to scream with frustration. All those hours of high-powered drugs and he was exactly the same?

"The good news," the nurse said, "is he isn't any worse. He's holding his own."

Sam would take the good news where she could find it.

"I enjoyed the photos from your wedding," the nurse added with a shy smile. "You made for a beautiful bride and groom."

"That's nice of you to say," Sam said. The wedding seemed like such a long time ago. "If we leave for a couple of hours, he won't die, will he?"

"I can't say for sure, but I don't think he's in any danger of dying at the moment. If anything changes, we could certainly call you."

"We'd appreciate that," Nick said. "Let's go for a while, babe."

Sam leaned over the bed to kiss her father's forehead. She liked to think he could feel it, that he knew she was there. "I'll be back soon," she said. "Hang in there, Skippy, you hear me? Don't give up."

Straightening, she was relieved to feel Nick's arm around her shoulders. In the waiting room, Tracy jumped up when she saw them coming. "How is he?"

"The same," Sam said, "which is apparently a good thing." She repeated what the nurse had told her.

"That's something anyway," Tracy said. "You guys should go home for a while."

"We are. Call me if anything changes? Anything at all?"

"I will," Tracy said, hugging them both.

Sam and Nick walked through the quiet hospital to the parking lot.

"Why don't you leave your car here?" he said. "I'll bring you back in the morning."

Since Sam was dead on her feet, she gladly agreed with his plan and sank into the comfort of his BMW. Her mind was racing with everything that'd happened that day. It was unlike her to be indecisive about next steps, especially in a murder investigation, but the worries about her father had scrambled her brain and shot her legendary concentration all to hell.

Hanging over everything was that damned promise she'd made him at a time when she would've given anything to have him live for one more day.

"What is it, Samantha? I can hear you churning over there."

Did she dare tell him? No, because then it would be his burden, too. If she ever had to keep her promise and there was trouble over it, he could honestly say he hadn't known about it. That would be better for him politically, even if it went against her effort to be more forthright with him.

"The woman who was murdered—I know her from somewhere, but I can't figure out where."

"I'm sure you'll think of it when you have less on your mind."

"Yeah, I guess. Tomorrow we'll dig into her friends, and maybe something will pop there." She looked out the window at the city rushing by as they headed for Capitol Hill. "Am I doing the right thing continuing to work while my dad is in there?"

"He'd hate to have you keeping a vigil at his bedside. He'd much rather have you out there solving a murder."

"What about my sisters and Celia? Will they think I'm horrible if I keep working?"

"I was with them all night, and I never heard the first hint of anything like that. They know how your job is and that your dad would want you seeking justice for the woman who was killed."

"I wish I could run this one by him. I have all this crap in my head about the new case, this lead Gardner gave us about my dad's shooting, the creepy cards. It's all floating around in my brain refusing to come to any kind of order."

"It's only natural you'd be off your game right now, Sam. This thing with your dad has to have you totally freaked out, even if you're trying hard to hide that from everyone."

Of course he saw right through her. Didn't he always?

He parked at the curb outside their Ninth Street townhouse.

Emerging from the car, Sam noticed the lights were on at her dad's house. "I'm going to check on Celia. I'll be right there."

"All right, but don't be long. You need to sleep."

124 | MARIE FORCE

What she needed was to burrow into his loving embrace and let it all go for a few hours. Nothing cured what ailed her more than sleeping in his arms. "Yes, dear."

He rolled his eyes at her and headed for their place.

On the short walk to her father's house, Sam glanced around at the murky shadows, hyper-vigilant since her ex-husband had waylaid her the night before the wedding. An odd sensation crept down her spine, and Sam was almost certain someone was watching her. She raced up the ramp to her father's place and rapped on the door. "Celia, it's me."

The door swung open. "What've I told you about knocking here?" Her stepmother looked like she was ready to drop from exhaustion.

"I didn't want to scare you."

"Don't be silly. Come in."

"I saw the lights and figured I'd check on you."

"That's sweet of you, honey."

"How're you holding up?"

"Oh well, you know. Not so hot. I finally manage to get myself married and now he's in the hospital fighting for his life."

She was so dejected that Sam crossed the room and wrapped her stepmother in a tight hug.

Celia returned the hug, and the two of them stood there like that for a long time. "Of course I knew we might get very little time when I married him," Celia said, wiping a tear from her face. "But I still want more. We haven't had enough."

"The nurse said it's a good sign he hasn't gotten any worse."

"Yes," Celia, a nurse herself, agreed. "It is. But if he's not much better by this time tomorrow, it means the antibiotics aren't working. We may have to make some tough decisions."

Just the thought of it made Sam sick to her stomach.

"You still have the prescription, right?"

Startled, Sam stared at her. "What do you mean?"

"Don't play dumb with me. I know all about it."

"Oh, well…"

"If we need it, I want to know we have it. I'll take care of everything. Don't worry."

"All day today," Sam said, "I've been thinking about the promise I made to him at a time when we had no clue whether he'd have any quality of life at all. Since then, he's had a rough go of it, but it hasn't been all bad. I can't help but think he'd want us to do everything possible to get him through this so he can come home and get back to his life with you."

"I agree he's not the same man he was days after the shooting when everything seemed so grim." The two of them had been secretly dating before the shooting, which is why Celia had volunteered to oversee his care at home. "But as his wife and next of kin, I won't allow him to exist tied to machines that are breathing for him."

Sam had never heard her sweet, unassuming stepmother speak so forcefully.

"I want you to get that prescription from wherever you've stashed it, and bring it to me. The moment it's in my hands it's off your shoulders. Do you understand me?"

Stunned by the exchange, Sam couldn't seem to form the words she needed. "But you won't, you know, unless he's..."

"I wouldn't begin to consider it until I know there's no hope of him recovering in any meaningful way."

"And you know to be careful, to make sure no one would ever know."

"I'm a nurse, Sam. I know exactly what to do, and as his wife, I'd ensure there's no autopsy." She put a hand on Sam's arm and squeezed. "Let me relieve you of this burden."

Sam held her stepmother's gaze for a long moment before she nodded. "Okay. I'll get it for you tomorrow."

Celia let out an audible sigh of relief. "Thank you."

"I'll see you in the morning," Sam said, heading for the door.

"Oh, honey," she said, sounding more like the Celia Sam knew. "Before you go, there's more mail for you."

Sam's stomach dropped. *"More?"*

Celia went to the kitchen and returned with a plastic shopping bag full of envelopes. "It keeps coming."

"Great," Sam muttered, taking the bag from her.

"Try to get some sleep."

"You too," Sam said, even though she doubted either of them would sleep at all that night.

On the short walk home, she replayed the conversation with Celia. She'd never seen such steel in her stepmother's backbone before, but in hindsight, she probably should've suspected it was there all along. Sam's phone chimed with a text message. She retrieved it from her pocket and flipped it open.

Too bad someone had to die because of you. Who will be next? An old friend.

Sam stopped short on the sidewalk. "What the hell?" She took another long look around, still having the odd sense she was being watched the way she used to before she learned her ex-husband had, in fact, been stalking her. With a couple of stints in jail and a restraining order in place, she figured he'd know better than to screw with her again, but Peter never had been known for his common sense.

Of course the sender's number was unavailable, but she'd have it traced anyway. She walked up the ramp to their house and used her key in the door. Once inside, she called HQ and instructed a third-shift detective to trace the source of the text message.

Wearing only a pair of gym shorts, Nick came downstairs as she was finishing up the call.

She took a moment to enjoy the splendid sight of her husband's muscular chest. Only his presence could make her mind go blank, which was rather welcome after the day she'd had.

"What's going on, babe?"

"Weird text message." She'd learned the hard way that telling him the truth about the crazy crap she encountered through her job made for a more harmonious relationship.

"Let me see." He held out a hand, and she gave him her phone.

She watched his amiable expression harden. "What the hell does that mean?"

"I wish I knew. Are they saying Crystal Trainer died today

because of me? I swear I know her from somewhere, but I can't remember where."

"Don't be ridiculous, Sam. What could you have possibly had to do with the death of a woman you don't even know? So what if you recognized her. Think of all the people you've met during twelve years on the force, not to mention growing up here and living in the city for almost thirty-five years. You could know her from anywhere."

"True."

"Don't take this on, babe." He handed the phone back to her and extended his arms.

Sam went to him and rested her head on that chest she loved so much. Soft dark hair brushed against her face. "What if they're referring to someone else besides Crystal? Maybe someone else has been killed, and I don't know it yet."

"If that's the case, you'll hear about it soon enough."

"I suppose."

"Let's go to bed. You're exhausted."

Since she couldn't argue with that, she let him lead her upstairs. She decided to take a quick shower, and by the time she emerged from the bathroom he was already in bed. As she crawled in next to him, she decided being married was about the best thing since diet soda, a thought she shared with him.

Without opening his eyes, he chuckled. "That's quite a compliment coming from the diet-cola queen." He held out his arm, inviting her to come closer.

"I miss my soda," she said with a sigh as she snuggled up to him.

Nick ran a hand up and down her back in a gesture that soothed and comforted her. It also turned her on, which she hadn't expected after the day from hell. She slid a leg between his and pressed kisses to his chest.

"What're you up to, Mrs. Cappuano?" he muttered, sounding half-asleep. One part of him, however, was very much awake.

"You haven't gotten your daily dose today."

"You've got other things on your mind tonight."

"I did have other things on my mind, but then I got in bed with you, and it seems I have only one thing on my mind." As she spoke, she curled her hand around his burgeoning erection.

One gorgeous hazel eye popped open, probably to gauge her intent.

"But if you're too tired…"

Before she knew what hit her, he was on top of her, poised between her legs.

"The day I'm too tired for this," he said, peppering his words with kisses, "is the day I'm no longer breathing."

Sam combed her fingers into his hair, holding him still so he'd continue kissing her, and raised her hips, inviting him in.

He teased her, denying her what she wanted, until she let out a squeak of frustration that made him laugh.

Sam took matters into her own hands by reaching down and putting him where she wanted him.

Nick let out a gasp as she clutched his backside and took what she wanted from him. His forehead landed on her shoulder as he slid into her.

She loved him this way, overcome by the heat they generated together. If she knew him, he'd rally in a minute and take her where no one else ever had. Only he could drive the thoughts of the day and the worries about her dad from her mind. She rolled his earlobe between her teeth and whispered, "I love you. More than anything."

"Samantha." He pushed into her again and stayed there, filling her with everything she needed to survive. His arms came around her, her legs encircled his waist and they rocked together as his mouth came down on hers once again.

She wouldn't have thought she could climax like this, but he was hitting all the right spots, and sure enough the familiar tingle began to grow.

He never stopped kissing her as they continued to move together. Her orgasm broke suddenly and triggered his explosive release. For a long time afterward, they stayed right where they were, joined and breathing the same air. Touching his lips lightly to hers, he said, "I love you, too."

Today had totally sucked. Tomorrow would no doubt be worse. But tonight—tonight had been bliss.

CHAPTER FIFTEEN

"I've been thinking," Nick said the next morning as he forced some eggs and toast on her.

Sam would've preferred to skip breakfast so she could get to the hospital earlier. A call to the nurses' station had yielded the news that nothing had changed overnight. "About what?"

"Scotty."

"What about him?"

"Remember how we decided I would talk to him during the trip to Boston about possibly coming to live with us?"

"Yeah."

"Well, with your dad in the hospital and everything, it doesn't seem like the right time."

"It'll never be the right time. Something will always be going on. If we're going to do this, then let's do it. We'll work it out somehow."

"Are you sure?"

Leaning over to kiss him, she said, "I'm very sure. You can't keep running back and forth to Richmond when you have a campaign to think about."

He took her hand and kissed the diamond band she wore without her engagement ring when she was working. "And a new wife to tend to."

"That, too. Of course."

Smiling, he released her hand and downed the last of his coffee. "I'll drive you back to the hospital to get your car. I'd like to check on Skip, too."

"Don't you have to get to work?"

"I have a committee meeting at ten, but nothing before that, so let's go."

Grateful he was coming with her, she helped him clean up the kitchen before they left together.

AFTER NICK LEFT for the Capitol, Sam spent another hour with her dad before Celia shooed her along to work, promising to call if there was even the slightest change in his condition. In Sam's opinion, his breathing seemed less labored than it had the day before, but she wasn't sure if that was wishful thinking. Because she suspected it was the latter, she didn't mention it to Celia.

Sam's sister Tracy was on her way in as Sam was leaving. They embraced in the hallway.

"How is he?" Tracy asked.

"About the same, although if you ask me, he seems to be breathing easier."

"That's good." Tracy glanced up at her younger sister, who towered over her. "I wasn't ready for this."

"I wasn't either. But he's been living on borrowed time for two years now."

"Still."

"I know. Believe me."

"Are you going to work?"

Sam nodded. "I feel bad leaving—"

"Dad would want you to go catch the person who killed that poor woman in Chevy Chase."

"You really think so?"

"I know so." She hugged her sister again. "Go. I'll be here with Celia."

"Thanks, Trace. I'll be back as soon as I can."

"We'll be here."

Sam felt less guilty about leaving after receiving her sister's blessing. On the way to her car, she sent a text ordering a staff meeting in thirty minutes at HQ. She needed to get her team together and shift all these investigations into high gear. Her first stop when she arrived at HQ was the morgue.

"Hey," Lindsey said when Sam came through the double doors. "Did you get my email from last night?"

"Not yet. Haven't been near a computer."

"Before we get to that, how's your dad?"

"They say about the same, but he seemed to be breathing easier in my educated opinion."

Lindsey smiled. "I'm glad to hear that. Everyone here is pulling for him."

"I appreciate the concern. So what've you got for me?"

Lindsey explained the findings of the autopsy and her theory about a hammer as the probable murder weapon. "No defensive wounds, no skin under her nails. I believe she was attacked from behind and never saw it coming."

"Thanks for the quick work, Doc."

"Wish I could've given you more to go on."

"I do too. I've got a well-liked woman killed in her own home while in the midst of reconciling with a man who'd cheated on her but seemed genuinely distraught over her death."

"You're not looking at him?"

"His alibi checked out. Cruz was running the financials last night. We'll see if he found anything. He could've hired someone to knock her off if he was faking the reconciliation thing."

"I suppose anything's possible."

"I'll be heading back to Chevy Chase today to see if the Trainer family hammer is missing."

"Before you go, I wanted to tell you—I saw Terry last night."

"How'd it go?"

"Quite well," Lindsey said, her pale skin flushing with color. "Are you *blushing?*"

"I don't know." Lindsey raised her hands to her face. "Am I?"

Sam leaned in for a closer look. "Yep. Must've been some night."

"It was just pizza. Nothing special."

"Then why are you blushing?"

Lindsey laughed. "You're a pain in the ass."

"So I'm told—often. Does this mean you've decided to give him a chance?"

"I've decided to take it slow and see what happens."

"That sounds like a smart move."

"I guess we'll find out if it was smart or the stupidest thing I've ever done."

"Even though I can't stand all this cross-pollination between my husband's world and mine, I hope it works out for you."

"Gee, thanks. I think."

Sam laughed. "Well, come on! First Gonzo gets engaged to Nick's chief of staff, and now you're dating his deputy chief of staff. Where does it end?"

"While I can understand your dismay over the cross-pollination, don't forget I spend most of my time with dead people. I gotta grab hold of a live one whenever I can."

"When you put it that way…"

"Keep me posted on your dad."

"Will do. Keep me posted on your boyfriend."

"He's *not* my boyfriend," Lindsey said.

"Yet," Sam shot over her shoulder as she exited through the double doors.

NICK WAS GETTING ready for a hearing of the Senate Homeland Security Committee when the receptionist let him know Irene Littlefield, the director of the home where Scotty lived, was on the phone for him. Right away, Nick was worried something had happened to the boy.

"Mrs. Littlefield?"

"Good morning, Senator. Thank you so much for taking my call, and please accept my profound thanks for your help in getting our funding restored for the coming year."

Nick relaxed a bit when he realized there was no emergency. "It was my pleasure. Your program is extremely worthy."

"I'm glad you think so. These children mean the world to all of us, which is why I'm calling. You're coming later to pick up Scotty, am I right?"

"Yes, I'm due to pick him up around seven. Were you able to clear the day off tomorrow with the school?"

"I spoke to the principal. This is the first day he'll miss this year, so she was fine with it."

"Ouch," Nick said with a wince. "He didn't tell me he'd be ending his perfect attendance record."

"To go to Fenway Park? I think it's safe to say he's okay with it."

Nick laughed. "I suppose he's probably a little excited."

"Just a little. I wondered if you might be able to get here a few minutes early tonight. There's something I'd like to speak with you about."

"I hope there's nothing wrong."

"No, no. Nothing like that. I know you're awfully busy, and I'll only keep you a minute."

"Of course. No problem. I'll see you about six forty-five if the traffic cooperates."

"Thank you very much, Senator."

Now what was that all about, Nick wondered, as he gathered his files and headed to the hearing.

SAM HAD enough time to set up a murder board for Crystal Trainer before the meeting she had called.

Freddie ambled in carrying a couple of donuts and looking well rested. "Hey," he said. "How's Skip?"

Sam filled him in and then took a minute to study his face. "Did you talk to your mom?"

"Nope." Putting his feet up on the conference table, he took a bite of his donut. "She called a couple of times, but I'm not ready to talk to her."

"You know she'll worry if you don't call her back."

Freddie shrugged. "I'm sure she's keeping so busy hanging out with my dad behind my back that she won't have time to worry about me."

Sam frowned her disapproval.

"I'm moving in with Elin."

Her mouth fell open at that news. "Since when?"

"Since last night. We talked about it, and we agreed it's what we both want."

How had he gone from seeing other women the day before to making a huge commitment to Elin? The shock of seeing his mother with his father had clearly addled his brain. "Freddie, are you sure—" Before she could finish the thought, Gonzo came into the room with his partner, Detective Arnold. Jeannie and Tyrone were right behind them with Captain Malone bringing up the rear. The conversation with Freddie would have to wait until they were alone.

"Thanks for coming in," Sam said, gesturing to the murder board. "I want to go over what we've got so far on the Trainer murder. Cruz, what did the financials show?"

He wiped the donut residue from his lips with the sleeve of his shirt. "Nothing out of the ordinary for any of their accounts. No large sums of money in or out in the last twelve months."

"That rules out the husband paying someone to kill her," Sam said, picking up Lindsey's report. "Dr. McNamara has determined the murder weapon was a hammer or a similar flat-surfaced weapon. She places time of death right around noon, which was three hours before her daughter came home and found her. Cruz and I will be heading back to Chevy Chase today to talk to Mrs. Trainer's friends and to look into the places where she did volunteer work. Moving on to baffling mystery number two, Gonzo, where are we with the cards?"

"No word yet from the lab. They're backed up and the exact words of the admin were 'We've got real cases and don't have time to work on pranks.'"

"What the hell?" Freddie asked. "Since when do threats against a police officer and a United States senator not count as not a real case?"

"They're only perceived threats," Sam said, and Gonzo nodded in agreement.

"I'll see what I can do to move things along," the captain said from the back of the room.

"I'd appreciate that," Sam said. She gestured to the bag of cards that had arrived at her dad's, to which she'd added the new batch delivered to her own house. "We've got more."

Gonzo groaned. "Why do you two have to be so popular?"

"I ask myself that question every single day."

"We'll go through them," he said, eyeing the full bag with disdain.

"Um, remember to keep all the envelopes." This was so embarrassing! "Nick has to acknowledge a lot of them."

Gonzo rolled his eyes.

Before he could crack a joke about her new status as a senator's wife, Sam turned her attention to Jeannie. "What've you got on the Fitzgerald case?"

Jeannie glanced at her partner before meeting Sam's gaze. "Nothing yet. We talked to the parents yesterday, and we plan to speak to one of the brothers today."

Sam nodded. "Stick around for a minute when we're done, please."

"Yes, ma'am," Jeannie said.

"All right, everyone," Sam said. "We've all got work to do. Let's get to it." They began to file out of the room. "Gonzo? Give me a minute with McBride and then I need you."

"You got it, L.T." He closed the door, leaving Sam alone with Jeannie.

"How's it going?" Sam asked her.

"Fine."

"I was sort of surprised to see you back again today. Are you sure you're up for being back full time?"

"I'm taking it a day at a time. For right now, I'm feeling okay."

"Good. Just make sure you're not overdoing it."

"Yes, ma'am." Jeannie pursed her lips, as if there was something else she wanted to say.

"Something on your mind, Detective?"

"I was wondering…"

"About?"

"Why didn't you ever look into the Fitzgerald case yourself?"

"I'd always planned to when I got around to it, but then my dad got shot and finding his shooter has sucked up all my extra time—such as it is. Plus he told me not to bother, that he'd exhausted every avenue, and it was a waste of time to reopen that one."

An odd look flashed across Jeannie's face, but then it was gone as fast as it had come. "Oh, I see. That makes sense."

"Something else you want to talk about?"

"No, I'm good."

"Then I'll let you get to work."

Sam watched her go, wondering what her friend wasn't telling her. Something. But the last thing she wanted to do was push her when Jeannie had been so fragile lately.

Gonzo came in and closed the door. "What's up, Lieutenant?"

"What've you found on Leroy?"

"We've got more than two hundred active records with the name Leroy."

"*Seriously?* It's not that common of a name."

"I ran first and last names, since Gardner only gave us that one name."

"Good thinking."

"I'm working my way through them," Gonzo added. "So far I have two possibilities. I'll keep you posted."

"Thanks, and sorry to stick you with card duty, but I need to keep working the Trainer case."

"Yeah, yeah. You'd rather work a murder than open wedding cards. You can't fool me."

Sam laughed. "You are *so* right about that."

Gonzo's scowl only fueled her amusement.

"How's the baby?" He'd recently learned he'd fathered a baby with a woman with whom he'd had a brief relationship. After a contentious hearing, he'd been granted temporary custody of the boy he'd named Alejandro or Alex, as Gonzo called him. To say his life had been turned upside down was putting it mildly.

"He's great. I can't believe how big he's getting."

"Happens fast the first year."

"So I'm told."

Sam cleared her throat, knowing she needed to show interest, but damn this colliding worlds thing bugged the shit out of her. "And the wedding plans?" He was engaged to Christina Billings, Nick's chief of staff.

"Coming along. We're looking at next spring. We're moving in together in the next month or two."

"Sheesh, it's an epidemic."

"What'd you mean?"

"Cruz is shacking up, too."

"With Elin?"

"So he says."

"Wow. Is that a good idea?"

"Your guess is as good as mine."

"Very interesting."

"By the way, any movement on figuring out who's pissed about the wedding?"

"He hasn't talked to you yet?"

"Who?" Sam asked, confused.

Looking annoyed Gonzo went to the door. "Arnold! Get in here."

Gonzo's partner came running from the pit. "What's up?"

"You were supposed to tell her something."

"Oh. Yeah. Um, well, the whole wedding invitation thing with Stahl is probably my fault."

"How so?" Sam asked the young detective.

"Well, the day of your wedding, I was, um, taking a leak in the men's room along with another officer, and I made a crack about getting stuck working so everyone else could go to your wedding. Then a toilet flushed and Stahl came out with this creepy smile on his face. My stomach sank because I knew he'd probably find a way to use that against you. I'm sorry, Lieutenant."

"Don't worry about it. I'm sorry I wasn't able to invite you."

"Oh, please, it's fine. I know you couldn't have everyone, and I didn't mind working that day at all. Really. I was totally kidding around."

"Thanks for clearing that up."

Arnold scurried out the door.

"Mystery solved," Sam said to Gonzo. "Thanks for getting to the bottom of it."

"No problem. I about smacked him upside the head when I realized what he'd done." He walked over to pick up the bag full of cards. "Better get to work."

"Thanks again for dealing with the cards."

"You owe me one—a big one."

"Put it on my tab."

CHAPTER SIXTEEN

*D*arren Taber from the *Washington Star* was waiting for Sam when she emerged from HQ on her way to Chevy Chase.

"Not now, Darren."

"I need a minute, Sam."

Since he'd done her a favor or two in the past, she slowed to a normal pace as she headed with Freddie to the parking lot. "What?"

"Is there any truth to the rumor you've received threatening mail?"

"Where'd you hear that?"

"Answer the question."

"Off the record?"

"Aw, come on, Sam."

"Off the record or no deal."

"Fine." He jammed the reporter's notebook into his back pocket and held up his hands.

"We received a few strange messages in some wedding cards sent here and to Nick's office while we were away."

"Define *strange*."

"We're looking into it. That's all I'm saying. Now tell me how you heard about it."

"Phone call to the paper's tip line."

At that Sam stopped walking and turned to face him. "Explain."

"We got a call that you've received threatening mail, and the caller was wondering why they hadn't seen any mention of it in the media."

"Is that right? So our pen pal is looking for some publicity. Was the caller a man or woman?"

"We couldn't tell. I listened to it four times, and I still wasn't sure."

"Did you make me a copy?"

"Sam, you insult me." He withdrew a thumb drive from his pocket and handed it to her.

She took it from him before he could change his mind. "I hate being indebted to you."

"I know," he said with a big grin.

"What's this going to cost me?" Sam asked.

"What've you got on the housewife murder in Chevy Chase?"

"Not a damned thing yet."

"When you do, how about an exclusive for your favorite reporter?"

"I'll see what I can do. Now, we've got to get to work."

Darren stepped aside to let them pass.

"Hey, Darren?" Sam called over her shoulder. "Thanks."

"No problem."

"He's not as bad as some of them," Freddie said when they were out of earshot from Darren.

"True." Sam would never forget how Darren had tipped them off that one of the rags was going to run a story about her near-abortion years ago. Thanks to the tip, they'd been able to get ahead of the rag with the truth—that she'd suffered a miscarriage.

When they were in the car, Freddie pulled his laptop out of his bag and plugged in the thumb drive. They listened to the recording five times, and neither of them could place the voice as someone they knew. Nor could they tell if it was a man or woman. As Darren had indicated, the caller was clearly looking for some publicity about the letters.

"Seriously narcissistic," Sam said.

"No kidding."

On the way to Chevy Chase, Sam tried to come up with a tactful way to broach the subject of Freddie's plans to move in with Elin. "Are you sure you're ready to shack up with Elin?" Okay, so tact wasn't her thing. "You've only known her a couple of months."

"You got married after a three-month relationship."

He had her there. "We're older," Sam said. "And more experienced." That sounded lame, even to her. Apparently, he thought so too because he snorted.

"I'm sorry you don't approve, but I'd appreciate you dropping it. I'm through with doing what everyone else wants me to do. It's my life, and I'm going to live it the way I see fit."

Sam glanced over at him, wondering where her sweet, accommodating partner had gone. Seeing his mother with his father had clearly contributed to this new hard edge. "Did you tell Elin about seeing your mom with your dad?"

"Nah. It's got nothing to do with what happened with her."

"Except you weren't even thinking about shacking up until yesterday."

"You don't know that."

"Whatever."

"I know you think you're looking out for me and all that, but let it go, okay? I'm doing what I want to do, and that's the end of it."

"I still say you need to talk to your mother."

"And I will. When I'm good and ready, and not one second before."

"It's not fair for you to make her worry."

"I sent her a text this morning to let her know I'm busy, and I'll call her when I can."

That was something, anyway. "Good."

"Now, can we drop it?"

"Whatever you want."

They passed the rest of the ride in unusual and uncomfortable silence. As they'd requested, Jed Trainer was waiting for them outside the house. He was leaning against his silver sedan staring at the house when they pulled up. Crime Scene detectives had finished their work, but the yard was still roped off with yellow police tape.

As Sam and Freddie approached him, Trainer stood up straight. He looked like he hadn't slept a wink, and yesterday's polished exterior had been replaced by an old T-shirt and jeans. His face was unshaven and his hair stood on end. Judging by his appearance he was taking the death of his wife hard.

"Thank you for meeting us," Sam said.

"Anything it takes to find out who did this to Crystal."

"How are the kids doing?" Freddie asked. The question was one she expected from old Freddie, so it was a relief to hear him ask it.

"Horrible. They were up crying all night. It's a nightmare."

"We're sorry for your loss," Sam said. She always felt awkward speaking to the family members of murder victims. Nothing she could say would ever be enough. "Do you have tools in the house?"

He seemed surprised by the question. "The usual stuff."

"Can you show us?"

"Sure," he said, seeming confused. "Right this way."

He led them to a basement work area with a pegboard boasting a variety of screwdrivers, wrenches and pliers. A hammer was held up by two hooks, one on either side of the handle.

Sam nodded to Freddie, who pulled on latex gloves and put the hammer into an evidence bag. "Take the sledgehammer, too," she said.

"I don't understand," Jed said. "Why are you taking them?"

"The medical examiner has determined your wife died of a single hit to the back of the head, administered by a flat-surfaced instrument, such as a hammer. We'll be asking the lab to determine whether either of these hammers were used in the attack."

He slumped against the bench. "Someone smacked her in the back of the head with a hammer. *Why?*"

"That's what we'd like to know. While we're here, could you

take another look to make sure none of the valuables are missing? Cash, jewelry, silver if you have it. That kind of stuff."

"I did that yesterday with the Crime Scene detectives, but I'll look again."

"We'd appreciate that."

They accompanied him through the house as he investigated Mrs. Trainer's jewelry box where he pointed to her wedding rings. "Would it be possible," he said, his voice catching, "to have her buried with her wedding ring? I'd like to save her engagement ring for my son to give his wife someday."

"Go ahead and take it," Sam said, touched by his overwhelming grief. She couldn't imagine what it would be like to have screwed up a marriage so royally and be on the road to fixing the damage only to lose a spouse to murder. As a newlywed, the idea of such a staggering loss sent a shiver down her spine.

"Are you all right?" Freddie asked her as they followed Jed to the office downstairs.

"I'm fine."

When Jed had confirmed nothing of any value had been taken, they let him go back to his kids, whom he'd left with his parents. They asked him to stay local and to keep them apprised of the funeral plans.

"I feel so bad for them," Freddie said, sounding more like the Freddie Sam knew so well.

"I do, too."

"Those poor kids will never be the same."

"No kidding."

Their next stop was Alice Deal Middle School where the grief-stricken principal, Mrs. Nesbitt, confirmed Crystal Trainer had been a tireless volunteer and a well-loved member of the school community.

"Did she have issues with anyone that you know of?" Sam asked.

"She was very well liked by the other parents and the faculty. We all appreciated how much she did to raise extra money for the school. It was her idea for each classroom to sponsor a theme basket to raffle off during our winter festival. That fund-raiser brought in more revenue than anything we've ever done. I can't imagine what we'll do without her."

"Is it possible," Freddie said, "another parent was put out by Mrs. Trainer's success as a volunteer?"

Mrs. Nesbitt thought about that for a moment. "I can't think of anyone who'd be jealous. We're all working toward the same goal of making sure the kids have what they need, especially in the last few years during the economic downturn. A lot of our families were adversely affected, and volunteers like Mrs. Trainer were indispensable to us."

Sam left her card with Mrs. Nesbitt in case she thought of anyone who might've had a problem with the oh-so-perfect Crystal Trainer.

"Do you know anyone," Sam asked Freddie on the way back to the car, "who's as universally well liked as this woman was?"

"Other than yourself, of course." He smirked and drew a laugh from Sam. "I'd have to say only my mother would qualify. I don't know of anyone who doesn't adore her."

"Except for you at the moment."

That made him smile, as she'd hoped it would. "What's next?"

"I want to talk to Donna Kasperian," Sam said. "Jed listed her as Crystal's best friend."

They drove to the address several blocks from the Trainers' home. A number of cars were parked in the Kasperians' driveway. An older woman was approaching the door carrying a covered plate when Sam and Freddie pulled up to the curb.

"Ugh," Sam said. "Grief central. I hate this."

"I do, too. Let's get it over with."

When a man answered the door, they flashed their badges.

"Mr. Kasperian?"

"Yes."

"I'm Lieutenant Holland. This is my partner, Detective Cruz. We'd like to have a word with Mrs. Kasperian."

"She's not well at the moment. Would it be possible to do this another time?"

"I'm sorry," Sam said, "but this is a murder investigation. We need to speak to her."

"Come in." He stepped aside to admit them and showed them into a nicely furnished living room. "I'll get her."

A low murmur of voices from another room was the only sound in the otherwise quiet house. The man who'd admitted them returned with his arm around a woman who was clearly relying on him to hold her up. She had short blond hair and green eyes gone red from crying.

"Mrs. Kasperian," Sam said, "I'm Lieutenant Holland—"

"I know who you are. Crystal and I watched the coverage of your wedding together."

"Oh, I, um, thank you. This is my partner, Detective Cruz. We're sorry to intrude during this difficult time."

"Who could've done this?" Donna asked, her eyes swimming with tears.

"That's what we're trying to find out. Could we sit for a moment?"

"Yes, of course." She and her husband took one sofa while Sam and Freddie perched on the other.

"When was the last time you spoke with Mrs. Trainer?"

"Yesterday morning. It was her day 'off' with no outside commitments. She had a hair appointment and then she was going to yoga. We'd talked about taking a walk after dinner, but…"

"And you'd been friends for some time?"

"Since the girls were in kindergarten. Our Melanie is in Nicole's class. We volunteered together. Our families became friends. It's so hard to believe."

"Can you think of anyone who might've wished to harm her?"

"No! She didn't have an enemy in the world!"

"Did she ever mention problems with people from before you knew her?"

Donna shook her head. "Never."

"Would she have told you? If something had happened in the past?"

"In more than ten years of friendship, there was no subject we didn't cover." She tried but failed to stifle a sob, and her husband patted her knee with his free hand. "She was the best friend everyone wished they had."

"You were aware then of the problems in her marriage?"

Donna seemed to sag a bit, and her husband scowled. "We were so shocked when we heard about Jed's affair," she said. "Even all this time later, we still can't believe it. They had a marriage others envied. You know the type—still affectionate with each other even after a decade of marriage. It was a total shock to everyone who knew them."

"They were working to reconcile?"

"They'd been going to counseling for quite some time."

"How was that going?"

"Depends on what day it was. On one day she'd say they were getting back together and then on the next she would wonder how she could ever trust him again. It was a roller-coaster ride."

"Did he seem genuinely committed to putting the marriage back on track?"

"Yes," Donna said softly. "He was extremely contrite and willing to do whatever she asked of him. In fact, the other day, I told her it might be time to give him a break or cut him loose. It was sucking the life out of her."

"He knew he'd screwed up," Mr. Kasperian interjected. "He was determined to do whatever it took to fix it."

"Was there any chance she'd told him their marriage was over?"

The couple exchanged glances. "If she did," Donna said, "she didn't tell me she planned to do that, and she would have. We would've talked about it first."

Sam stood, and Freddie followed her lead. "Thank you for your time. We appreciate you speaking with us."

"Find the person who did this to her. Please."

"We're doing our best." When they were outside, Sam turned to Freddie. "We need to talk to their marriage counselor."

"You read my mind, Lieutenant."

. . .

THE OFFICES of Dr. Taylor Kingsley were located in a brick building on Connecticut Avenue. After asking Jed Trainer to call ahead and give consent for her to speak with them, Sam and Freddie caught her between patients.

Tall with shoulder-length brown hair and hazel eyes, the doctor stood to greet them with handshakes.

"You spoke to Mr. Trainer?" Sam asked.

She nodded. "I'm still in shock over this whole thing. Ever since I saw the news on TV last night, I've been reeling. She was such a lovely person."

"So we've heard. What can you tell us about their sessions with you?"

"Since I have his permission, I can tell you they were working very hard to put the pieces of their marriage back together. She'd been terribly hurt and disappointed by his infidelity, and he was ashamed, contrite. They were making real progress."

"One of her friends called it a roller-coaster ride."

The doctor thought about that for a second. "That's an apt description. She went back and forth with the trust issues. That was the major sticking point for her—whether she'd be able to trust him to be faithful in the future if she allowed him back into her life. They still had a long way to go, but as I said, they were definitely getting there." She paused before she added, "He's not a suspect, is he?"

"Not at this time, but we haven't completely ruled out anyone."

"Judging from what I saw in here, he was very devoted to her. Other than one short-lived affair, he'd been faithful."

"Or so he said." Sam was unable to keep a hint of sarcasm from infecting her tone.

"Or so he said," the doctor acknowledged.

"Did she ever talk about anyone from her past who she might've had a problem with?"

"After I heard the news last night, I reread all my notes in their file because I figured you'd want to speak to me eventually.

I found no references to problems with anyone other than her husband."

Sam handed her a business card. "Please call if you think of anything else that might aid in our investigation."

On the way back to the car, Sam called Celia to check in. "Any change?"

"His fever has broken," Celia said, sounding euphoric.

Sam had to stop walking for a second as relief flooded through her. "That's great news."

"He's not out of the woods yet. Not by a long stretch, but it's a good sign."

"Yes," Sam said. "I'll be back as soon as I can."

"No problem, honey. You're where he'd want you to be."

"Good news?" Freddie asked when she ended the call with her stepmother.

"His fever has broken."

"I'm so glad to hear that."

"I'll meet you at the car in a minute, okay?"

"Sure."

After he walked away, Sam called Nick's cell.

"Hey, babe, what's up?" When she didn't answer, he said, "Sam?"

"I'm here."

"What is it, honey?"

"My dad's fever broke."

Nick let out a low whistle. "That's terrific news. What a relief."

"He's got a long way to go, but it's a good sign."

"Yes, it is. Are you okay?"

"I'm just... I'm afraid to get my hopes up, you know?"

"I can understand that, but this is a good sign. It's probably okay to feel a little optimistic now."

"I suppose."

"How's the case going?"

"It's going nowhere fast, like the Carl's case. I've yet to hear anyone utter a bad word about any of our victims."

"Did you figure out how you know her?"

"Nope. It's hovering on the periphery."

"I hate when that happens."

Sam laughed. "Sure, like it ever happens to you who never forgets a face or a name."

"Now that is not true."

"Sure, Senator. Whatever you say."

"Speaking of the Senate, I've got to go vote on the new energy bill. Will you be okay?"

"I'm much better now that I've talked to you."

"Good. I'll see you tonight when I get home from Richmond with Scotty."

"Can't wait to see him—and you."

"Be careful out there today."

"Always am. Love you."

"Love you, too."

CHAPTER SEVENTEEN

*J*eannie and Will found Caleb Fitzgerald at work at a small accounting firm on Massachusetts Avenue.

"I don't have much time," he said when he joined them in the conference room. "Tax season."

He looked much as Jeannie suspected his slain brother would've looked had he lived to adulthood. Tall with a muscular build, short brown hair and warm brown eyes, Caleb studied them with a wary edge, as if he was afraid of what they were there to tell him.

"I heard you talked to my parents yesterday. What's with the renewed interest in my brother's case? We haven't heard a word from the MPD in years, and now suddenly, twice in two days?"

"Our lieutenant asked us to take a fresh look at the case," Jeannie said.

"Look, we appreciate the interest and the attention, but I can't deal with watching my parents get their hopes up again only to see them dashed when nothing comes of it."

"Could we ask you about your brother Cameron?" she said.

Caleb went rigidly still. "What about him?"

"When was the last time you spoke to him?"

"I don't know. A month ago maybe."

"So you're not close?"

"Not particularly. He has his life. I have mine."

"You were both with Tyler the night he was abducted?"

Caleb's face tightened with tension and a muscle ticked in his cheek. He gave a short nod in reply to the question.

"What do you remember from that night?"

"I don't like to think about it. I try not to remember anything."

"If you could tell us the sequence of events, from the time the three of you left your home until the moment you realized Tyler was missing—"

"I've given that statement a hundred times since it happened. I don't see the need to do it again."

"We're taking a fresh look," Will said. "We might hear something the others missed."

"Mr. Fitzgerald," Jeannie said, injecting her tone with compassion. "I know it's a terribly difficult thing to talk about—"

"How would you know?" His eyes flashed with anger and despair. "Every time I think I've managed to move past it, something happens to rip open the wound again. It goes on and on. It doesn't end. We never get any peace."

"I'm so sorry to be reopening that wound," Jeannie said. "It's not my intention to cause you more pain. If we could finally close this case, maybe then your family can find some peace."

Caleb seemed to be considering that. He dropped into a chair and leaned forward to rest his elbows on his knees. Propping his head on his hands, he was quiet for so long Jeannie wondered if he was going to give them what they'd come for.

"My parents wanted me and Cam to take Tyler to the playground," he finally said.

Jeannie glanced at Will.

He nodded, seeming encouraged, and gestured for her to take the lead.

"He'd been stuck inside all day because it'd been raining. I didn't mind taking him, but Cam was pissed."

"How come?" Jeannie asked. It was all coming back to her— the rhythm of the interview, the flow of the questions. She had to admit it felt good to be back in the groove.

"He had a girlfriend, and he was supposed to meet her, but my parents said he couldn't go out until he spent some time with Tyler."

"Did they often force the two of you to spend time with him?"

"They never had to force me. Ty and I were always close, even though I was quite a bit older. He didn't get on my nerves the way he got on Cam's."

"So they'd had issues?"

"I wouldn't call it that. It was more that Ty bugged Cam. He was always getting into his stuff, ratting him out. You know, typical little brother crap."

"Did he do the same stuff to you?"

"Yeah, but it didn't bother me the way it bothered Cam." Still hunched over in the chair, Caleb linked his fingers and seemed far away from the conference room. "They'd had a big fight because Ty told my mother Cam's girlfriend had been in his bedroom when Mom was at work. My mom hit the roof, and Cameron got grounded from seeing his girlfriend for a week."

This was all news to Jeannie. None of that had been included in previous reports about the events leading up to Tyler's death. "Did you tell the other officers all of this?"

"Yeah, I guess. I'm not sure who I've told what to. I've told this story so many times."

A knock on the door interrupted them. An older man stuck his head in, glancing first at Jeannie and Will and then at Caleb. "Everything all right, Mr. Fitzgerald?"

Caleb had sat up straighter when the other man appeared. "Yes, sir, Mr. Barrett. I'm sorry for the interruption. I'll only be another minute."

"Are you in some sort of trouble? We don't want any trouble here."

"Mr. Fitzgerald is helping us with an old case," Jeannie said. "He's not in any trouble."

Barrett didn't seem entirely convinced, but he nodded briskly. "Carry on then."

"Fabulous," Caleb muttered. "I've never told anyone here about what happened to my brother."

"You don't have to now if you don't wish to," Will said.

"I'd rather tell them than have them speculating."

"You were saying how Tyler had gotten Cameron in trouble," Jeannie said.

"That's right," Caleb said, glancing at the door.

Jeannie realized she'd lost him the minute his boss interrupted them. The rest of what happened that night was in the files. The brothers had gone to the park and played a game of cops and robbers, during which Tyler had gone missing in the dark. "Who's idea was it to play cops and robbers at the park?"

"I don't remember. It wasn't mine, but I don't know which one of them suggested it."

"At some point, you became separated from your brothers, is that right?"

"They were the robbers. I was the cop. I was looking for them, when Cam came running back, all freaked out because he couldn't find Tyler."

This was the same story they'd heard the day before from Mr. and Mrs. Fitzgerald—the story that wasn't included anywhere in Skip Holland's reports.

"What did you do then?"

"I went with Cam to try to find him." He rubbed a hand over his jaw. "We looked everywhere, but we couldn't find him."

"What did Cameron tell you about what happened?"

"He said they were running away from the base, and he was in the lead. When he looked back to tell Tyler to hurry up, he was gone. Cam turned back, calling for him, but he'd vanished."

"Did either of you see anyone else on the way to the playground or in the aftermath of Tyler's disappearance?"

"No."

Jeannie glanced again at Will, who nodded, as if to give her permission to ask what they both wanted to know, the question that had been on their minds since the day before.

"Caleb, do you think there's any chance Cameron could've harmed Tyler?"

"No! Of course not! They'd had their problems, but Cameron would never *hurt* him." Even as he proclaimed his brother's innocence, Jeannie saw the fear. The thought had definitely crossed his mind. "He wouldn't do that."

"You're sure of that?"

"Please," he said, his eyes imploring. "It wasn't Cameron. I don't know how you could even ask me that."

"We know this is so difficult—"

Caleb stood. "I'm done. If you're targeting my brother, you'll do it without my help." He strode purposely from the room, but turned back at the doorway. "Leave my parents alone. They've been through enough. If you go after Cameron, it'll destroy them. Keep that in mind before you start a witch hunt."

The moment they were alone, Jeannie said, "We need to talk to Cameron Fitzgerald."

"I WAS THINKING," Sam said when she and Freddie were back in the car.

"About?"

"What if the chick at work wasn't the only one Trainer was banging."

"An interesting theory."

Sam reached for her cell phone and handed it to him. "Get him on the phone."

"You're going to come right out and ask him?"

"Hell yes, I am. Let me tell you something about men, my friend. There are those who cheat, and there're those who don't. You're one or the other. Nothing in the middle, no gray area. My research has shown that those who cheat, *cheat.* You follow?"

"You're a regular *font* of knowledge, Lieutenant."

Sam laughed. "Aren't you lucky I share so much of it with you?"

"Very lucky," he said drolly as he dialed the number. "Mr. Trainer, this is Detective Cruz. Please hold for Lieutenant Holland." He handed the phone to her.

"Mr. Trainer, I'm sorry to disturb you, but I have another question I need to ask you."

"Whatever I can do to help with the investigation."

"I need to know if Janet Nealson was the only woman you were seeing outside your marriage."

"Of course she was! What kind of question is that?"

"It's a fair question. Your affair with Ms. Nealson was only uncovered because someone told your wife, so you came clean. That's not to say you don't have other skeletons sitting in your closet."

"I don't have to put up with this abuse. My wife, the *love of my life*, was viciously murdered in our home. I've got traumatized children and devastated in-laws to contend with. Having the rest of my life ripped apart is the last thing I need right now."

"I understand this is a difficult time for you, but you can either come clean with me now or I can bring you in for a polygraph. If you think I'm ripping apart your life now, wait 'til I *really* get going."

Freddie smirked at her from the passenger seat.

A long moment of silence passed.

"What's it going to be, Mr. Trainer? The easy way or my way?"

"I've heard you were a heartless bitch, you know that? I told my friends last night that your reputation wasn't fair because you'd been nothing but nice to us."

"I'm devastated to hear I'm known as a heartless bitch." Glancing over at Freddie as she navigated the car through traffic, she added, "Isn't that awful, Detective Cruz? He agrees that's a terrible insult, Mr. Trainer."

"I can tell you're having a good laugh at my expense."

"I'm not finding anything funny about a murdered mother with a philandering husband who refuses to share information that could be vital to my investigation into the murder of a woman he claimed to love."

"I did love her."

"I never said you didn't."

Now he was blubbering. Sam held the phone away from her ear.

"You don't understand."

"You're right. I don't. I'm married to a man who would never, *ever* cheat on me." There were few things in life she was absolutely sure of. That she'd married a man who wouldn't stray was one of them.

"You think so now," Trainer said. "Talk to me in a few years."

"I could talk to you every year for a hundred years, and that would never change."

"You sanctimonious bitch."

"I'm losing my patience, Mr. Trainer. Are you going to tell me what I already know or should I have Patrol come by to pick you up?"

"Fine," he snarled. "There were others."

Sam flashed a thumbs-up to her partner. "Are we talking one? Two? Or a baseball team?"

Freddie choked back a laugh.

"A few."

"I need names, addresses, phone numbers, dates you saw them, promises you might've made them. Do me a favor and rank them—most significant to least." Sam couldn't deny she was enjoying this. Hey, he'd called her a bitch. Twice! "You can send your dirty laundry list to my email. Are you ready for the address? Here it is." She rattled it off. "Have it to me in thirty minutes, or you'll be spending the night in the city jail."

"Will this be all over the media?"

"I suppose that'll depend on whether one of your ex-lovers killed your ex-wife with a hammer."

"She wasn't my *ex*-wife."

"Which was too bad for her. Twenty-nine minutes." Sam slapped her phone closed. "Damn, that was fun."

"It was fun to listen to."

"I aim to not only enlighten but to also entertain." She swung into the parking lot at HQ. "Let's regroup and figure out what's next."

. . .

NICK ARRIVED at the state home for children in Richmond twenty minutes before seven. While he was excited to see Scotty and to take him on his first plane ride as well as his first trip to Fenway Park, he was nervous about why Mrs. Littlefield wanted to see him. He parked on the street and took the cement stairs to the door. Buzzing the intercom, he gave his name to the security officer.

"Come in, Senator."

Even all these months later, Nick still wanted to look over his shoulder for John when someone called him that.

"Nice to see you again, sir," the guard said.

"Likewise." Nick had become a familiar face around the home since he'd met Scotty on a visit a few months ago and bonded instantly with the boy.

The guard gestured to a door. "Mrs. Littlefield is expecting you."

"Thank you." Feeling almost like he'd been summoned to the principal's office, Nick knocked on her closed door.

"Come in."

Nick stepped into an austere room where the older woman waited for him. She wore a sensible navy-blue suit and kept her steel-gray hair cut short.

She stood up and extended her hand. "Thank you so much for coming early."

"Not a problem," he said, even though it had required a mad sprint through hellish rush-hour traffic.

"Have a seat, please. Can I get you a drink? Soda or water?"

"No, thank you. I'm good."

"The reason I asked you to come in is I wanted to talk to you about Scotty."

"Is everything all right? He promised he'd get all his school-work done early so he wouldn't fall behind by missing tomorrow."

She smiled. "He's got it all done."

"Oh, good," Nick said, relaxing slightly.

Propping her chin on the tips of her fingers, she seemed to

choose her words carefully. "You know how much we appreciate your help with our funding."

"I was doing my job."

"We appreciate it. And we appreciate all the time and attention you've given to Scotty."

His gut tightened with an odd sense of dread. "But?"

"With all due respect, I'm interested in your intentions toward him, Senator."

Of all the things he'd thought she might say, that hadn't been one of them. He couldn't help but laugh. "My wife's father once asked me the same question." Referring to Sam as his wife never got old. He suspected it never would.

Mrs. Littlefield returned his smile. "Please don't misunderstand me. You and your wife have been wonderful friends to him. He talks about you both all the time. I can see he's getting attached, and while I'm so happy for him to have made such lovely new friends, I worry, too. He's had so much heartache in his short life. I couldn't bear to see him hurt if you were to suddenly lose interest."

"Let me put your mind at ease. Sam and I intend to adopt him if he'll have us."

"Oh," she said, her hand covering her heart. "Oh really?"

"I was planning to speak to him about it on this trip, in fact." Nick's announcement seemed to have sucked the life out of her. "I thought you'd be happy to see him settled with a family."

"Of course I'm thrilled for him. And not just any family, but a senator and decorated police officer."

"We may have interesting jobs, but at the end of the day we're regular people, and we've come to love him very much. I want to give him the chance to play baseball and hockey and anything else he wants or needs. I want to give him everything."

Mrs. Littlefield brushed subtly at a tear. "I'm sorry," she said. "Your news caught me off guard. I feel I need to explain my reaction. You see, I too have become extremely attached to him. I can't imagine this place without him."

"There's no reason you couldn't see him anytime you wish to."

"That's very kind of you to say, but it wouldn't be the same as seeing him every day." She picked up a pen from her desk and balanced it between her fingers. "I can't help but wonder…"

Because she seemed embarrassed by whatever she'd been about to say, Nick said, "Please, feel free to speak your mind."

"You've only gotten married. Are you sure you're prepared to take on the responsibility of a child so soon?"

"That's a fair question and one we've asked ourselves. We've come to the conclusion that just as we didn't expect to find love when we did with each other, we didn't expect to find it with him, either. Yet there it was, and now we want to make him part of our family."

"You keep reducing me to tears," she said, reaching for a tissue. "He's a lucky boy to have two such fine people interested in being his parents."

"We're the lucky ones."

"Well, I won't keep you any longer. I appreciate your honesty."

"So I can count on your support with the state and the social workers?"

"Absolutely."

Nick stood and extended his hand. "Thank you."

She shook his hand. "He gave up on ever finding a family a long time ago, so thank *you*."

"Every minute with him has been my pleasure."

"Have a good time in Boston."

"I'm sure we will. I'll talk to you when we get back on Sunday."

"I'll see you then."

Nick stepped out of the office as Scotty came through the doorway to the reception area. His face lit up with pleasure when he saw Nick waiting for him.

When Nick held out his arms, Scotty ran to him. Only one other time in his life had Nick felt the instant connection to another human being that he'd experienced when he first met Scotty—and that was the night he met Sam. Holding the boy close to him, Nick was overcome by the rightness of having this child in his life. They'd become close pals, but he wanted so much more. He wanted the boy to be his son.

"Good to see you, buddy," Nick said as he released Scotty.

"You, too. I thought today would *never* get here."

Nick took Scotty's backpack from him. "I don't think you really want to go to Fenway."

"That's so funny I forgot to laugh."

"Scotty."

The boy turned to Mrs. Littlefield. "Sorry, Mrs. L. I'm so excited I forgot to say goodbye."

"I'll forgive you this one time." She smiled as she put a new fitted Red Sox cap on the boy's head.

"Oh wow! Thanks!" He gave her a hug. "That's so awesome!"

"You can't go to Fenway for the first time with that ratty old hat," she said, gesturing to the one hanging from his backpack. "Be a good boy this weekend."

"I will. I promise."

Over the boy's head, Nick shared a smile with Mrs. Littlefield.

Outside, Nick held the passenger door for Scotty who'd insisted he could ride in the front seat now that he was officially twelve. When he got into the driver's seat, Nick switched off the passenger-side airbag, just in case.

"I'm afraid I'll forget to tell you when we get back that this was the best weekend of my whole life."

For a brief moment, Nick couldn't find the words. "I know it'll be one of the best weekends of my life, too."

Scotty glanced over at him, hesitant. "Really?"

"You bet. It's not every day I get to take one of my favorite pals on his first-ever trip to Fenway."

"And his first plane ride."

"That, too. Before we go, there's something I have to tell you about what's going on at home. Sam's dad is in the hospital."

"Oh." Nick watched the boy process the information. "Is he okay?"

"He's pretty sick. We hope he'll be okay, but we don't know for sure yet."

"She must be freaking out. They're super close, right?"

"Yes, they are."

Scotty fiddled with the strap on his backpack. "I'd understand if this wasn't a good time for you to go to Boston. You must want to be with her."

Nick was pleased and touched by his insight. "That's good of you to say, but we talked about it, and we agreed Skip would want us to go on our trip. She told me he helped her get the tickets, and he'd hate to see you disappointed."

"Are you sure? Because I'd totally understand if this isn't a good time for you to go."

"Sam has her family all around her. And I don't want to hear about it from Skip when he wakes up and finds out I didn't take you to this game because of him. He'd hate that." Nick started the car. "What do you say we get this show on the road?"

"Let's go," Scotty said.

Nick could tell he was still thinking over what Nick had told him. It pleased Nick that he saw the big picture and was willing to sacrifice his own dream coming true if it meant doing what was best for his friends. Who wouldn't love a boy like that?

CHAPTER EIGHTEEN

*W*hen Sam and Freddie returned to HQ they ran smack into Chief Farnsworth in the lobby.

"Lieutenant," he said in that stern voice he did so well. Sometimes it still made her want to giggle, because the "Uncle Joe" she'd known as a child was anything but stern. "What've you got on the mail situation?"

"Nothing yet, sir. The lab has been dragging its feet, and we've been working the Chevy Chase homicide."

"Anything there?"

"Not a damned thing. We've got a wife and mother loved by all who knew her. The husband was a serial philanderer so we're looking into the girlfriends next."

"Keep me posted, and let me know if there's any more mail I should be concerned about."

"I will, sir."

"Officers Hernandez and St. James miss you," he said with a teasing grin. The two officers had been assigned to tail her when she'd been threatened during the call-girl investigation. "They'd love nothing more than to be back on your detail."

Sam glowered at him. "I'm sure they have much better things to be doing than following me around."

"I can't think of anything more important than protecting one of my top detectives. Officer Hernandez said something about 'enjoying the view' on his last assignment. I can't imagine what he means by that. Can you?"

As Freddie wisely choked back a snicker, Sam said, "Where's Lieutenant Stahl when I need him? I'm being sexually harassed by my superior officer."

Farnsworth chuckled. "Speaking of Stahl, I hear he's up in your grill again."

Sam had almost forgotten about the summons to the IAB hearing. "Over who I chose to invite to my own wedding! Can you make it go away?"

"I'm doing what I can. I hate to see department resources wasted on foolishness."

"So do I."

"But as always where you're concerned, I'm walking a fine line. If I get too involved, he'll scream foul over our longtime personal relationship."

"So much for everyone thinking I get away with murder because my Uncle Joe is the chief," Sam muttered.

"You often do get away with murder, but not because I'm your Uncle Joe. It's because your case closure rate is so high. Keep up the good work, Lieutenant, and keep me posted." He nodded to Freddie. "Detective."

Sam and Freddie continued on to the pit.

Gonzo saw them coming and gestured for Sam to join him in the conference room. Her stomach dropped when she saw another card encased in a plastic evidence bag. "What now?"

"A first anniversary card," Gonzo said, handing it to her.

Inside, the sicko had written, "After so much happiness, let's hope you get to celebrate your anniversary. From, An Old Friend."

"Jeez," Freddie said from over her shoulder. "That's nice."

"This is starting to seriously piss me off," Sam said. After all she'd been through with her father being shot and her miserable marriage to Peter, didn't she deserve a tiny bit of happiness with Nick? Didn't she deserve a small interlude in which no one was out to get either of them? A month? Maybe two? Was that too much to ask? "I'm going to talk to Peter on the way home."

Speaking of feeling sick. The idea of spending even a minute in her ex-husband's presence was enough to make her seriously ill. Sam reached up to touch the diamond key necklace Nick had given her as a wedding gift, drawing on the strength he'd brought to her life. It seemed like she'd need it before this day was out.

"Any word yet from the lab?" Freddie asked.

Gonzo shook his head. "Captain Malone leaned on them, but it doesn't seem to have done any good."

"Do me a favor and let the chief know about this latest card," Sam said to Gonzo. "Might go over better coming from you."

When his cell phone rang, Gonzo glanced at the caller ID. "Sorry, I need to take this but don't go away. I have something else for you." He moved farther into the room to take the call, which seemed to be from his fiancée Christina who, from the sound of his side of the conversation, was having trouble with Gonzo's baby son. He gave her a couple of suggestions and ended the call by saying he'd be home soon.

"Sorry about that," he said. "Alex is teething. It's a nightmare."

"Ouch," Freddie said.

"Good thing we can't remember getting teeth," Gonzo said. He turned to Sam. "So I dug deeper into this Leroy dude that Gardner gave us."

Apparently, the news wasn't good or Gonzo would've led with it, knowing how badly she wanted to catch her father's shooter—especially right now.

Gonzo reached for a folder on the conference room table and withdrew a photo of a strapping black man. "Leroy Augustine."

"What do we have on him?"

"A rap sheet a mile long."

"This is awesome," Sam said. "Let me see it."

Gonzo glanced at Freddie. "Sam…"

"What?"

Reaching into the folder again, he pulled out a second photo of Leroy Augustine, this one taken in the morgue.

"You gotta be fucking kidding me," she said as she took the photo from him and dropped into a chair.

"Shit," Freddie muttered from behind her. Since he saved curse words for only the most extreme of circumstances the single word told Sam he was as upset by this news as she was.

"Killed by a drive-by shooter a year ago," Gonzo said, filling in the blanks.

"If we weren't talking about my dad and the person who made him a quadriplegic, this would be funny, wouldn't it?"

"We'll get a break, Sam," Gonzo said. "One of these days, someone will come forward with information."

"No, they won't," she said. "It's been more than two years. Almost two-and-a-half. This case is colder than an Alaskan mountaintop."

"I'll track down some of Augustine's known associates and see what they can tell me. Maybe he bragged about the shooting, and now that he's dead, people might be more willing to talk."

"Do we know who shot him?"

Gonzo shook his head. "That case is also open."

"Of course it is."

"I'll talk to the detectives who worked that case as well as Augustine's associates. You worry about your dad and leave this to me." Gonzo's dark eyes were fierce with emotion—and anger. Skip Holland was well loved by everyone who knew him. "I'm on it."

Sam stood to face her colleague and close friend. "Thank you." She simply didn't have the mental capacity to take on another thing at the moment. "I need to get to the hospital."

"Keep us posted on how he is," Freddie said.

"I will."

"I'll get the list of Trainer's girlfriends from your email and get going on that," Freddie added.

"Good, thanks." Sam glanced at her watch. How had it gotten to be seven already? Nick would be getting home with Scotty soon, and she was anxious to see them. "Give it another hour and then go home. I'll see you back here in the morning."

"You got it, L.T."

To Gonzo, she said, "Go home to your family. It'll keep until the morning."

"I'll give it another hour, too."

"You guys are the best of the best," Sam said in a rare moment of sentiment. "Thanks for all you do." She stopped in her office to collect her belongings and was on her way out when Jeannie and Will came into the pit.

"Oh good, Lieutenant," Jeannie said. "I'm glad we caught you."

"What's up?" Sam asked, taking a close look at the other woman. Jeannie seemed tired, but her eyes were more alive than Sam had seen them since the attack.

"We need authorization to travel to Cincinnati," Jeannie said. "To talk to Cameron Fitzgerald."

"Tyler's older brother?"

"That's right. He was the last one to see Tyler alive, and we have some questions for him."

"Walk with me," Sam said, anxious to get to the hospital. "Hasn't he been interviewed before?"

"Yes, but we have some new questions for him."

"Like what?"

Out of the corner of her eye, Sam watched her detectives exchange glances.

"If it's just the same with you," Will said, "we'd prefer to give you a full report when we complete our investigation."

As Sam thought that over, they pushed through double doors leading to the parking lot. "All right. I'll authorize the travel." Normally, she would've allowed only one of them to go, as she was always mindful of her limited travel budget. But there was no way she was sending Jeannie anywhere alone, and since her traumatized detective was clearly engaged in the investigation she didn't have the heart to send just Will.

"Thank you, Lieutenant. I'll forward our itinerary as soon as we have it."

"Keep me posted." She took another minute to study Jeannie. "You doing all right?"

Jeannie nodded. "It's good to be back to work."

"Don't overdo it."

"Yes, ma'am."

"I'm keeping a close eye on her," Will said.

"Shut up, Will," Jeannie said.

"What? I *am* keeping an eye on you."

"Get your eyes off me before Michael has you killed," Jeannie retorted.

"I'll let you two work this out on your own," Sam said, unlocking her car. They were still bickering when she drove past them and out of the parking lot. Will had been so deeply distressed by what happened to his partner. Sam had no doubt he was indeed keeping close tabs on her now that she was back to work and seemingly coming back to life at the same time. It made Sam feel better to know her wounded detective had such a fiercely loyal partner looking out for her at this critical juncture in her recovery.

On the way to the hospital, Sam called Nick. After hearing the news that another promising lead in her father's investigation had led nowhere, she wanted to hear his voice.

"Hey, babe," he said. "Where are you?"

"Leaving work on the way to see my dad. You?"

"Stuck in traffic outside Springfield."

"Going or coming?"

"On the way back to the city with Scotty."

"How is he? Excited?"

"Just a tad, although he's also concerned about Skip."

"You didn't need to tell him about that."

"I thought he should know, and he offered to stay home with you if that's where I thought we should be."

Hearing that, Sam couldn't help but smile. What a sweet kid he was. "You told him Skippy would have a cow if you did that?"

"Yes, indeed. I'll see you at home in a bit?"

"Yep. After I see my dad there's one other thing I have to do and then I'll be home."

"We'll be waiting. I've been coerced into pizza for dinner."

"Sounds good to me."

"Love you, babe."

"Love you, too. Both of you."

"I'll pass that on."

"Please do."

"See you soon."

At the hospital, Sam learned Skip was much improved and the doctors were considering removing the ventilator in the morning if he continued to make progress overnight. He'd also been moved from ICU into a regular room. Celia, Tracy and Angela were elated by the good news, but Sam refused to get her hopes up until Skip opened one of those blue eyes and said something about how foolish they were being for blubbering over him. Then, and only then, would Sam be able to breathe again.

Maybe tomorrow, she thought more than an hour later, as she stood by his bed and ran her fingers through his wiry gray hair.

"So many things I need to talk to you about. Nick picked up Scotty for the trip to Boston. How excited do you think he is?" Imagining it, Sam smiled. "I've spent so much time trying to have a baby. Now this twelve-year-old kid has come into my life, and all I can think about is how cool it would be to get the chance to be his mom. We could do so much for him, you know? All of us. Not just Nick and me, but you, Celia, Tracy, Ang, Nick's dad, the O'Connors. I told Nick Scotty would be surrounded by a village, and you're a big part of it. You know that, don't you?"

Sam bent to rest her forehead on his chest, relieved to hear the wheezing had subsided considerably since the day before. "We had another big lead on your case blow up in our faces. Just when I think we're getting close…" Suddenly, she was exhausted —mentally, physically, emotionally. Only a few days back to work and it was like the lovely vacation had never happened.

"Sam, honey," Celia said, resting her hand on Sam's back. "Why don't you go on home? There's nothing you can do here, and I can only imagine how tired you must be."

Sam stood up straight and turned to face her stepmother. "What about you? You have to be on your last legs. Let me give you a ride home?"

"I'm going to stay." Celia glanced at her husband. "Just in case he needs me."

Sam understood that. No way would she go home if Nick had been the one in that bed. Shuddering at the thought, she hugged Celia. "Try to get some rest."

"I've been grabbing catnaps when I can."

As Sam released her stepmother, she let out a gasp of surprise when Nick and Scotty appeared in the doorway.

Nick had his hands on Scotty's shoulders as his eyes met hers. "He wanted to see Skip."

Scotty looked nervous but determined.

"Hi, buddy," Sam said, reaching for him.

He stepped into her embrace and held on tight.

She pressed a kiss to his soft hair. "Good to see you."

"You too, Sam. I'm sorry about your dad being sick." He hugged Celia and stepped closer to Skip's bed. "Does it hurt? Whatever he's got?"

"No, honey," Celia said. "They've given him lots of medicine."

While Scotty spent a moment with her dad, Sam went to her husband.

Nick put his arms around her, giving her the comfort she needed.

Sam breathed him in, comforted by his presence, his scent and the muscular chest that provided the perfect place to land after another hellish day. She put her arms around him and closed her eyes.

Too bad she still had to drive home because she could doze off right here and be perfectly content.

"Samantha." She felt his lips on her forehead. "Babe, are you with me?"

"I'm here." Had she fallen asleep? Sam forced herself back into the moment and gave Nick one more squeeze before she turned to kiss her dad goodnight. "See you in the morning, Skippy." Lowering her voice even further, she whispered, "I love you."

On the way out of the hospital, Nick held her hand and kept up a steady stream of chatter with Scotty who seemed to be making an effort to curb his excitement over the trip in light of Skip's illness.

"Are you okay to drive home?" Nick asked when they arrived at Sam's car.

"Of course I am."

"You say that as if you didn't just fall asleep on your feet."

Sam scoffed at him. "I wasn't asleep. I was *relaxed*."

When Nick rolled his eyes at her, Scotty giggled.

"You were *so* asleep, Sam," Scotty said.

"I can see whose side you're on."

"He's taking me to Fenway," Scotty said with a teasing grin.

"Hey!" Sam cried. "Who got you the tickets?"

"Oh, that was you? I'd forgotten about that."

Sam wrestled him into a headlock. By the time she let him go, Scotty was laughing hysterically.

"You think you're *so* funny, don't you?" she asked.

"I am pretty funny."

Sam glanced at Nick and found him enjoying the show. His smile warmed her all the way through. "I'll see you boys at home."

"Didn't you have something else you needed to do?" Nick asked.

Sam thought of her ex-husband and the conversation she needed to have with him. All she wanted at the moment was to be home with her new husband and the boy they wanted to make their son. "I can take care of it in the morning."

CHAPTER NINETEEN

*N*ick came into their bedroom, closed the door, locked it and leaned back against it. He wore a T-shirt with gym shorts and looked almost as sexy as he did in a suit and tie, which was Sam's favorite look on him.

Well, that wasn't entirely true. She most preferred him in nothing at all.

"If you'd asked me to bet on whether or not he'd sleep tonight, I would've said no way."

"And?"

"Out like a light."

"Oh good. I didn't want him exhausted for his first trip to Fenway."

He moved from the door to the adjoining bathroom. "You were so cute with him earlier. I love watching the two of you together."

"Then you know how I feel watching you with him. I was lying here thinking about how he fits with us. He just fits."

Nick finished brushing his teeth and returned to the bedroom.

Sam got to watch him peel off the shirt and shorts before he crawled into bed with her. "Mmm," she said as he reached for her. "Best part of my day."

"Mine, too," he said, leaning in to kiss her. "I count the hours until I can feel you next to me."

His hand never left her hip, but he managed to set every inch of her on fire using only his lips and tongue. "You're so tired."

"Not too tired for you."

"You fell asleep standing up."

"I did not."

"Yes," he said, kissing her again as his eyes danced with amusement, "you did."

"Well, I'm wide awake now." Sam kissed her way from his lips to his chest. Pushing him onto his back, she continued her trip south. When her hair brushed against his erection, he jolted.

"Sam."

"Hmm?"

"We don't have to... Oh *shit*."

She took his cock deep into her mouth, stroking him with her tongue and hand, loving the taste and feel of him. "Mmm," she said, knowing how the vibration of her lips against his shaft would drive him crazy.

His fingers tightened in her hair. "Come here, babe," he said, sounding breathless. "Let's do this together."

Sam thought about finishing him off this way, but his offer was too appealing to be ignored. After a few final lashes of her tongue, she straddled him. His eyes were closed, his breathing heavy, but he rallied, cupping her ass and surging into her.

Nothing in the world could compare to the way he made her feel—desired, sexy, powerful and loved. Always loved. Even when he suddenly turned them so he was on top, even when he surrounded and possessed her, she felt his love in every look, every touch, every breath.

The orgasm that had been so unattainable in past relationships hovered below the surface, waiting to overwhelm her with sensation. When he took her this way, with such utter abandon, she held back, wanting to prolong the moment rather than rush to the finish. But then he bent his head and sucked her nipple into his mouth. The combination shattered her control and sent her flying.

His arms tightened around her and his mouth found hers as he surged into her one last time, hot and deep and powerful. "Jesus," he whispered against her lips. His head dropped to her shoulder.

Sam kept one arm tight around him while she ran the fingers of her other hand through his thick hair. "We're going to ruin our unbroken streak of married sex tomorrow night," she said after a long period of silence. The thought of spending a single night without him was nearly unbearable, not that she'd ever tell him that. He felt bad enough about taking this trip with her dad still in the hospital.

"Believe me, I know. I have half a mind to change our tickets to come home tomorrow night."

"Don't do that. I think it's important you take him to Lowell on Saturday and show him where you're from." She'd seen the humble home he'd shared with his grandmother when they'd gone to Boston for Julian Sinclair's funeral earlier in the year. "Let him see you weren't born the successful senator you are today."

"Are you sure you're okay with me talking to him about coming to live with us when it's just him and me? I keep feeling like that's something we should do together."

"It all started with the two of you, so it's probably fitting you take the next step with him. He'll know it's coming from both of us."

"As long as you're sure that's the right way to handle it."

Sam laughed at that. "I'm not sure of anything. We're talking about *adopting* a child. It's so huge."

Stealing one more kiss, Nick withdrew from her and shifted to his back, bringing her with him. "It is huge, and I feel that, too. Don't get me wrong."

"But?"

"Because it's him, it doesn't feel as overwhelming to me as it probably should. It feels meant to be." He ran a hand through his hair. "I'm not saying it right."

"No, you are. I know what you mean because I feel the same way. Like he belongs here with us, and the rest is details."

"Exactly," he said, sounding relieved. "I love that you understand."

"I love that you met this boy and you saw something in him from the first day and you nurtured it and brought him to me and made us a family."

He turned on his side and cupped her face before kissing her softly. "Just when I think I can't love you any more than I already do, you go and top yourself."

Sam smiled. "My goal in life."

"So about our unbroken streak…" He raised himself up so he could see the bedside clock. "It's five after twelve."

She smothered a yawn. "So?"

"If we get in another round now, we won't miss a day, and the streak will remain intact."

"You gotta be kidding me."

He cupped her breast and tweaked her nipple between his fingers. "Does it look like I'm kidding?" For emphasis, he pressed his reawakened erection against her hip.

Sam moaned and then gasped when he replaced his fingers with his lips.

"It's for the record, babe," he said against her breast.

"Well, when you put it that way, I suppose I could be persuaded."

"That's my girl."

"I DON'T UNDERSTAND why *you* have to go to Cincinnati," Michael said as he followed Jeannie into the walk-in closet. "Why can't they send Will?"

"Because. This is *my* case. Sam assigned it to me."

"Three days ago you wouldn't leave the house, and now you're going to Cincinnati? I don't get it, Jeannie."

"Are you mad at me because I'm getting back to my routine?"

Standing with his hands on his hips, Michael stared at her. "I am not *mad* at you. I'm confused about what suddenly happened to make it possible for you to not only go back to work but travel too when a few days ago I couldn't get you to meet me for lunch."

Unable to bear the confusion she felt coming from him she averted her gaze. "I can't say exactly what happened. The lieutenant asked me to look into this cold case, and it's caught my interest. It feels good to be interested in something again."

"I'm worried."

"About?"

"That you're doing too much too soon. I don't want to see you have a setback." He crossed his arms and stepped closer to her. "What if something happens and you're all the way out in Ohio? What if you need me, and I can't get to you?"

"Michael…" She met him halfway and slipped her arms around him.

Returning her embrace, he held her close. "Let Will do the interview. There's nothing you can do that he can't do too."

She drew back from him so she could look up at his face. "I understand what you're saying, and I appreciate why you're saying it, but I need to do this. I *need* it, Michael. I need you to kiss me goodbye in the morning the way you used to and send me on my way like everything is normal."

"I don't know if I can do that."

She patted his chest. "Please try." Turning away from him she began rifling through the clothes she had at his place, hoping to find something appropriate for a day of travel.

"This one," Michael said, reaching over her shoulder for a blue dress shirt that had gotten stuck between two other hangers. "Black pants." On the top shelf he found a black sweater and handed it to her. "In case it's cold on the plane."

As he picked out the clothes, tears stung her eyes. "Thank you."

"I still don't like it."

"I know."

"But I get it." He turned her to face him and kissed her. "You've got a long day ahead of you. Let's get to bed."

"I'll be right there." When she was alone, Jeannie leaned back against the wall. Still grasping the shirt he'd chosen for her, she focused on breathing—in through her nose, out through her mouth. She could do this. She *had* to do this.

While she hoped she was ready to take the trip, she *really* hoped she was ready to deal with whatever she might learn there.

THE DREAM RETURNED with relentless disregard for Sam's newfound happiness or her efforts to put the darkness behind her. Gunfire echoed through the rundown house where Marquis Johnson ran his drug operation. His young son Quentin wasn't supposed to be there. In all the months Sam had spend under-cover with the Johnsons, she'd never once seen Quentin there. So why now, on the night when they'd finally decided they had enough to prosecute and could raid the house, why had Marquis decided to bring his son there?

Every instinct in Sam was crying out to turn and run, to get out of there before anyone else got hurt. But her job here tonight was to arrest Marquis, to confiscate the evidence of his far-reaching drug ring, to close the case she'd devoted her life to for half a year.

But the shrieks of the crying child were all she could hear. *What was he doing here?* She almost called off the whole opera-tion, but they were too far along to stop now. Doing so might cost the life of one of her people, which was an unacceptable risk. So she pressed on and ordered her officers to return fire. With her own weapon leading the way, she moved stealthily through the darkened house, following the sounds of the screaming child. All at once the child went silent, and the father began to scream. The sounds coming from Marquis were unlike anything she'd ever heard from him or anyone else for that matter.

Swinging around the corner into the bedroom where he'd kept the lion's share of his drug stash, the first thing Sam saw was the blood. So much blood. Sitting on the floor, Marquis kept up the inhuman screams, but when she looked down to the bloody child in his lap, it wasn't Quentin she saw. No. God. No.

Scotty.

"Samantha. Baby, wake up."

Sam jolted awake, a scream dying on her lips as she realized where she was, who she was with and what had happened —again.

"I'm here, babe. I've got you. It's okay. Just a dream."

She couldn't seem to draw air into her lungs. Every time she tried, her mind took her back to the scene in that squalid room, the broken and bloodied child. This time her child. Her son. The boy she loved. *Not just a dream.* Her greatest nightmare.

"Nick."

He held her so close she could feel his heart beating in time with hers. "I'm right here."

"What if…"

"What, honey?"

"If we take him in and we love him and something happens?"

His lips were soft against her forehead. "Nothing will happen. We'll take such good care of him. We'll keep him safe always."

She took comfort in his words, but the nagging worry remained.

"You're starting to feel like a mother," Nick said.

A mother. After so many miscarriages, she'd given up on ever having that title attached to her name.

"Would he be safe with us? Look at what's going on with these damned cards. People are always threatening me. I can't expose an innocent child to that kind of danger. We should think about this some more."

Nick raised himself up. In the faint light from the street filtering in through the blinds she could see him well enough to know he was looking at her with concern. "Do you have any plans to take our son to a crackhouse?"

"Of course not." The idea of it sent a shudder rippling through her.

"We'll do everything we can to keep him safe. We'll surround him with love and family and baseball and hockey and all the things he doesn't have now. He'll be fine, Sam."

"But what if—"

Nick kissed the question right off her lips. "He'll be *fine.*" He settled her head on his chest and kept his arms around her. "Now go back to sleep. You never have the dream twice in the same night. It's okay to sleep."

Sam blew out a deep breath, but the anxiety refused to let go. Her cell phone rang, and even though she was used to middle-of-the-night calls, they took on new meaning with her dad in the hospital.

Nick released her so she could grab the phone from her bedside table.

Her heart stopped beating for a second as she glanced at the phone and saw the number for Dispatch. "Work," she said for Nick's benefit. "Holland," she said into the phone.

"Lieutenant, we have a report of a possible homicide in Mount Pleasant." The dispatcher rattled off the address.

"Got it. On my way." Sam ended that call and rang Freddie. When he answered she passed along the information.

"Okay."

"Are you awake?"

"What? Yeah. I'm awake. See you there."

Since she was looking at another long day, Sam took a two-minute shower and pulled on jeans along with a long-sleeved T-shirt. In the closet Nick had made for her in one of the spare bedrooms, she topped off the ensemble with a Washington Redskins sweatshirt and running shoes.

Nick was sitting up in bed when she returned to their bedroom.

"Sorry to wake you before," she said, sitting on the bed to tie her shoes.

"Don't apologize for that. I hate the way those dreams plague you."

"I do, too."

"Am I still talking to Scotty about the adoption while we're on the trip?"

Sam thought about that for a second. "I guess so. I can't let fear run my life, right?"

"Right," he said, as he hugged her from behind.

She turned to him and looped her arms around his neck. "Have the best time in Boston. Enjoy every minute and take lots of pictures for me."

"I will." He kissed her. "Wish you were coming."

"Next time. This one is for you and your boy."

"My boy. I love the sound of that."

Knowing how he'd yearned for a family to call his own, Sam loved the sound of it, too. "I'll see you, Senator."

"Yes, you will. Day after tomorrow. I'll be back before you have time to miss me."

She kissed him one last time and stood up to wrap her hair into the clip she wore to work. From the bedside table, she retrieved her weapon and strapped it on, slipping her badge and cuffs into her pockets. "No, you won't."

"Go on before I drag you back to bed."

"I'm going," she said, leaving him with a jaunty wave. "Love you."

"Love you too, babe. Be careful out there."

"Always am."

She ran down the stairs and out the door, doing a time check on her phone as she went. Ten minutes from call to the car—with a shower. Not bad.

CHAPTER TWENTY

Sam drove northwest toward an address off 16th Street, arriving along with the medical examiner. Nodding to the deputy ME, she ducked under the yellow crime-scene tape and headed up the stairs at the well-kept Cape Cod-style home. The smell of death smacked her face the second she crossed the threshold.

Making an effort not to gag from the odor, Sam took a quick look around at a tidy living room on one side of the center staircase. A dining room was on the other side. In the kitchen, she found disarray and the sign of a possible struggle. "What've we got?" she asked the Patrol officer who met her as she took in toppled chairs and broken glass on the floor next to the body of an older man.

"Raymond Jeffries, age seventy-three," the officer said, consulting his notes. "A phone call from his daughter, Sabrina Campion in Albany, New York brought us here on a well-being check." The young officer was clearly battling the need to vomit. "When we got no response, the daughter asked us to enter the home. We found the front door unlocked and entered the dwelling. The odor indicated the homeowner was most likely deceased. We investigated further and found him here in the kitchen." The officer placed a handkerchief over his mouth and nose.

Over the years, Sam had trained herself to breathe through her mouth at times like these. She tugged latex gloves from her pockets and pulled them on.

"It appears," the patrolman continued, "as if he was pushed or fell and possibly hit his head on the table." The officer pointed to a wound on the side of the dead man's head.

"Possibly," Sam said, squatting for a closer look. He had wiry gray hair, a beak of a nose and lips that had turned blue in death.

"He had something cooking on the stove that burned. We turned off the heat."

"Lucky the place didn't burn down," said Deputy Chief Medical Examiner Byron Tomlinson when he joined them. Handsome, arrogant and far too brash for Sam's liking, she put up with him since Lindsey couldn't work twenty-four hours a day. "Judging by the smell, he's been dead awhile. Maybe thirty-six hours or more."

"While you do your thing, I'd like to talk to the daughter," Sam said, rising.

The patrolman produced his cell phone and handed it to Sam. "Press Send. She was the last call I made. She's rather distraught, naturally."

"Thank you, Officer…"

"Huff."

Sam nodded and took the phone outside where she could breathe normally.

Freddie ambled across the lawn, looking half-asleep and rumpled.

"Take a look," Sam said. "Plug your nose."

"Oh God, one of those?"

"Yep." Sam pressed Send on the cell phone and closed her eyes while she waited for the daughter to answer. She hated making calls to victims' families.

"Hello?"

Sam wasn't expecting a man to answer. "This is Lieutenant Holland, Metropolitan Washington Police. May I please speak with Sabrina Campion?"

"One moment please."

The woman who came to the phone a moment later was crying so hard Sam could barely understand her.

"Ms. Campion, I'm sorry for your loss. I realize this is an extremely difficult time for you, but I need your help in determining what happened to your father."

"I just talked to him," she said between sobs.

Sam rubbed her tired eyes. "When was the last time you spoke to him?"

"Two days ago. Maybe three."

"Can you try to be exact?" Sam told herself to be patient. Wasn't she worried about her own father at the moment?

"Monday night. Yes, it was Monday because I'd been to book club and called him on the way home."

Three days ago.

"That's helpful, ma'am. Did he live alone?"

"For the last five years since my mother passed." That set off a new round of crying. "I can't believe they're both gone. How can they both be gone?"

Since Sam had no answer that would satisfy the grieving woman, she pressed on with the questions. "What else can you tell me about your father and his routine?"

"He was a retired high school chemistry teacher."

"Which school?"

"Roosevelt." Sam stood up a little straighter. This was the second time recently that Roosevelt High School had been mentioned during a homicide investigation. "How long had he been retired?"

"Twelve years."

"Any health problems that you knew of?"

"Nothing major. He was on medication for cholesterol, but that was it. He was still very active, played golf and tennis. He was in good health."

"Can you tell me about a typical day for him? Any problems he might've had with his neighbors or anyone else?"

Sam was treated to a ten-minute dissertation of a rather ordinary life with no particular issues that his daughter knew of. "If he had problems, would you know?"

"Yes, of course. I was his only living child. My brother, Jimmy, a marine, was killed in the Beirut barracks bombing in the '80s."

"I'm sorry to hear that."

"It was a long time ago," Sabrina said softly. "I was after Dad to move here to be with us, but he always said his whole life was in Washington. I teased him about that, about how it hurt my feelings that he'd rather be there than here with me. But I knew he didn't mean it that way. Now…" She faltered. "I'm sorry, but I need to go be with my family. I'll be traveling there tomorrow if you have other questions."

"I may need to speak with you again. Could I give you my cell number so you can call me when you're free?"

"Let me find a pen."

While Sam waited for her to return, Freddie emerged from the house looking pale and wide awake. He took deep, gulping breaths of the cool air.

"Brutal," he said.

Sam nodded in agreement.

"I'll never take fresh air for granted again."

Sabrina Campion returned with a pen, and Sam gave her the number. "I'm sorry for your loss. I'll speak with you tomorrow."

"Could I ask you…?"

"Anything you need to."

"Did he suffer?"

"It's hard to say for sure, but at first glance, it doesn't seem so."

"That's good."

Sam waited a moment in case the other woman wanted to ask anything else.

"Are you the officer who married the senator?"

Sam winced. If she lived to be a hundred years old she'd never be comfortable with all the attention she and Nick received. "That'd be me."

"I'm glad you're the one assigned to my dad's case. You seem like a real nice person."

"Well. I try to be. We'll do everything we can to figure out what happened."

"Thank you."

Sam ended the call and turned to Freddie. "Impressions?"

"Are we sure this is a homicide?"

Sam smiled to herself. Her young protégé was coming along rather nicely. "Not entirely. No."

"I can see two chairs toppled over if he falls, but how do you account for the third one?"

"Maybe he stumbled, grabbed one, it went over, and then he fell against the other two."

"I suppose that's possible, but there'd have to be a physical cause for him to fall, right?"

"Yep. That's what we'll need the ME to tell us."

"So what do we do now?"

Sam glanced at the predictable gathering of people outside the crime-scene tape and noticed one of the Patrol officers taking a video of the crowd to refer back to later, if necessary. "Let's speak to the neighbors, find out if they heard a disturbance or know of any problems he might've been having, and then we go home."

"Really?"

"We'll let Crime Scene do their thing and the ME do his thing, and then we'll see what we've got in the a.m."

"So we're going home? In the middle of the night. When we might have a homicide."

Sam laughed at his befuddled expression. "Don't get used to it. Most of the time we're pretty damned sure when we've got a murder on our hands. But this time..." Sam shrugged. "I don't know."

"Well, then let's get to it. I want to go back to bed."

"You want to get back to your girlfriend."

He flashed her a shit-eating grin. "That too, Lieutenant. That, too."

. . .

"WELL, that was a gigantic waste of time," Freddie said. They had conducted an hour's worth of interviews and had as much at the end as they'd had when they started.

"No kidding. Go on back to your love shack. I'll see you at…" Sam checked the time on her phone. Three-thirty. "Nine." Normally they were on duty at eight so they could piggyback all three shifts.

"Your generosity knows no bounds."

"I agree."

"I've got some stuff on Trainer's other ladies that we need to go over in the morning."

"Sounds like a plan." When he hesitated, she said, "Why aren't you running for your car?"

"How's your dad?"

"Out of ICU and doing better."

"How about you? You have to be disappointed over what we heard earlier. About Leroy."

"At this point, I'd be shocked if something went our way."

"It will. Eventually. Probably when we're not even looking. You know how these things go."

"Yes, I do, and I appreciate the concern. But I'm okay."

"I'm glad to hear it."

"So while we're being all mushy here, I want you to do something for me."

"Whatever you need."

Expecting that reply, she smiled. Sure, she was being sneaky, but if she got the result she wanted… "I want you to call your mother."

"Oh jeez—"

"Wait. Hear me out." Sam took a moment to get her thoughts together. "On the day my dad was shot, we had one of the biggest fights we've ever had."

"I can't imagine the two of you fighting. You get along so well."

"We always have."

"So what happened that day?"

"I told him I wanted to take another look at the Fitzgerald case. To say he reacted badly would be an understatement."

"Did he say why he was so opposed?"

"We never got that far. He told me to butt the hell out and he stormed off. That was the last time I ever saw him walking and moving normally. The next time I saw him was in the hospital. For three of the longest days of my life, I didn't know if my last words to him would be, 'You stubborn old bastard.'" She looked up at Freddie. "I've never told anyone about the fight we had. Do you get why I told you?"

"I think so."

"Call her, Freddie. Find out what she's doing with him. Give her a chance to explain." Sam rested a hand on his arm. "You never know what's waiting right around the next corner. What happened that day with my dad taught me to allow nothing to go unsaid. The most important person in my entire life could've *died*, and those would've been my last words to him." Her heart ached just thinking about it. "How would I've lived with that?"

Freddie rubbed at the stubble on his chin. "I'll call her."

Sam nodded. "Good."

"What'll you tell your dad about reopening the Fitzgerald case now?"

The stomach that used to run her life chose that moment to make its presence known. "I haven't decided yet."

"He's apt to still be angry."

"Maybe McBride and Tyrone will tell me what he's got to be angry about." She rested a hand over her churning belly. "I'm sort of afraid of what they might uncover."

"Whatever it is, we'll figure out what to do about it. You don't have to deal with it on your own."

For some reason that made her feel a thousand times better. "Thanks. Go on home. Get some sleep while you can."

"You, too." As Sam left Mount Pleasant a few minutes later, she pondered her options. Since she'd already said goodbye to Nick, she decided to take care of another matter she'd been postponing.

The apartment her ex-husband had rented after their separation and divorce was located only a few blocks from her Ninth Street home. Peter had, of course, done that to goad her. In the two years that followed their divorce, she'd done her best to ignore him until he'd strapped bombs to her car and Nick's. When her car exploded a few days before Christmas, injuring her and Nick, it had blown the cover off her then-secret relationship with Nick as well as Peter's ongoing obsession with her.

Sam hadn't seen him since the night before her wedding to Nick when Peter had confronted her on the street outside her home to let her know their relationship would never be over. Thankfully, Nick had put an ex-cop on retainer to keep an eye on the newly released Peter, which had saved her ass.

The idea of willingly seeking out Peter's company for any reason made her sick. Thinking about what Nick would have to say about this middle-of-the-night visit filled her with anxiety. Despite that, Sam parallel-parked on the street outside Peter's building, locked her car and checked her weapon to ensure it was easily accessible should the need arise.

She took the stairs to his third-floor apartment and rapped on the door. When he didn't answer, she pounded harder. A minute later she heard him shuffling to the door so she held up her badge over the peephole. As the locks disengaged, all she could think about was how Nick would fucking flip when he heard about this.

Peter pulled open the door. "Don't tell me you're already sick of your fancy new husband. If you're here for a booty call—"

"Shut up, Peter." As she took in his graying hair and bitter expression, she tried once again to remember what she'd ever seen in him.

"Still cranky when you don't get enough sleep, I see."

"Shut up and listen. Whatever crap you think you're pulling, cut it out. You're way past pathetic and cruising straight to laughable, you got me?"

"If you're done hurling insults at me, maybe you can tell me what the hell you're talking about."

"As if you don't know."

"I have no freaking clue."

A door across the hall opened. "People are sleeping around here, asshole."

"Fuck off," Peter replied.

"Eat shit and shut the fuck up," his neighbor said, slamming the door.

"Nice," Sam said, making an effort to lower her voice.

"I know you'd love to pin something on me to get me out of the picture. I'm sorry to disappoint you, sweetheart, but whatever you're fishing for, it's not me. Maybe whatever you think I've done is the work of some other dude you banged who's put out by all the press you've been getting lately. I had no idea you were such an attention whore."

"Peter," a female voice said from inside the apartment. "Who is it?"

He reached behind him for the blonde bimbo. "My ex-wife. She misses me."

Sam flashed her badge. "Do yourself a favor, sweetheart." Sam leaned in closer to the startled young woman. "*Run.* As fast and as far away as you can."

"That's it," Peter said, thrusting the girl back into his apartment. "Conversation over."

When he would've slammed the door in her face, Sam stopped it with her hand. "Don't fuck with me or mine, or I swear I'll make your life a living hell."

"Too late. You already have."

Since she'd said what she needed to, she let him have the last word. Unfortunately, she believed him when he said he had no idea what she was talking about. If he wasn't her vindictive pen pal, who was?

CHAPTER TWENTY-ONE

*T*hrilled to be on his way home and longing for his bed and his girl, Freddie parked outside his apartment building and jogged to the door. The second he became aware of a dark shadow in the entryway, he reached for his weapon. "Freeze!"

"It's me, Frederico," his mother said.

"For God's sake, Mom! What're you doing? It's five in the morning. I could've shot you."

"You haven't answered my calls, so I was hoping to catch you before work."

He reholstered his gun. "Were you planning to skulk around out here for two more hours?"

She folded her arms and gave him her best mulish expression. "If I had to. You're avoiding me. Want to tell me why?"

A jolt of anger lanced through him, and he fought it back. This was his mother, and as furious as he was with her at the moment, he refused to show her an ounce of disrespect. She'd raised him better than that.

Juliette Cruz reached up to caress his face. "What is it, Freddie?"

"What're you doing with him? I saw you!" The words tumbled from his mouth in a rush of emotion, and suddenly he was ten

years old again and wondering what he'd done to drive his father from their lives.

"Oh, honey," she said with a sigh as her hand dropped to her side. "I'm so sorry you were caught off guard."

"*Off guard?* Seeing you with him was one of the most shocking moments of my entire life. Tell me you're not back with him, Mom. I swear to God—"

"Don't swear to God." She linked her arm through his and drew him away from the building, away from the windows of sleeping neighbors. "Take a walk with me."

Even though he feared what he might hear and craved Elin's warm body, Freddie went with his mother. The conversation with Sam echoed in his mind, reminding him of his promise to address the issue with his mother.

"Are you back with him, Mom? That's all I want to know."

Juliette hesitated before she answered. "It's complicated."

Freddie let out a huff of disbelief and tugged his arm free. "You have to be kidding me. *He left us!* You had to work three jobs to support us, and you had no life of your own for years because all you did was work. If you tell me you're taking him back after all that—"

"Frederico Cruz, *listen to me!*"

Chastened by her unusually stern tone, Freddie forced himself to breathe normally and listen to what she had to say.

"I ran into him at a restaurant about six months ago."

"Six months? When were you going to tell me?"

"Soon. I'd planned to talk to you about this very soon."

"Sure," he said, not bothering to hide the bitterness.

Even though he could tell she didn't care for his tone, she pressed on. "Needless to say, I was shocked to see him. I had no idea he was back in town."

Freddie stared at her. "Did you know where he was? All the time he was gone, did you know?"

She shook her head. "I only suspected he was probably in the Midwest with his mother's family. He was always close to them and had talked about wanting to move back there someday. When he disappeared, I assumed that's where he'd gone."

"If you knew where he was, why didn't you try to find him?"

"Because he left, Freddie. I refused to go chasing after him. Clearly, he preferred to be elsewhere."

Freddie's mind was spinning as he tried to process it all.

"The night I saw him, in the restaurant, he asked if he could have thirty minutes of my time. At first I said no, but he said it was important and I needed to hear what he had to say."

"It's probably a pack of lies. You shouldn't have let him suck you in."

"Do you know why I did?"

"I can't imagine."

"I did it for you. So I could get some answers to the questions you used to ask me when you were little. Do you remember?"

A stab of pain struck him right in the heart as he traveled back in time. *Doesn't my daddy love me? Why did he leave me? What did I do? When will he be back?* He'd asked the questions over and over for years until she pleaded with him not to anymore. She didn't have any of the answers he'd needed.

"Yes," he said softly, not sure he was any more prepared to hear the answers now than he'd been then.

"When I finally agreed to meet with him, he told me something I'd never heard before." She took a deep breath and under the glow of the streetlight he noticed her hands were shaking. "When he was twenty-one, he was diagnosed with bipolar disorder. Do you know what that is?"

Freddie nodded. He'd seen plenty of it on the job.

"Apparently at that time, he had a major breakdown and was hospitalized for a few months. Afterward, he was able to manage his illness with medication. In all the years we were together, I never knew. That's something I'm still coming to terms with— how I could've been married to a man coping with something so significant and not had the first inkling of what he dealt with every day of his life."

"If he was well medicated, what was he dealing with?" Freddie asked, unwilling to forgive and forget.

"The fear of it coming back. Even when he was in the midst of the first breakdown, he was still somewhat aware of what was happening to him, that his behavior wasn't normal. He said it was the most frightening thing he's ever been through, and he lived in mortal fear of another episode for years after the first one."

Freddie had no idea what to make of any of this. "Why didn't he say anything?"

"You have to remember, son, this was twenty years ago. People went to great lengths to hide mental health disorders because of the stigma attached to them. We've made great strides since then, but back then…" She shrugged. "I wish I could say I would've been supportive and understanding, but more than anything, I probably would've been terrified."

"So what does he want? Why did he come back?"

"You may find this hard to believe, but he's concerned about you."

Everything in him tried to rise up and reject any overture from his deadbeat father, but the ten-year-old living deep inside couldn't help being intrigued by his father's interest in him. "Why me?"

"Bipolar disorder can run in families."

Freddie let that settle for a minute. "I'm not bipolar."

"I know, and I told him that. He was extremely relieved."

Freddie shook his head in disbelief. "I find it hard to swallow he's suddenly concerned about me when he left without a word twenty years ago and hasn't shown a lick of interest in me since."

"He left because he had another breakdown. He was in the hospital for a year this time, and by the time he was released he figured he wouldn't be welcome with us, which was probably true."

Freddie stood with his hands on his hips, every inch of him rigid with tension and despair and a multitude of other emotions he couldn't begin to identify. "And you believe all of this? Where's the proof?"

"He showed me the records from both hospitalizations as well as a third one from five years ago. He's telling the truth, Freddie." Her quiet dignity in the face of what had to be life-altering information for her, too, struck him as odd, but then again she'd had months to absorb what he was only now hearing. Then she dropped the final bomb. "He wants to see you."

"No. Absolutely not." The words erupted from his mouth.

"I told him you'd say that, and he understood. He wants you to know he's so proud of you and how you grew up to be such a fine man and outstanding police officer. I told him how you'd been shot earlier this year, and he was very upset to hear that." She paused before she added, "And I told him I think you might be in love for the first time."

Startled by her acknowledgement, Freddie let his gaze meet hers. "Did you tell him how much you hate her or how difficult you've made things for me?" Freddie knew it wasn't fair to lash out at her, that none of this was her fault—except the part about her hating Elin—but he couldn't seem to stop himself.

"That's between you and me," his mother said. "It's our business."

"And Elin's, since she's the one I love and you hate."

"I don't hate her or anyone."

"You certainly act like you hate her, but that's your problem not mine. I love her, she loves me and we're moving in together."

Juliette gasped. "But you're not married!"

"No, we're not. Maybe we would've gotten married if my mother hadn't hated her so much, but whatever."

"Honestly, Freddie, I feel like I don't even know you anymore."

"Ditto."

They stood there staring at each other for a long moment until he finally looked away, unable to bear the pain he saw in her eyes.

"I need to go to bed," he said. "I have to be back to work in a couple of hours."

"Will you think about seeing your father? He's only asking for a few minutes of your time."

"He's asking for much more than that, and you know it as well as I do. I won't see him, and as long as you're seeing him, I won't see you, either."

"Freddie! For goodness sakes! What has gotten into you?"

"Take care, Mom." Since they had ended up by her car, he walked away with a heavy heart. Even as he said no to seeing his father, a small part of him was curious. "Curiosity killed the cat," he muttered as he entered the building and took the stairs two at a time. In his apartment, he shed his clothes in the living room, set the alarm on his phone and slid into bed with his girl. Her warm softness cured what ailed him.

Even though he was exhausted and emotionally drained after the exchange with his mother, he lay awake for a long time thinking about what she'd told him. By the time sleep finally claimed him, he still had no idea what he was going to do about it.

JEANNIE GOT UP EARLY to take a shower. The trembling began as she squeezed liquid soap into a loofa. Recognizing the signs of the panic attacks that had plagued her since the rape, she stepped out of the shower and gripped the sink. Her heart raced, her stomach surged with nausea and her legs were so unsteady she sank down to the closed toilet. As she struggled to get air to her lungs, tears poured from her eyes, an unstoppable river of pain.

That was where Michael found her.

She had no idea how long she'd been there by then.

He, too, had become accustomed to the attacks and scooped her up into his arms to carry her into the bedroom. Sitting on the bed, he kept her on his lap. "Breathe, baby," he said. "*Breathe, Jeannie.*"

Focusing on the sound of his voice, she forced air into her lungs. One breath at a time, her heart rate returned to normal but the trembling continued.

"Keep breathing," he said.

Jeannie clutched the hand he offered, holding on for dear life. At some point she'd lost her towel, and suddenly she was cold.

Michael reached for a blanket at the foot of the bed and covered her.

"Sorry," she said through chattering teeth.

"Don't apologize. Ever. None of this is your fault."

"Need to get ready. Will's going to be here soon."

"Baby, come on. You can't go today. The trip caused the panic attack. Don't you see that?"

"It's my case. I have to go."

"You don't have to go. Send Will. He can handle it. You know that. What if this happens again while you're away?"

Jeannie was about to argue with him, but then she noticed the dampness on his face.

Using the corner of the blanket, he dried the tears from his cheeks.

"Michael…"

"I can't bear to see you suffer. I can't bear it."

Hearing her strong, fearless boyfriend so defeated made her ache. "I won't go."

"Not because of me."

"Because you're right. I'm not ready."

Michael tightened his arms around her. "I'll stay home today, too. We'll spend the day together."

"Are you sure you can do that?"

"It's fine."

"Let me call Will." Jeannie attempted to get up from his lap but her legs faltered.

Michael got up and steadied her. "Sit. I'll get you the phone."

Jeannie made the call and then slid into bed, feeling worn out from the battle. She'd been so certain yesterday that she had beaten back her demons, that she'd be able to go to Cincinnati and come back with the information Sam had asked her to get.

Michael called his office and then joined her in bed. His body was warm and comforting as he wrapped his arms around her. "You're going to be okay, Jeannie. You're not quite there yet, but you're getting closer."

"You sure about that?"

"Mmm hmm."

Suddenly she became aware they were both naked, and he was aroused. She shifted to her back so she could see his face. His eyes were closed, but his jaw twitched with tension. She hated she was putting him through such a painful ordeal. Her hand found its way to his face where she attempted to caress away the tension.

"Feels good," he whispered, "to have you touch me again."

Jeannie leaned in to press her lips to his.

His eyes flew open. He kept his gaze locked on hers as their lips met.

She ran her tongue over his bottom lip, drawing a gasp from him.

He stayed perfectly still, letting her take the lead as the kiss became more sensual, as tongues met and mated.

"Touch me, Michael," she said, breathless from the passionate kiss.

"Are you sure?"

She nodded and went back for more as his arms encircled her. As his hands moved slowly over her back, she realized he was making an effort to hold back, to keep from scaring her. The knowledge saddened her, especially when she remembered the passionate no-holds-barred lover he'd been before she was brutally raped.

"What?" he asked.

Startled by the question, she raised her head to look him in the eye.

"You got tense all of a sudden. What're you thinking?" He brushed the hair back from her face and ran a finger over her lips.

"I want you. I want *this*. I'm afraid I'll freak out at the last minute like I did the other night. I don't want to ruin it again."

"I told you—we'll keep trying until we get it right. However long it takes. I'm not going anywhere, Jeannie. No matter what." He shifted his hand to the back of her neck and drew her into another kiss.

A sharp tingle of desire settled between her legs, making her itchy with need. She ran her hand down his back to his muscular backside.

His tortured groan told her how much it was costing him to hold back.

With her hands on his face she directed him to her breast, and sighed with satisfaction when he drew her nipple into his mouth.

Jeannie arched into him, wanting more. Her hand found him hard and throbbing and ready. "Michael," she said as she stroked him. "Make love to me."

He surprised her when he shifted to his back and encouraged her to straddle him. "Like this. You're in control, baby. Whatever you want."

Her heart ached with love, while another part of her ached with the familiar desire he'd stirred in her from the first night they met. She slid her moist heat back and forth over his substantial length, watching his reaction with delight and anticipation. All the while, she kept waiting for the panic to return. She waited for the memories of a yellow room to resurface and ruin this for both of them. But she forced herself to keep those memories where they belonged and to remain present in *this* moment.

Michael's hands shifted from her hips to her bottom, encouraging her to take whatever she wanted from him. "Do we need protection?"

"I never stopped taking the pill." She glanced at him and found him watching her intently and warily, as if he too was waiting for the demons to return. Thinking of the ring he'd shown her the night before, of the promises he'd made, of the unconditional love he'd given her at the lowest point in her life, she was able to keep the demons at bay as she took him in slowly, reveling in each inch as she slid down on him.

"Oh *God*, that feels good," he said.

Nothing about this had anything to do with what had happened to her. She kept telling herself that over and over again as she raised herself up and came down on him again, this time pivoting her hips to take him even deeper.

"Yes, Jeannie. *Yes*. I love you so much."

Tears filled her eyes at his sweet words.

He sat up and worked her legs around his hips, bringing his chest in tight against hers. "Is this okay?"

She nodded, loving the feel of his skin, loving the feel of him buried deep inside her, loving him more than she'd ever imagined possible.

Keeping a hand on her bottom, he urged her to move as he drew her nipple into his mouth again. The combination had often sent her over the edge into mindless orgasm, but tonight it was enough to have gotten this far, to be able to give him this much.

She surrendered to the sensations, to the love and the relief at having been able to do this.

"I can't hold back, baby," he said, gasping as she came down on him again.

"Don't. Don't hold back." She urged him into another deep kiss and felt him go rigid beneath her as he came hard, surging into her with a cry ripped from his very soul.

His forehead landed on her shoulder as he sucked in one deep breath after another. He stayed like that for a long time before he lifted his head and found her eyes. "You're so beautiful, and I love you."

"I love you, too. Thanks for being patient with me."

"My pleasure." His goofy smile reminded her of the carefree days before a madman attacked her and changed both their lives. "Speaking of pleasure," he said, kissing his way down her neck, "one of us got more than the other just now."

"That's okay," she said.

He smoothly shifted them so she was on her back. Withdrawing from her, he kissed his way down the front of her. "No, it isn't."

CHAPTER TWENTY-TWO

*O*n the way to HQ, Sam decided she needed to call Nick. This new "full disclosure" policy with her husband went against everything she believed in, but it helped to keep the peace with him.

"Samantha," he said when he answered the phone.

"You're rather chipper at this ungodly hour."

"You weren't my first call this morning."

"Oh. Really?" Her stomach pitched and rolled. Something about his tone set her on edge. "What does that mean?"

"Something you want to tell me?"

Sam scowled. Of course he already knew she'd been to Peter's. "I thought you said you weren't going to have him watched anymore."

"When did I say that?"

"I told you I didn't want you wasting your money on having someone watching him. Remember? We were in that bar in Bora Bora."

"You mean the one time we left our room?"

"Yes! I knew you remembered!"

"I remember you saying that, but I don't recall agreeing to anything."

Sam let out a frustrated growl. "You did, too."

"Did not." He seemed to be enjoying this a lot more than she was. "Do you want to tell me what the hell you were doing there?"

"I was sure it was him sending the cards."

"So you thought it would be a good idea to go over there in the middle of the night by yourself to confront a man who has—at last count—stalked you, bombed you and pulled a gun on you?"

"My gun is bigger."

"I'm not fucking around here, Sam. What the hell were you thinking?"

Startled by his tone and choice of words, she chose hers carefully. "I was thinking I was going to pin this pen pal shit on him and be done with it."

"And if he'd come at you again? What then? You're there in the middle of the night with, as far as you knew, no backup, and no one even knowing where you were."

"It seemed like a good time to check it off my to-do list."

"You're making me seriously mad, Samantha."

"Yeah, I got that." She rubbed the bridge of her nose where a headache had formed. The nights without sleep were catching up to her all of a sudden. "Look, I'm sorry I went over there by myself. Call me crazy that I chose not to trot out my dirty laundry to my coworkers. Peter has put on enough shows in front of the people I work with to last me a lifetime."

"He's an unbalanced psychopath, and you know it." He paused and softened his tone. "It's bad enough I have to worry about something happening to you every time you walk out the door, but when you go looking for it… That makes me crazy."

Sam pulled into her parking space in the HQ lot and killed the engine. "I hate that you worry so much."

"I hate how you're always in some sort of danger, and there's not a goddamned thing I can do to protect you."

"I don't need you to protect me."

"What about what I need?"

"Nick…"

"Forget it. I know you're doing your job, and to you he's an annoyance that has to be dealt with. But to me, he's the guy who'd rather see my wife dead than with anyone but him."

She leaned her head against the wheel. "I'm sorry. You're absolutely right. I shouldn't have been there by myself."

"Wait, back up. What did you say?"

Even though she hated to give an inch, she couldn't help the small smile that made her lips quiver. "You heard me the first time."

"I'd love to hear it again."

"Dream on. You said the *F* word."

"You drove me to it."

"Do you promise to stay mad until you get home tomorrow so we can have make-up sex?"

He snorted with laughter. "I'll see what I can do."

"Is Scotty up yet?"

"Up, showered—without being told—and fully decked out in Red Sox attire. I'd better get him some breakfast and get to the airport before he busts his buttons."

"Could I talk to him? Just for a sec?"

"Sure, let me get him. Before I let you go, I love you, and you'd better behave while I'm gone, got me?"

"Whatever you say."

"No more unnecessary chances?"

"I'll do my best."

"For some strange reason, I love you more than life itself."

"Back atcha, Senator, which is why you're getting security for the campaign trail. In fact, I'll be arranging it while you're away."

"Wait a minute—"

"You don't get to do all the bossing in this family. Put Scotty on."

"We're not done with this subject."

"Yes, we are. Hello, Scotty?"

"Let me go get him," Nick said stiffly.

"Hi, Sam," Scotty said a minute later. "What did you say to make Nick mad?"

"I didn't let him get his own way."

"Ahh, well, he's pretty steamed."

"Good. That was my intention. How are you?"

"I'm so excited. I was awake at like five o'clock."

Sam couldn't help but smile. He was so adorable. "I want you to have the best time ever, and make sure Nick behaves, okay?"

Scotty giggled, and in the background, she could hear Nick asking what she was saying.

"Don't tell him. Our secret."

"You got it."

"Tell him to put his BlackBerry to good use and send me lots of pictures."

"We will."

"See you tomorrow."

"Thanks again for the tickets. This is going to be the best day of my whole life."

"Enjoy every minute." She ended the call and sat there for a moment thinking about Nick and Scotty and the family they were becoming. Before she went into HQ, she called the hospital to check on her father and learned he'd had a good night. They were expecting him to be awake later in the day. Sam couldn't wait to talk to him. She couldn't believe how much she'd missed him after only a few days without him.

She went into HQ and ran into Lieutenant Stahl in the lobby.

"Ah, Lieutenant Holland," he said with a smarmy grin that made his jowls jiggle. "I'm looking forward to our meeting this afternoon."

Sam pretended to pay significant attention to her phone so she wouldn't have to look at him. As she tried to read a text message from her sister, the words swam before her eyes. Goddamned dyslexia. "What're you talking about?" she asked Stahl, not that she cared.

"The administrative hearing? About your wedding?"

"I'm running multiple investigations at the moment. What makes you think I have time for your foolishness?" She glanced up in time to watch his face turn the delightful shade of purple she so enjoyed. "Get out of my way. Unlike you, I have real work to do."

"You'd better be there at 2:00 p.m. sharp, or I'll bring you up on charges."

"Do what you gotta do, Lieutenant." She left him fuming and headed for the pit, which was surprisingly quiet a few minutes before shift change. Grateful for the peace, Sam went into her office, dropped into her chair and gave in to the headache for a few minutes.

"Big night out?" Captain Malone asked.

Sam startled, astounded to realize she'd dozed off at work. She sat up straight and rubbed the sleep from her face. "Middle-of-the-night call."

"Homicide?"

"Not entirely sure." Sam brought him up to speed on the Raymond Jeffries case. "Waiting on the ME's report to tell me what we've got."

"It's an odd day when we can't say for sure if a DOA is a homicide."

"No kidding."

"What's the latest on your pen pal?"

"Nothing yet from the lab, and we haven't gotten any more mail, but I want to arrange security for Nick while he's campaigning. All I can think about is that 'bang bang you're dead' line. It would be so easy for some lunatic to take him out."

"Conklin has all kinds of contacts in the government. I'll ask him to look into it."

"That'd be great. Make sure he tells them we're dealing with a hostile candidate who doesn't think he needs protection."

"Got it," Malone said with a chuckle. "Where are we with the Carl's and Chevy Chase murders? The press is all over us."

Dreaming of blissful days and nights in Bora Bora, Sam smoothed her hands over the hair she'd clipped up for work. "In the Chevy Chase case, we're digging into the husband's stable of mistresses today. Nothing new with the Carl's case. I have all this crap circulating in my head, making me feel like I'm missing something obvious in all three cases. But what?"

"I wish I could tell you, but I have no doubt you'll figure it out. How's Skip?"

"Better. They said he could be awake later today, but of course I'll be stuck in Stahl's stupid hearing rather than with my father."

"So blow off the hearing."

Sam wondered if she'd heard him right. "Are you seriously telling me to blow off a summons from IAB?"

"Everyone knows it's part of Stahl's witch hunt against you. What's he going to do if you don't show?"

"Um, bring me up on charges?"

"And who will care?"

"The media will jump all over it."

"Only if it is leaked, and he's the only one who would do that —and he knows it."

"I gotta say—I like the way you think, Captain."

"I figured you might. Keep this between us, but the chief is trying to get Stahl to take early retirement."

"Oh my God. That's the best news I've heard all day."

"Apparently, he's resisting, so don't get your hopes up."

"Of course he is, because he has no life outside the department."

Lindsey McNamara appeared at the door. "Oh, sorry to interrupt," she said when she saw Captain Malone. "I'll wait out here."

"Come in, Doc," the captain said. "Tell us what you've got on our maybe-homicide."

"Not much, I'm afraid." She handed a file folder containing the autopsy report to Sam. "The head injury killed Mr. Jeffries, and the injury is consistent with him striking the table with some velocity. Unfortunately, I can't tell you if he fell on his own or if he was pushed."

"So we're right back to square one," Sam said. "The fact that three chairs were toppled is bothering me. I can see someone falling and taking out two chairs around a table, but not three."

"Not much to build a case on," Malone commented.

"Hopefully Crime Scene can give me something else I can use. In the meantime, what do I tell his daughter when she gets here later today?"

"The same thing we always tell them—we're looking into it, and we'll let you know when we have more," Malone said.

Sam nodded in agreement.

Malone stood. "I'll let you ladies get back to work. Keep me posted."

"Will do."

After the captain left, Lindsey took the chair he'd vacated.

"What's up?" Sam asked, noting the other woman looked unusually fatigued. "Boyfriend trouble?"

"He's *not* my boyfriend."

"Methinks she doth protest too much."

Lindsey laughed. "Lighten up, Shakespeare."

"Have you seen him?"

"Not since the night we had pizza. I was supposed to call him, but…" She shrugged.

Sam couldn't believe she felt a little sorry for Terry O'Connor, a man she'd once suspected of murder. "What's stopping you?"

"You know."

"I can understand your reluctance in light of your family history. Maybe you should call it a day with him if it's too much for you to deal with."

"I would, except… There's something there. You know what I mean?"

Sam nodded. She knew all too well what Lindsey meant. That "something" was how she'd ended up married three months after reconnecting with a guy from her past whom she'd never forgotten. "So what're you going to do?"

Lindsey sighed. "I have no idea."

"What do you *want* to do?"

"I don't know that either." Lindsey moaned. "This is *so* not me. I'm not an indecisive twit who doesn't know what she wants."

"It's not like you don't have good reason to be concerned."

"I know."

Sam massaged her temples as the headache took a turn for the worse. "I can't believe I'm going to say this, but, maybe you need to dive in and see where it takes you. Worst case, you get your heart broken. Best case, you get everything."

Lindsey seemed to brighten a bit as she considered what Sam had said. "When you put it like that, it doesn't seem quite so scary."

Sam shrugged. "Sometimes you gotta say what the hell and go for it."

"That strategy worked out pretty well for you."

"Yes, it did, but I fought it at first because it was so big and scary. When you're with the right person, big doesn't stay scary for long." Putting what she felt for Nick into words, even abstract words, made her wish he was there with her.

Seeming reenergized by the conversation, Lindsey stood. "I think I know what I need to do. Thanks, Sam."

"Anytime." As she watched Lindsey leave her office, she hoped she hadn't made a mistake by encouraging her friend to pursue a relationship with Terry. That whole "worlds colliding" thing continued to nag at her, but with her skull being split in two by a worsening headache, she had bigger problems at the moment. She was rooting around in her top drawer in search of pills when Gonzo came in.

"We got the report from the lab on the cards," he said, handing it to her. "Of the prints they were able to get, none were in the system. The cards were bought at various locations around the city, curiously all in places that don't have any kind of consumer program where you have to scan a card that would identify the purchaser."

She tried to read the report but once again the words appeared scrambled. "Because that would've been too easy." Sam closed her eyes, took a deep breath and tried again. No luck.

Gonzo frowned as he studied her. "What's wrong with you?"

"Bad headache." Which was the truth. Only Freddie knew about the dyslexia that plagued her.

"You look like hell."

"Gee, thanks." Sam finally located two ibuprofen pills and downed them using a bottle of water left over from God knows when. A surge of nausea made her wonder if they'd be coming right back up. She managed to keep them down, but the battle only intensified the drumbeat in her head. "Wow, I've never had a headache like this before."

"Do you think it's a migraine?"

"I don't know. Maybe."

"You should go home."

"Too much to do. We're looking at Trainer's girlfriends today. How much you want to bet that one of his chicks got pissed he went back to his wife and took her out?"

"Wouldn't be the first time," Gonzo said. "Give me the list. I'll dig in a bit while you take thirty to see if those pills work."

"I'm okay."

"No, you're not. Your face is so white it's see-through." He held out his hand. "The list?"

Sam reluctantly handed it over to him. "Don't tell anyone what I'm doing in here."

"Your secret is safe with me." He went out and closed the door behind him.

Sam heard him telling someone the lieutenant was not to be disturbed for the next thirty minutes because she was in a meeting. She smiled to herself as she tipped her head back, seeking relief from the blinding pain. It was good to have friends who looked out for her, even if being sick at work and taking a nap went against everything she believed in. But she felt so shitty at the moment, she doubted she could even get herself home.

As she closed her eyes, she told herself she would rest for a minute or two. Then she'd get back to work.

CHAPTER TWENTY-THREE

*W*ill Tyrone found Cameron Fitzgerald working in a warehouse outside of Cincinnati. Taking this trip alone had turned Will into a nervous wreck. In his two years as a detective, he'd never once interviewed a suspect by himself. Sure, maybe his more experienced partner had spoiled him by holding his hand a bit, but he hadn't objected. Will swallowed hard as he watched the blond man hoist boxes. The muscles bulged on Fitzgerald's tattooed arms as he worked.

What if he screwed this up somehow and the lieutenant got pissed? He had so much respect for her. She was one bad-assed chick, but he'd rather swallow his own tongue than express such a thought to her. The idea of somehow messing up a case that had meant so much to her father was unimaginable to him.

"So don't screw it up," he muttered to himself, grateful for the noise in the warehouse.

"What's he done now?" asked the supervisor who'd led Will onto the floor.

"Nothing. I need to speak with him for a few minutes."

The supervisor checked his watch. "He's due for a break. Tell him he can take five."

Will nodded and headed over to Cameron Fitzgerald. Whereas Caleb had been smooth and refined, Cameron was all hard edges. He had long sideburns and rough stubble on his jaw.

"Mr. Fitzgerald?" Will said.

"Yep," he said without so much as a glance at Will.

"I'm Detective Will Tyrone, Metropolitan Police Department in Washington, D.C."

Cameron briefly shifted his eyes to rest on Will before he returned his attention to the boxes he was moving. "What'd you want?"

"We've reopened your brother's case, and I need a few minutes of your time."

A box slipped through Cameron's hands, startling both men when it crashed to the floor.

Cameron cast a nervous glance at his supervisor.

"Take it easy, Fitzgerald!" the guy yelled across the floor.

Cameron signaled for someone to take his place and pulled off his work gloves. "Come with me," he snapped at Will as he wiped sweat from his brow.

He led Will into a dingy break room, bought a bottle of water from the vending machine and downed the whole thing before he turned to Will. "Why now?"

Will shrugged. "My lieutenant asked me to take a fresh look. That's what I'm doing."

"You've read all the reports. You've seen my statement. There's nothing I can tell you that I haven't already told ten other cops."

Here goes nothing, Will thought. "Your brother Caleb mentioned you had gotten in trouble earlier in the day Tyler went missing. He'd told your parents you'd had your girlfriend in your bedroom when they weren't home."

Cameron's already hard eyes got even harder. "Caleb said that, did he?"

"We talked to him yesterday and asked him what he remembered about that day."

Cameron put his hands on his hips. "And how is my dear brother? Busy and successful as always?"

"You don't talk to him?"

"Only on the first Sunday of the month when he calls like

clockwork. Sometimes I take the call, other times I don't. Depends on my mood."

"Were you angry with Tyler for telling on you to your parents?"

"Of course I was. He was a constant pain in my ass, always ratting me out for one thing or another."

"And you were the last person to see him alive?"

"I guess I was." He ran a hand over the stubble on his jaw.

"What do you remember from that night?"

Cameron eyed him warily. "I really gotta go through this again?"

"If you wouldn't mind."

He told the same story Caleb had shared about the game of cops and robbers and how Tyler had gone missing while they were running away from Caleb, the cop. "I looked back over my shoulder, and he was gone. So I backtracked, calling for him. I figured he was hiding from me, which would've been like him. That kid loved to push my buttons."

"Did that bother you?"

"Sometimes."

"Like when he told your parents about your girlfriend being in your bedroom?"

"That pissed me off," he said, his face tightening with anger. Will decided in that moment he wouldn't want to cross Cameron Fitzgerald without his weapon handy.

"What was your girlfriend's name?"

The question seemed to startle Cameron. "What's that got to do with anything?"

"Maybe nothing." Will's heart was beating so rapidly he wondered how he managed to breathe normally. "I'd still like to know her name."

"Lauren Holbrooke."

"Spell the last name, please."

Cameron did so through gritted teeth. "I don't get why you have to drag her into this."

Will couldn't believe it'd taken this long to drag her into it.

"You went into the military two days after your brother went missing."

"So?"

"Why so quick?"

"It'd been in the works before my brother disappeared. My parents and I didn't see any reason to postpone it."

"Your brother had been kidnapped and was missing, yet you decided to leave your family at that difficult time."

Cameron's stare made Will's blood run cold. The other man moved toward the door. "If you're insinuating I killed my brother, prove it. Until you can, leave me and my family alone. My parents have been through enough." Cameron stalked out of the room, slamming the door behind him.

Will didn't know if they'd ever be able to prove it, but he felt like he'd looked directly into the eyes of a killer.

GONZO STARED at the card on his desk, wishing he hadn't been so diligent about staying on top of the mail flooding in for the lieutenant and her new husband. If they'd had any doubt about whether someone was playing a joke or wanting to cause serious harm, they didn't have to wonder anymore.

"Dear Sam" the sicko had written. "What do I have to do to get your attention? I've already started killing all the people who've pissed me off over the years, but no one seems to care, even the police officers like you who are paid to care. I suppose I'll have to strike a little closer to home to get your attention. In the meantime, I want to see you out telling the media all about the spate of murders that have broken out in your fair city. If I don't see you out there at the microphone today, someone else will have to die. Let's hope it's not someone you love this time. Signed, An Old Friend."

Gonzo was on his feet and heading for Sam's office before he reached the last line. "Lieutenant," he said when he opened the door. "We've got a problem." He took one look at her and realized he had an even bigger problem. "Someone call for paramedics! Hurry!"

Her face was devoid of all color, her lips were bluish and when he pressed his hand to her forehead, she was cold and clammy. His partner rushed through the door.

"What's wrong with her?" Arnold asked.

"I don't know," Gonzo said. "Sam, wake up. Sam?" He checked her pulse and found it rapid and irregular. "Jesus Christ, what's taking so long?"

"They're on their way," Arnold said, staring at their boss.

"Shh," Sam finally said. "Bad headache. Need quiet."

"You're okay, Sam. Help is on the way." He looked over his shoulder. "Keep everyone out of here and let Malone know."

Arnold scurried out of the office, and Gonzo returned his attention to her. He eyed her cell phone on her desk and wondered if he should call Nick.

She clutched his arm. "Don't." Her voice was so faint it came out as a whisper. "Don't let anyone call him. Scotty's big day."

"Whatever you want, Sam." The greenish tint to her skin was scaring the hell out of him. "Just hang in there."

"Out of the way, Detective," the lead paramedic said as she rushed into the office.

Gonzo stood back to watch them quickly assess Sam's condition and load her onto a gurney.

"We're taking her to GW," the paramedic said to Gonzo on the way out.

They passed Captain Malone as he came running into the pit. "What the hell happened?" he asked Gonzo.

"She said she had a bad headache, so I suggested she take a break." Gonzo realized his hands were shaking so he jammed them into his pockets. "When I went back in a few minutes later, she was totally out of it. They're taking her to GW."

Malone spun around to follow the paramedics. "I'll go with her."

"Wait! Sir. Before you go, she got another card." Gonzo grabbed the bagged card off Sam's desk and thrust it at the captain.

"This is a whole new ballgame," the captain growled as he read it. "We need people on every member of the lieutenant's immediate family. Get that set up right away." He glanced at Gonzo. "You'll need to talk to your fiancée about the senator's schedule and work out security arrangements. Talk to Deputy Chief Conklin. He's already been in touch with the Capitol Police."

"Yes, sir, I'll take care of it." Gonzo wished his hands would quit shaking. "Will you let me know the minute you hear anything about Sam?"

Malone answered with a curt nod and bolted from the pit.

"Holy shit," Arnold muttered when he and Gonzo were left alone in the pit. "She's going to be okay, right? There can't be anything seriously wrong with the lieutenant."

"I'm sure she'll be fine," Gonzo said with more confidence than he felt. "But until we know more, we've got work to do."

FREDDIE WOKE AHEAD of the alarm he'd set for 8:00 a.m. Since Elin was still sleeping he stared at the ceiling and rehashed the odd pre-dawn conversation with his mother. His father wanted to see him. That was the only part Freddie could seem to focus on as the words ran through his mind like a refrain from a favorite song.

What would it be like, Freddie wondered, to come face-to-face with the man who'd left them without a word more than twenty years ago? What would it be like to have a chance to talk to him, to hear his voice, to see his face up close? If he'd seen the man somewhere other than with his mother would he have recognized him as the father he'd once loved with his whole heart?

"What're you thinking about?" Elin asked, her voice husky with sleep.

"Nothing," he said, turning to her.

"Did you know," she said, reaching out to run a finger over the furrow of his brow, "that when you're not telling the full truth, you get a line right here."

"I do?" Freddie asked, startled by the revelation.

"Uh huh."

"Well, that's not fair. How do I know when you're not telling the truth?"

She flashed a saucy smile that made his blood race. "You'll have to figure that out for yourself."

He slid an arm around her to bring her closer to him, but she resisted.

"Don't try to change the subject by distracting me."

"Is that what I'm doing?"

She once again traced the line between his brows as she nodded. "Tell me."

So he did. He told her about the father who had suddenly reappeared in his life twenty years after checking out. He told her his father wanted to see him and that he'd said no.

"That's a mistake," she said without hesitation.

"How can you say that? He left us without—"

Elin pressed her fingers to his lips. "I'd give everything I have, everything I'll ever have, for one more day with my dad. Just one day."

Freddie knew her father had died of a heart attack when she was twelve and a part of her had never recovered from the shock of the sudden loss.

"It's not the same thing," he said.

"Isn't it? The only difference is your father's ailment didn't kill him."

God, when she put it like that… "I don't know if I could do it. What would I say?"

"You don't have to say anything. Just listen." She snuggled into his embrace, her head on his chest and her arm around his waist.

Normally when she was close to him like this, he had one thing on his mind. This time, however, he was comforted by her closeness and the simple wisdom of what she'd said. "You really think I should see him?"

"I really do. What if something happens and you never get the chance to talk to him? Won't you always wonder what he would've said? How it would've changed things?"

"That's sort of what I'm afraid of—it'll change things."

"Maybe that wouldn't be so bad."

"What if I let him back in and he does the same thing again?"

Elin was quiet for a long moment as she pondered that. "I have to think you'd be better equipped to deal with it as a thirty-year-old man than you were as a ten-year-old boy."

He wasn't at all sure that was true.

She tipped her head up to kiss him. "Think about it. You don't have to do anything today. See how you feel about it in a couple of days. Maybe once the shock of him wanting to see you wears off a bit, it won't seem so overwhelming."

In a move he considered rather smooth, Freddie turned so he was on top of her, looking down at her brilliant blue eyes. "When did you get so wise?"

"I've always been wise. You're too busy thinking you're wiser to listen to me."

Shocked by the statement, he stared at her. "That is not true."

"Oh, yes, it is," she said, giggling. "Mr. Wise Detective, who knows everything about everything."

"Are you trying to piss me off?"

She ran her hands down his back to cup his ass. Her smile was nothing short of victorious when she realized she'd turned him to putty under her hands. "Don't forget you love me."

He planted a kiss on her pouty lips. "As if I could ever forget that." Just as he was about to show her how much he loved her, his phone rang. "Ugh. She said I could have until nine," he muttered as he reached for the phone on the bedside table.

Elin continued to knead his rear end until he was so hard he could pound nails.

A quick glance at the caller ID showed Gonzo's number. "What?" Freddie growled.

"Something's wrong with Sam."

CHAPTER TWENTY-FOUR

A bright light aimed at her eyes brought Sam back to reality. The searing pain that followed the flash of light made her wish she were dead. Why was he yelling at her? Why wouldn't he stop yelling? Her stomach heaved, and Sam was forced to decide between focusing on the stabbing pain in her head or the fact that she was going to puke any second. The head pain won.

"It's all right, Sam," a familiar voice said. She couldn't work up the focus to figure out who it was.

"Stomach," she muttered as a final surge of nausea led to vomiting that nearly split her head right down the middle.

Someone held her head, which was the only thing that kept it attached to her neck. When the heaving finally stopped, Sam opened her eyes and discovered she was in the hospital, surrounded by medical personnel. The voice she recognized belonged to Captain Malone. God, this was embarrassing. He'd watched her puke up her guts.

"Sam, can you hear me?"

She looked up at Nick's friend, Dr. Harry. "Where'd you come from?"

"Heard they brought you in."

Sam fought against whatever was restraining her as she tried to sit. Her head fought back against the movement. "Don't call Nick," she said to Harry. "Don't let anyone call him."

"But Sam—"

"Don't call him." Each word cost her everything she had. "Scotty's day."

"Someone needs to know you're here."

"Tracy. Call her."

"Tell me what hurts," Harry said.

"Head. Like it's gonna explode."

"Just relax. We'll take good care of you."

The next time Sam opened her eyes, her sister was hovering by her bedside. "Hey," Sam said, her voice gravely.

Tracy reached for her sister's hand. "Are you okay?"

"Not sure. What happened?"

"Harry says it's a severe migraine."

"Jesus. I had no idea they were this bad." Sam felt a tiny bit better than she had before, but her head was still pounding. Thankfully, they'd turned the lights way down in the room. "Why would I get one now when I've never had one before?"

"They aren't sure, but Harry said the fact that you've had two recent concussions might've triggered something."

"Fabulous." Sam tried to get more comfortable and closed her eyes when her head nearly exploded. "I guess dyslexia, a lousy stomach and infertility wasn't enough. How's Dad?"

"Better. Groggy and out of it but conscious."

"At least one of us is."

"If you're joking, that's a good sign."

"No one called Nick, did they?"

"Not that I'm aware of. Harry said you didn't want us to call him."

"Scotty's big day in Boston. I didn't want to ruin it."

Tracy patted Sam's hand. "Don't worry about anything. Get some rest."

"I want to go home."

"Harry is keeping you overnight for observation."

"No. Give me a ride home?"

"Sam—"

"Please."

"Let me talk to the nurse."

SITTING in her office in the lab, Lindsey stared at the phone for a long time. If she made this call she'd be committing to an actual relationship with Terry. He'd put the ball in her court. She could make the call. Or not. The conversation with Sam earlier had been on Lindsey's mind all day.

She'd had her heart broken once before, and it was an experience she wouldn't wish on her worst enemy. But she'd never managed to have everything with any guy. She'd never met anyone who'd come close to that for her. Until now. From the first time she ever talked to Terry she'd felt something different for him.

She picked up the phone and then put it back down. Her deputy, Byron Tomlinson, appeared at the door. "What's up?"

"We've got a call. Want me to take it?"

"I thought you had a hot date tonight."

Byron shrugged. "She knows what I do."

Lindsey glanced at the phone one last time, relieved to have the decision taken out of her hands—at least for now. "That's all right," she said. "I'm not doing anything tonight. I'll take it."

"Are you sure?"

"Yep."

"Did you hear about Lieutenant Holland?"

Lindsey stopped short. "What about her?"

"She got sick in her office, and they took her to the ER. I heard it was a severe migraine."

"Oh my God. I'll check on her later." Lindsey grabbed her field kit and locked her office. "See you tomorrow."

She drove to the address in the northwestern corner of the Woodley Park neighborhood, thinking of Sam and wondering how she was. Emergency vehicles had gathered outside yet another well-appointed suburban home. This was becoming a pattern lately. Nice house, regular people, no criminal connec-

220 | MARIE FORCE

tions and vexing, unexplainable murders. She had a feeling this one would be more of the same.

Detective Gonzales greeted her outside the house.

"What've we got?"

Gonzo led her through the nice house to the backyard where a body floated in the pool. "James Lynch, age forty. According to his wife, Amanda, who found him, he was terrified of water and stayed far away from the pool." Another officer was comforting Amanda, who was hysterical. "Apparently, he nearly drowned as a kid, and ever since then he never went near the water."

"So how'd he end up in the pool?"

"Good question. Because she was so adamant that he'd never go near it on his own, Patrol called us in."

Mr. Lynch was dressed in what appeared to be work clothes —dark gray slacks, a pale blue dress shirt and still had his shoes on.

Lindsey grimaced as she waded into the shallow end of the pool and made her way to the body. As she turned him over, his wife screamed and then broke down into gut-wrenching sobs.

"Jimmy! *No!*"

Lindsey glanced up at Gonzo, imploring him to get the woman out of there.

He signaled to the patrolman to take the woman inside.

"Thanks," Lindsey said when they were gone. "Help me get him out of here."

Between the two of them, they lifted him out of the pool and laid the dark-haired man on the pool deck. On first glance, the body showed no obvious signs of trauma or injury. Lindsey would need to transport him back to the lab to determine the cause of death.

"Why do I have a feeling this one is going to go like the last two?" Gonzo said. "A well-liked guy who didn't have an enemy in the world."

"Clearly someone had a problem with him." Lindsey examined Lynch's eyes and mouth. "Any word on how Sam is?"

"Last I heard she was in the ER with a severe migraine."

"Poor kid. She's got enough going on with this crazy pen pal and her dad in the hospital."

"I heard he's a little better today."

"That's good." Lindsey closed Mr. Lynch's eyes. "I'm ready to transport him." She stood and tugged off her gloves, signaling to the team that had accompanied her.

"Can you stick around for a minute, Doc?" Gonzo asked, eyeing the house warily.

"Sure. What do you need?"

"We're short-handed today, so I'm here by myself. I could use a more senior witness to the interview with the wife than the probie who's with her."

"And you don't deal well with hysterical females, am I right?"

"I never said that," Gonzo said, feigning offense.

"Lead the way, Detective." Lindsey followed him inside even though she'd rather be anywhere other than at ground zero of Amanda Lynch's grief. She instructed her people to load the body in the truck and wait for her outside.

Mrs. Lynch was inconsolable.

Gonzo glanced at Lindsey, seeming to be asking for her help.

"Is there someone we could call for you, Mrs. Lynch?" Lindsey asked. "A friend or relative maybe?"

Amanda shook her head. "If I call people, I'll have to tell them. I can't tell them."

"You'll have to eventually, ma'am," Gonzo said gently.

"Not yet."

"Do you have children?" Lindsey asked.

"No, it was just Jimmy and me."

"If your husband was terrified of water, I have to ask why you have a pool," Gonzo said.

"We moved in a month ago. We'd planned to have it drained and filled in. I fell in love with the house, so he said we shouldn't let the pool stop us from buying it. And now…" She looked up at them, her pretty face a mask of devastation. "What'll I do without him? He was my whole world."

"Can you think of anyone who might've wanted to hurt him —or you?"

"No," she said, shaking her head. "Everyone loved Jimmy. He had so many friends. I had trouble keeping track of them all."

"What did he do?"

"He's a lawyer. A partner in a firm in Bethesda."

Amanda's use of the present tense pained Lindsey and made her sad to think about the journey this woman had ahead of her as she learned to live without her husband.

"What kind of law did he practice?" Gonzo asked.

She wiped new tears from her face. "Civil litigation."

"Has he been involved in anything particularly contentious?"

"Nothing," she said, shaking her head. "In fact, he'd complained lately of being bored and had even said it might be time to quit his job and pursue his lifelong goal of writing a legal thriller." It seemed to settle on her all of a sudden that he'd never reach that goal now. "How can he be gone? He was just here. This morning. We had breakfast together."

"Where were you today?"

Amanda stared at him, her face frozen in shock. "What does that have to do with anything? I came home and found my husband dead in our pool."

Gonzo swallowed hard, and Lindsey felt for him. He had to go down this road, but it couldn't be easy to insinuate that the obviously devastated woman might've had something to do with her husband's murder.

"We'll need to confirm your whereabouts to rule you out as a suspect."

Grief turned to outrage in the fraction of an instant. "That is ridiculous! I could no more harm him than I could myself!"

To his credit, Gonzo didn't waver. "I need to know where you were so I can rule you out."

Amanda glanced at Lindsey, as if to ask if he was for real. "It's a formality, Mrs. Lynch," Lindsey said. "If you can answer the question, we can get busy finding out who did this to your husband."

Gonzo sent her a grateful look and refocused on Amanda.

After a long moment of silence, she said, "I was at the hospital having tests." She spoke so softly they had to strain to hear. "Jimmy and I... We'd been trying for a long time to have a baby. We're running out of time." Her voice caught on a sob. "Because I just turned forty. I never thought... This wasn't supposed to happen."

"Did your husband know where you were?"

She shook her head. "We...I...had a miscarriage last year, and it was so devastating to both of us. I didn't want to get his hopes up."

"Could you please write down the name and address of your doctor?" Gonzo asked, extending his notebook and pen to her.

She scowled at him, snatched the pad from his hand and wrote down the information.

"Please also add the name and address of your husband's firm."

Amanda did as instructed and thrust the pad back at him.

Lindsey glanced at Gonzo. "May I?"

He gestured for her to go ahead.

"Mrs. Lynch, do you by any chance know Crystal Trainer or Raymond Jeffries?"

"Crystal Trainer's name is familiar, but I've never heard of Raymond Jeffries."

"Is it possible you heard Mrs. Trainer's name in the media in recent days?"

"Oh, yes, she's the mother who was killed in Chevy Chase. Such an awful tragedy." Amanda's eyes widened all at once. "Do you think there's a connection between her murder and what happened to my husband?"

"We don't know yet," Gonzo said. "But there are some similarities that require further scrutiny before we can say for sure if they're connected."

"Who is Raymond Jeffries?" Amanda asked.

"He was found dead in his home last night," Gonzo replied. "He's a retired chemistry teacher. Taught at Roosevelt—"

"I went to Roosevelt," Amanda said, her eyes widening. "But I don't remember Mr. Jeffries. Then again, I never took chemistry."

"I need you to think if there was anyone who might've had a

conflict with you or your husband, anyone with a score to settle or a grudge," Gonzo said. "Perhaps someone involved with one of his lawsuits at work or someone you met through your work."

"I haven't worked since Jimmy and I got married six years ago. He wanted to take care of me, and I'd worked for so long by then I was happy to let him. Of course, we thought we'd have a family by now, but that never happened."

"There's no one else you can think of? Someone who might've begrudged your happiness together—an old boyfriend or girlfriend maybe—or someone through his work."

Amanda shook her head the whole time he was talking. "Nothing like that. We're low-key people. We have friends we enjoy but prefer to keep to ourselves most of the time. We're happiest when we're together, just the two of us."

Lindsey's heart broke for her.

Gonzo handed Amanda his card. "If you think of anything he might've mentioned about problems with other people or at work, please let me know."

"Find the person who did this to my Jimmy," she said. "Please find them."

"We'll do all we can. There has to be someone we can call. I don't feel comfortable leaving you here by yourself."

"I'll be fine."

Lindsey noticed an eerie sense of calm had come over the grief-stricken woman and saw Gonzo had tuned into it, as well. She followed him out of the house.

"I don't feel right leaving her," he said.

"Call Dr. Trulo," Lindsey said, meaning the department psychologist. "He'll be able to hook you up with grief counselors."

"Good idea." Gonzo looked around at the upscale suburban neighborhood. "Is it odd she has *no one* to call when her husband has been murdered?"

Freddie Cruz ambled up the lawn to join them. "I've been working on Trainer and Jeffries all day. Just heard about this one."

"How's Sam?" Gonzo asked.

"She was diagnosed with a severe migraine and checked herself out of the hospital against medical advice because she didn't need to be observed overnight."

"Sounds like she's feisty," Lindsey said. "That's a relief."

"For sure," Gonzo added. "Finding her like that scared the shit out of me."

"What've we got here?" Cruz asked.

Gonzo brought him up to speed and outlined their dilemma about leaving the man's widow alone in the house where he'd been found dead.

"My mom volunteers at a grief group at our church," Freddie said. "I could give her a call and see if they can send someone over to be with Mrs. Lynch."

"That'd be great," Gonzo said. "Thanks."

As Freddie stepped aside to make the call, Lindsey turned to Gonzo. "I'm going to head in to HQ and get going on the autopsy. I'll let you know what I've got the minute I'm done."

"Thanks for staying."

"Anytime." Lindsey headed for the curb and climbed into the back of the ME's truck to accompany Mr. Lynch to the lab. She rapped on the window to give her guys the go-ahead. As the truck lurched forward, she studied the face of the man Amanda Lynch had loved with her whole heart. Lindsey wanted to know what that was like, to love so completely and to be loved the same way in return.

Without allowing herself another minute to ponder the implications or to consider all the reasons why making this call might be the worst thing she'd ever done, Lindsey found Terry's number on her list of contacts and pressed Send.

"Hey, gorgeous," he said when he answered, making her smile.

"Hi, there."

"Funny, I was just thinking about you."

"What about me?"

"I was wondering if your legs are as long as they look. I hope I get the chance to find out."

Even though the truck was kept cold in deference to the

cargo, Lindsey was suddenly on fire. "I have a few more hours at work, but I was wondering if you might be free later."

"I've got a few more hours to go, too, but I've got nothing going on later."

"How about I give you a call when I'm done?"

"Sounds like a plan." He paused for a long moment. "Lindsey?"

"Yeah?"

"I'm really glad you called."

CHAPTER TWENTY-FIVE

*W*hile he waited for the Crime Scene detectives to finish their work at the Lynch house and for Cruz's mom to show up—she'd insisted on coming herself—Gonzo took another look at his watch and realized he was going to be late. Again. Christina was awesome about stepping up to help with his baby son when he needed the assistance, but lately he knew he'd been taking advantage of her. He kept waiting for her to say enough already. With that in mind, he placed a call to her.

"Hi, hon."

"Hey, where are you? Alex and I just got to your place."

"Thanks for picking him up again. I appreciate it."

"I don't mind. You know that."

He closed his eyes and released a sigh of relief. "I keep waiting for you to tell me he isn't your problem."

"Why in the world would I do that?"

"Because, technically, he isn't your problem."

"I love him, Tommy, and I love you. I'm not going to suddenly get annoyed because you need me to help you with your son. I know your hours are crazy and unpredictable."

"So are yours." As Nick's chief of staff, she put in long hours at the office and on the campaign trail.

"What you're doing is more important."

"I don't know what I did to get so lucky to find you."

"Well, it didn't hurt that you're hot."

Gonzo smiled. "Back atcha, baby. I caught a homicide late in my tour."

"In that case, I'll feed Alex and give him a bath. Hopefully, you'll be home in time to say good-night."

"I hope so." He lived for his evenings with her and his son.

"If not, I'll wait up for you. Go do what you need to do, Tommy. It's okay."

"Love you." He loved her so damned much he couldn't recall how he'd ever lived without her. Freddie's mom pulled up to the curb and got out of the car. "I've got to go, hon. I'll be home as soon as I can." Jamming his phone in his pocket, he crossed the lawn to meet Freddie and his mom.

"You remember Gonzo, right, Mom?" Freddie said.

"Of course. Good to see you again, Tommy."

Gonzo shook her outstretched hand. "Thanks for coming, Mrs. Cruz." He told her about Mrs. Lynch and her terrible loss.

"Don't worry. I'll take care of her."

Gonzo knocked lightly on the front door and found Amanda Lynch right where they'd left her. He introduced her to Freddie and Juliette Cruz and asked if she'd be willing to speak with her for a couple of minutes.

"Is it about Jimmy's case?" Amanda asked.

"No, ma'am. She's here for you." Thankfully, Juliette stepped forward and took over before Gonzo had to explain further.

Once the women were seated together talking, Gonzo and Cruz stepped outside again.

"Thanks a lot for getting her over here," Gonzo said.

"No problem. Are you thinking this one is related to Trainer and Jeffries?"

"Hard to tell, but there are similarities. We've got a connection to Roosevelt High School with all three murders. Tomorrow we'll dig a little deeper on that."

"I spent all day interviewing Jed Trainer's girlfriends. The guy was a total man whore. I can't believe he only got caught once."

"Anything pop?" Gonzo asked.

"Not a thing. They all have airtight alibis."

Frustrated, Gonzo ran his hands through his hair. "What the hell is going on with all these low-key, well-liked people ending up dead? I don't get it."

"We don't even know if they're related in some way."

"Sam got another card today that said something about being disappointed there hasn't been more media coverage of the letter-writing campaign."

"You think the pen pal case is related to the three murders?"

"I don't know what to think. Everything about all three of these cases feels off to me."

"We need one of Sam's threads to pull. Something to tie them together."

"We'll start digging in the a.m. As soon as Crime Scene is done, I'm going back to HQ to do the paperwork on this one before I head home."

"I'll to stick around here and wait for my mom, so go on ahead."

"Really?"

"Sure. I don't mind."

"All right then," Gonzo said. "See you in the morning."

"If not before," Cruz said, referring to the odd spate of murders that had struck their city in recent days.

"If not before." Gonzo jogged to his car with renewed hope that he might get home in time to see his son before bed after all.

SAM TRUDGED into the house and made a beeline for the kitchen. After she plugged her phone into the charger, she poured a glass of ice water and downed a big swallow.

"Go easy, tiger," Tracy said. "Your stomach is totally empty."

"I'm so thirsty." She checked her text messages and saw a quick note from Jeannie expressing concern about Sam's health and mentioning she'd like to talk to Sam when she felt better. "I've got McBride looking into the Fitzgerald case."

Tracy seemed shocked to hear that. "Why?"

"I know it bothers Dad that he was never able to solve it. I thought it was time for a fresh look."

"Does he know that?"

"I decided to do it after he got sick. Why?"

"No reason." Tracy got busy putting dishes away. "How about some toast or something? Remember how Mom always fed us cinnamon toast when we had the stomach bug?"

Sam hadn't thought about that in a long time. "Yeah." While her head was still pounding, they'd given her something that made her feel woozy and mellow. Whatever it was had taken the edge off the god-awful pain from earlier.

"So you want some?"

"I couldn't keep it down." She refilled her glass and leaned unsteadily against the counter. "I got a wedding card from her."

Tracy looked up from the text message she was sending. "From who?"

"Mom." Sam now had her sister's full attention.

"What'd it say?"

"The usual stuff. She said we made for a beautiful bride and groom, and she'd love to meet Nick sometime."

"Wow."

"You ever hear from her?"

Tracy shrugged. "Here and there. Nothing regular."

"You never told me that. I figured she didn't bother with any of us."

"Ang went to see her last fall."

Sam stared at her sister. "Are you *kidding* me? Why didn't she say anything?"

"We both know how you feel about her."

"I thought you felt the same way. After what she put Dad through…"

"It wasn't all her, Sam. He played a part in it, too. You were too young to remember a lot of it."

She had no idea what her sister was talking about. "A lot of what?"

"That's a conversation for another time. Let's get you upstairs to bed."

Even though she wanted to finish the conversation, Sam's legs were on the verge of collapse, so she let Tracy guide her upstairs. On the way, though, she recalled encouraging Freddie to make amends with his mother. Was it time for her to take her own advice? That would be something she'd have to think about once this case was closed. "I need a shower. I smell like puke."

"Sit here for a minute," Tracy said, guiding Sam to the bed. "I'll get you some clothes and help you into the shower."

"You must have stuff to do. I can take it from here."

"I'm not leaving you alone. I signed a form that gave me custody of you, so you have to do what I say."

"Oh jeez," Sam said, shuddering. "Just like the old days."

"You got it, little sister. Sit tight."

Sam watched her sister leave the room and cross the hall to the bedroom that had been made into a closet.

Tracy stopped, raised her hands to her face and let out a shriek. "Oh, my God! *Oh, my God!*"

Sam struggled to her feet and staggered to where her sister stood watch over the shredded remains of Sam's clothes. At first, Sam couldn't figure out what had happened, but then she took a closer look. Her eyes landed on the gorgeous wedding gown Vera Wang had made just for her, which lay in tatters on the floor next to the ice-blue gown she'd worn the night Nick proposed to her in the White House Rose Garden.

"Oh," Sam said as a new wave of nausea demanded her full attention. She fought it back, reached for the weapon still holstered to her hip with one hand and grabbed her sister with the other hand. "Get out." The headache began a new relentless tempo as she half dragged Tracy to the stairs. "Might still be in the house. Go. Now."

"What about you?" Tracy whispered, her eyes wide with fear and shock.

"I'm coming, too." Under normal circumstances, Sam would do a full canvass herself to make sure the house was clear. But at the moment she couldn't decide if she was going to puke or pass out, so getting her sister out of there was her top priority.

Ignoring the pounding pain in her brain, Sam steered Tracy

downstairs and out the front door. "Call it in," she said, breathing through the pain.

Tracy, who seemed frozen, fumbled with her phone and finally succeeded in calling 911. "What the fuck, Sam?" she asked when she ended the call. "Who would do that to you?"

"God only knows."

"How'd they get in?"

"The alarm wasn't on, so it wouldn't have been all that difficult." She couldn't believe Nick had failed to set the alarm when he left. That wasn't like him. If anyone were going to forget, it would usually be her. Scotty must've had him seriously distracted to miss that step. Thinking of how upset he'd be when he heard about what'd happened made her sad. He would blame himself, of course.

The idea of someone breaking into her house and shredding her clothes... Who could possibly hate her that much? A lot of people, she conceded, recalling the huge pile of folders containing all her case files. So many people had reason to hate her. How would they ever narrow it down to one suspect?

Dots danced before her eyes, returning her attention to the headache from hell. She must've stumbled because Tracy grabbed her arm.

"Sit," she said, guiding Sam to the curb as the scream of sirens filled the early evening air.

Sam dropped her pounding head into her hands, trying not to think of her glorious wedding gown reduced to shreds. Tears burned her eyes, but she blinked them back. She wouldn't allow her colleagues to find her bawling on the curb when they arrived. Right now she needed to be a cop. She could be a devastated recent bride later.

NICK SAT across from Scotty at one of his favorite Italian restaurants in Boston's North End. The boy's face was slightly sunburned from the afternoon in Fenway Park's Green Monster seats, his mouth was red from spaghetti sauce and his brown eyes still danced with excitement. Nick had enjoyed every minute of watching Scotty's awe at flying for the first time and visiting Fenway Park—also for the first time. It had been quite a day for both of them.

"What was your favorite part of today?" Nick asked as he nursed a beer while Scotty devoured his second plate of spaghetti.

Scotty rolled his eyes. "Duh."

Amused, Nick said, "Don't talk with your mouth full."

Scotty swallowed the huge mouthful of spaghetti and wiped his face, succeeding in better smearing the sauce on his face.

Nick leaned over and finished the job.

"Thanks," Scotty said with a chagrinned smile. "Meeting Big Papi was the best part of the day. You still haven't told me how you made that happen."

"I'm friends with a senator from Massachusetts. He went to college with one of the team owners, and they helped me arrange it."

"Seriously, I almost passed out when I realized we were going to meet him."

Nick laughed. "I had to remind you to breathe, remember?"

"It was the coolest thing *ever*. I'll never forget it."

"Neither will I." Nick had no doubt he'd always remember the awestruck expression on Scotty's face when David Ortiz strolled toward them, and Scotty got that he was coming to talk to them. What was even more priceless was the worshipful expression he'd directed at Nick when he realized his friend had arranged the meeting in advance.

"So, listen," Nick said. "There's something I want to talk to you about." He'd asked for a private corner in the restaurant so they wouldn't be overheard.

Scotty put down his fork, and his entire demeanor changed. "Did I do something wrong?"

"No, buddy. Of course not. It's nothing bad."

"Oh, good," Scotty said, visibly relieved. "I would hate it if you didn't want to be friends with me anymore."

"Scotty…" Nick's heart broke at the fear he heard in Scotty's voice. "That's not going to happen." Nick reached out to put his hand on top of Scotty's. "There is nothing you could ever do that would make me—or Sam—not want to be your friends anymore. Nothing."

He looked up at Nick with big eyes. "Really?"

"Really. That's kind of what I wanted to talk to you about." *Here goes nothing,* Nick thought, suddenly as nervous as he'd ever been in his life.

"If it's nothing bad, why do you look so freaked out?"

Nick laughed, which helped to defray the nerves a bit. "Because it's not every day I ask a boy who has become my very best friend if he'd like to come and live with me and my wife."

Scotty's mouth fell open, and his eyes got even wider. "You... you guys want me to *live* with you? Like every day?"

Nick was besieged by a thousand different emotions that settled into a lump in his throat. Clearing it away, he nodded. "Sam and I love you very much. We'd like to make you part of our family—officially. Not just occasional weekend visits."

Scotty took a full minute to process that. "So you want to like adopt me?"

"If you'll have us."

"And she wants me, too?"

"Very much so. We talked about whether we should ask you together, but we decided I should talk to you about it when it was just us guys. But she wants you to know how much she loves you and wants you in her life—not once in a while but all the time."

"Wow," Scotty said, seeming blown away. "It's a lot to think about."

"I know it is, and you should take your time and think it over. We'd give you everything we have—and I don't mean money, but our time and attention and the love of a big, extended family."

Scotty's eyes filled. "That's nice of you guys, but I wonder..."

"What?"

"Why me?"

"Aww, buddy, we love you. But that's not the only reason."

Nick propped his chin on his fist and studied the handsome boy. "Have I ever told you about when I was a kid?"

"You said you grew up in Massachusetts, but that's it."

"I was going to tell you about it tomorrow when I take you to Lowell to see the house where I lived, but I suppose I can tell you now." Nick took a deep breath and made an effort to keep his emotions in check. Revisiting his childhood was something he did as infrequently as possible. "My parents were still in high school when they had me, so my father's mother ended up raising me. She was a nice enough lady, but she'd already raised her family, so she wasn't thrilled with the idea of having another child to take care of."

"That must've been hard for you."

Nick nodded in agreement. "I was about ten when I realized she didn't want me around. I was kind of oblivious before that. So I asked if I could go live with my dad."

"He seems really nice."

"He is—now—but then he was in his twenties, enjoying the single life. He didn't want to be weighed down with a kid. The one thing he did for me—and it was a big thing at the time—was send the money I needed to play hockey. That was my favorite thing to do, and he paid for it."

"How about your mom?"

"She's another story—I barely saw her when I was growing up." Nick thought of her showing up uninvited at their wedding and how Sam had sent her away before she could ruin the day for him. Thinking of Sam sticking up for him like that made him miss her like he hadn't seen her in a week rather than the few hours they'd been apart. "My mother never wanted me and didn't do much to try and hide that. Everything changed for me when I got into Harvard on a scholarship and met John O'Connor. His father, Senator O'Connor, who you've met, was the first one to make me believe I could make something of my life."

Scotty hung on his every word.

"Are you surprised to hear this?"

"Sort of. I didn't know you'd been through all that."

"I wanted you to know I wasn't born a senator. I had to work hard—for a lot of years—and then my best friend died suddenly and tragically, creating an opening in the Senate that I was asked to fill. I've never run for office before, and who knows what'll happen between now and November? I could end up a regular guy again if the people of Virginia don't like the job I'm doing."

"That won't happen," Scotty said confidently. "You have a sixty-five point lead over the Republican dude."

Astounded, Nick stared at him. "How do you know that?"

"I read the paper."

Nick tossed his head back and laughed. "You are too much."

"So you want to do for me what Senator O'Connor did for you. Is that right?"

"Yes," Nick said softly, appreciating that Scotty got the connection. "I want that very much. I want you to be able to play Little League or hockey or whatever else appeals to you. I want you to have your own room and all the posters on your wall that you can fit. Hell, you can even put them on the ceiling if you want to."

Scotty smiled at the reminder of their first meeting when Nick had been annoyed the boy wasn't allowed to hang posters on his wall in the state home. "I want you to know… I appreciate you and Sam want me to come live with you."

A pang of fear struck Nick just below his heart. "Why do I hear a 'but' in there?"

"Would we still be friends if I don't come live with you?"

"Of course we would. Don't ever worry about that. You're stuck with me."

"Oh good. That's good."

"Talk to me," Nick said even though he wasn't sure he wanted to hear what was on Scotty's mind. "There's nothing you can't say to me."

"It's just, you know, I've gotten used to where I live now. I have a family there. I know it's not a regular family, but the other kids and Mrs. Littlefield and all the people who work there are like my family, and they need me. I've been there a long time. I barely remember living with my mom and grandpa."

Nick hadn't entertained the possibility that Scotty might say no to their offer, that he'd be reluctant to leave the only home he'd ever known, which, in hindsight Nick should've considered. "I can understand how leaving there would be scary, but Sam and I would do everything we could to make it as smooth as possible for you. And of course we would take you to Richmond to visit anytime you wanted."

"It's a really nice offer," Scotty said softly.

Nick's cell phone rang, but since he didn't recognize the number in the 202 area code, he let the call go to voice mail. "Let's make a deal, okay?" he said to Scotty.

The boy nodded.

"Think about it. You don't have to decide anything right now, okay?"

"Okay," Scotty said, looking relieved.

"I promise no matter what you decide, Sam and I will always be your friends, and we'll always be there for you." He squeezed Scotty's hand. "I promise."

Scotty surprised Nick when he got up, came around the table and hugged him. "You're the best friend I've ever had."

Tears filled Nick's eyes as he returned the embrace. "Back atcha, buddy." He released the boy and looked up at him. "What do you say we get to our hotel? I hear there's a pool."

"Awesome!"

Nick's phone rang again, and he saw the call was from the same number. Just in case it was Sam borrowing someone's phone, he took it. "Nick Cappuano."

"This is Darren Tabor."

Nick was immediately sorry he'd taken the call. "Not now, Darren. I'm busy."

"What's wrong with Sam? No one will tell me."

Nick sat up straight. They'd tried to call her as they left Fenway, but she hadn't picked up. Since she was at work, he hadn't thought anything of it. "What do you mean?"

"You haven't heard? They took her out of HQ on a stretcher. I haven't heard what was wrong with her, but a 911 call from your house came over the scanner. What's going on? Senator? Are you there?"

Nick hung up on Darren and tried Sam's phone again. When he got her voice mail, he also tried Freddie, Tracy, Angela and Christina, but no one answered.

As his heart jackhammered in his chest, Nick pocketed his phone, tossed some bills on the table, grabbed Scotty's hand and made for the door. "Sorry, buddy, but we've got to go home."

CHAPTER TWENTY-SIX

$\mathcal{W}$hile Jeannie had been disappointed to miss the trip to Cincinnati, the day with Michael had done them a lot of good. They'd talked and laughed and made love again before taking a long nap. While there was still an undercurrent of strain between them, she could feel them edging toward a new version of normal.

She was slowly realizing her attacker had changed her life forever, and there would be no going back to the way things had been before. They could only go forward and define a new future as they went. It was a relief, however, to know they'd be going forward together. A lot of guys wouldn't have stuck around after what happened to her. She was grateful her guy was stronger than that. Turning onto her side in bed, she studied Michael's face as he slept. The poor guy had worried himself sick over her in the last few weeks and was no doubt exhausted.

Jeannie eased out of bed so she wouldn't disturb him and headed for the shower. Afterward, she pulled on yoga pants and a long-sleeved T-shirt. Grabbing the Fitzgerald case files, she went downstairs to find her cell phone. Will had texted a short time ago that he had landed and was anxious to speak with her. Rather than reply by text, she called her partner.

"Hey," he said when he answered.

"Where are you?"

"Just leaving Reagan on the Metro. Do you mind if I come by on the way home?"

"Sure, no problem. See you in a few." Jeannie went to turn on the porch light for him. In the past, she might've propped open the door, but now she kept it locked.

While she waited for Will, she looked up the phone number for retired medical examiner Dr. Norman Morganthau and placed a call to him. He answered on the third ring.

"Dr. Morganthau, this is Detective Jeannie McBride with the MPD. I wondered if you might have a minute to answer a couple of questions about an old case?"

"You're the one who was kidnapped."

Jeannie closed her eyes. Would that word always be attached to her name now? "Yes, sir."

"How are you doing, honey?" he asked, his voice softening.

His compassion brought tears to her eyes. "Good days. Bad days. But overall, I'm better. Thank you very much for asking."

"The entire brotherhood—and sisterhood—stands behind one of its own in a time of need. I hope you've felt the support of your colleagues."

"Very much so."

"Glad to hear it. Now what can I do for you today?"

Jeannie explained about reopening the Tyler Fitzgerald case.

"Ahhh," Morganthau said with a deep sigh. "That was a tough one."

"So I'm hearing from everyone we've talked to."

"How can I help?"

"I wondered if you might be able to share any impressions from that time. If you tell me what you remember, I might hear something I don't already know."

"That's a wise strategy, young lady. You have good instincts."

Jeannie smiled and wished she'd gone to see the old man in person rather than calling him. "Thank you, sir."

"Let's see," he said. "I got the call that a body had been found in the landfill late on a Thursday night."

"Did you have jurisdictional issues because he was found in Maryland?"

"Since the body was a child, and we'd been overseeing the search for Tyler Fitzgerald, Maryland State Police called us in as a courtesy. It was obvious to them it was him based on the clothing and other distinguishing characteristics."

"I have your autopsy report in the file, but if you could tell me in your own words—"

"You might hear something new."

"That's right," Jeannie said, amused by him.

"Tyler had been manually strangled. Unfortunately, after a few days in the landfill we were unable to get usable prints off his neck. The only other trauma to the body was from exposure to the elements." He paused and cleared his throat. "That one stayed with me. I have children of my own, grandchildren. It bothered me we were never able to get the bastard who killed him. Pardon my language."

"No pardon necessary. I happen to agree with you. Was there any talk of Tyler's brothers as suspects?"

"Not that I ever heard. That doesn't mean they weren't considered. If they were, I wasn't privy to the conversations."

"Talk to me about Skip Holland."

"What about him?"

"I'm interested in your impressions of him and his handling of the case."

"He was a good cop. Thorough. We always worked well together."

"Was that true during the Fitzgerald case, too?" The long pause that followed her question set Jeannie's nerves on edge. If she uncovered something untoward about Sam's sainted father, how would she ever tell Sam that? "Dr. Morganthau?"

"I have nothing but the utmost respect for Skip Holland."

"But?"

"He was going through a rough patch around the time of the Fitzgerald case." Jeannie wanted to put her head down and moan. While part of her wanted to hear what he had to say, the part that considered Skip's daughter a close friend wished she'd never made this call.

"Rough in what way?"

"This is between us, right?"

"Are you aware his daughter is now our lieutenant?"

"I am."

"I'll have to brief her at some point on what we've uncovered."

The doctor released another rattling sigh. "I find myself between a rock and a hard place."

"In what way?"

"Do I share things my friend told me in confidence if they could help to break an old case, or do I keep my mouth shut the way I have for years?"

"Doctor Morganthau, if you know something that could help us find Tyler's killer—"

"I don't know anything about who killed that boy. I never would've sat on information like that. What I do know is Skip was going through a tough time around then, and that's all I'm going to say. You can leave it up to his daughter to decide whether or not she wishes to pursue it further with him."

"Thank you very much for your time."

"I'm sorry I couldn't give you more."

"I understand." Jeannie put down the phone and leaned her head back against the sofa, processing what she'd learned. The ringing doorbell interrupted her thoughts. She got up to let Will in.

"Hey," he said.

"Come in."

He seemed a bit uncertain as he took a seat on the sofa. "Are you okay?"

Jeannie sat next to him and curled her legs up under her. "I'm good. I'm sorry I couldn't go today."

"That's okay."

"Were you nervous about interviewing Cameron on your own?"

"Hell, yes, I was nervous." Will recapped the conversation with Cameron.

"Sounds like you covered all the bases. What're your impressions?"

"I think he had something to do with it."

"Now all we have to do is prove it."

"I'd love to get him on a polygraph."

"We can check tomorrow with the AUSA to see if we have enough to make that happen," Jeannie said.

"What'll we tell Sam?"

Jeannie brought him up to speed on what had happened to Sam earlier in the day as well as the conversation with Morganthau.

"We need to talk to her before we go to the U.S. Attorney."

"Agreed. I'll do that as soon as she feels up to working again."

"This whole thing is freaking me out," Will said. "We all know how close she is to her dad. What if he bungled this case and we have to be the ones to tell her?"

"Let's hope it doesn't come to that."

THE SECOND THEIR flight touched down at Reagan National Airport, Nick powered up his phone and tried to reach Sam again. Her voice mail picked up, which made Nick want to scream with frustration. With Scotty watching his every move, Nick was forced to keep himself in check so he wouldn't scare the boy.

He called Christina next. "Senator," she said, sounding breathless when she answered. "I'm so sorry I missed your earlier calls. I was giving Alex a bath, and then I fell asleep with him."

"Have you heard anything about something happening to Sam at work today?"

"No, I haven't. I talked to Tommy a couple of hours ago, but he didn't mention it."

"I hate to ask you this, but would you call him and see what you can find out? Her phone is going straight to voice mail." Sam would be furious at him for using Christina and Gonzo to gain information about her, but he needed to know what the hell was going on.

"Sure, hold on. I'll call him."

While she clicked over to the other line, Nick glanced at Scotty who was watching him with big eyes.

"Is Sam okay?"

"I'm sure she's fine. There must be a good reason why she hasn't been answering her phone." At least there had better be a good reason, or he was going to raise holy hell with her.

Christina clicked back on. "Ahhh, he said she told everyone not to call you because she didn't want to ruin Scotty's big day. Apparently, she got sick at work, but she's okay. Gonzo said there's something going on at your house. He didn't have the details, but he's on his way over there now."

Nick thanked her for the info and ended the call, his mind racing with worries.

As the captain announced a delay in reaching their gate because the other flight hadn't yet departed, Nick wondered if he was having a heart attack. His chest was tight, and he couldn't seem to breathe.

"It's okay," Scotty said, patting his arm. "If something was really wrong, she would've called you."

Nick blew out a deep breath. "You're right. I know. I'm sure she didn't want to mess with our day in Boston, but she knows I hate when she keeps stuff from me."

"She did it for a good reason today."

Forcing himself to relax since he had no choice, he eyed Scotty. "If you come to live with us, I'll need you to be on my side during all disagreements. You were my friend first."

Scotty laughed, which Nick had hoped he would. "I don't play favorites."

"Now you tell me," Nick grumbled.

"I want you to know… It's cool you and Sam like me so much you want to adopt me. I'm afraid I didn't say it right before."

"No, you did. We're asking you to change your whole life, and it's only natural you'd want some time to think about it."

"Will you tell Sam I really appreciate that you asked me?"

"I will, buddy."

The plane lurched forward, delivering them to the gate. Since they were in the front of the plane, they were the first ones off. Two Capitol Police officers met them.

"Senator? I'm Officer Clarkson. This is Officer Griffin. We're under orders to escort you home."

Stunned, Nick stared at them. "Why?"

"We've received a credible threat against you and Lieutenant Holland. The two of you, along with your immediate families, have been placed under protection."

"What kind of threat?"

Officer Clarkson glanced at Scotty and then at Nick. "I'd rather not get into the details right now. If you can please come with us, we'll get you home."

Nick glanced down to find Scotty giving him that wide-eyed look again. "It's okay, buddy," he said. "Whatever it is, I'm sure Sam is taking care of it." At least he hoped that was true. Either way, she had some serious explaining to do.

LINDSEY FELT like a teenager waiting for her first boyfriend to come over. She'd changed her clothes three times so far, and still wasn't entirely thrilled with the outfit she'd settled on. The scoop-neck top showed too much skin and the jeans she'd chosen were extra snug. She didn't want him to think she was easy.

"Oh my God," she said as she blew out half the candles she'd lit earlier, fearing she was giving him the wrong idea. "Will you stop it already?"

By the time the doorbell rang ten minutes later, she was on the verge of a complete meltdown. Was she really about to officially start a relationship with a recovering alcoholic after the way she'd grown up? Was she out of her freaking mind? Since it was too late to back out now, she gritted her teeth and opened the door, prepared to get rid of him as quickly as she could without being rude.

All thoughts of getting rid of him dissolved when she saw the dozen pale pink roses he'd brought for her. "Oh," she said as the wind left her sails in one big exhale.

"I know," he said with an adorably boyish grin. "Totally cliché, but I wanted to bring you something."

"They're beautiful," she said, finally daring to make eye contact with him. Oh, boy… She led him into the kitchen where she found a vase for the flowers. Grateful to have something to do with her shaky hands, she trimmed the stems and arranged them. "Thank you. I love the color."

He tucked a strand of hair behind her ear and traced a finger lightly over her cheek. "It reminded me of you. The exact shade of your skin when you blush."

Lindsey swallowed hard as her heart beat frantically.

"Come here," he said, his voice gruff.

"I'm here."

"Closer."

"I, um, Terry…"

"I won't bite. At least not yet."

Her eyes darted up to find his dancing with amusement. He held out a hand to her. Lindsey studied that hand for a long, charged moment, knowing if she put her hand in his, the attraction zinging between them would become something more. Something significant.

"Trust me, Lindsey. I promise I won't let you down."

Everything in her was drawn to him. Like a magnet that couldn't resist the pull, her hand landed in his, and she let him bring her into his embrace. He held her close, but not too close.

Her mind had gone blank, and her arms hung awkwardly by her side.

He ran his hands down her arms, urging her to put them around him. "There," he said. "That's better."

Lindsey rested her face against his chest and closed her eyes to listen to the rapid beat of his heart. They stood there like that for a long time. Lindsey had no idea how long. All she knew was it felt good to be held by him. It felt right.

When he started to pull back from her, she resisted, which made him laugh.

She looked up at him, and their eyes met in a heated moment of awareness that sent desire rippling through her.

His gaze shifted to her lips. "Is it okay if I—"

Lindsey slipped a hand around his neck and pulled him to her for a kiss that went from zero to ninety in about two seconds flat. In the single most explosive moment of her life, he took her mouth like a man who'd been starving and she was the only thing that could sate his hunger.

His tongue teased and enticed. One of his hands was buried in her hair while the other slid down her back to better align their bodies.

Lindsey had never before experienced passion like this and had to pull herself out of the moment to remember how a few short minutes ago she'd been thinking of ways to get rid of him. Breathing hard, she broke the kiss and turned her face away.

He took advantage of the opportunity to explore her neck, which made the rest of her throb with need. "Terry..."

"What?" he whispered, his breath hot against her sensitive skin.

"We, I..."

"Say the word if you want me to stop."

She was under some sort of hypnosis. That was the only possible explanation for why she didn't stop him as his lips laid a trail from her neck to her throat. His hands shifted from her hips to her breasts. He cupped them and ran his thumbs over the tight buds of her nipples, sending a shudder all the way through her.

And then his mouth was devouring hers again. His hands were under her top and pushing up her bra to free her breasts.

The word *stop* hovered on her lips, but somehow she never said it. As he pinched her nipples between his fingers and caressed her lips with bold strokes of his tongue, the last thing in the world she wanted was for this feeling to stop.

"Lindsey," he gasped, his face warm against hers. "Tell me to stop or find us a bed." He maneuvered them so her back was against the counter and pushed his erection against her.

She'd never wanted a man the way she wanted him, and even as alarms went off in her mind that it was too much too soon, she took his hand and led him upstairs to her bedroom.

Once there, he held her from behind, his erection nestled in the cleft of her ass. He reached for the hem of her top and drew it up and over her head. Unclipping her bra, he removed it too, and then proceeded to drive her mad with his hands on her breasts and his lips on her neck. When she tried to turn to face him, he stopped her and made her moan with frustration.

"Easy, baby. Just feel."

She'd begun to wonder how much longer her legs would support her weight when his hand traveled to the button of her jeans. He had the button open and the zipper down so fast she had no time to prepare before his hand was inside her panties, exploring the slick heat between her legs.

She was so primed, so ready, it took only a few strokes of his fingers over her clit to send her flying into orgasm so intense that her legs finally buckled beneath her.

His arms tightened around her, keeping her standing as he continued to stroke her sensitive skin. "Again," he whispered.

"I can't."

"Yes, you can." He set out to prove her wrong with relentless determination, and before long she was climbing again.

The second explosion was even greater than the first, rocking through her with such force that she cried out from the shock of it. Still in a daze, she was barely aware of him removing her jeans and panties and lowering her to the bed. Focused on catching her breath, she managed to keep her eyes open as he unbuttoned the dress shirt he'd worn to work and dropped it on the floor. His undershirt, pants and boxers followed before he stretched out on the bed next to her.

"Hey," he said, resting a hand on her belly. "Fancy meeting you here."

Lindsey laughed, but as she let her eyes travel over his chest and belly and below, her mouth went dry. Oh, my.

"You sure about this?" he asked.

"I wasn't." She forced her gaze up to meet his and found him watching her face intently. "But somewhere between the kitchen and the second orgasm I stopped worrying about all the reasons this is a bad idea and started focusing on all the reasons it's a good idea."

Smiling, he propped himself up on one elbow and bent to kiss her softly, gently. "I think it's the best idea we've ever had."

"You do, huh?"

He nodded as he started all over again with drugging kisses and teasing caresses that soon had her primed and ready for more.

"Terry," she gasped. "Please."

"What do you want?" he asked in a playful tone.

"You know."

"Tell me."

She found his impressive erection and stroked the length of him once and then again, drawing a groan from him. "I want you. Now."

"Hold that thought." He got up and found his pants on the floor, withdrew his wallet and found a strip of three condoms. Ripping off one, he threw the other two on the bedside table.

"You came prepared."

"I've been carrying them since the day after I met you."

For some reason, she was ridiculously flattered by that. "Such confidence," she teased.

He brought her to the edge of the bed and settled between her legs. "It was more hope than confidence." Bending over her, he kissed her again. "I've been anything but confident where you were concerned."

Lindsey smoothed her hands over his back. "I didn't mean to drive you crazy."

"Yes, you did," he said, chuckling as he entered her.

She closed her eyes and floated on a cloud of sensation.

"Look at me."

Opening her eyes, she found him watching her.

"Good?" he asked.

"Soooo good."

"I knew it would be."

Lindsey reached up to run her fingers through his hair. "I think I knew too, which is why I was so freaked out."

"No need to be freaked out. We'll take it slow."

In light of what they were currently doing, the statement made her laugh. "Not too slow I hope," she said, lifting her hips to meet his thrusts. That seemed to make him a little crazy, and he picked up the pace.

Lindsey held on for the ride as he drove them both to an explosive finish.

CHAPTER TWENTY-SEVEN

*E*mergency vehicles lined Ninth Street as cops secured Sam's home and scoured for evidence. Normally, she'd be in the thick of the investigation, but the blinding headache wouldn't allow her to do anything other than sit on the curb and try not to vomit again.

"Looks like they jimmied a window in the back of the house to get in," Captain Malone reported. Only about twenty minutes had passed since Tracy and Sam discovered the carnage in her closet, but it felt like a year to Sam. The lights, the sirens, the people and the activity all around her made her want to weep from the agonizing pain.

"Let me take you to Dad's so you can lie down," Tracy said.

"I should wait. They might need to talk to me." The idea of her home, her private sanctuary, invaded by a stranger and now crawling with cops was enough to make her sick on its own, even without the headache.

"We'll be fine, Sam," Malone said. "Your sister is right. You need to be in bed."

Sam wanted to argue with them, but she couldn't seem to find the words. Between the pain and the medication they'd given her in the hospital, she was totally out of it.

Tracy helped her stand, guided her to their father's house

and up the stairs to the bedroom that had been Sam's from the time of her father's shooting until the recent move up the street.

Sam drifted in and out, grateful for the quiet and the darkened room. Somewhere in the back of her mind it occurred to her she should probably call Nick. But then she remembered he was in Boston with Scotty and decided she'd tell him when he got home. That would be soon enough.

WHEN NICK SAW the emergency vehicles lining Ninth Street, he nearly stopped breathing. "Oh my God." He turned to Scotty. "Wait here. I'll be back for you."

"But Nick—"

"Wait." To one of the Capitol Police officers, Nick said, "Will you stay here with him?"

"Of course, Senator. Not a problem."

Nick ran down the street and grabbed the first cop he encountered, a patrolman he didn't recognize. "What's going on?"

"Ah, Senator, let me get the captain for you." The young man gestured to Malone and pointed to Nick.

Captain Malone walked over to them.

"Where's Sam?" Nick asked. "What's happened?"

"She's at her father's. Someone broke into your house and from what we can tell they had one thing in mind—shredding every ounce of clothing she owns, including her wedding gown."

Nick tried to process it. "But the house is alarmed. How did someone get in?"

"Apparently, the alarm wasn't set."

"That's not possible. I set it myself." He ran through the morning in his mind, thinking of Scotty's excitement and nonstop chatter as they'd prepared to leave. Of course he'd set the alarm. He'd never forget something so important.

"All I can tell you is when the lieutenant and her sister arrived home earlier, the alarm wasn't on."

Nick suddenly felt sick. "I need to see Sam." He strode

purposefully down the street and up the ramp to Skip and Celia's place.

Tracy was coming down the stairs as he came in. "What're you doing here?" she asked, clearly surprised to see him.

"What's wrong with Sam?"

"Severe migraine that came on out of nowhere at work earlier. How did you hear?"

"I got a call from a reporter that Sam had been taken to the hospital and something was wrong at the house, so we came home early."

"I'm sorry you had to find out that way. She asked us all not to call you because she didn't want to ruin Scotty's day."

"That's what I figured. I need a favor." He explained about leaving Scotty with the police officer.

"I'll go get him."

"Thanks, Tracy." Nick ran upstairs to his wife. In the doorway to the room where so many significant moments had transpired between them, he took a moment to drink in the sight of her. Watching the rise and fall of her chest filled him with relief. Despite the workings of his rather active imagination, the thing he most feared hadn't happened. She was fine, and as a result, so was he.

Mindful of the pain she must be in, he moved carefully to stretch out next to her, linking his hand with hers. After three of the longest hours of his life, he was finally able to breathe normally again.

"Who called you?" she murmured.

"Shh. Don't talk. Just rest."

"Are you mad?"

"No." He brought her hand to his lips. Normally, he'd be furious she hadn't called him, but he knew she'd been making a sincere effort to be more forthcoming with him. Today she'd held back for Scotty's sake, so he couldn't fault her for that.

"Where's Scotty?"

"With Tracy."

"We should get him out of here."

"Everything's fine. Don't worry."

"Everything's not fine," she said, her voice barely a whisper. "Someone was in the house."

"Your people are all over it. They'll figure out what's going on."

"People keep dying. Tied to me somehow. What did I do?"

He hated the pain and bewilderment he heard in her voice. "Nothing, babe. You didn't do anything."

A tear slipped from her closed eye and ran down her cheek. "They ruined my beautiful wedding dress."

Nick brushed away the tear. "I'll buy you a new one."

"Won't be the same."

"They can ruin everything we have, but they can't touch us unless we let them."

"Hurts." He knew she meant more than the migraine.

"I know."

"Need you."

"I'm here, baby. I'm right here."

She turned gingerly onto her side and brought their joined hands to her chest. "I stink like puke."

Smiling, he pressed his lips to her forehead. "No, you don't. Where does it hurt?"

She pointed to her temple.

Nick replaced her finger with two of his, massaging the area as gently as he could. "Is that good?"

"Yeah. Don't stop."

"I won't." He massaged her temple for a long time, until he felt her drift off to sleep. As he held her, he thought of what she'd told him and the staggering implications. People were dying, and somehow it was all linked to her? What crazy person from her past had come back to torment her? How would they ever narrow down the suspects? And most important of all, how would he keep her safe until they did?

NICK WAITED until he was sure she was asleep before he got up to check on Scotty. He had to be concerned about what was going on with Sam, especially since they'd arrived home to emergency vehicles all over the street. Nick went downstairs where Scotty was enjoying a big bowl of ice cream under Tracy's watchful eye.

He brightened when he saw Nick. "Is Sam okay?"

"She will be." Nick ruffled the boy's hair. "She had a bad headache."

"A migraine, right?"

"You know about migraines?"

"Uh huh. Mrs. Littlefield gets them sometimes. She has special pills she has to take when she feels them coming on. Can we get some for Sam? I can find out what it is."

"That'd be helpful."

Scotty shoveled in another scoop of ice cream. "I'll ask her."

"How's your dad?" Nick asked Tracy.

"Much better today. Celia said they might let him come home in a couple of days. She's on her way home now."

"Did you tell her we've invaded her house?"

"Yes, and of course she's fine with it."

Nick turned a kitchen chair and straddled it to face Scotty. "Buddy, there's some weird stuff going on with Sam's work—"

"That's why the police are here."

He said it so matter-of-factly that Nick was taken aback. "Yes, that's why. Until we know what we're dealing with, we're going to have some extra police around. If Sam wasn't so sick, I'd run you home tonight to get you out of here, but I can't leave her."

"I don't want you to leave her. I'm fine with being here with you guys. Don't worry about me."

"Sam is worried about you, and so am I. We'd never want to put you in any kind of danger."

"I know that. So what happened at your house?"

Nick glanced at Tracy, who nodded. He was past the age of sugarcoating the truth. "Someone broke in and cut up Sam's clothes."

Scotty's mouth fell open and his spoon froze midscoop. "Why would they do that?"

"We don't know, but the other detectives are looking into it. I have no doubt they'll find the person who did it."

"They haven't found the person who shot Skip," Scotty reminded him.

"Don't let Sam hear you say that. She's been trying to solve that case since the day it happened."

"She'll solve it." Scotty choked back a yawn. "I know she will."

"Time for you to hit the hay," Nick said.

"Already?"

"You've had a long day."

"The best day ever. Until Sam got sick and everything."

Nick walked Scotty upstairs, made sure he brushed his teeth and tucked him into one of the spare bedrooms. He'd considered sending the boy to Tracy's for the night, but decided against it, preferring to have him close by. When Nick looked in on him a few minutes later, he was already asleep. He checked on Sam before he went downstairs and then outside looking for information—but stayed right near Skip's front door.

Gonzo was consulting with Captain Malone on the sidewalk. Keeping one eye on the house where Sam and Scotty were sleeping, Nick went over to them. "What've you got?"

"Oh, Senator, I didn't see you there," Malone said, startled. He looked tired and furious. Sam was one of his, and he would take an attack on her personally.

"Any idea who could've done this?" Nick asked.

"I wish I had answers for you, but we believe this is a calculated campaign," Malone said. "Someone is exacting revenge on people who've done him or her wrong in the past. In the morning, we're going to start looking at connections between the various victims."

"How do you know this is revenge, and how is Sam involved?"

Malone and Gonzo exchanged glances.

"What aren't you telling me?"

"Show him," Malone said.

Gonzo produced a photocopy of a greeting card with a handwritten message.

Nick took it and, still facing Skip's house, he tipped the paper so he could use the streetlight. A stab of fear went through him as he read the chilling words. "Has Sam seen this?"

"Not yet," Gonzo said. "She got sick before I could show it to her."

"May I keep this?"

"Sure," Gonzo said.

Nick tucked the page into the back pocket of his jeans. "So this is why the Capitol Police met my flight." The two officers were standing in the street watching his every move.

"Yes," Malone said. "Until we know more about what we're dealing with, it might be a good idea to avoid large public gatherings. Stick close to home and your office."

"I'm in the middle of a campaign. How do you suggest I avoid public gatherings?"

"Hopefully, it won't take long to get to the bottom of this. When you look at the totality of the messages the two of you have received, it's clear to us you're being targeted."

"If someone's looking to exact revenge on Sam," Gonzo added, "you'd be a handy target."

"Fine, I'll tone down the campaign for a few days. But I'm far more interested in what's being done to protect Sam from this lunatic."

"We've ordered twenty-four-hour protection for her and every member of her immediate family."

"Does that include Skip in the hospital?"

"It does. We have two men positioned outside his room."

"Good, because if someone is trying to hurt Sam, they probably know he's a weak spot."

"Agreed," Malone said. "I know the threats against Sam have to be getting tiresome, Senator, but we're doing everything we can to get to the bottom of this situation and to figure out who is targeting you and Sam."

Nick had a lot of things he'd like to say about why his wife was constantly being threatened, but he knew Sam wouldn't want him to go there. "I'd appreciate being kept in the loop."

"Of course. It would help us if you could take a look through the house and let us know if anything else has been disturbed or if you notice anything missing."

"I'll take a quick look, but I don't want to be away from Sam any longer than I have to."

"We understand. We'll make it quick."

Nick glanced at Skip's. "Will one of you keep an eye on things here while I'm in there?"

"I will," Gonzo said. "Go on ahead."

Nick moved quickly through the home he shared with Sam, focusing on things of value that might've been stolen by an intruder. "I don't see anything else disturbed," Nick said to Malone, who had accompanied him.

In the room he'd had made into a closet for Sam's vast wardrobe and shoe collection, Nick was overwhelmed with sadness as he studied what remained of her gorgeous wedding gown. He made a mental note to contact their wedding planner, Shelby Faircloth, to see about having it replaced. It wouldn't be the same, of course, but he had to do something to make this right, especially since it was his fault it'd happened in the first place. He winced when he saw the wrecked remains of her prized Jimmy Choos and the new Manolos he'd bought her to wear the night they got engaged. He'd replace them as fast as he could.

"Senator?" Malone asked after Nick had stood in the doorway to the closet for several minutes.

Nick tore his eyes off the shredded silk and moved on to check every other room of the double-sized townhouse. "As far as missing items," he said as they went downstairs, "I can't say for sure, but it doesn't look like anything was touched except for Sam's clothes and shoes." An icy ball of dread settled in his gut as the implications registered—this was a calculated, *personal* attack on his wife.

"We'll find the person who did this, Senator," Malone said, his tone fierce and angry. "He or she has come after one of our own. We'll find them."

Nick wanted to quiz the captain on the plan of attack, but he was far more anxious to get back to Sam in case she woke up.

Tomorrow would be soon enough to get the details. Tonight he would watch over his family.

FREDDIE SPENT the night in his car outside the Lynch home. Even though he and his mother were in an odd place in their relationship at the moment, no way would he leave her unprotected in a place where murder had occurred earlier in the day—even when his partner's home had been broken into. He'd followed the radio traffic about the incident on Ninth Street all night, and had heard from Gonzo that Sam was sleeping through most of the drama.

While he was tired after multiple sleepless nights this week, he kept a watchful eye on the Lynch house, which is why he saw his mother step outside and gaze up at the stars. Freddie got out of his car and shut the door with a thwack so she'd know he was there.

In the moonlight, he saw her tip her head and her expression soften at the sight of him. "What're you doing here?"

"Keeping an eye on things. How's Mrs. Lynch?"

"Not so good." Juliette gathered her long hair into a ponytail that she secured with a tie as she sat on the porch swing. "The poor thing cried herself to sleep. She's got a long road ahead of her."

"I appreciate you coming."

"I was glad—and surprised—you called."

Freddie shrugged. "I figured you'd know someone who could help Mrs. Lynch."

"I hate having all this conflict between us."

"I do, too." Freddie sat next to her on the swing and gave it a gentle push. "It was like he died, wasn't it?"

"Your father?"

Freddie nodded.

"Yes."

"For years after he left, I tried to figure out what I'd done to drive him away."

"Oh, Freddie." She rested her head on his shoulder and

wrapped her hand around his. "It still breaks my heart to hear you say that." Her voice caught. "He loved you so much. From the first instant he ever saw you…"

They sat in the darkness, swinging and listening to the chorus of crickets and frogs.

"I'm told I owe you an apology," she said after a long period of contented silence.

"Who told you that?"

"Your father."

Freddie didn't want to be curious, but he couldn't help it.

"He told me I was wrong in the way I've acted toward Elin—and toward you since you've been with her."

"Is that so?"

She nodded. "He reminded me when we were first together, my father didn't approve of him and how difficult that was for us. I'd forgotten. It was such a long time ago, but I haven't forgotten how it felt to be torn between the two most important people in my life."

Flabbergasted by her revelation, Freddie had no idea what to say.

"I haven't given her a fair chance, and I've put you in a terrible spot. I'm sorry for that."

"You're freaking me out here. Have you been abducted by aliens or something?"

Juliette laughed. "I'm trying to practice what I preach by treating others the way I'd want to be treated. That extends to my precious son, as well. I've been unkind to someone you care for, and I'm ashamed of that."

"Aw, Mom, stop. You're killing me here."

"Do you forgive me?"

Freddie raised his arm and put it around her. "Yeah."

She snuggled into his embrace. "It's been just the two of us for such a long time. I was unprepared to share you with someone else."

"And my father helped you to see all this?"

"He did."

"Huh."

"After he came back, the first time we talked, he wanted to know everything I could think of about you. I wish you could've seen his face when I told him you were a police officer, and a Homicide detective, no less. He was proud. So, so proud."

Freddie felt the walls tumbling down around him. He was once again ten years old and desperate for his father's approval. "He really wants to see me?"

"Oh, Freddie, he wants that more than anything. He wants the chance to explain what happened and why."

"I don't want to know what happened twenty years ago. You told me about that. I want to know about the future. If I see him, if I let him back into my life, will the same thing happen again?"

"I wish I could tell you his troubles are behind him, and you can trust him to not let you down again, but I can't do that. He has an illness—a serious and often debilitating illness. Right now, it's under control. Will it still be in six months or a year? No one knows. It's a gamble—for both of us—to allow him back in. I've decided the risk is worth it. You have to decide that for yourself."

Freddie pushed the swing as he processed what she'd said. "I'd like to see him. No promises about anything beyond a single meeting."

"That's fair enough."

"I'm doing this for you."

"Don't do it for me, honey. Do it for you. If nothing else, maybe you'll get some closure."

"Maybe." Freddie looked up at the star-filled sky. "Remember that camping trip when Dad taught me all the constellations?"

"Sure I do."

"I wanted to sleep outside, but you were afraid I'd get eaten alive by mosquitos. He talked you into letting us sleep out there." Freddie studied the stars, remembering the long-ago night. "I think about that every time I look up at the stars."

"You should tell him. It would mean a lot to him to hear that."

"Maybe I will."

She patted his leg. "You ought to go home and get some sleep."

"I'm not going anywhere as long as you're here. Someone was killed here today, and the person who did it is still out there."

"Then come inside and stretch out on the sofa. No reason you can't be comfortable while you stand watch over your mama."

Freddie let her take his hand and lead him into the house.

CHAPTER TWENTY-EIGHT

*S*am opened her eyes slowly, anticipating the blast of pain that had ruined her day yesterday, but the only pain that registered was in her heart as she remembered the shredded remains of her wedding gown.

She found Nick standing by the window, wearing only a pair of well-worn jeans. Hands in pockets, he stared intently through the glass.

"Hey," she said.

Turning to her, he smiled but his eyes were troubled. "Oh, you're awake."

Sam focused on the ridiculously sexy stubble on his usually smooth jaw. He hadn't shaved once on their honeymoon, and she'd discovered she loved him a little scruffy. "What time is it?"

"Just after six."

She noticed he also seemed tired and haggard, a look she'd never seen on him before.

"Did you sleep?"

"Some."

"What's wrong?"

He sat on the bed next to her and reached for her hand. "How do you feel?"

"I asked first."

Shaking his head, he looked down at their joined hands. "I've been over it and over it in my mind and for the life of me, I can't remember setting the alarm yesterday morning. Scotty was all excited, he was talking a mile a minute—"

Sam reached up to rest a finger over his lips. "It's not your fault. How often do I leave without giving a thought to the alarm?"

"But you were going to be there alone last night. What if they'd still been in the house when you got home? What if—"

"Nick…come here." She held out her arms to him and wrapped them around him. When he dropped his head to her chest, she ran her fingers through his hair.

"If anything had happened to you… I don't know what I'd do, Samantha. After all we've had together, how would I ever live without you?"

"Stop." She framed his face and forced him to look at her. "I'm right here, and I'm fine. I'm also a little relieved to find out that contrary to past evidence, you are indeed like the rest of us."

"What's that supposed to mean?"

"You *forgot* something. You *never* forget things. It's rather annoying to live with. This proves you're as human as the rest of us."

"What a thing to forget, something that could've gotten my wife killed."

Sam pressed a kiss to his pouting lips. "Get over it. I know it's a terrible shock to discover you aren't perfect, but you'll be glad to know you're still perfect for me."

That earned her a small, reluctant smile. He leaned his forehead against hers. "We have stuff we need to talk about."

"First, I want to hear about Boston."

Nick stretched out next to her but kept a firm grip on her hand. "It was fantastic. He was so cute and appreciative."

"What did he think of meeting Big Papi?"

"Just what you'd imagine. For a minute there, I thought he might pass out from the shock."

"You came home early so you didn't get to take him to Lowell."

"No, but I told him about it."

"Did you ask him about coming to live with us?"

Nick nodded.

"And?"

"And, I think he said no."

Sam stared at him, incredulous. "Really?"

"Yep." Nick relayed the highlights of the conversation with Scotty. "I loved that he got the connection between what Graham did for me and what I want to do for him without me having to draw him a map. But I guess he's too entrenched in Richmond to shake things up now."

"I never imagined he'd say no."

"Neither did I."

"You're disappointed."

"Hell, yes, I'm disappointed. I'd gotten my hopes up, you know?"

Sam rested her head on his chest and put her arm around him. "Yes, I know. Maybe when he has some time to think about it he'll change his mind."

"Maybe." He brought their joined hands to his lips. "We need to talk about what happened at our place yesterday."

"Do we have to?"

"We got another card."

That got her full attention. "What did this one say?"

Nick tugged the sheet of paper Gonzo had given him from his back pocket and handed it to her.

Sam skimmed it and gasped. "Oh my God, it's all related. When did we get this? I need to make a statement to the press, or someone else is going to die!" She sat up quickly and was hit with a head rush that stopped her short.

Nick's hands on her shoulders steadied her. "Babe, hang on. You've been really sick. You need to take it easy."

"I need to stop this person before they kill someone else." As she got up, her stomach let out a huge growl. In the boxes Celia had packed for her, Sam found an old pair of jeans, some underwear and a T-shirt. She'd have to make due with yesterday's bra. "Did you check the rest of the house last night?"

"Quickly. I didn't see anything else missing, but we'll have to check closer when we have more time."

In the shower, she washed her hair and was loading it with conditioner when Nick stepped in behind her. "Don't start any funny business," she warned. "I need to get to work."

He filled his hands with liquid soap and washed her back. "You think my business is funny?"

Despite the lingering effects of the migraine, the investigation that had taken a turn for the personal and the disappointment over Scotty's decision, he still made her smile.

She turned to face him. "You know what I like best about being married?"

He put his arms around her and brought her in close to him. "What's that?"

As his nearness made her tingle with desire, Sam wished she had more time. She went up on tiptoes and planted a lingering kiss on him. "I can do that anytime I want."

"You could do that anytime you wanted before we were married."

"But now no one else can ever do it but me. I like that."

"I like it, too."

She kissed him once more. "Gotta go, Senator." They dried off and threw on clothes.

Downstairs they found Scotty devouring bacon and eggs that Celia had made for him.

"You guys are up early," Sam said.

"Oh, Sam, honey, how're you feeling?" Celia asked, rushing over to hug her stepdaughter.

"Much better. How's Dad?"

"Also much better. He had a good night, and they're talking about letting him come home maybe tomorrow. We'll see how he's doing twenty-four hours from now."

Sam nearly swooned with relief. "That's such great news. Tell him I'll get over there as soon as I can today."

"I will. How about some breakfast?"

"I'd love some. I'm starving."

"We can fix that. Sit."

"You don't have to wait on me."

"Sit," Celia said, pointing to a chair. To Nick, she added, "You, too."

"Yes, ma'am," Nick said.

Scotty snickered at the exchange and then zeroed in on Sam. "Are you really okay? We were worried."

"I'm fine. I'm sorry you got cheated out of a night in the hotel."

"That's okay. As long as you're better that's all that matters."

"Thanks, pal. I heard you had a great time in Boston." Sam listened to his animated report as she ate as fast as she could without making herself sick again and downed two tall glasses of ice water. "I hate to say it, but I've got to get to work."

"But it's Saturday," Scotty said.

"Unfortunately, criminals never take a day off." She bent to press a kiss to the boy's forehead. "I'm glad you had a great time at the game."

"It was awesome. Thanks again for getting the tickets."

"My pleasure." She kissed Nick and thanked Celia for breakfast. "I'll see you boys when I get home. Try to stay out of trouble."

"Can we go to the farm to ride horses?" Scotty asked Nick.

He glanced at Sam, troubled.

"There's nothing you can do here today, so go on ahead. We've all got protection."

"My officer is *adorable*," Celia said, blushing.

"Easy, Mrs. Robinson," Sam said on her way to the front door. She was almost to a clean escape when her sisters rushed in, bearing shopping bags.

Angela hugged her. "I can't believe what that psycho did. Tracy and I were out early to get you some essentials. The slutty stuff was her idea. She reminded me you're still a newlywed."

Sam rested a hand on her sister's pregnant belly. "You need your rest more than I need new clothes."

"Don't be silly. An excuse to shop with Nick's credit card? I was all over that."

Sam should've guessed he'd had something to do with it.

"Thanks, guys." She hugged them both. "I appreciate it. I gotta get to it, but I'll see you later?"

"We'll be with Dad," Angela said.

"Are you sure you feel up to working today?" Tracy asked. "You were in rough shape yesterday."

"I don't have any choice. Either I show my face to the media or some other innocent person is going to die."

"God, your job sucks the big fat one," Angela said.

"Sometimes, it really does. Later." She was outside in the street when she realized her car was at HQ. "Goddamn it."

"Good morning, Lieutenant Holland. It's a pleasure to see you again."

Confronted by the officers who'd been assigned to her detail, she groaned. Officers Hernandez and St. James, the same two fresh-faced recruits who'd guarded her during the last investigation, were back for another tour.

"We meet again, Lieutenant," Hernandez, the cheekier of the two, said. Sam had suspected he was lusting after her the last time around.

"Great," Sam muttered. "Make yourselves useful and give me a ride to HQ, will you?"

"Yes, ma'am," they said in unison, snapping to. St. James held open the back door of their Patrol car for her while Hernandez rushed around to the driver's seat. They practically fell over themselves in their haste to do her bidding.

This was going to be a *long* day.

After Mrs. Lynch's sister arrived, Freddie saw his mother home and then went to his own place to shower and change. Elin had already left for work, which was a relief because he had so many thoughts cluttering up his brain at the moment he feared he'd make for lousy company.

He'd replayed the middle-of-the-night conversation with his mother a million times, and while he was anxious to tell Elin about his mother's change of heart, he was still trying to process it himself. And he'd agreed to see his father. That thought sent a wave of panic all the way through him. What would they say to each other after all these years? How could he risk letting his father back into his life when he'd caused such pain in the past?

The questions had kept him awake for what'd remained of the night on Mrs. Lynch's sofa.

As he was getting ready to leave for work, he called Sam. "How're you feeling?" he asked when she answered.

"Better. I'm on my way to HQ now. Tweedldee and Tweedledum are back on my detail."

"Awww, that's so sweet. They must be thrilled. I think Dee was totally in love with you last time. Or was that Dum? Hmm."

"Are you through?"

Freddie laughed. "Yeah, I think I am."

"Good because I've requested protection for you, too."

"Why me?"

"This whole thing has taken a personal turn, and whether I like it or not, you're...you know...personal. To me."

"Oh. Well. Okay then." He cleared his throat. "I need to talk to you. Some stuff has happened. I don't know what to do."

"We'll talk when you get in."

"I'm going to interview the staff at Lynch's office before I come in. Just making sure you're cool with that."

"Good. We need to find someone who didn't love him. If we can find one person any of our vics was having problems with, we'll probably be able to link all these killings."

"I'm on it, boss."

"Watch your back. Someone's gunning for me, which puts you in jeopardy, too."

"I'll be careful."

"See you when you get back to HQ."

Freddie vowed to put aside his personal turmoil and focus on closing this baffling case before anyone else had to die.

TERRY O'CONNOR woke with an armload of soft woman and an erection so hard it hurt. Checking his watch, he was glad he still had some time before the daily AA meeting he attended on Capitol Hill.

"Does this mean you're happy to see me?" Lindsey asked sleepily as she wrapped her hand around his cock and stroked him.

Terry gritted his teeth and stopped the movement of her hand.

"You don't like?"

"Like it too much."

"Ahh, I see." She grabbed their last remaining condom from the bedside table and made quick work of rolling it on him. Straddling his hips, she took him in.

Terry rested his hands on her hips as he watched her ride him, her small breasts bouncing in time with the movement of her hips. He'd never seen anything more provocative than the blush that stained Lindsey McNamara's fair skin when she was aroused.

She threw her head back and sent them both spiraling into orgasm in no time at all. Panting, she fell forward onto his chest.

Surrounded by her scent, the soft cascade of her red hair and riding the aftershocks of their coupling, Terry had never been more content—or more afraid. Here, finally, was everything he'd ever wanted. No doubt he'd find some way to screw it up. He always did.

"I hate to say it, but I have to go."

"So early? You have to work on Saturday?"

"No, but I have a meeting to go to. Every day."

"Oh." She shifted off him and settled next to him.

Here it comes, he thought as he waited for her to say something.

"Could I go with you sometime?"

Startled by the question, Terry glanced at her. "If you want to. Sure."

"You wouldn't mind?"

Terry shrugged. "I have no secrets, least of all from you."

"You mean that?"

"I've spent most of the last decade screwing up my life. I

don't want to live like that anymore. I have a job I love, a reason to get up in the morning that doesn't revolve around getting loaded. My father is looking at me with respect again, the way he used to before I destroyed my life. And now," he said, turning on his side and putting his arm around her, "I have you. So please, come to AA. Hear my story and you'll know why I never want to be that guy again."

"Could I maybe come today?"

As she looked at him with big eyes and a seemingly open heart, he looped a strand of her long hair around his finger. "Yeah, you can come today."

CHAPTER TWENTY-NINE

*C*hief Farnsworth was waiting for Sam when she arrived at HQ. "Lieutenant, a moment of your time please." He gestured for her to follow him to his office.

Sam glanced at the sergeant working the reception desk, hoping he might throw her a lifeline. Instead he chuckled and shook his head to tell her she was on her own. Fabulous. The chief walked purposefully into his office where a man in a suit waited for him.

"Lieutenant Sam Holland meet Special Agent Avery Hill."

As Sam stared at the movie-star gorgeous FBI agent in the sharp dark blue suit, her stomach turned. "You called in the *Feds?* What the hell?"

"We have a serial killer targeting people in my city, and from what I hear from everyone other than the lieutenant in charge of my Homicide detectives, the same killer is targeting the lieutenant in charge of my Homicide detectives."

Sam swallowed hard. "I only found out it's all related this morning, sir. You couldn't give me a *day* to figure this thing out?"

"Last I knew you were flattened by a migraine. I need to stop a killer, and I had no idea if you'd be able to work today."

"But my team—"

"Is stumped. Agent Hill isn't here to take over your investigation. He's here to assist as needed."

Sam scowled at the smugly handsome agent. "Sure he is."

"I'm wounded, Lieutenant."

"Sure you are."

"As the chief said, I'm here to help in any way I can. You're the boss."

"See you don't forget that. I have work to do." Sam headed for the door, but the chief called her back.

"How's your father?"

"Much better from what I'm told. I've been the world's worst daughter since he's been in the hospital."

"He wouldn't see it that way, and you shouldn't either. You've been doing exactly what he'd want you to be doing."

Even though she was still annoyed with him for calling in the Feds, she appreciated the kind words. "Thank you, sir." She cleared her throat. "Let's go, Hill. Time's wasting and I have a press conference to host."

"We're with you, Lieutenant," Farnsworth said as the two men followed her to the courtyard outside the main doors of HQ where the media waited like wild animals anticipating feeding time at the zoo.

At the sight of her, the TV reporters positioned their cameras to capture the briefing.

Darren Tabor from the *Washington Star* began the feeding frenzy. "We've heard there was a break-in at your home, Lieutenant. What can you tell us about that?"

"I'd like to take you through it from the beginning, if I might," Sam said and watched their faces register shock as they realized she planned to be unusually forthcoming. Stonewalling them was one of her favorite pastimes. "On the night before I returned to work after two weeks off, I was called to a double homicide at Carl's Burger World on Massachusetts Avenue. There I found seventeen-year-old Daniel Alvarez and sixty-two-year-old Carl Olivo. Both victims were found locked inside the freezer. A deposit bag full of cash was found on the counter next to some items belonging to the victims. Chief Medical Examiner Dr. Lindsey McNamara determined the victims asphyxiated in the freezer before Mr. Alvarez's father discovered them."

The reporters were writing frantically. Smiling to herself, Sam continued in the same flat tone. "Upon returning to HQ the next morning, I discovered an enormous amount of mail had been sent to myself and Senator Cappuano while we were away. Among the thousands of wedding cards that wished us well, were a few from 'an old friend' who hoped we 'lived long enough' to enjoy our happiness. We immediately went through the rest of the mail we'd received and found a few other cards that indicated our old friend was anything but happy for us."

"Can you tell us exactly what the threatening cards said?" one of the TV reporters asked.

"We'll get you the full text of the cards after this press conference. We were then called to the Chevy Chase home of Crystal Trainer, age thirty-five. She was found dead on her back patio by her daughter Nicole, age twelve, when the daughter arrived home from school. Mrs. Trainer was well liked in her community, was an active volunteer in her children's school and was, by all accounts, a devoted mother. Dr. McNamara determined the cause of death to be blunt force trauma, most likely caused by the single strike of a hammer or other flat-faced object.

"Our next victim was Raymond Jeffries, age seventy-three. He was found on the floor of his dining room in Mount Pleasant and had been dead for some time when officers went to his house at the request of his daughter in New York who'd been unable to reach him. Deputy Chief Medical Examiner Dr. Byron Tomlinson determined Mr. Jeffries died from a blow to the head, possibly caused when he hit his head on the table during a fall. We're not one hundred percent certain Mr. Jeffries was murdered."

"How can you not know that?" Tabor asked, his expression rife with skepticism.

"The only signs of struggle were three toppled dining room chairs. Because three chairs had been turned over, we deduced someone else had been in the house, but again, that's supposition on our part. Like our earlier victims, Mr. Jeffries, a retired chemistry teacher at Roosevelt High School, was well regarded by family, friends and colleagues. We could find no one in his immediate circle of acquaintances who knew of any problems he had with other people."

"Where did Mrs. Trainer go to school?" a blonde TV reporter asked.

"Roosevelt. The school has come up several times over the course of the investigation, and we're looking into connections the various victims had to the school. The final victim, James Lynch, age forty, was found floating in his backyard swimming pool in Woodley Park. From all reports, Mr. Lynch had a life-long fear of the water and never would've gone near the pool on his own."

"If he was afraid of the water, why did he have a pool?"

"We asked his wife that question, and she said they fell in love with the house and planned to have the pool filled in at a future date."

"What's this got to do with the threatening mail?"

"I'm getting to that." Sam gripped the podium and forced herself to finish the story. Baring her soul to the media went against everything she believed in, but if it saved a life and helped to crack the case, so be it. "Yesterday, we received a new card that was the first solid indication we've had that all of this is related." Sam flattened the photocopied page on the podium and tried to keep her voice steady as she read the chilling message.

"That explains the lieutenant's unusual frankness," Darren quipped to chuckles from the others.

"Last night," Sam said, "I returned home to find someone had entered my house and shredded most of my clothing."

A gasp went through the gaggle of reporters.

"Just about everything I own was ruined. As far as we can tell, nothing else in the house was disturbed."

They fired a flurry of questions at her.

Sam held up her hands to quiet them. "I've told you everything we know so far. I'll keep you posted as more information becomes available."

Agent Hill was right on her heels as she headed back inside.

"Now you're all caught up, Agent Hill," Sam said, affecting an unusually sweet tone.

"So it seems," Hill replied.

Freddie joined them as they approached the door.

"How'd you make out with Lynch's coworkers?" she asked.

"Same story we've heard on all the others—he was well liked by his colleagues, well respected by his peers, even opposing counsel. He's been involved in a few high-stakes litigations, but nothing someone would kill over."

"I think this could go down as the most baffling case of our careers," Sam said.

"We've certainly never seen less motive for murder than we have this week."

"Which is why I'm here," Hill said, introducing himself to Cruz who shot Sam a confused look.

She shrugged. "Take it up with the chief."

Gonzo was waiting for them in the pit. He too stopped short at the sight of the agent.

"Gonzo, Agent Hill," Sam muttered.

"What's he doing here?" Gonzo asked.

"Beats me."

"Your chief thought y'all could use some help," he said in a honeyed Southern accent that made Sam's hackles rise. She couldn't stand guys who played the Southern gentleman role and then stabbed you in the back at the first opportunity.

Still eyeing Hill with suspicion, Gonzo said, "I've been through the financials of all our vics, and nothing unusual stands out."

"Of course it doesn't." Sam smoothed her hands over the hair she'd clipped up. "Give me fifteen minutes, and then let's gather in the conference room. We'll start from the beginning and hopefully find some new threads to pull."

"Sounds good, L.T.," Gonzo said, studying her. "You feeling better today?"

"I feel beat up, like I've been through the wringer or something, but at least I'm able to function."

Gonzo turned his back to the agent and lowered his voice. "Scared the crap outta me."

"Sorry." If there was anything she hated more than being the center of attention, she couldn't think of what it might be. Oh wait, she hated flying more. And needles. Yeah, needles were at the very top of her list of hated things. No wait, she hated Lt. Stahl more than needles.

As if she'd conjured him, he came storming into the pit, jowls wiggling with righteous indignation. "Lieutenant, you missed a critical IAB hearing yesterday."

"Not sure if you heard, but I was in the *hospital* during your precious hearing."

"No doubt you manufactured this incident to get out of answering for your bad behavior."

"Now wait a minute," Gonzo said.

Sam stopped him with a hand to his chest. The last thing she needed was one of her most valued detectives taking an insubordination rap. "Please feel free to check with the emergency room doctors at George Washington. They'll attest to the status of my health yesterday afternoon. Tell them to call me if they need me to sign something. Now, if you don't mind, I have real work to do, something I know is a foreign concept to you." She loved watching his face get all purple with rage. Making that happen was becoming her favorite pastime.

He shoved a piece of paper at her.

Since she'd rather be shot than have him touch her, she snatched it from him before he made contact.

"The hearing has been rescheduled for tomorrow at three. Be there or be suspended."

Sam turned, dropped the paper into the closest trashcan and continued into her office, slamming the door behind her. The faint tingles of pain in her forehead forced her into her chair where she took deep breaths. No way could she afford a return engagement of the headache from hell today. With a few minutes until the meeting she had called, she dialed in to her voice mail to get her messages from yesterday and this morning.

Predictably, there were messages from Joseph Alvarez, Jed Trainer, Carl Olivo's oldest son and Raymond Jeffries's daughter, all looking for updates on the investigation. She wrote down their numbers with the intention of returning the calls as soon as she had something more concrete to tell them.

The next message made her blood run cold. It had come in a few minutes after she concluded her press conference and the voice was the same techno-sounding tone from the last time. "Very impressive rundown this morning, Lieutenant. It took you long enough to figure out it's all related. Now let's see how smart you are in figuring out who could possibly be committing these random crimes. Oh and by the way, your inventory of victims was missing one or two. Better get to work. Bye now."

Before the recording finished, Sam was out of her seat and running for the door. "Someone get Archie down here right away." Lt. Archelotta ran the department's IT division and was the only fellow cop Sam had ever dallied with romantically, but that had happened years ago, after her split with Peter.

"What've we got, L.T.?" Gonzo asked as Cruz made the call.

"Come listen." She replayed the message for him and then again when Cruz and Hill joined them.

"Same voice as the earlier call," Cruz said.

"I want it traced," Sam said, writing down the exact time the call had come through the department's voice-mail system.

"You rang," Archie said as he came in looking as tall, dark and handsome as always. "I had a note to call you because that text you asked us to trace led to a throw-away phone."

"Figures. Listen to this." After she replayed the message, Sam filled him in on what they needed and handed him the page with the time.

"I'm on it," Archie said, flying out the door.

"So we've got bodies we haven't found yet," Sam said. "That's just fabulous."

Detective Arnold came to the door. "Lieutenant, your father is on line four. He says it's urgent."

"My dad's in the hospital."

Arnold shrugged. "Sounded like him to me."

Sam picked up the phone and punched the flashing number four. "Dad?"

"Sam, you need to get over here right away." His voice was congested and strained, but it was definitely Skip Holland. She dropped into her chair, overcome with relief at the sound of his voice.

"Dad," she said softly. "It's so good to hear your voice. You've had us so worried."

"We can talk about all that later, baby girl. This is about the case. I saw your press conference this morning, and I think I might know who your perp is."

"Who?"

"Come. Quickly."

"On my way." She put down the phone and grabbed her portable. "Cruz and Gonzales, come with me."

"Wait a minute," Hill said. "Where're you going?"

"To see my dad in the hospital," Sam said. "Is that okay with you?"

"Why're they going with you?" he asked, gesturing to Gonzo and Cruz.

"Because they're friends with my dad. Is *that* okay with you?"

Hill kept his hands on his hips as he eyed her with suspicion. His crisp white dress shirt stretched taut over a broad chest. In another life, Sam might've found him attractive—that is if he hadn't been a Fed and if she hadn't been married to the love of her life.

"Let's go," Sam said.

The three of them ran from the pit and were in the lobby when McBride and Tyrone came through the main door.

"Lieutenant," McBride said. "I need to speak with you. It's somewhat urgent."

Wasn't everything somewhat urgent today?

"I need an hour. Maybe two. Can we do it then?"

The two detectives exchanged glances.

Sam turned to Gonzo, who most likely would be promoted to detective sergeant when the list was posted any day now. "You take care of them."

"It, um, it needs to be you, Lieutenant," Tyrone said, shifting from one foot to the other.

Sam felt like she was made of clay and being pulled in every possible direction.

"Does it involve the current spate of homicides?"

"No," Jeannie said. "It's about the cold case."

"I'll be back in an hour. We'll do it then." To Gonzo and Cruz, she said, "Let's go."

On the way to GW, Sam ran the case through her mind every which way, but nothing clicked for her. Leave it to her paralyzed, pneumonia-weakened father to emerge from his illness as sharp as ever. Thank God, she thought, blinking back tears when she thought of how close they'd come to losing him.

In the rearview mirror, she noticed Tweedle Dee and Tweedle Dum following close behind her in a squad car. She'd totally forgotten they were tailing her.

"My father wants to see me," Freddie blurted out, breaking the tense silence in the car.

"*What?*" Gonzo said from the backseat. "When did this happen?"

Freddie brought him up to speed on what had happened recently and told them both about the two late-night conversations with his mother.

"Wow," Sam said. "What're you going to do?"

"I told my mother I'd see him. She seems to really want me to, and after everything she's done for me…" He shrugged.

"God, man," Gonzo said. "I can't imagine how weird that must be for you. The guy disappears off the face of the earth twenty years ago and then reappears with a story about being mentally ill."

"So you think it's a story?" Cruz asked. "That's what I thought, too."

"No," Sam said. "I don't believe that. Why would he make that up? Especially knowing what you do for a living. It's not like you couldn't do a little digging and verify his story. We're all trained to be cynical, but don't let that carry over into your personal lives. There's no place for it there. The guy wants to see his son. He wants to make amends. Don't make it about anything other than that until you have reason to."

"See?" Cruz said to Gonzo. "This is what I get to work with every day. She never fails to amaze me with her wisdom and spot-on advice."

"Bite me, Cruz, and quit sucking up."

"And she talks dirty to me. Life is good."

Gonzo howled with laughter.

Sam choked back her own need to laugh. She wouldn't give her partner the satisfaction. It would only encourage him. They parked at the hospital and hustled to Skip's room on the fourth floor.

Celia, Tracy and Angela were with him when they arrived.

"Oh thank goodness you're here," Celia said. "He's been driving us crazy wondering what was taking you so long."

Sam stepped up to her father's bedside as he looked up at her with blue eyes the exact same shade as hers. "Nice to have you back, Skippy." She dropped her head to rest it on his shoulder. "Scared me," she whispered.

"Sorry about that, baby girl. It's gonna take more than a coupla nasty germs to take out your old man. Now, enough of the maudlin stuff. Let's talk shop."

"That's our cue," Tracy said, signaling her sister and step-mother to step out with her.

"No," Skip said. "Stay. You girls might be able to help."

"How so?" Ang asked.

"Let me lay out my theory. Tell me what you think."

Sam stood up straight and took a step back so she could better see his face, but she kept a firm hold on his right hand, the one place below his neck where he retained some sensation.

"Melissa Morgan," Skip said.

"No way," Sam said, snorting with disbelief. "Come on! She's a total drama queen but not a *murderer*."

"Really, Dad," Tracy added. "There's no way."

"Let me finish," Skip said, choking on a cough.

Celia ran her fingers through his hair. "Take it easy, Skip. You shouldn't get too worked up after being so sick."

"If they would listen to me," he said with a pointed look for Sam and her sisters, "I wouldn't need to get worked up."

"Girls," Celia said sternly, "listen to your father."

"Okay, Dad," Sam said, deciding to humor him. "We're listening. Lay it on us."

"She went to Roosevelt High School and worked for Carl Olivo. Do you remember why she left that job?"

"Not off the top of my head," Sam said as an itch of discomfort began to niggle at her.

"He fired her when her drawer kept coming up short. Remember how furious she was about that because she needed the job to pay for her dance classes? She had some big idea about being a professional dancer."

"Yeah," Sam said as it all came back to her. To be honest, after she and Melissa had a falling out a few years ago, she'd been so relieved to be rid of the nonstop drama, she'd barely given the woman a thought. "Then she wanted to be a doctor for a while."

"That was before she flunked chemistry in high school," Skip reminded her.

Sam sucked in a sharp deep breath. "Most of all she wanted to be famous, remember that? Famous dancer, famous doctor, famous actress."

Tracy nodded in agreement. "She thought she was going to grow up to be some sort of star. We used to make fun of that."

"Yes!" Sam said.

"I bet if you do a little digging, you'll find out Raymond Jeffries was her teacher."

"Oh, my God," Angela said. "So she's going around systematically getting rid of everyone who's ever done her wrong?"

Sam's mind raced as she tried to process the possibility that someone she'd once considered a close friend was capable of mass murder. "What's the connection to Crystal Trainer?"

"Not sure about that one or James Lynch, but I bet it won't take you long to find it."

"I know I've met Crystal somewhere before," Sam said. "It was probably through Melissa." Adrenaline zipped through her body as all the pieces began to fall into place.

"But what's she got against you, Sam?" Tracy asked. "You two were always such good friends."

"No, we weren't," Sam said. "She kept pulling these weird disappearing acts on me. The first time was after high school. She didn't speak to me for years and then popped up and asked me to be in her wedding. Oh! Oh my God! That's it! I met Crystal and her husband at Melissa's wedding. That's why they looked so familiar to me!"

"Remember the dress thing at her wedding?" Tracy asked.

"Yes!" Sam said, adding for the others, "She picked out this frilly, lacy dress and then accused me of trying to steal her thunder at the wedding because the dress looked good on me."

"I remember you being so pissed about that," Tracy said. "And then there was the incident with the ATM card."

"Right," Sam said, thinking back.

"What?" Angela asked.

"She got ahold of Sam's ATM card and tried to use it to withdraw money from her account," Tracy said. "The bank called Sam, asked her to come in and view the video, and she saw it was Melissa."

"But when I confronted her, she denied it. That's when I stopped talking to her."

"I remember now," Angela said. "You had to talk Dad out of pressing charges against her."

"I was ready to nail her ass," Skip said.

Sam turned to Freddie. "Was her name on the list of Trainer's bimbos?"

"No Melissa Morgan, but there was a Melissa Woodmansee."

"That's her married name! What was her alibi?"

"She claimed to be out of town that day. She had train tickets to prove it."

"I bet she never stepped foot on a train that day." To Gonzo, she said, "Put out an APB for Melissa Morgan Woodmansee."

"She's not married anymore," Skip said. "Celia and I ran into her mother at the grocery store a couple of months ago. She said Melissa got divorced, and her ex-husband got custody of her children."

"We need protection on the husband and children immediately," Sam said. "Justin Woodmansee. They lived in Gaithersburg the last I knew." To Cruz, she said, "Use both names on the APB, but keep it off the airwaves. I want our people looking for her, but I don't want her to know we're on to her yet."

"I'll take care of that," Cruz said, reaching for his cell phone.

"I still don't understand why she has a beef with you," Ang said. "She tried to steal from you, not the other way around."

"Remember Debbie Donahue?"

Her sisters nodded.

For the sake of Gonzo and Cruz, Sam said, "A mutual friend of mine and Melissa's had a cookout a couple of years ago and she invited me. I found out afterward Melissa had asked her to have a party and invite us both. Melissa was looking for a way to talk to me again after years of silence. Poor Debbie didn't know anything about all the crap Melissa had pulled on me. When I got there and saw Melissa was there, I told Debbie I couldn't stay—and I told her why. Melissa chased after me, but I refused to speak to her. I'd had enough, you know?"

"I can understand that," Tracy said. "I had no idea she'd pulled all that crap with you."

"It was a total cry for attention," Sam said. "Typical Melissa." Sam shook her head. "I can't believe she'd do something like this. To kill innocent people all because they did her wrong in some way."

"She had an awful time with her parents, remember?" Angela said. "How many times did she run away from home when she was in high school and end up at our house?"

"Too many to count." Sam leaned over her father's bed and kissed his forehead. "It's a good thing you got better when you did, Skippy. You've probably saved some lives today. Good work, Deputy Chief."

He beamed with pleasure, which made Sam as happy as she'd been since before he got sick.

"Good work, Deputy Chief Holland," Gonzo said, squeezing Skip's right hand on his way out of the room.

"Thank you, sir," Freddie said, saluting Skip before he followed Gonzo.

"Go to work, Lieutenant," Skip said.

"See you at home, Dad."

"I'll be there."

Sam left the room and had to take a moment to absorb the implications. Her friend, her once close friend, had become a serial killer. What did that say about Sam's ability to judge people? And what did it mean that she'd needed her dad to connect the dots for her? She liked to think she would've figured it out eventually, but it would've taken a lot longer without his help.

As she navigated the hallways on her way to the parking lot, she ran through the whole thing in her mind and wondered how she could've missed it. Everything from the murders themselves to the threatening cards to the demand for Sam to spell out the case to the media was a classic Melissa cry for attention.

Gonzo and Freddie were waiting for her in the car, both talking on their cell phones.

"I've updated Malone," Gonzo said when he ended his call.

"Good, thanks."

"What's our first move?" Freddie asked when he completed his call.

"I want to see her parents." Sean and Frieda Morgan had always reminded Sam of fire and ice. Sean had a larger-than-life personality that mortified his daughter while his uptight, rigid wife tried to control Melissa's every thought and action. Melissa was a combination of both, warm one minute and frosty the next. The three of them had fought over everything—Melissa's clothes, her taste in music, her grades, her choice of friends. Sam remembered how devastated Melissa had been the summer before their junior year when her parents had moved her from Wilson High to Roosevelt, supposedly to get their daughter away from the influence of the group of kids she'd become friendly with at Wilson, including Sam.

Interestingly, Sam thought as she drove to the Morgans' home several blocks north of Capitol Hill, that particular group had gone on to have successful lives and careers whereas Melissa had never figured out what she wanted to be when she grew up.

While she had a minute, she called Nick to bring him up to date.

"Wow," he said when she'd laid out the case for him. "So you never thought of this woman as a possible suspect."

"Not for one second, although once my dad put it all together for me, it made perfect sense."

"Don't beat yourself up, babe. Why would you think someone you once considered a close friend would be capable of this?"

"It's so freaking obvious—now. If only I'd talked to her that night at Debbie's. Maybe none of this would've happened."

"If she was this unglued, it wasn't only because of you."

Sam wanted to believe him, but she couldn't help but take some of the blame. "Are you out at the farm?" she asked, meaning the O'Connor's Leesburg home.

"Yeah. You should see Scotty riding. He's come a long way in the last few weeks."

Hearing the pride in his voice made her smile. "Do me a favor and stay put there for the night, will you?"

"Dream on, babe. I'm coming home to sleep with my wife."

"I might not make it home tonight."

"Either way, I'll be there whenever you get home."

"Leave Scotty there. I don't want him anywhere near what's going on here. Will you do that?"

"That's not a bad idea. I'm sure Graham and Laine would be happy to have him."

"I'd feel much better if he was out of the city. You, too, but I'm not going to argue with you."

"There's a change."

"Don't get used to it. I've got to go. I'll see you when I see you."

"Let me know if I can help in some way."

"You'll be the first to know."

"Be careful with my wife, Samantha. I love her very much."

His softly spoken words made her insides go all soft and gooey. "Will do."

CHAPTER THIRTY

*N*ick ended the call and stashed the phone in his
pocket. His every nerve felt raw and exposed after
the story Sam had relayed about her former friend Melissa.

"Everything all right?" Graham O'Connor asked. They stood
at the rail overlooking the practice ring where Scotty rode the
gentle mare he'd befriended on his first visit to the farm
weeks ago.

"Sam's in the midst of a weird case that apparently involves a
former friend who's got a grudge to settle against her."

"So naturally you're worried."

"Seems like I'm always worried since she and I got together.
I'm starting to accept it as a permanent fact of my life now."
Nick waved at Scotty as he trotted by. "He's gotten the hang
of it."

"He's a natural. I've said that all along. All he needed was a bit
of confidence." Graham studied Nick. "You're not yourself
tonight. You weren't even before the call from Sam. What's on
your mind, Senator?"

As Nick watched Scotty's infectious joy on the horse, his
heart ached a little when he thought of how badly he'd wanted
to make the boy his son. "I talked to him about coming to live
with Sam and me."

"And?"

"He turned me down."

"No."

"I think it might be too late. He's too old to start all over again with a new family. He's happy with the one he's created for himself at the home in Richmond."

"That's a load of horse pucky," Graham said with a vehemence that surprised Nick.

"What'd you mean?"

"The poor kid is scared shitless—not of leaving his home or coming to live with the two of you. I've seen him with you guys. He loves you both with all his heart."

"Then what is it?"

"He's afraid if he allows you to see the full scope of his love for you and takes this huge risk to come live with you that you'll change your mind about him at some point. Then where will he go?"

"But that'll never happen!"

"You know that, and I know that, but does he? It has to be on his mind."

Nick thought about the conversation they'd had in the restaurant. Had he come right out and told Scotty his offer was a forever proposition? Had he done a good enough job of letting Scotty know how much he and Sam had come to love him? If Graham was right, clearly he hadn't.

"I'll talk to him again."

"Don't give up on him. Maybe he needs to see you mean it when you say you're not going anywhere before he'll feel comfortable to committing to a permanent arrangement."

"That's certainly a better scenario than the alternative."

"It'll all work out. He'd be damned lucky to have the two of you as parents. Don't think he doesn't know that."

"Thanks for the vote of confidence."

"Anytime." Graham returned his attention to the ring. "Thatta boy, Scotty. Show her you're in charge. That's the way."

The winning grin Scotty sent to Graham went straight to Nick's overcommitted heart. "Could I ask a favor?"

"Anything."

"Would it be okay if I left him here with you and Laine for the night? Sam's concerned about him being in the city with this investigation coming to a head."

"Of course he can stay. We'd love to have him."

"I'll have to clear it with Mrs. Littlefield."

"Make sure you refer to me as *Senator* O'Connor."

Laughing, Nick said, "Will do. Thanks, Graham."

Graham squeezed Nick's shoulder. "Our pleasure, son."

"MY NAME IS TERRY, and I'm an alcoholic."

From the third row of chairs in the church hall on Capitol Hill, Lindsey watched him intently, rubbing her sweaty palms on her jeans as her heart beat so fast she wondered if she might be having a heart attack. Why had she asked to come? What had she been trying to prove? That she could handle this better as an adult than she had as a kid?

She'd been to her share of AA and Al-Anon meetings. Heard her share of stories. Shed her share of tears. What the hell was she doing here again? Just as the panic was about to get the better of her, she looked up at him, met his gaze, and the eye contact calmed her. That was why she was here. Because of him. For him. But for her, too. She needed to hear his story.

"For years," he said with a self-deprecating grin that didn't quite reach his dark eyes, "I was the heir apparent, the one slated to run for my father's Senate seat when he retired after forty years. While I waited for my turn, I was given the Ivy League education and the pampered life of a rich man's son. After college, I went around this town with a sense of entitlement. That Senate seat was *mine*. I'd been groomed for it all my life. I'd *earned* it by being born, and the powerful people in this city sucked up to me because they knew my day was coming. I was invited everywhere. I had all the women I could handle. My campaign war chest was fat with cash. I was the next senator from Virginia, and I had the world by the balls as my father's final term wound down. Everything in my life had led me to this moment, and nothing was going to stop me. Until one night three weeks before I was due to declare my candidacy, I got loaded with a couple of college friends and thought it would be a good idea to drive home afterward."

Lindsey's heart ached at the hurt she heard in his voice. Gone was the arrogance he'd begun with. It had been replaced by raw pain.

"I got caught on the 14th Street Bridge of all places." He uttered an ironic chuckle. "You gotta love the symbolism. I was halfway between Virginia and Washington when the life I'd planned for myself went up in smoke. I was charged with driving under the influence, and my blood alcohol level was twice the legal limit. All the political influence in the world couldn't get me out of that. Overnight I went from the anointed one to persona non grata. I didn't just stumble. I went into free fall. The same people who'd clogged my phone with messages the day before my arrest acted like I had leprosy the next day. My mug shot was all over the Washington papers. The same news programs that had once fought to book me now mocked me. The silence from my 'friends' was deafening."

At some point, Lindsey became aware he was speaking directly to her. Even though she was undone by his naked honesty, she couldn't look away from his intense gaze.

"Worst of all, however, was my father's disappointment. The only thing I'd ever wanted was to make him proud of me. I'll never forget, for the rest of my life, the look on his face when he came to bail me out of jail. Even my mother couldn't seem to look me in the eye. When everyone else seemed to have abandoned me, my good friends whiskey and beer were there for me. The three of us became the very best of friends." Terry paused, took a drink of water and still, he never took his eyes off her.

"My father turned away from me, and suddenly my younger brother was the heir apparent even though he had absolutely no interest in running for elected office. He was the co-owner of a successful business and wanted nothing to do with politics. However, our father is a persuasive man, and when he wants something, it's damned difficult to say no to him. My brother finally buckled under enormous pressure and agreed to run. He had just turned thirty, so he barely qualified. On the night my brother declared his intent to seek the office our father had held for four decades, the office that was supposed to be *mine*, I drank myself into a blackout for the first time."

Tears rolled unchecked down Lindsey's face.

"Of course my brother won. With my father's machine behind him, he was almost unbeatable. I don't remember much of the next five years. All I cared about was getting drunk and staying drunk so I didn't have to watch my brother do the job I should've been doing—the job he didn't even want. The job I'd wanted with every fiber of my being. I was a constant source of disappointment and shame to my parents and family. My father got me a job at a lobby firm downtown. They gave me an office and a title but nothing of any substance to do. That gave me plenty of time—and money—to feed my addiction. And feed it I did. I lost entire days to blackouts. I often woke up in strange places with strange people and had absolutely no idea how I'd gotten there. I was completely and totally out of control. After a couple of years of this my parents and siblings stopped trying to get me to stop. They quit begging me to seek treatment. They left me to find rock bottom all on my own."

Lindsey brushed frantically at the tears that cascaded down her face.

"And then my brother was murdered in his Washington apartment, and I was considered a prime suspect in part because he was killed on the eve of his first major legislative victory. I was outraged by the accusation that I could've had something to do with the murder of my own brother, but why not me? People have killed for a lot less than the kind of jealousy I'd harbored for years by then. I was questioned by the police and was unable to tell them who I'd spent the night with, because I couldn't remember. I knew I'd been with a woman, partied with her, had sex with her, but I couldn't remember a single thing about her or where we'd been. So here I was with plenty of motivation and no alibi.

"If I thought I'd disappointed my father before, that was nothing compared to this. On the day my brother was killed, when he realized I couldn't produce my alibi witness because I'd been too drunk to remember her, he looked at me with such disdain and revulsion. I have no doubt he was thinking if he'd had to lose one of his sons, why couldn't it have been this loser rather than the golden boy who was such a source of pride to him. To be honest, I couldn't blame him. I would've felt the same way in his shoes. I spent the next few days frantically trying to retrace my steps that night. I went to all my usual places, talked to the bartenders, the people I drank with all the time. No one could remember seeing me leave with a woman. I went days without a drink, and the withdrawals nearly killed me. My hands were shaking so hard I could barely drive, and I was awake for four days straight, gripped in utter panic."

He took a deep breath, and Lindsey noticed his hands were trembling, but still, he never looked away from her. "The reason I was so panic-stricken is because I couldn't say for sure I *hadn't* killed my brother. It wasn't like I hadn't wished him dead a couple thousand times since he 'stole' my life. It wasn't like I hadn't fantasized about what it would be like to choke the life out of him so maybe my father would once again look at me the way he used to. By then I'd rewritten history so it was my brother's fault my life had fallen apart. *He* was the root of all evil. My first thought upon hearing my brother had been killed was oh God, did I do it? The lowest point, my rock bottom, was when the police hauled me out of my parents' home at dawn and arrested me for suspicion of murder. As if my parents weren't going through enough planning a funeral for their younger son. Now their older son was looking at murder charges for killing his brother. I spent ninety of the longest minutes of my life being interrogated by one of the best homicide detectives in the nation, and the whole time I was proclaiming my innocence I wasn't entirely sure I *was* innocent. Other than vague recollections of a party and a woman, I couldn't remember a single thing about that night.

"Luckily, the police didn't have a shred of evidence tying me to the crime. Later I heard the woman I was with that night came forward after she saw on the news I'd been arrested. I still don't know her name or what she looks like or where we were that night. I was released from custody and sent home to join my family for my brother's funeral. My brother's best friend and chief of staff was tapped to complete the last year of his Senate term. I went to his swearing in because I knew my parents expected me to be there, and I was tired of disappointing them. Afterward, the new senator took me aside and asked me a question that, to this day, I still can't believe. He asked me to be his deputy chief of staff. He said he wanted my political acumen on his team. After I picked myself up off the floor and started breathing again, I accepted his offer. It came with one condition —thirty days in-patient alcohol rehab or no deal. I took the deal and spent sixty days in rehab, to make sure I was ready to face life without booze.

"I haven't had a drink in the nearly one hundred days since my brother was murdered. I finished rehab and started my new job, which also includes running the senator's campaign for reelection. I'm back in the game I love. I get up every day with a sense of purpose I've never had before. I have new people in my life." He paused to collect himself. "I have new people who make me feel things I've never experienced before. My father calls me every day to find out what I'm working on and to talk about the issues. He values my opinion, and I value his wisdom. He no longer looks at me as if I'm the biggest disappointment in his life. I can't imagine any scenario in which I'd start drinking again or return to the go-nowhere life I was leading before. I've learned no one is entitled to anything, and the best things in life are love and respect and hard work. This program saved my life, and I'm grateful every day for the life I have now. Thanks for listening."

The gathered group applauded as Terry returned to his seat next to Lindsey. She didn't trust herself to look at him just then, so she reached for his hand and held it between both of hers.

"YOU LOOKED great out there today, buddy," Nick said as he supervised Scotty washing up for dinner. He'd spent an hour on the phone with Christina and Terry, rearranging his campaign appearances per the request of the Capitol Police. "Graham says you're a natural on a horse."

The boy's face lit up with pleasure at the compliment. "Really?"

"Yep, and he knows what he's talking about."

"They told me I should call them Graham and Laine, but I don't feel right doing that. Mrs. Littlefield says it's disrespectful to call adults by their first names, especially older people."

"You call Sam and me by our first names."

"That's different."

Leaning against the vanity in the bathroom, Nick crossed his arms. "How is that different?"

"It's you and Sam. You're different."

A warm sense of rightness filled Nick as he studied the boy he'd come to love so much. "Is that so?"

"Uh-huh." He ventured a glance up at Nick. "I was thinking about what you said. Yesterday."

Play it cool, Nick thought. "What about it?"

"Well, there's something I want to ask you, but I don't want you to think I'm taking advantage of you or anything because we're friends. You've already done so much for me."

"Whatever it is, all you have to do is ask. I'll never think you're taking advantage of me. Why do you think I asked you to come live with me? Sam and I want to do everything for you." So much for playing it cool.

"That's so nice of you. I still can't believe you guys feel that way about me."

"Well, we do, and here's something else you need to know— our love and our friendship is forever. No matter what you decide about coming to live with us, we'll always be there for you in whatever capacity you want."

"That's really cool," Scotty said softly, his big brown eyes shining with unshed tears.

Looking to lighten the moment, Nick ruffled his dark hair. "Now, take advantage of me. What do you want to ask?"

Scotty hesitated for a moment and then took a deep breath.

"One of my friends at school is going to this insanely cool baseball day camp in D.C. this summer. It's three weeks, and I'm sure it's too expensive—"

"Of course you can go. I don't care how much it costs."

"That's not a responsible answer. Mrs. Littlefield says you should always know how much something costs before you agree to buy it."

Laughing, Nick couldn't resist the urge to hug the boy. "Mrs. Littlefield is absolutely right about that."

Scotty's arms encircled his waist, and he held on tight. Nick hoped he'd never let go. "If it's okay with you guys, maybe I could stay with you and Sam during the camp, and we could see how it goes?"

"Yes, buddy," Nick said, closing his eyes tight against the emotional wallop. "We'd love that."

SAM PULLED up in front of the Morgans' home, a place where she'd once spent a considerable amount of time, although she'd never felt entirely comfortable there.

"What's the plan?" Freddie asked.

"I'll go to the door and act like I was in the neighborhood," Sam said. "See if I can find out where Melissa might be."

"What if she's in there waiting for you?"

"She won't be."

"And how do you know that?" Gonzo asked.

"That would be too anti-climatic," Sam said, in the zone and tugging the thread her father had given her. "She'd want a big scene, something dramatic. A standoff at her parents' house won't feed her narcissistic need for glory."

"Still," Freddie said, "I don't think you should go up there alone."

"Fine. Stand outside the car and provide backup, but stay out of sight." Sam got out of the car and headed up the front stairs to a spacious porch decorated with white wicker furniture and pots full of colorful blooms. She knocked on the door and tried to peek in a window, but couldn't see through the sheer curtains.

After she knocked again, she looked around at nearby houses. An older woman was watering plants on the porch next door.

"Haven't seen them around in a couple of days," the woman said.

"Is that unusual?"

"Somewhat. They normally tell me if they're going to be away so I can water their plants and take in the mail. We do that for each other. Have for thirty some years now."

"Has their daughter been around at all?"

The woman's sunny smile turned to a frown. "Not that I've seen. Why, is something wrong?"

"We're not sure." Sam showed the woman her badge. "Would you happen to have a key?"

"Why yes, but I don't know..." She fussed with the collar of her housedress. "I wouldn't feel right letting a stranger into their home."

"I'm a police officer, ma'am. Lieutenant Sam Holland with the Metro Police Department."

"Oh! You're the one who married that handsome senator!"

Sam felt her face heat up. "Yes, ma'am."

The woman leaned over the rail of her porch. "Is he as handsome in real life as he is in the pictures?"

"Yes, ma'am."

"I thought so." She fanned her face. "You're a lucky gal."

"Yes, I am. Now, about that key?"

"Since I feel like I know you, I'm sure the Morgans wouldn't mind if I let you in. I'll be right back."

As she scurried off, Sam turned to find Freddie and Gonzo crippled with silent laughter. "Shut up," Sam said through gritted teeth.

"Soooo famous," Gonzo said.

"I said to shut up."

"Personally, I think he's more handsome in the pictures than he is in person," Freddie deadpanned.

Sam flipped him the bird, which set the two of them off again. It was her lot in life to be surrounded by clowns.

The neighbor returned and came down her stairs, nodding to Freddie and Gonzo as she made her way next door. She joined Sam on the Morgans' porch and produced the key.

"I'm going to need you to wait out here," Sam said. "Just in case."

"In case of what?"

"I don't know yet." An uneasy sensation worked its way down her spine, and Sam had learned to trust those feelings. She inserted the key in the door and pushed it open. The stench of death smacked her square in the face.

Apparently, the neighbor smelled it too because she gasped and let out a squeal of dismay.

"Cruz, Gonzales," Sam said, "please take care of her and call for backup. Now." With her hand over her mouth and nose, Sam stepped into hell. If Melissa's other murders had been marked by their sparseness, here she'd gone for high drama as if to leave no doubt that *these* people were, in fact, murdered. Blood stained the floors, walls and carpeting.

Mr. Morgan lay prone in the front room his wife had always reserved for company. From what Sam could see, he'd been bludgeoned with a blunt object.

Breathing through her mouth, Sam ventured farther into the house where nothing much had changed in the twenty years since she'd last been there. She found Mrs. Morgan, also bludgeoned, in the kitchen. On the floor next to her was a two-foot piece of metal pipe covered with blood and brain matter.

Sam was overwhelmed by sadness. They'd been difficult, rigid parents, but no one deserved this. "Oh, Melissa," Sam whispered. "Why?"

"Holy Moses," Freddie said when he joined her and took in the carnage. "Quite different from the others, huh?"

"I was thinking the same thing. She wanted there to be no doubt here."

"Gonzo got word from Patrol that Melissa's ex-husband and children are out of town on vacation this week."

"And the source is certain they went on the trip?"

"Drove them to the airport."

"Thank goodness," Sam said. "That vacation probably saved his life, if not all of them."

They took photographs of the victims and worked the scene in silence until Lindsey McNamara joined them.

"What've we got?" she asked.

Sam asked Freddie to start a canvass of the neighborhood before she brought Lindsey up to speed on the case and what they'd learned about Melissa.

Lindsey took it all in without comment and went right to work, first on Mrs. Morgan and then, after her body had been removed from the home, Mr. Morgan. "I'd estimate the time of death as sometime early yesterday. I can narrow it down for you when I get them back to the lab."

"Everything all right, Doc?" Sam asked.

Lindsey looked up at her. "Why do you ask?"

"You seem a little preoccupied."

Lindsey returned her attention to Mr. Morgan.

"Have you seen Terry?"

Lindsey nodded. "You could say that."

"Ohhh, well... How was it?"

"Astounding."

Sam started to laugh but reined in her amusement in deference to where they were and what they were doing. "I'm glad for you. Both of you."

"I went with him to an AA meeting today and heard his story." She looked up at Sam, her expression fraught with emotion. "I had no idea what he'd been through. The best part was he totally *owned* it, you know? No excuses, no woe-is-me stuff."

"That's promising."

Lindsey nodded. "I was afraid I'd hear a litany of excuses and blame passing like my father used to do, but there was none of that."

"He seems to have turned his life around, but I wonder..."

"What?"

"He hasn't been out of rehab all that long. I'd hate to see you hurt if he relapses."

Lindsey stood and tugged off her latex gloves. "I guess I have to own that possibility. At least I'm going into it with my eyes wide open." She gestured for her assistants to go ahead and remove the body.

"I hope it works out for you," Sam said as they watched Mr. Morgan be removed from the house.

"I guess we'll see."

Sam turned the house over to Crime Scene detectives and met Malone, Gonzales and Cruz at the curb. She brought Malone up to date. "We need to keep the fact that we've found her parents out of the media," Sam said with a meaningful look for Tweedle Dee and Tweedle Dum, who were wide-eyed and white-faced after watching the bodies be removed from the house.

"I'll take care of that," Malone said.

"What's the plan, L.T.?" Gonzo asked.

"Give me a minute," Sam said. "Let me think." Pacing the sidewalk in front of the Morgans' home, under the watchful eyes of her colleagues and the Morgans' neighbors, she thought about the woman she'd once known so well, the woman she'd once counted among her closest friends until being her friend had become too much work.

While she paced, Malone talked to the neighbors, probably asking them not to speak to the media.

She and Melissa had been silly teenagers together, suffered through crushes and first loves together, and shared every detail of their lives with each other until the day when it all stopped for no apparent reason. Melissa quit returning Sam's calls and put an end to their friendship for reasons Sam hadn't understood then and still didn't understand now.

Then, several years later when they were in college, Melissa reappeared and acted like nothing had ever happened. She told Sam she was getting married and asked her to be a bridesmaid in the wedding. Sam had been surprised—and saddened—that Melissa had no other friends she was closer to by then. Even though she hadn't wanted to be in the wedding, she'd gone along with it. That was where she'd met Crystal and Jed Trainer. The memory was sharper now that Sam recalled where the meeting had occurred. Crystal had been a college friend of Melissa's. Sam wondered if she too had grown tired of the drama that came with being Melissa's friend and paid for that with her life. Tomorrow, she'd ask Jed Trainer about that and get the details of his affair with Melissa.

After her wedding, Melissa kept in sporadic touch over the next few years. When Sam married Peter, she invited Melissa to the wedding, but she'd refused to attend because Sam hadn't asked her to be in the wedding party. This next time she reappeared, she'd gained twenty pounds and had two children she was having trouble managing. Her marriage wasn't working, and the husband she'd been so wildly in love with had turned into a major disappointment—or so she said.

Sam had endured a couple of visits with Melissa and her unruly children. This time when Melissa pulled her disappearing act, Sam was almost relieved. She'd been busy getting her career in the police department off the ground, and the last thing she needed was Melissa's brand of drama.

Years had passed before Melissa once again reappeared, asking Debbie to orchestrate the meeting after Sam ignored several phone calls from Melissa. Once Sam realized Melissa had manipulated her and Debbie, she'd left the party without a word for Melissa. She hadn't seen or heard from her since, but couldn't help but wonder at the timing of Melissa's killing spree, weeks after the wedding Sam hadn't invited her to.

As that staggering thought registered, Sam came to a halt in front of her three colleagues. "I need to see Amanda Lynch."

CHAPTER THIRTY-ONE

*A*fter waiting four hours for her to reappear, Jeannie and Will gave up on Sam coming back to talk to them about the Fitzgerald case.

"You think she knows we need to tell her something she doesn't want to hear about her dad?" Will asked as they shared a sandwich at eight o'clock that night in the conference room.

"I doubt it's even on her radar. She gave me the case because she wanted to get me back to work but didn't want it to be high stress and pressure the way an active case would be. If she'd known how he basically bungled this case, she never would've asked us to look into it."

"True. Everyone knows how tight the two of them are."

"Um, excuse me, Detective McBride?"

Jeannie wiped her mouth and got up.

"I'm Sam's sister Tracy. We met at the shower?"

"Yes, of course. Come in. My partner Will Tyrone."

Tracy nodded to Will. "Nice to meet you."

"What can we do for you?" Jeannie asked, ushering Tracy into a chair.

"Sam's not here, is she?"

"Not at the moment."

"Good," Tracy said, folding and unfolding her hands.

"Is everything all right, Tracy?"

"Sam told me she asked you to look into the Fitzgerald case."

"That's right."

"I wondered...Were you able to learn anything new about what might've happened to Tyler?"

"We have our suspicions," Jeannie said, glancing at Will. "But nothing we can prove."

"My dad worked hard on that case."

"We could tell that from his notes."

"It was...a, uh, a rough time for him."

This was now the second time she'd heard that, Jeannie thought. "How do you mean?"

"This is all off the record right? You won't tell Sam?"

Jeannie shifted her gaze to Will and then back to Tracy. "You're putting us in a tough spot asking us to keep things from our lieutenant. I get that she's your sister, but—"

"I understand, and I know I shouldn't even be here, but...I wanted you to know... My father was going through some stuff during that case. It had nothing to do with the case or work." Tracy took a breath and seemed to be fighting for composure. "That was the first time my mother left him. I heard them fighting. She accused him of all kinds of things. She said he'd been unfaithful, he'd been drinking too much, he was married to his work. I remember her saying she couldn't live like that anymore.

"The next day when we woke up she was gone. Dad said she went away on a trip with her girlfriends, and my sisters bought that, but I knew that wasn't where she was. He was a mess for weeks afterward, all during the Fitzgerald investigation. I heard him on the phone saying he had a suspect but couldn't make a case against the person. He said if he was able to nail that person it would destroy the Fitzgerald family even more than they already were. He sounded so terribly torn. I don't know what any of it meant. I only know what I heard."

She cleared her throat and looked up at them. "I have no idea what you've learned about the investigation, but I wanted you to know my dad always tried to be a good cop and a good man."

"We haven't found anything to the contrary," Jeannie said,

telling Tracy what she needed to hear. "Sam doesn't know about any of this?"

Tracy shook her head. "She idolizes him. I'd never take that away from her, and I hope you won't either. The way people treat him here...it sustains him since the shooting."

"We'll keep the information you've shared out of the report," Jeannie said.

"I appreciate that. My father has given so much to this department."

"Yes, he has. We're relieved to hear he's feeling better."

"We are, too." Tracy stood up to go. "Thank you for your time and discretion."

"Thanks for coming in. You've given us a lot to think about."

After Tracy left the two detectives sat in silence for a long time, processing what they'd been told.

"What the hell do we do now?" Will asked.

"Damned if I know."

SAM DROPPED Freddie and Gonzo at HQ to begin tracking down Melissa and headed for Woodley Park. At the Lynch home, Sam found Amanda in the care of her sister. They'd returned from picking out a casket for Mr. Lynch, and judging from Amanda's ravaged face, she hadn't slept much since Sam saw her the day before.

"I'm sorry to bother you again, Mrs. Lynch," Sam said, "but I have a couple of follow-up questions that couldn't wait."

Amanda waved a hand in a helpless gesture that tugged at Sam. What did she care if Sam had questions? Her life had been destroyed, and nothing Sam said or did would ever change that. Putting herself in Amanda's place made Sam feel sick, so she didn't allow herself to go there.

"Do you know a woman named Melissa Morgan?"

Amanda thought about it for a minute and then shook her head. "The only Melissa I know is a Melissa Woodmansee." Her face clouded. "A total bitch who came on to my husband, and when we confronted her about it, she tried to blame *us* for her husband leaving her."

Sam's heart sank. She'd known there was a connection, but hearing it spelled out made her ache for what she'd have to tell Amanda.

"What?" Amanda asked. "You know something. Tell me. Please."

Sam took a deep breath and reached for Amanda's hand. "We have reason to believe Melissa killed your husband."

Amanda Lynch's keening wail brought tears to Sam's eyes. In the past, she'd always empathized with the loved ones of any murder victim. But now that she had Nick, she had a whole new level of sympathy for victims like Amanda, who'd lost the love of her life.

"*Why?*" Amanda asked, her eyes searching Sam's for answers she didn't have. "*Why would she kill my Jimmy?* We hadn't seen her in years!"

"Because you shut her out. You stopped talking to her."

"Of course I did! She tried to get my husband to sleep with her. We were disgusted that she thought she could take him away from me. She had no idea how much he loved me, how much we loved each other." A sob hiccupped through her. "She had no idea."

"I knew her, too. Years ago. I also stopped talking to her."

"Did she come after your husband, too?"

The question was a knife to Sam's heart. As she shook her head it registered that Nick's trip to Boston with Scotty had quite possibly saved his life. Her heart ached, and her stomach lurched at the thought of it. "She broke into my house and shredded every piece of clothing I have, including my wedding gown."

Amanda grimaced with dismay. "She's sick. I always told Jimmy something was wrong with her, but he said she was a drama queen."

"He was right about that." Sam squeezed the other woman's hand. "I'm going to get her—for you and for Jimmy and for all the other people whose lives she's ruined."

"Whatever you do, don't let her take your husband, Lieutenant. I wouldn't wish this pain on anyone."

"She'll have to go through me to get to him."

Sam had Nick on the phone before she was through the Lynchs' front door. "Where are you?" she asked, filled with relief at the sound of his voice.

"On the way home from the farm. How about you?"

"Still working. I need you to do something for me."

"Anything."

"Meet me at HQ."

"This late? What's up?"

"I'll tell you when I get there." Thankful she'd reached him before he went home, Sam drove to HQ with one purpose in mind—getting to Nick and keeping him close until Melissa was in custody.

"I SWEAR TO GOD, it's a sickness," Sam said when she reached her office and saw that her husband had once again brought his anal retentiveness to her desk. In truth she was so happy to see him, he could've cleaned the place from top to bottom and she wouldn't have cared. "You have a sickness."

He flashed the grin that never failed to make her knees go weak. "You had it all cleaned up before the wedding. What happened?"

"Murder happened," she said, bending to kiss him.

He hooked a hand around her neck and held her in place for a more serious kiss.

"No PDA at work, Senator," she said, even though her eyes were closed and blood zinged through her veins.

When someone knocked on the door, Sam pulled away from him. She turned to find Jeannie McBride and Will Tyrone waiting for her along with an angry Agent Hill. "Shit," Sam said when she saw McBride and Tyrone. "I was gone much longer than an hour, wasn't I?"

"And from what I hear," Hill said, "you weren't at the hospital all that long."

"What can I say? Duty called. We've got this one nailed, Agent Hill, so you can go back to Quantico or wherever you normally hang your hat."

"I'm not going anywhere until Chief Farnsworth tells me I'm no longer needed here."

"You're no longer needed here, Hill," Farnsworth said from behind him. "I was premature calling you in, but I appreciate your assistance."

Sam sent Hill a smug smile. He left her with a glare and stormed out of the pit. She had a feeling she'd be seeing him again sometime.

"Lieutenant," Farnsworth said, "I understand you've figured out who our murderer is."

"My father did." Sam filled him in on how Skip had connected the dots.

"Is that right?" Farnsworth said, his expression full of pride and pleasure. "The old man's still got it, huh?"

"That he does, and thank God we've still got him." To Jeannie and Will, Sam said, "You two have waited long enough to talk to me. Let's go to the conference room."

Jeannie looked at Will, and he nodded. "We've gone over all the case files and re-interviewed witnesses," she said. "We were unable to add any new insight to the case."

Disappointed, Sam took the stack of folders from Jeannie. She would've like to have been able to tell her dad they'd closed this one for him. "Well, thanks for trying. Never hurts to put new eyes on a cold case."

"Lieutenant," Farnsworth said in the stern voice he did so well, "please tell me you have a plan for arresting the woman who's been murdering innocent people in my city."

Sam flashed him a winning smile. "Of course I do, Chief." Turning to Nick, she said, "We're having a party, Senator."

BY THE TIME all the plans were in place, contingency plans were considered and backup plans formed, it was after 1:00 a.m. They'd sent the pipe found at the Morgans' house to the lab for analysis, but the report wasn't back yet. Tracing her credit cards, Gonzo had found Melissa holed up in a motel outside of town, and Sam had ordered a couple of third-shift detectives to keep an eye on her. Sam would've preferred to arrest her tonight, but since they didn't have a scrap of evidence tying Melissa directly to any of the murders, they needed a confession. Tapping into her understanding of how Melissa's mind worked and her need for attention, Sam had hatched her plan.

Sam sent a text message to Melissa saying she was having a gathering of old friends so they could meet her new husband at four the next day and hoped Melissa could make it. She included her Ninth Street address. At the "party," Sam intended to back Melissa into a confession. Sam ordered her team to report to her house by three o'clock the next day and sent them home, telling them to get some sleep.

"Will she try to kill again in the meantime?" Farnsworth asked after she'd laid out the plan.

"I don't think so." At least she hoped not. "The whole purpose of her vendetta was to get rid of the people who'd done her wrong in the past and to get my attention. I believe she saved her parents—and me—for last."

"And if she doesn't confess?"

"Then we'll go with a plan B."

"Which is what?"

"Don't know yet, but if I need a plan B, I'll get one."

"Keep me informed."

"Yes, sir."

She was so tired she didn't put up much of an argument when Nick insisted on driving her home.

They were in the lobby on the way to the parking lot when Joseph Alvarez came through the main door.

"Oh God," Sam muttered when she thought of what she'd have to tell this poor man about his son's death.

"Lieutenant," he said, surprised to see her. "I wasn't expecting to find you here at this hour on a Saturday." He glanced around the deserted lobby. "I couldn't sleep. I was hoping maybe someone could tell me the latest on the case."

"Mr. Alvarez, this is my husband, Nick Cappuano."

The two men shook hands.

"Pleasure to meet you, Senator."

"Likewise. I'm sorry for your loss."

The expression of sympathy brought tears to the other man's eyes. "Thank you."

Sam gestured to a sitting area outside the door that led to the inner offices. "Nick, would you mind giving us a minute?"

"That's not necessary," Mr. Alvarez said. "No reason he can't hear this. Heck, he probably already knows."

Sam glanced up at Nick who fortified her with the empathetic gaze he sent her way.

When they were seated, Sam took a deep breath. "We know who killed your son."

Taken aback by the news, Mr. Alvarez said, "Oh."

In as few words as possible, Sam explained about Melissa backtracking to exact revenge for old hurts.

"But what's that got to do with my Danny?" he asked, confused.

"Nothing at all," Sam said softly. "I'm sorry to say he was in the wrong place at the wrong time."

Mr. Alvarez dropped his head to his chest and broke down.

Sam rested a hand on his shoulder. "He was a good kid, Mr. Alvarez. I couldn't find a single person who had a bad thing to say about him. We suspected all along this wasn't about him."

"Thank you." He wiped the tears from his face. "I appreciate you working so fast to get me some answers. Doesn't change anything, but it helps to know why."

"I'll get in touch as soon as we have her in custody."

Mr. Alvarez stood and offered her his hand. "Thank you."

Sam shook his hand. "I'm sorry again for your terrible loss."

He shifted his eyes to include Nick. "Take good care of each other."

"We will," Nick said, standing to shake the other man's hand again.

As Mr. Alvarez headed for the door, Sam let her husband put

his arm around her and bring her in close to him even though she normally prohibited PDA at work.

"Brutal," Nick said, brushing a kiss over the top of her head.

"Yes."

"You did good, babe."

"What do you even say in a situation like this?"

"He needed the truth, and you gave it to him."

"Let's go home. Please."

CHAPTER THIRTY-TWO

*H*and-in-hand, they walked to the parking lot where Nick held the door to his car for Sam.

She slid into the buttery-soft leather seat and put her head back.

"What if she doesn't show?" Nick asked as he drove them home.

"She'll show. She'll be too curious not to."

"She has to know by now that you're on to her."

"Not necessarily. She thinks she's been so clever—and to be honest, she has been. Other than her parents, these were clean, efficient executions with no evidence left behind. In her mind, she's holding all the cards, and she's got me chasing my tail, which is exactly what she wanted."

They arrived at home, and Nick took her jacket to hang it in the closet while Sam glanced at the sofa where she would've tossed it.

"Was Scotty okay about staying at the farm tonight?"

"Are you kidding? He was thrilled. When I left Laine was teaching him how to make ice cream with an old-fashioned butter churner. He was loving every minute of it."

"That's great. I love he's having fun and trying new things."

"I do, too. You should see him on the horse. He's gotten

confident. Graham says he's a natural." As he spoke, Nick kneaded the tension from her shoulders.

Her eyes fluttered closed as he chased away the tension.

"So get this—he asked me about going to a baseball camp here in the city for three weeks this summer and if it would be okay if he stayed with us."

Sam's eyes flew open and she spun around to face him. "Seriously?"

Nick's face glowed with pleasure. "Yep. You should've seen how cute he was asking me about the camp. One of his friends from school is going, and that's how he heard about it. He was worried about asking me because it's supposedly expensive, and he was afraid I'd think he's taking advantage of me."

"I hope you told him you don't give a fig about how much the camp costs."

"I did, and I was told that's an irresponsible answer."

They shared a laugh that turned serious when their eyes met and held. "Is this really happening?" she asked in a whisper.

"God, I hope so. We'll have to show him how great it could be living with us all the time."

"We can do that. Is Graham taking him home tomorrow?"

He nodded. "I told Scotty we'd be down to see him next weekend."

"Good. Something to look forward to."

Nick took her hand. "Come with me. I have a surprise for you."

"Is that a come-on line?"

Laughing, he led her upstairs to their bedroom. "Wait right here." He crossed the hall and returned with the red-and-white polka-dot bikini she'd worn on their honeymoon. He'd liked it so much the first time he saw it, they'd ended up back in bed before they finally made it to the beach.

Sam smiled at the memory and wished she could close her eyes and be back in Bora Bora where everything was so much simpler. "I'm glad to see at least one thing escaped Melissa's wrath."

"It was still in the suitcase."

"I told you there was no need to unpack the minute we got home."

He tweaked her nose. "Go put this on and come with me." Bending to kiss her, he added, "I know you're beat, but trust me, you'll like this."

She had no doubt she'd like anything having to do with him, especially when it put that boyishly handsome smile on his face. Sam went into the bathroom and changed into the skimpy bikini Angela had talked her into when they'd gone shopping for Sam's honeymoon. At first Sam had thought it was too revealing, but Ang had assured her Nick would love it. She'd been right about that.

Sam brushed her hair and teeth before she rejoined him. He'd changed into one of the bathing suits he'd worn in Bora Bora, and Sam took a moment to admire his finely sculpted chest. "Mmm, that view never gets old."

Embarrassed as always when she commented on his supreme hotness, Nick reached for her hand. "Close your eyes and come with me."

"Where're we going?"

"You'll see. Keep your eyes closed. I've got you."

Even though she'd go anywhere he chose to take her, she couldn't make this too easy on him. "You know I don't like surprises."

"I promise you'll like this one."

They went upstairs to the empty loft that made up the top floor of the townhouse.

"What's up here?" she asked, trying to figure out why she could suddenly smell the beach. It took all her self-control to keep her eyes closed so she wouldn't ruin this for him.

"Stay right there a minute."

Sam did as she was told, but it wasn't easy. While she'd been totally wiped out a few short minutes ago, now she was wide-awake and dying to see his surprise.

He came back a minute later, put his arms around her from behind and pressed a kiss to her neck that woke up some of her other parts. "You can look now."

Sam opened her eyes and had to blink a couple of times when she saw he'd transformed the loft to resemble their favorite beach in Bora Bora, complete with fake palm trees and a double-sized lounge chair similar to the one they'd enjoyed on their honeymoon. The only light in the room was an array of candles he'd arranged on a table next to the lounge. On one wall, the pictures they'd taken on their trip ran as a slideshow. Traditional Tahitian music played in the background, the sound of which took her right back to the blissful days and nights in Bora Bora.

"You like?" he asked.

Sam was flabbergasted. "*When* did you do this?"

"I got the idea the other day when you said you'd give anything to go back to Bora Bora. I figured if we had this place tucked away up here, we could go back anytime we want to."

Sam turned to him. "This is the best surprise *ever*. I love it, and I love you." She went up on tiptoes to kiss him. "I have the best husband in the whole world."

Pleased by her reaction, he hugged her. "I hope you'll always think so."

"I know I will. How'd you get it to smell like the beach?"

"Candles." He produced a tube of sunscreen. "Do my back?"

Laughing, Sam took it from him and enjoyed every second of running her hands over his finely muscled back. "Turn around."

His hazel eyes were heated when he turned to face her.

She took her time smoothing sunscreen on his warm skin, exploring every inch of the chest that dominated her fantasies. His belly quivered under the movement of her fingers, and the scent of the sunscreen took her right back to the beach.

Taking the tube from her, he said, "My turn." He too took his time and set her on fire with the gentle movement of his fingers over her fevered skin, like he had on their trip. More than once the application of sunscreen had led to passionate lovemaking.

"I don't think I'll ever look at sunscreen the same way after our trip."

"Who knew it was such an aphrodisiac?"

He was making her breathless with the slide of his fingers

over the tops of her breasts before moving to her belly and then to her legs. Sam was boneless by the time he was finished with her.

"There," he said. "That ought to keep you from getting burned. Now, have a seat while I see about getting us some drinks."

"No wait staff at this resort?"

"Just yours truly."

In one corner of the big room he'd stashed a small refrigerator and blender.

"Jeez, you thought of everything! When did you have time to do this?"

"I couldn't go back to sleep after you left the other night, so I got up and got busy. Only took a couple of hours. With everything open twenty-four hours these days, I had it all done and was at work on time. I couldn't wait to show you."

"Just when I think I've already seen the full extent of your awesomeness, you go and top yourself."

He brought them each a frozen margarita and stretched out next to her on the lounge. "I shall seek to top myself for the next sixty years."

Sam leaned over to kiss his cold lips. "I'll look forward to that."

As they sipped their drinks, they watched the slideshow and relived the exquisite beauty of Bora Bora.

"Does it bother you that it would never occur to me to do something like this?" Sam asked.

"If you did something like this, I'd think you were having an affair."

"Hey!" she said, outraged and amused at the same time. He knew her *so* well. "I'm not *that* unromantic."

"Um, yes you are, babe. But I wouldn't have you any other way."

"That sounds like a challenge to me."

Nick snorted out a laugh. "Knock yourself out." He took her drink and put it with his on the table next to the lounge. "Come here."

"No, I'm mad at you."

Still laughing, he tugged her to him, startling her when his cold hands made contact with her warm skin. His lips were as cold but that didn't keep Sam from arching into him as he focused on her neck. "This bikini makes me crazy. Any time you make me mad, which I expect to be often, put that on and all will be forgiven."

"Is that so?" she asked, smiling.

"Oh yeah." He sat up and, never taking his eyes off her, reached for his glass and took another sip of the frozen drink as he untied the bikini top to free her breasts. Bending his head he captured her nipple between ice-cold lips, making her gasp when he ran his equally cold tongue back and forth over the rigid tip.

The sensations were so overpowering Sam could barely breathe. As he kissed his way down the front of her, her entire body was on fire for him. Her fingers threaded through his hair. "Wait," she said, breathless. "Come up here."

"Not yet. Relax, babe. Let me love you."

When he settled between her legs, her hands fell away from his hair and landed on either side of her hips. He ran his hands from her knees to inner thighs, opening her as he went. His lips followed the same path, focusing briefly on the juncture before moving to the other side.

Sam squirmed, trying to direct him to where she wanted him most, but he had his own agenda and refused to deviate. The second time he returned to the middle, he lingered, tonguing her through the fabric of her bathing suit. And then his hands were on her bottom, lifting her tighter against his hot mouth. He kept that up until she was on the brink and then backed off but only long enough to untie the bows at her hips and remove the two triangles of fabric that covered her.

Coming back for more, he hooked her legs over his broad shoulders, forcing them even farther apart. With his hands once again cupping her bottom to hold her where he wanted her, Sam had no choice but to go along for the ride as his tongue and lips worked their magic. And that was the only word to describe the way he made her feel—pure *magic*. He drove her crazy taking her to the edge and backing off until he finally zeroed in on the heart of her desire and sent her screaming into orgasm so intense it brought tears to her eyes.

Without giving her time to recover, he turned her over and kissed his way from her spine to the small of her back, restarting the tingling desire between her legs. She wouldn't have thought it possible to come again so soon, but she'd learned not to underestimate him in that regard.

"Nick," she said, the single word sounding almost like a sob.

"Can't talk right now. I'm busy paying homage to your gorgeous ass."

He shocked her senseless when he ran a finger down the cleft of her ass as his lips once again found her clit, making her come again. Completing the assault on her senses he entered her from behind, taking her by surprise as he held her hips and surged into her in one deep stroke.

"Oh, *God*," he said with a groan. "So hot."

Only his arm around her waist kept her legs from collapsing. His free hand continued to explore the cleft of her ass as he pumped into her in long hard strokes. He kept it up until they came together in a combustible moment of utter harmony and then collapsed into a heaving pile on the lounge.

Sam held his hand to her chest and focused on getting air to her lungs. The aroma of beach and sunscreen and sex filled her senses while love for him filled her heart to overflowing. "Thank you for this."

He kissed her shoulder and then her cheek. "My pleasure."

FREDDIE WOKE up early on Sunday morning and turned over to cuddle up to Elin's warm soft body.

"Why are you awake so early when you don't have to work until later?" she mumbled.

"Why are you awake?"

Her hand covered his. "Because you are."

"Sorry if I woke you."

"It's okay. What're you thinking about?"

"Moving. Your place or mine?"

"I think we should find a place together and start fresh somewhere new."

"That's a good idea," he said, pleased she'd obviously given it some thought.

"Speaking of starting fresh, I had a rather amazing conversation with my mother last night during which she said she's been wrong to treat you the way she has and she wants the chance to get to know you better." He waited expectantly, imagining what Elin would have to say about that.

"I'm glad for you that she's decided to stop giving us such a hard time."

"That's not what I thought you would say."

"What were you expecting?"

"Maybe something like 'good for her, I'm not interested.'"

Elin turned over so she could see him. "I know how much you love her. I'd never say that. I love you too much to do that to you."

Freddie felt like he'd been hit by a Taser. Hearing her say the words so freely and confidently was incredible. He cupped her face and leaned in to kiss her. "You want to say that one more time so I can be sure I heard it right?"

"I love you, Freddie. I didn't plan to love you, but you're so damned persistent and kinda cute, too."

He furrowed his brows. "Just kinda?"

"I can't tell you the truth. You'd be downright unlivable then."

Thrilled with what she'd given him, he kissed her again and glanced at the clock. "I've got to go."

"Where?"

"Church."

For real? We finally have a day when we can stay in bed and you're going to church?" She ran a finger straight down the middle of his chest to his belly and below to let him know what he'd be missing.

His body responded predictably.

She wrapped her hand around his cock and stroked him. "You can't miss *one* week?"

He stopped the movement of her hand. "I'm going to see my father after the service."

She looked up at him. "You are?"

Nodding, he tried to ignore the sudden gallop of his heart at the thought of seeing his father after twenty years of silence.

"Could I maybe come with you?"

Surprised, he stared at her. "To church?"

"To church, to see your dad, the whole thing."

"You really want to?"

"Yes, Freddie, I really want to."

Freddie linked their fingers. "I'd like that."

CHAPTER THIRTY-THREE

*B*y three-thirty, everything was ready. Food and drinks and music, all the signs of a party, and Sam was battling nerves. What if Melissa didn't show? What if she came and Sam couldn't get her to confess to the spate of murders?

Nick approached her from behind and got busy massaging the tension from her shoulders. He was *so* good at that and knew where the stress collected. "I had you all loose before, and now you're all locked up again."

"I'm afraid I've played this one all wrong."

"How do you mean?"

"Well, if she doesn't show—"

"Lieutenant," Freddie said when he came into the kitchen, "we got word from her detail. She's on the move, fifteen minutes from here."

Sam let out a sigh of relief. "Show time." To Nick she said, "Would you mind letting everyone know?" The house was full of cops posing as party guests. "I need to speak to Cruz for a minute."

"Sure." Nick gave her a quick kiss and left her alone with her partner.

"What'd I do now?" Freddie asked, helping himself to a cream puff.

"You tell me. Why do you look weird in the eyes?"

He paused midchew and stared at her. "I do?"

Sam nodded. She watched him swallow the treat and wipe his mouth with a napkin. "Everything all right?"

"I saw my father today."

"Oh man. How was it?"

"It was…you know…kind of overwhelming. He was just as I remembered, older of course, but still him."

Sam crossed the room and put a hand on his arm. "I can't imagine what that must've been like for you."

"This one part of me wanted to be mad with him, you know?"

She nodded. "I can totally understand that."

"But then there was this other part of me, the ten-year-old I was the last time I saw him, who was thrilled that all he wanted to talk about was me and my life and my work and my girl. Elin came with me."

"Sounds like he's making a real effort."

"Yeah."

"That's good, right?"

"Sure, it is. I guess my worry is what if I let him back in and he does it again?"

Sam thought of how many times she'd let Melissa back in only to get burned again. "I think you need to let him know if it happens again, he won't get a third chance."

"So I come right out and say that?"

"Why not? You're not ten anymore. You can set your own rules this time."

"That's true."

"For what it's worth, I think you want to give him a chance. Don't be afraid to take a risk. The payoff could be so worth it."

"That's good advice. Thanks. On the plus side, my mother has decided to give Elin a chance."

"Good for her and good for you."

Gonzo came into the kitchen. "She's just about here, L.T."

To Freddie, Sam said, "Let's close this sucker."

.   .   .

MELISSA HAD GAINED a significant amount of weight since the last time Sam saw her. Her once shiny dark hair had been cut to an unfortunate length that only accentuated her pudgy face. Sam wasn't sure she would've recognized her old friend if she'd run into her somewhere else. She'd once been stylish, but today she wore a bulky sweater over black pants.

"Hey," Sam said, swallowing a burst of revulsion. "Come in. I'm so glad you could make it last minute."

"I had other plans," Melissa said stiffly, "but I was able to change them."

Sam's teeth ached from the effort it took to welcome a murderer into her home. All around them other officers were pretending to enjoy food and drink.

"I want you to meet my husband, Nick Cappuano."

Nick moved to her side and extended his hand to Melissa. "Good to meet you. Sam has told me a lot about you."

Melissa hesitated before she shook his hand. "She hasn't told me anything about you, *Senator*, but of course I've read *all* about the two of you."

The comment was another bit of insight into what had sent Melissa over the edge. She who'd always wanted to be famous wouldn't like that Sam was getting so much attention.

"Can I get you a drink?" Nick asked, always the gracious host.

"No. I can't stay long." Melissa took a measuring look around the room, as if she hadn't been there once before on a clothes-shredding mission. "Nice place."

"Thanks," Nick said.

"A lot of space for two people."

Nick put his arm around Sam. "We hope it won't be the two of us for long."

"I thought you couldn't have kids," Melissa said, seeming unhappy to hear otherwise.

The last thing Sam wanted to do was discuss her fertility struggles with this woman. "I thought so, too. I found out otherwise recently."

"Were you *pregnant?*"

Nick tightened his grip on Sam's shoulder. "Briefly." It still hurt so badly to think about the baby they'd recently lost. "How are your children?"

She shrugged. "With their father."

"You don't see them?"

"Occasionally. I heard your dad got shot."

Boy, she was going for the jugular. "Yes."

"Did you get the guy who did it?"

"Not yet," Sam said, forcing herself to keep her tone friendly.

"That must get the goat of a rock-star detective like you."

"It doesn't make me happy that he's stuck in a wheelchair when the person who shot him walks free." Sam crossed her hands to keep from grabbing Melissa by the throat and beating the confession out of her. "How're your parents?"

"Same as always," Melissa said without missing a beat. "Carping at me about one thing or another. Nothing I ever do is good enough for them. Same old story."

"My dad said he saw your mom recently in the grocery store."

"She didn't mention it."

"Are you sure you don't want something to eat or drink?"

Melissa turned away from them all of a sudden, startling Sam and Nick as well as the other cops in the room who were instantly on alert. "I have to go."

"So soon?"

"I shouldn't have come here."

"Why not?"

"Because the last thing I want to hear about is your happy life with your handsome senator husband and your successful career. It's enough to make me sick."

"I'm sorry you feel that way."

"Tell me something—why didn't you want to be friends with me anymore?"

"Um, well, I got tired of you breezing in and out of my life like our friendship meant nothing to you." *Oh and the fact you tried to steal from me was a bit of an issue too,* Sam thought, but chose not to say.

"It meant everything to me!" The room went silent as the others gave up the pretense of pretending they weren't watching the two women intently. "You were the one person I always thought would be there for me no matter what, but you were like everyone else. People pretended to be my friend, and then they'd abandon me. I expected better from you."

"I'm sorry I let you down."

"That's all right," Melissa said with a deceptively angelic smile. "But I can't let you have it all when I have nothing."

"Melissa—"

She whipped off the bulky sweater to reveal a vest full of wires that Sam instantly recognized as a bomb. Melissa held the detonator above her head, waving it erratically.

"Clear the room," Sam screamed. "Run!" No one moved, except Melissa who spun around to find a dozen weapons aimed at her.

"Isn't it amazing what you can buy on the Internet these days?" Melissa asked.

"Sam," Nick said, his voice tense. "Let's get the hell out of here."

"No."

"Samantha—"

"See what it feels like to have nothing?" Melissa's eyes glittered with insanity and rage and defiance. "I showed that rat bastard Jed Trainer what it feels like to lose everything. He made me *promises.* He never intended to leave her, the perfect little wife and mother. Too bad she was frigid in the bedroom. I showed him what he was missing."

Sam forced air into her lungs as her heart beat erratically. Fifteen, no twenty, of her people were in the house. She couldn't let them all be killed. Her mind raced with scenarios, but she couldn't seem to get past Melissa Morgan standing two feet from Nick with a bomb strapped to her chest.

"What did James Lynch do to you?" Sam asked, hoping to buy some time to figure a way out of this.

"He and his wife *ruined* my marriage. They said I came on to him, and my husband believed them and left me." Melissa's eyes glittered with evil. "Poor Jimmy cried like a baby when I forced him into that pool."

Melissa continued to wave the detonator over her head, almost taunting Sam to come after it. "What's the bad-ass star detective going to do now? If she can't find the person who shot her own father, I hope none of you are counting on her to get you out of this alive."

A shot rang out and blew Melissa's left hand right off her arm.

She let out an inhumane shriek as blood spurted from the stump.

Nick lunged for the detonator as Gonzo took Melissa down at the knees.

"Call the bomb squad and the EMTs," Sam ordered as she bent to free the weapon she'd stashed under her pants leg before the "party."

"Already done," Jeannie said from the kitchen. Assistant U.S. Attorney Faith Miller stood next to her, looking shell-shocked. Sam had asked her to be there to witness the confession she still planned to extract from Melissa.

Nick gently placed the detonator in Sam's hand.

She knelt down next to Melissa who continued to scream as tears rolled down her face. "I bet that hurts."

"You fucking bitch!" she sobbed. "You know it hurts!"

Sam reached out and put her hand on the wound, pressing hard to stop the bleeding and inflict maximum pain.

Melissa's screams got even louder.

"You want it to stop hurting?"

"Yes," Melissa said in a pleading tone. "Make it stop hurting. *Please make it stop.*"

"Tell me what you did to Crystal and Mr. Jeffries and your parents."

"I won't tell you. I'd rather be dead than go to jail."

"No one's going to die today," Sam said, pressing harder. "So start talking or keep hurting."

Paramedics appeared at the door, but Sam shook her head to

keep them from coming in until she had what she needed to close the case.

"Give me something for the pain!"

"Not until you tell me what you did."

"I hit Crystal with a hammer and pushed Mr. Jeffries over. It was so easy to pay them back for what they did to me." A sob hiccupped through her as tears and snot wet her face. "My parents had it coming. They wouldn't leave me alone. You had it coming, too. You ignored me!"

Sam kept up the pressure on the wound. "What did Carl Olivo and Danny Alvarez do to you?"

"He fired me because I took a little of his precious money. Do you know how much that place makes every day?"

Sam had what she needed so she released her hold on Melissa's mangled arm. The other woman's eyes bugged, and she let out a soundless scream as the blood began to flow again. Sam signaled to the paramedics to take over.

Turning to the others in the room, she said, "Who fired that shot?"

All eyes shifted to Freddie.

With his weapon still in his hand, his arm hung limply at his side, his eyes big with shock. It was, Sam knew, the first time he'd discharged his weapon in the line of duty.

"Freddie."

"I shot her hand off."

"Yes, you did, and you saved all our lives. Everyone in this room owes you a debt of gratitude."

He got even paler, so Sam took the weapon from him, jammed it into the back of her jeans and pushed Freddie into a chair, holding his head between his knees. "Breathe."

"I can't believe I shot her hand off."

Sam looked over and met Nick's gaze.

He sent her a small, relieved smile.

The house was soon crawling with detectives, bomb-squad officers and department brass. Sam and her team retold the story at least six times until the chief was satisfied he had a complete picture of what'd transpired.

"I understand Lieutenant Stahl wasn't happy you missed another hearing," Farnsworth said, clasping his hands behind his back.

"Yes, sir. Busting my chops seems to be his primary job description since he landed in IAB."

"I took care of this latest situation, but see what you can do to stay out of his crosshairs going forward."

Imagining Stahl's reaction to Farnsworth's interference made Sam want to giggle, which she went to great lengths to hide from the chief. "I will, sir."

"Detective Cruz," Farnsworth bellowed.

"Sir. Yes, sir."

Poor Freddie was still pale and shaky, but Sam was bursting with pride over what her protégé had done.

"You believe the shot was justified?"

"Yes, sir, I do. The way she was waving that detonator around, she was going to kill us all."

Farnsworth held out his hand. "I'll need your badge and weapon."

Freddie's mouth fell open. "Sir? Why?" With trembling hands he turned over his badge.

Sam pulled his gun from the waistband of her jeans and gave it to the chief.

"Routine investigation," Farnsworth said. "I expect not only will you have them back in no time, but I see a commendation in your future. Well done, Detective."

"Oh, um, thank you, sir."

"Detective Gonzales also showed incredible bravery," Sam said to Farnsworth. "He tackled her with no thought to his own safety."

"Well done, Detective," Farnsworth said to Gonzo, who seemed embarrassed by the praise. "Have your reports on my desk by twelve hundred tomorrow. Good work, everyone." Pointing to the door, he added, "Lieutenant, the media awaits a statement."

"Would you mind asking Darren Tabor to come in?" Sam said. "I owe him a favor."

"As you wish, Lieutenant," Farnsworth said with a fond smile for Sam. "On behalf of the department, I apologize to you and the senator for bringing this madness into your home."

"Thank you, sir."

He shook hands with every member of Sam's team on his way out the door.

"Before you talk to Darren, I need a minute," Nick said, taking Sam's hand and half dragging her into the kitchen. Once there, he wrapped his arms around her so tightly Sam had trouble breathing, but she didn't dare complain. "Holy shit." His voice was unsteady, and she could feel a slight tremor in his muscles. "Holy *freaking* shit."

"Look at it this way—never a dull moment."

That drew a reluctant chuckle from her husband. "Dull is boring and overrated."

"I'd love the opportunity to find out."

Tipping her chin up to receive his kiss, he said, "Not gonna happen in this lifetime, babe."

Sam smiled and took a moment to enjoy the kiss, thankful she had a lifetime to spend with him.

$\sim$

Continue the Fatal Series with book 5, *Fatal Deception*.

ALSO BY MARIE FORCE

Romantic Suspense Novels Available from Marie Force

Contemporary Romances Available from Marie Force

The Wild Widows Series

Book 1: Someone Like You

The Gansett Island Series

Book 1: Maid for Love (*Mac & Maddie*)

Book 2: Fool for Love (*Joe & Janey*)

Book 3: Ready for Love (*Luke & Sydney*)

Book 4: Falling for Love (*Grant & Stephanie*)

Book 5: Hoping for Love (*Evan & Grace*)

Book 6: Season for Love (*Owen & Laura*)

Book 7: Longing for Love (*Blaine & Tiffany*)

Book 8: Waiting for Love (*Adam & Abby*)

Book 9: Time for Love (*David & Daisy*)

Book 10: Meant for Love (*Jenny & Alex*)

Book 10.5: Chance for Love, *A Gansett Island Novella* (*Jared & Lizzie*)

Book 11: Gansett After Dark (*Owen & Laura*)

Book 12: Kisses After Dark (*Shane & Katie*)

Book 13: Love After Dark (*Paul & Hope*)

Book 14: Celebration After Dark (*Big Mac & Linda*)

Book 15: Desire After Dark (*Slim & Erin*)

Book 16: Light After Dark (*Mallory & Quinn*)

Book 17: Victoria & Shannon (Episode 1)

Book 18: Kevin & Chelsea (Episode 2)

A Gansett Island Christmas Novella

Book 19: Mine After Dark (*Riley & Nikki*)

Book 20: Yours After Dark (*Finn & Chloe*)

Book 21: Trouble After Dark (*Deacon & Julia*)

Book 22: Rescue After Dark (*Mason & Jordan*)

Book 23: Blackout After Dark (*Full Cast*)

Book 24: Temptation After Dark (*Gigi & Cooper*)

The Green Mountain Series

Book 1: All You Need Is Love *(Will & Cameron)*

Book 2: I Want to Hold Your Hand *(Nolan & Hannah)*

Book 3: I Saw Her Standing There *(Colton & Lucy)*

Book 4: And I Love Her *(Hunter & Megan)*

Novella: You'll Be Mine *(Will & Cam's Wedding)*

Book 5: It's Only Love *(Gavin & Ella)*

Book 6: Ain't She Sweet *(Tyler & Charlotte)*

The Butler, Vermont Series

(Continuation of Green Mountain)

Book 1: Every Little Thing *(Grayson & Emma)*

Book 2: Can't Buy Me Love *(Mary & Patrick)*

Book 3: Here Comes the Sun *(Wade & Mia)*

Book 4: Till There Was You *(Lucas & Dani)*

Book 5: All My Loving *(Landon & Amanda)*

Book 6: Let It Be *(Lincoln & Molly)*

Book 7: Come Together *(Noah & Brianna)*

Book 8: Here, There and Everywhere *(Izzy & Cabot)*

The Quantum Series

Book 1: Virtuous *(Flynn & Natalie)*

Book 2: Valorous *(Flynn & Natalie)*

Book 3: Victorious *(Flynn & Natalie)*

Book 4: Rapturous *(Addie & Hayden)*

Book 5: Ravenous *(Jasper & Ellie)*

Book 6: Delirious *(Kristian & Aileen)*

Book 7: Outrageous *(Emmett & Leah)*

Book 8: Famous *(Marlowe & Sebastian)*

The Treading Water Series

Book 1: Treading Water

Book 2: Marking Time

Book 3: Starting Over

Book 4: Coming Home

Book 5: Finding Forever

The Miami Nights Series

Book 1: How Much I Feel *(Carmen & Jason)*

Book 2: How Much I Care *(Maria & Austin)*

Book 3: How Much I Love *(Dee & Wyatt)*

Single Titles

Five Years Gone

One Year Home

Sex Machine

Sex God

Georgia on My Mind

True North

The Fall

The Wreck

Love at First Flight

Everyone Loves a Hero

Line of Scrimmage

Historical Romance Available from Marie Force

The Gilded Series

Book 1: Duchess by Deception

Book 2: Deceived by Desire

ABOUT THE AUTHOR

Marie Force is the *New York Times* best-selling author of contemporary romance, romantic suspense and erotic romance. Her series include Fatal, First Family, Gansett Island, Butler Vermont, Quantum, Treading Water, Miami Nights and Wild Widows.

Her books have sold more than 10 million copies worldwide, have been translated into more than a dozen languages and have appeared on the *New York Times* bestseller more than 30 times. She is also a *USA Today* and *Wall Street Journal* bestseller, as well as a Spiegel bestseller in Germany.

Her goals in life are simple—to finish raising two happy, healthy, productive young adults, to keep writing books for as long as she possibly can and to never be on a flight that makes the news.

Join Marie's mailing list on her website at *marieforce.com* for news about new books and upcoming appearances in your area. Follow her on Facebook at *www.Facebook.com/MarieForceAuthor* and on Instagram at *www.instagram.com/marieforceauthor/*. Contact Marie at *marie@marieforce.com*.

CPSIA information can be obtained
at www.ICGtesting.com
Printed in the USA
BVHW031706061022
648853BV00007B/78

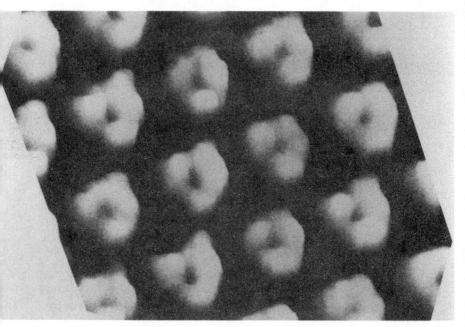

A scanning tunneling micrograph of benzene molecules lined up on a supporting metal surface. Each white lump is a single ring-shaped molecule, with a dark smudge indicating the hole through its center. COURTESY OF IBM RESEARCH

PALM BEACH COMM. COLLEGE
EISSEY CAMPUS - LLRC
3160 PGA BOULEVARD
PALM BEACH GARDENS, FL 33410

An oxygen atom on a gallium arsenide surface looks like a hill or a valley, depending on the direction of the electron flow from the surface to the STM probe. COURTESY OF RANDALL M. FEENSTRA